Running In The Shadows

Memoirs Of A Living Dead Girl

By Niki Gregory

This is a work of fiction. Names, characters, places and incidents are the products of the author's imagination or are used fictitiously. Any resemblance to actual events or locales or persons, living or dead, is entirely coincidental.

Copyright ©2022 by Niki Gregory
www.nikigregory.com

All rights reserved, including the right of reproduction in whole or in part in any form. No part of this book maybe used or reproduced in any manner whatsoever without written consent of the Author.
Published in the United States of America

Publishing by Practically Magic, LLC

Editing by Melanie Lopata (Get It Write Editing Co.)

Author Photo taken by Madison Jobe

Dedication

This book is for my mom and dad. I am forever thankful to them for making my childhood great.

In loving memory of my father. He was my hero, and I miss him every day. 09/04/1999

Acknowledgments

I want to start by thanking my husband. (He doesn't like attention, so I won't mention his name.) I am so blessed to have such a wonderful man in my life. I appreciate that he loves me without ever trying to change me.

I want to express my gratitude to my children, Madison, Ethan and Avery. Being their mom has always pushed me to work hard to be successful. They inspire me every day.

A very special thank you to my oldest sister, Gena, who shares my love of Halloween. She has inspired my fascination of spooky stories since I was a little girl.

Thank you to my family for cheering me on.

My good friend and fellow Sagittarius, Natasha. I appreciate her being my first "official" reader.

My editor and favorite New Yorker, Melanie. I am indebted to her for her assistance throughout the editing process.

~ Thank you to my readers for allowing me to share a piece of my imagination with you! ~

Chapter One
The Little Lost Dead Girl

Some people light a candle as they pray for an ailing friend or while praying for a recently departed loved one. Sometimes we make a wish and blow on a dandelion in hopes that our wish will come true. People have been known to carry lucky charms to ward off evil and jealousy or bring good luck or protection for themselves.

Some people use vision boards and chant daily affirmations. Is this low-key witchcraft by definition? I have been told we shouldn't look at tarot cards; we shouldn't talk to the deceased; we shouldn't practice astrology. Are these things not as innocent and harmless as blowing out candles on a birthday cake and making a wish? Would making a wish on a birthday candle also be low-key witchcraft by definition?

Some religions pick and choose, I guess. I suppose some look down on innocent magic, but then they celebrate the resurrection on the Sunday after the first full moon. They drink the wine; they eat the bread that represents the blood and the body. Organized religions shamed us for centuries for our gifts and called out things to be witchcraft when they are just as innocent as the church's rituals and traditions.

I personally believe that, early on, organized religion wanted us to be afraid to fend for ourselves and have our own spiritual connections and expressions free of their walls. How can using our own gifts God blessed us with be a sin? Is it just because we wouldn't need the church if we weren't so afraid of our own divine gifts from God? These are just a few things I jotted down in a journal my granny gave me the summer before I died when I was twelve, almost thirteen.

Death isn't easy. The departure from life can be a long process that takes years. Our bodies are dying a slow death each day. We were born to die—to leave this life for the next. When I died, it was unexpected. I'd always thought death was supposed to be peaceful. When I was younger, I heard things about death. Things like, your life flashing before your eyes, white lights, and angels. When I passed away, it was much more chaotic than that—for me, anyway.

I had an unexpected passing, so unfortunately, there was an element of surprise and an even larger element of panic and fear for me. I was relatively young when I passed away. I will explain what happened to me later. I'm sure you are probably more curious about my experience as I began transitioning from our living world and going into the next world and the hellish witch that led me there, so I will begin my story there.

The best way I can describe my departure is this way: Once the initial panic of passing away lulled, and I accepted that I was, in fact, dying, my fear—as well as pain and anxiety around death—subsided. This was not a lengthy process once I accepted death defeated me. It's when we fight because we are afraid to die that we make it harder on ourselves.

Once I gave up, accepted my demise and began my journey of passing on, it was actually a relief. It is so much easier once your brain is no longer fighting to cling to a life that is inevitably over. I was at utter peace after the initial pain as the water filled my lungs and I was on my journey of exiting the world I knew. Now, to be honest, I don't know if this process is the same for everyone, but this was my experience as I gargled my last breath.

For me, I was almost in a dreamlike state when I was leaving my life behind. Oddly enough, in my subconscious frame of mind, I found myself at the most beautiful beach you can imagine. The water was pristine, and it was serene and very calm. I had never been to the beach when I was living. It took death for me to make it there.

As I was pushing out to sea, I felt happy and excited. I didn't have a care in the world, for the most part. In the pit of my stomach, I felt sad for my mom and sister, knowing how much they'd been through recently and how much they'd miss me.

I could see my loved ones on the shore, seeing me off on my

journey. They were sad and sobbing, but it didn't upset me. Somehow, I knew they were all going to be OK, even though I knew they would be upset; I knew they would miss me. Those emotions are all very natural as your family and friends mourn their loss of you, after all.

I experienced this when my father passed away, and then again when my grandmother passed on, so I related to my mother and sister's emotions. My loved ones were filled with a thick sense of sorrow—dejection from my passing. I suppose it was a little different when my daddy passed away. There was a sense of relief; we knew he was tired of suffering. He had been sick from a lengthy illness and ready to move along, but that wasn't the case for me.

As my journey took me out to the calm ocean, I could see the vast water on the other shoreline far off in the distance. I could see the loved ones that passed before me. They were rejoicing; exhilarated to see me again. I saw grandparents I had never met, yet I knew who they were. I saw my childhood dogs waiting for me. Death was very welcoming now.

I felt elated when I saw my dad and my grandmother after recently losing them both. They were healthy and youthful again. I could see that they were happy, but I felt a small amount of worry and sadness. They knew I was dying, and I could feel their disappointment because I was young, and I'm sure they felt a sense of loss—not only for my life but for the grief my mom and sister would be left to endure. Daddy and Granny were waving me in to meet them in the next life. I was so surprised to see my dad happy and healthy again, that I, for some unknown reason, made a mistake.

I was supposed to keep going toward him and the sunshine upon the beach, but I turned away to let my sister and mom know that Dad was OK, as I felt a strong urge to do so. In my childlike innocence, I wanted so badly to tell my mom that my father wasn't sad or sick anymore. I wanted her to find some solace after all she had endured.

Up to my passing, my mother had been so consumed by my father's illness and his slow, agonizing death. She had grieved so much, and I worried about her.

I should have kept going toward my dad and grandmother, but I didn't. I now felt a duty to let her know that Dad was fine again, and he was waiting for me, so she would have some comfort knowing that I would be alright after I died.

As I started, I could no longer see my mom or sister. I made an attempt to swim back to where they could see me, but the more I struggled, the bigger the waves grew and started to collapse over me, pulling me from the calm waters into chaos and a tempest within the waters. I wasn't drowning; I was already dead. The next thing I remember, I was in our house, watching my mother answer a ringing phone.

"Hello?" As she sat there, her arms began shaking. "What are you talking about?" She began to panic, screaming at the top of her lungs. The screams and shrieking are something I can never unhear again. As my mom fell to the floor, she was bawling. There was a knock on the door that would go unanswered by my mom.

My sister finally burst into the house only a moment later and was followed in by two gentlemen. They weren't in uniform, yet somehow, I knew they were police officers. My mom and sister were both shaking, and their faces almost seemed colorless. My sister was also crying and ran and huddled over my mom.

In soft whimpers, my mom told my sister, "This can't be the truth; I can't handle this, I can't handle this!" Her soft whimpers turned into rageful ranting. The floor was soaked in tears as my sister laid over my mom and held her as she uncontrollably sobbed.

The next memory I have is of my mom and sister at a pond where divers and volunteers were going into the water, looking for me. Regrettably, they would never be able to find my body. I knew, at that time, I was dead; the rescue efforts were really a recovery effort now. They unsuccessfully searched for my body for several days. It's hard to explain death, but I wasn't there with them the way I would have been if I were living. Time is like a blink of an eye when you are dead.

The ordeal was devastating for my mom and my sister that my body was never recovered. I think knowing I was in the water made my passing that much more unbearable for my mom. She had a mental break with reality and was a shell of a woman that she once was before she lost me. I was her baby. My passing left her in a conundrum.

My mother then desired to take her own life. After losing my dad, followed by her mother's passing and now me, she wanted to end her miserable feelings. My sister is what kept her alive. To be honest, I believe Mom would have killed herself had it not been for the responsibility of needing to be there for my sister, Mia.

Mom had no choice but to live for my sister since she treasured and adored her just as much as she did me. Knowing that my sister couldn't pick up the pieces by herself, she would never be able to forgive herself for leaving Mia alone.

The love of my sister, coupled with the sense of obligation, forced our mother to live a life she no longer loved. My mom was, in fact, living in Hell on earth. She was such an amazing wife and mother. She truly was a wonderful person; she didn't deserve the pain she was suffering. I hated that she was experiencing such agony.

I was around my mom a lot the first few days after I passed. I think you stay with your loved ones because you're all they think about and they grieve for you so hard. I was there for just the first three or four days.

I don't know when or how I drifted to the afterlife; it was difficult accounting for my time. It's like I was in limbo somehow. I had no way of controlling when I would go from one world to the next, but I felt as if I were hiding and afraid for some reason.

Honestly, to this day, I still don't know for sure how I was able to see my mom and sister after I died, though I have some guesses. Maybe this is normal for everyone who passes away, but I don't really believe that's the case. I believe I was between worlds, though I have no recollection whatsoever of *when* I was in limbo, in a state of purgatory, going from the afterlife to the living world. I was waiting for something, though I had no idea what. I can't explain how or why. The problem was, when I drifted to the afterlife the last time, so much time passed before I was able to make my way back to the living world again.

The even stranger thing is that I can recall seeing parts of my life that didn't happen yet. I sometimes saw myself as an adult in my memory. "Memory" may be the wrong word since it never came to be, I suppose, but I could see someone, and I knew it was me.

When I would have the flashes of the future, it looked like I could have had a happy life—all the little things I was supposed to experience but never had my chance to, the little details of my life. I saw high school football games, my graduation, the car I would have driven as a teenager, and getting dressed at my wedding. I even saw my sister and me at lunch with my mom, happy and laughing together. I saw about a thousand flashes of what my life may have held for me—a life that I would never know now, and I would never live because I, unfortunately, was dead. Sadly, I died before I was supposed to. I would see but would never live those days. It's almost like watching a movie that you're the star of, but it isn't really yours. Your would-be reality is now more like a fantasy that you wish you could live out. Even the shit days and sad days with your family are better than being dead and lost without them.

I never saw my funeral. In fact, the next time I came back after drifting away, it was very obvious it had been years after my death. In the afterlife, time isn't measurable. There are no days or years. By the time I came back to see my mom and sister, so much time had clearly passed. My sister was grown up and, if possible, even more beautiful than I remember. She had a little boy too. She was a mama now. I wish I had been there to see her get married and have a son, but I missed it all.

When I came back to the living world, my sister was in our childhood home, and she was packing my things, so I watched her from the corner of the room. I feel as if I returned due to her going through my things again and her strong emotions. I am unsure; it's only a guess.

Watching my sister felt like an out-of-body experience. If you ever experienced one before, that's pretty much what it seemed to be. I had those experiences occasionally growing up, so I knew it wasn't a dream.

The out-of-body experiences were different from the visions I would experience. The best way I can explain it is that it is comparable to Déjà vu. Instead of just a familiar feeling, I would see and sometimes hear little glimpses of something that would happen soon. Visions and feelings were quite regular for me growing up. I could read the room, I guess you could say.

I didn't have any idea how to pick and choose what I could see. I didn't have control of when I would see it either. I don't know if it was random or accidental when I would have visions or out-of-body experiences. They were almost like defense mechanisms and warnings.

Strangely enough, my wits and emotions were still with me. I could hear, see, think, and feel emotions; it was almost like I was alive again—minus having a body, which is actually a pretty important part of being alive, I suppose.

I don't really think I was a ghost. Maybe I was. I don't really know how to explain it, probably because there isn't a name or an explanation I can provide other than giving you my very best guess. "Ghost" just sounds like you're definitely dead. I guess there aren't many things as definite as death, but my awareness of my surroundings and my thought processing didn't make me feel like I was dead.

While my sister was in my room, I could hear everything around me. I could even smell my room. It smelled like a candle I had when I was a young girl. I had no clue how much time had passed, but my sister was not the teenager I knew when I was still living. She was grown up now.

Mia was sad and troubled while packing my short-lived life in boxes. Seeing her upset was very troublesome for me. I only wanted her to feel joy and happiness. I feel certain the array of emotions is what brought me back to her world.

"Jacob, come look at these pictures with me." She was thumbing through old polaroid photos. "Who is this, Jay?"

The little boy, who was probably three or maybe four, pointed to the photo. "My aunt Lucy."

My sister smiled big and hugged him so tight that he wiggled away a bit to catch a breath. "Yes, she would have loved you so much." She hugged her son again as tears flooded her beautiful blue eyes. The green fleck under her right pupil glistened. I remembered that green fleck. I had the same exact green fleck in my right eye. We were eye twins. We didn't look anything alike, really, but our eyes were unique.

In that sad moment of her grief, that green fleck made me feel happy. My mom could look into her eyes and still see a part of me too.

My mother walked into the room; she appeared to be so small compared to how I remembered her the last time I saw her at the pond. Her body was fragile, and her eyes still looked sad and tired. Her hair was now short and a shiny, lustrous silver color, which aged her. I remembered her thick brunette hair, so seeing her all gray was somewhat shocking.

She sniffled and tried to keep the tears in her eyes from sliding down her cheeks. "I haven't been in her room in years. I can never bring myself to come back here after that night. I haven't even dusted in here." Mom dragged her finger across a thick layer of dust that collected on my dresser, closing her eyes and thinking of that first night I was gone. Then she opened her eyes and looked at the bed that she lay in and cried and screamed into my pillows that same night. "I can't just leave her here in this room; I can't." My mom's voice shook as she tried her best to hold it together in front of Mia and her little boy.

My sister went to comfort her. "Mom! You can't, and you don't need to. Let me pack her room up; we are taking everything with us to your new house. Lucy isn't here, Mom; she is with Dad. These are just keepsakes. Take Jacob to get a burger. Let me work on getting the room put away."

My mom remained silent for a few minutes and then agreed. "Am I making a mistake? I feel awful leaving here. This is where my girls grew up. Your sister played here when she was alive. All her memories are in this house. I just don't know if leaving here is the right decision."

My sister reassured her that, with the neighborhood getting bad with crime, it was time to move on and that her memories belonged with her, not the house. After seeing my sister with her son and my mom growing old, I knew I didn't want to leave their world again. I felt like I kept trying to slip away, and I had to dig in and make myself present in each moment to avoid it.

I suddenly remembered something my grandmother told me long ago when she came to stay with us after my dad died. She said dolls were originally made for spirits to inhabit. Now, I don't know why that thought entered my mind while watching Mia pack my things—I don't even know for sure if that's true—but as soon as that memory came to mind, my sister picked up my Lucy doll. I had a flashback of receiving this doll in the mail for my birthday one year. I was so excited. Granny painted the doll's face to my likeness. Looking at it now, I see she really did a brilliant job with the doll. It did resemble me a lot as a young girl, especially the tiny green fleck in one of the doll's eyes. It was spot-on.

My sister stared at the doll. "Granny really did a great job making this doll look like Lucy," she said aloud, holding the doll close to her heart. "Lucy, I think about you every day. I miss you." She suddenly gasped. "Lucy?" She then shook her head as if dismissing her suspicion that I was in the room with her. If only she truly believed I was.

For generations, we have been taught and even forced to ignore our gifts and senses. We shut out our own intuitions and feelings, then dismiss them without a second thought. Each generation clings to superstitions or fear of our own abilities as if they are forbidden. We have closed our third eye. We disregard our own godliness and gifts of wonderment.

Believe me when I say our gifts were given to us for a reason, but it has been stripped away from us out of fear. Generation after generation, we move further and further away from our abilities. In early times, people—not just women—were burned to death, hanged, and stoned for their "magic" gifts. Truth be told, it was all just for greed and political reasons. Innocent people were treated as evil witches for selfish gains.

Men and women alike were accused of witchcraft. Here's the thing we must remember when we embrace our divination. We were taught to fear the witch more than those who burned her alive. One thing I am certain of is they wouldn't burn the witch if they weren't certain of her magic. I can't speak for you, but I know I have had magical experiences that make me believe there was more to it than just strange coincidences. I never believed in coincidences anyway.

Before you start thinking negatively about the word "witch," please let me explain. There are good people and extremists in every religion—every single religion, even with witches. Some practice dark magic for selfish gains and serve a very dark lord that was once the beautiful and highly favored angel who now serves eternity in the pit of Hell.

Some practice clean magic without intent, just using nature's bounty that our Creator has blessed us with. These witches embrace their gifts, which are practically magic. Their intent is to help people.

The guardian angels of nature. The champions of retribution.

My mind had its awakening some years back when I was an adolescent. This has been a curse ever since I can remember. I didn't know my experiences were considered a gift. Trust me; they seemed so much like a punishment at that time in my life. I never thought I was psychic, but people often told me I was.

I consider myself intuitive. The problem is that it's easy to lie to yourself so you don't have to listen when it's something you don't want to believe. Lying to myself sometimes felt more comfortable. I think we can all agree on that. We have all ignored gut feelings about people or situations we shouldn't have ignored.

My sister was also very intuitive—especially when she was younger—but she ignored her gifts. I believe she ignored them so much that they almost went entirely away. Somehow, she felt I was with her the day she cleaned my room. She always thought about me after my passing but never felt my presence around her until that day.

Mia didn't want to believe I was still in my room. My sister wanted to believe I had found peace and moved on. It did not comfort her to think that, day after day, year after year, I was still in my room. How sad would that be, after all? Mia couldn't bear the thought of me being a little ghost girl stuck in my room for all eternity. People love discovering ghosts, but how sad is that? Trapped in perpetual loneliness without being led to the light.

Fortunately, that wasn't the case for me. I wasn't trapped in my room, and I don't even remember anything about where I was. It was just a void of consciousness. I think when you're dead, you just accept that this is how it is now. Most people don't try to stay behind on purpose. I believe it is very different for those who cross over successfully. I was probably supposed to cross over and experience Heaven, but I do think when I turned back and tried to go to my mom, I somehow became stuck between worlds.

The living world and the afterworld is such a thin veil, after all. I couldn't be a part of either. Instead, I was now watching my sister and mom live their lives without me. I was alone in my world, but I was not afraid. I was not a kid anymore; my thought process was that of an adult now. Being there with my sister made me realize that maybe I was still growing up and maturing as if I were still alive.

I wandered the house, room to room, as my sister diligently packed my former life away; one last look as my mom was getting ready to move on with her life and leave the memories that haunted her. Sure, we had unbelievably wonderful memories there, but I imagine the sad memories weighed on her heart a little heavier.

I could see the entire house was being packed away. I saw our family picture at the very top of one box in the hallway that was taken about a year before my dad was sick and passed away. My mom looked happy. Her eyes that now carried dread and heartbreak used to be full of joy and pride in her family. I think you can only be as happy as your saddest child. Unfortunately for my mother, her baby was dead, so she could probably never experience complete and utter happiness again, which is really heartbreaking.

I went into the kitchen, where my mom used to spend so much time preparing delicious meals for our family. I went into the living room and reminisced on the times I played Nintendo with my dad. I looked at the windows and door that haunted me as a small child.

I had always been highly connected with other people's energies. Being able to know things you aren't supposed to can be very draining. If you have this "gift" you understand. Reading people's emotions sounds like it would give you an advantage to really know people. You would think you would want to possess a gift like this, but you must believe me when I say it isn't exactly a blessing.

You will never have a healthy relationship if you know everyone's secrets and shortcomings before having a chance to actually know the person first and then finding out their secrets and bullshit later. If you have this ability, you know you have to withdraw from many relationships early on before even giving the person a chance. All-knowing and all-seeing, you encounter a lot of icky people. I don't even just mean love interests; I mean friendships and work relationships. All of it.

Fortunately, it isn't something you pick up with all people. It happens almost unexpectedly. Sometimes it's immediate, and sometimes it takes a while. Usually, you pick up on it when they experience a moment of vulnerability, and their energy and mysteries are set free.

I didn't always possess these gifts; my gifts evolved with age. Usually, people dismiss their gifts and eventually they go away—for the most part. I always had a strong connection with my intuition. I guess to understand me, you'd have to know where it all started. What made me the "living dead girl" I am today.

I found myself thinking of my childhood. My initial encounter with a witch is where the strangeness in my life began. Her name was Ruby and she was from Mexico. I can assure you; this bitch didn't care about affecting others' freewill and their lives. She cared about one thing. Me. She wanted to ruin my life, and it gave her great pleasure to cause me turmoil. Why? I have no fucking idea why, but I grew to loath her as much as she did me.

As a young girl, I couldn't fathom why she took an interest in me. I had no idea what would motivate an adult woman to hate a child in the way that she hated me. The way she came into my life was just by chance. She knew my next-door neighbor from when they lived in Mexico together as young ladies.

The witch would occasionally come to stay for a few weeks on and off since I could remember. From my understanding, she owned the house but would sometimes go to her other home in Mexico too. When she would come to stay at the house, it was always hell for me.

Chapter Two
Eyes Upon Me

My first and most vivid memory of childhood was being too afraid to fall asleep in the living room of my home. This memory began when Ruby, the witch, came to stay at her house across the street. I didn't realize initially that was why I had these nightmares. It all started when I had the same recurring dream while dozing off on our couch. I didn't know then what I know now about these dreams—these nightmares.

Remember, I was a kid in a much more innocent and simple time. We didn't have access to the internet or cell phones like people do today. We had each other, our friends to play with, and our family to sit down and watch television with. We internalized our feelings and fears and didn't tell anyone what torment we were going through; or, at least, I didn't. Perhaps that was just me, but I think back then it was pretty normal.

I started having habitual nightmares at a very young age. I was young enough that I had no idea what a witch was. I mean, I remember seeing a cute witch in a cartoon and a lovely witch on a television show—nothing I would think of as frightening; nothing I would have associated as evil or negative in any way. I didn't know people were sinister, mean, or even selfish…not at that age, anyway.

Whenever I fell asleep on the couch, I would dream so clearly that an old lady was standing outside the window looking in on me. She was a witch; I knew that's what she was in my subconscious mind. I certainly knew what she was after in my encounters with her in my nightmares. This woman, this witch, would lightly tap her long fingernails on the window and call me by my name. "Lucy, let me in."

She was insistent that she be let in, and I would wake up paralyzed with fear. As I lay awake, too afraid to move, I heard movement on the porch, followed by sinister laughter fading from the window into the front yard and away. I would lay there frozen, ignoring the pleadings of the witch.

Any time I made the mistake of falling asleep in our living room, this would be my experience. Fear would take over my body when the tapping and pleadings for me to let her in began. I was too afraid to look at the small window squares at the top of the door, fearing that I would see something looking in on me. I could tell someone was waiting for me to open the door. I would see the shadows in the crack of the door move towards the window, and I would close my eyes so tight that tears would trickle down my cheeks. I could feel eyes upon me, watching me, drawing strength from my paralyzing fear. I didn't fall asleep on the couch often. It was rare because I was so afraid. I even talked to my mom about not letting me sleep in the living room anymore, though I didn't share my fears of nightmares with her.

I was quite the tomboy in my younger years. I would play in the Texas heat all day with my friends, and then I would shower and enjoy dinner with my family. We would watch whatever my dad wanted to watch on TV, of course. Let me just tell you, I know too much—against my will—about Star Trek and Barney Miller. Talk about torment. My dad was a pretty cool dude, though. I didn't realize that at the time, of course. I was just annoyed that I had to watch Barney Miller.

One evening, after playing too hard and being completely exhausted again, I accidentally fell asleep on the couch. My mom covered me with a blanket, ignoring my simple request of not letting me sleep in the living room. I was drifting into my dream when I heard the witch tapping on the window.

I guess I was sleeping, but it almost felt like the tapping carried on with soft whispers, growing into growling insistence to unlock the front door and let her in. I knew the witch wanted me, but I was just a kid; I didn't know why she harassed me so. But I knew, as I lay in a state of fear, that I didn't even want to open my eyes, and that she was getting angry at me for not allowing her in.

On the other side of the window, the taps turned to scratching and shrieking. This time was different from the times before. I realized I was already awake when it began. The witch was saying, "Lucita, come…open the door for me," in a thick, Hispanic accent.

My older sister, Mia, was a bit of a night owl and her timing that night was perfect. She tiptoed through the living room and asked if I wanted a piece of cake. I agreed that cake sounded pretty good and hopped off the couch to join her in the kitchen, knowing the witch was waiting for me on the porch. I told her I hated sleeping on the couch and asked if I could sleep with her. She didn't inquire why—probably just assumed it wasn't comfortable—so she just dismissed my statement. "Of course you can, but I think your bed is probably more comfortable than the couch," and then told me to stop falling asleep on the couch as if I did it on purpose.

Mia was the best big sister, and I admired her. She and I had the same biological parents, but we looked so different from one another. She had beautiful, luscious, long black hair, so dark it had hints of heliotrope. Her complexion was flawless with olive undertones, and she had brilliant blue eyes with that glimmering green fleck that shimmered. She strongly favored my mother, whereas my appearance was more like my father's side of the family. I had my dad's strawberry blonde hair, my sister's eyes, and peaches and cream complexion. The only similarity my sister Mia and I really shared were our eyes and our sass.

Mia was pretty cool. She listened to rock and roll and pushed back on everyone like any other typical teenager. Mia was very much a free spirit with a gypsy soul. I aspired to be like my older sister.

Right about the same time I was dealing with my night scares, my sister was dealing with her own troubles. It was probably typical behavior for her age, but Mia started spending time with the wrong crowd. For reasons only she could explain, she was reading about the occult and going through teenage struggles with depression.

In hindsight, she was battling her own demons, I guess. In many ways, she always felt that much of what she was involved with opened doors that should never have been opened. She believed she unknowingly introduced chaos into my life, impacting my whole family and breaking all of us. She always put the blame for our family misfortunes on herself, as though she thought she was being punished. None of that was true and certainly not her fault, of course.

As far as I was concerned, I was young, but I realized I had a witch that was very interested in me and haunted my thoughts. When I played in my front yard, I constantly felt her interruption. If I were alone, I would feel it. If I were playing with friends, I would feel it. She was inescapable. It was difficult to carry, especially as a little child. My attention would often wander to the house across the street because of the persistent calling of my name. I always tried to avoid looking at that framed, brown house with its white trim.

Ruby, the witch, would constantly stare at me through her screen door. Though I could not see her, I did see her shadow. I thought of her as an old witch, but looking back now, I don't think she was really old at all. She stood only five feet tall and maybe weighed ninety pounds with a small frame. Perhaps she was in her thirties, but when I caught a glimpse of her shadow, I assumed she was cruel and elderly.

Someone—a family member or friend, maybe?—came with Ruby from Mexico. She was a little older than Mia and not at all what I expected. Her name was Dulce, which means "candy" in Spanish; she was kindhearted and wore a big smile on her face.

Dulce told my sister that Ruby was deceitful and hateful. She warned, "Although Ruby may seem beautiful and have a non-threatening look about her, she is filled with hate, and that makes her very ugly to me."

Ruby remained very mysterious to us, but I could sense Dulce's fear of her. I could hear Dulce's inward cries, not wanting to go home as the evenings would begin to wind down.

Our neighbor to our left was also from Mexico, and they have been our neighbor's for as long as I can remember. My mom sometimes chatted with Maria, the woman who lived there, but her husband was very anti-social and controlling, so they didn't talk together too often. They would visit or gossip with each other when they were outside doing yard work or hanging laundry on the clothesline in the backyard.

I learned later that they were all connected to Ruby through marriage or old friendships in Mexico, which bonded them together—no blood relation, which made more sense, especially when it came to

Dulce. She had a beautiful presence about her. I could never understand how she could tolerate living with Ruby.

Oddly, Dulce never spent much time at the brown house during the day. She would only go there to sleep, though I know she never wanted to. It was almost like she slept there to keep a close eye on Ruby. I am certain Maria would have preferred Dulce to stay with her next door and would have made room for her. It seemed as though Maria shared her terror of Ruby. She seemed anxious, and I observed that she never gave the brown house a deliberate glance.

Dulce was usually reading and sometimes writing in her journal or diary of some kind. Sometimes she would visit my sister when she would come home from school and they would talk and laugh. They seemed to get along rather well. I saw Ruby watching from the shadows, and I could sense her disdain.

One day, I was outside, bored and without anyone to play with, and dreading school the following day. It was then that I first noticed Ruby interacting with me directly.

In my childish youth, I was being silly and began spinning my finger in a circular motion. I watched as the leaves started moving in the same circular motion as my finger, faster and faster. More leaves joined, and then more even still. When I stood up, I swiftly motioned my hand in one direction, and the leaves gusted in the same direction, then leaves poured off the trees behind me. This made me laugh.

But suddenly, I had the cold, familiar feeling of being watched from the screen door across the street. I turned and stared at the door, watching as the shadow moved and the door slowly shut. Did I do the thing with the leaves or did she, I wondered.

Then, my mom opened the door and called me in for dinner. As I turned to walk into my home, she laughed. "Lucy, what in the heck happened to your hair?" She attempted to tame my hair.

"Mom, it was the wind and leaves that blew all over me!!" As I proceeded to step into the house, my mom looked outside and pointed out the fact that it was not even windy outside and then told me to get cleaned up for dinner.

After that, I stopped playing in the front yard as frequently. Since I could see it wasn't a windy day, it seemed a little unsettling to me, as a young child, to be unable to explain what had happened.

Dulce came over and asked my mom if I was ok. Though my mom found the inquiry strange, she assured Dulce that I was fine. She seemed relieved and left. I watched her from the window and noticed she stopped and looked across the way at the witch's brown house. She stayed in the street almost as if she were in a trance, just staring over at the house where Ruby stood in the doorway.

Dulce quickly ran back to the porch and sat down on our steps. I hurried to tell my mom she was on the porch. My mom went to check to see if Dulce needed anything else, but she had already left by the time my mom reached the front door. It was strange to us.

I remember one rainy Saturday when my sister was running to her car with a jacket over her head. I was laughing at her through the window, and a strange feeling came over me. I looked across the way, and sure enough, there was the shadow of the wicked lady standing at her front door. I could hear faint whispers, and I felt uneasy, scared.

That night I had another dream. I was with one of my school friends, and we were at a strange place I had never seen before: a wide-open field with a huge pond that was dark green and almost swampy in appearance. In my dream, I was watching myself approaching the edge of the murky green water. The pond began to ripple which spread and widened.

When I thought about my dream, I remembered the waves were continually moving in the opposite direction. They would always start at my feet and strongly pull to the center of the pond. In my dream, I felt scared. My friend had backed away, but I was frozen and couldn't move away. I watched as the witch beckoned to me and tried to draw me in, but I was too terrified to do anything. As if to force me toward the pond, the wind increased. As I approached the lake, I tripped to the edge and felt the mud slip. It felt like the witch was pulling me into the pond with her. My feet were sliding in the mud as I tried to push away from the edge.

My nightmare ended when I was awakened by what sounded like pebbles being thrown at the window. It had begun raining, and the wind picked up, blowing aggressively, which startled me. The window began rattling as I laid there, and my sister came into my room.

"What are you doing?" she asked. She went to open the blinds.

My heart was pounding from my dream still. "A storm must be brewing. Look at this wind blowing all these leaves." Mia shut the blinds.

I still, to this day, have never seen anything like it. Leaves covered every inch of my window. My sister scooped me up and we went to her room to sleep, which as very quiet. I kind of think she was also a little afraid of the storm that blew out of nowhere.

"Well," she said as she turned the light out and looked out her window. "I guess the rainstorm has already calmed down." As she was walking to the bed, I could still hear pebbles and leaves and debris flying in the other room against my window. "It's the strangest thing. Why isn't anything hitting *my* window?" Mia shut off the light, and we walked to her front window to peak through the blinds. No wind, no leaves blowing.

Suddenly, I spotted the lady across the street, sitting on her steps, looking straight at me. My sister quickly shut her blinds and began laughing. "That lady thought we were looking at her!" I felt scared. I really hoped she hadn't thought we were spying on her! I would rather never lay my eyes on her again, truth be told.

We went to bed, and the next morning, my dad came to my sister's door and knocked to wake us. I felt so tired, but he hurried us outside. "I was getting ready to get cigarettes and noticed Lucy's window. Take a look at this," he said excitedly.

My window was covered in thick layers of leaves, caked on, with leaves on top of leaves, just on my window—no other windows on the house. Looking over to the brown house, I thought about the day I played in the yard with the leaves, and my gut told me the witch was responsible. I just knew she did it.

I know she was amusing herself with my fears of her. Playing in the front yard and sleeping in our living room were no longer things I wanted to do. I didn't even want to sleep in my own room. I got tired of being watched and interrupted by the calling from the brown house.

I was thinking about the leaves on my windows and the day I thought I was moving them. My little fingers began swirling around the leaves in my backyard because I knew the witch couldn't see me there. I was doing it; I was moving the leaves. They appeared to be moving by my will. My mom called for me to come in, and as she began speaking, I lost my concentration. The leaves stopped circulating and came to rest where I was sitting.

I went to the bathroom to wash up, and in my young mind, I only thought that was a funny and pretty silly coincidence. My logical mind knew there wasn't a way that I could cause the leaves to move by simply willing them to.

I went into the living room and saw my sister sitting with Dulce. I was excited to see them and asked Dulce if she was staying for dinner.

"I can't today. I was actually getting ready to leave," Dulce said to me.

Mia stood up. "I have to get ready for work." The two left, and I sat in my dad's recliner, which was quite comfy. I knew I could sit there until he got home, then I'd have to get up.

After my dad came home from work, I went to my mom's room and saw her and my sister, sitting on the bed, talking. I sat down against the door to wait and unintentionally eavesdropped. They were talking about Dulce. My sister told my mom that Dulce's aunt, Ruby, practices Santeria, which I now know is witchcraft. My mom listened without interruption. Ruby wasn't really her aunt, but that is how she explained her to the family. She was actually old friends with her father in Mexico.

I didn't realize at the time that my sister stopped short of telling my mom something that Dulce had said to her. "My aunt tells me Lucy would sell for a lot of money in Mexico with her strawberry blonde hair and light eyes. When I'm sleeping and having bad dreams about things happening to Lucy, I wake to see Aunt Ruby watching over me with an evil smile." As she pulled on her jacket, getting ready to leave, Dulce added, "Please don't tell your parents. Just watch over your sister. I don't want something bad to happen to her. I don't think Aunt Ruby likes Lucy. I wake up unable to breathe sometimes, and it weighs on me. I just couldn't let something happen to your sister."

It started very innocently, like most things do. I saw books in my sister's room with wizards and witches on the covers. There was a progression in the stack from innocent-looking book covers to books with scary demons on the cover. The artwork alone was quite frightful. I asked Mia why she was reading spooky books and wondered if it was because of Dulce's warnings. Maybe she was looking for ways to protect me or see what Santeria was really about.

"Oh, Lucy, are you being a fraidy cat?" She teased and taunted me with the books, of course playing it off. I know now she was only trying to ease my young mind by downplaying the ominous books she was delving into, but she assured me she wasn't reading them. She said she found them on the porch and kept them but that seemed strange to me.

I don't know why Mia was so unhappy. I would hear her crying and wailing into her pillow. I wasn't sure if it was boy trouble or just run-of-the-mill growing pains, but her eyes were always so sad. You can always see into a person's soul through their eyes.

I remember being surprised one night when Mia came home and how upset she was. My mom and I were in my room chatting, and Mia walked into the house, gathered the books, and tossed them into the trash bin. Then she sat on my bed. "I am getting rid of those books tomorrow morning." She was quite serious and upset and appeared to be very afraid.

My mom inquired, "Books…what books?"

Mia explained that when she came home from work one evening, she found a stack of books sitting on the front porch, so she looked through them. "I tried reading the books, but they were confusing, so I stopped. It's like they weren't really meant for me but someone else. I think they were sent here by mistake. I just feel like I need to get rid of them." She didn't believe the books called a demon to her, but she believed that her hanging around the wrong people and her growing anger may have opened her up to an unwanted encounter.

When Mia expressed that she had been unhappy lately, my mom asked me to leave the room. It was immature, but I threw a little fit. "UGH! It's MY room! I shouldn't have to leave."

Now in the 90's, your mom would tear your ass up for back-sassing. It was only child abuse if you could make it to the phone, so I knew not to push it too far. All joking aside, she would never hit me. But I still knew it was time to leave my room before she grounded me.

I left the room, closed my door behind me, then sat in the hallway so I could eavesdrop without them knowing.

My sister pressed on. "I think I'm just spending time with the wrong people at school. I feel very angry a lot of the time, and I'm struggling." She stopped for a second, then continued. "Mom, sometimes I just get so sick of these religious people with their better-than-everyone attitudes, and it makes me angry. Then I think things like, why does God let kids go hungry, and why does He let good people get sick? I have a lot of anger about God, and…look, I know I'm not supposed to feel anger towards God. I do, though. But I think I did something that I didn't really mean to, and now I am really afraid."

My mom cleared her throat. "I'm almost afraid to ask," she said with a worried tone.

My sister began explaining that she had been talking to people in the occult at school, and then she had an encounter that shook her. "I think—no, I know—I saw a demon. He came for me. He thought I was ready. I've been telling them I'm ready, and —"

My mom stopped her. "What are you saying? You wanted to see a demon?!!"

I'm pretty sure my mom was as scared as I was at hearing that. I cracked open the door and said, "I'm coming in!" I barged in and jumped on my bed. To be honest, that scared the shit out of me, and I wasn't about to keep hiding in the dark hallway. My sister shook her head and shrugged her shoulders.

"No, I think this just got out of hand. I've been reading these books, and…yeah, I guess I've been saying I'm ready to know the truth. I wasn't asking to see a demon, but he came to me tonight." Mom and I stared at her wide-eyed. She continued. "I have a friend at school that says he is strong now and doesn't even see himself in the mirror anymore. He sees something else. No one picks on him; he has control and power. I don't exactly know if that's true, but I guess I've also wanted control and power. I have been feeling powerless, you know?" Mom nodded, affirming what my sister was saying.

"So, tonight I went to the store, and a long black limo pulled right up to me. The windows were so dark, but somehow, I could still see the person inside perfectly. He didn't look human but was human-like. I stood there, frozen, as he stared at me, almost like he was examining me. He was the ugliest thing I have ever seen!! All I could think of was, no, I'm not ready for this!! I was shaking so much I felt my teeth chatter!

"I didn't want to know anymore. He knew it, and I could feel his disappointment. Fear rushed over me. The anger he felt went through me and made me feel nauseous. Mom, he shook his head with disgust. I know it's because I brought him to me and then became afraid. I was still shaking with fear as the limo pulled away." My sister paused to catch her breath, then groaned. "I know I summoned him, and I wasn't ready. I never really wanted to go down that path. I just started getting too far down the rabbit hole with this. I am 100% certain this was a demon."

I guess you could say that my mom was spiritual but not what you would call religious. She and my sister continued their discussions well into the evening hours. I don't remember when I fell asleep on a halfway made-up bed. The next morning, my sister told me Mom wanted her to stop hanging out with her friends and reading all this crap. She apologized if she had been a shitty sister to me. She was going to begin focusing on getting a new job and doing things that would make her happy. Like, not hanging around people that brought out the toxic traits in her own personality. My sister took her books that she tossed in the kitchen trash out to the trash cans outside the following morning. She was done with the evil she allowed into her life.

My sister wasn't very descriptive of what she saw, yet I knew. I saw him watching her. I had a vision of their encounter, and it was disturbing. I couldn't see clearly, but with the moonlight shining in his lap, I could see long fingernails. They weren't dirty; they were pristinely clean. I could also see a tail, as weird as it sounds. I couldn't quite see his face, just the shape of the structure of his elongated facial features. He had an exceptionally long skull, and his face had a rather large, thick bone structure. As I pictured him watching my sister in my mind, I was suddenly jolted as he pulled away.

I visioned her staring at him, and she was paralyzed with fear. He was getting pleasure out of making her feel afraid. I could also see the rage building as she would not approach. When I felt the jolt as he pulled off, it was jarring. There was so much anger and disgust in him. I don't know why I envisioned it; I certainly wasn't there, but it was almost as if I was reading my sister's thoughts. Maybe just using my imagination, I was unsure, but to be candid, I was too afraid to ask her about it.

I won't lie to you. I was scared that the demon wanted to engage and interact with my sister, but I was not afraid of the books—they're just books. I did feel that they had some sort of magic to them, and I felt like I needed to keep them. It was as if they were calling to me. She wanted to rid of anything around witchcraft, magic, or sorcery that could have opened the door to the demon.

I took the books out of the trashcan and snuck them into my bedroom. I didn't read them back then; they were definitely adult material, but I thumbed through them. They were handwritten and lovely. I thought there would be no harm in keeping them just in case I needed to look up information on how to get rid of Ruby somehow. They were my fallback plan if I needed to resort to magic, I suppose.

Chapter Three
El Diablo

Several months passed, and my dreams ceased. Coincidentally, the witch, Ruby, went to Mexico, and while she was gone, it was very peaceful. I could play with my friends and not feel the weight of her hateful energy upon my shoulders.

My mom motioned me inside as I watched an old beat-up truck pull up to the neighbor's house. I hoped Dulce would return to live with our neighbor, Maria, so she didn't have to stay with Ruby anymore. I despised Ruby, and I know Dulce was also afraid of her. Dulce went away for school, and I missed seeing her gracious smile, but at the same time, I was glad she could escape Ruby's watchful eye. Truth be told, her life was better without Ruby in it, and so was mine. Ruby being gone was a wonderful blessing for all of us.

To my utter disappointment, Dulce wasn't in the truck. A guy, probably in his mid-twenties, stepped out of the truck and looked around, briefly making eye contact with me. He reached into the truck's bed, pulled out two duffle bags, and off he went into Ruby's house. He was staying at Ruby's while she was away. He was there a short bit before he left abruptly. I never even saw him except for the day he arrived. I only saw his white truck, which stayed where he pulled up the day he arrived. I guess he kept to himself and didn't intend to make friends since he wasn't staying long.

The next day was like any other day. I was ready to play in my front yard with my friends. I went to the kitchen to exit that way to the yard and heard my mom and dad talking in their room nearby. My mom was upset. I never heard her voice tremble while she tried to choke back tears until that day. Her voice was full of fear. My mother was a brave woman, so I was surprised to see her so terribly frightened.

My dad opened the door, then paused when he saw us and said good morning as I walked behind my sister into my mom's room. "What's wrong, Mom?" I asked. I did not like seeing my mom so upset. She looked at me and assured me she was OK and asked me to go into the kitchen for a few minutes so she could talk to my sister.

Instead, I went to the backyard with my dad, who was staring up at a big Oak tree with luscious green leaves. I loved that tree. I have always loved to play on this tree since before I was even in kindergarten. Only then, the tree was without its leaves, and the bark appeared gray and brittle.

"What happened to our tree?" I inquired.

"I don't know, sugar, but it looks like maybe lightning struck it and killed it overnight." My dad was in awe of how quickly the tree went from being healthy to looking diseased and weakened. It was sad to see something once so strong and lovely turn into something weak and brittle seemingly overnight.

My mom was watching me play with my dog when the neighbor, Maria, started approaching our yard. "Well, Frank, that young man staying across the street left first thing this morning. He thinks his ex-girlfriend's family sent El diablo after him." Maria laughed only momentarily before continuing. "I saw him in your tree too."

My mom approached her. "The devil, I don't know. I thought it was a demon."

The two looked over at me. I was pretending not to listen while playing with my dog. They walked over to the tree, both in shock that it just died overnight. My dad said lightning might have hit it, which was strange to me since we didn't have any troubling weather that evening. I think we all knew what killed it, and it wasn't lightning.

My mom told Maria in a low voice that she looked out the window last night and saw something fly into the tree. She explained that she only got a glimpse of it, but it was horribly disfigured with large wings, and even though she saw it briefly, she could see its large veins pulsating. She said it almost reminded her of an insect, like a man-sized locust. Only, it was larger than a man; it was massive in size as it stood upon the tree. My mother felt, without a doubt, it was evil and responsible for causing the tree to perish.

Maria quietly listened to my mother. My mom was starting to worry that Maria was thinking she imagined it when Maria quietly said, "Frank was terrified. He wouldn't tell anyone where he was going. He was just very frightened of el Diablo." her voice trailed off. "The Devil." She quietly muttered.

Maria explained that Frank would stay with Ruby a lot when he was in Mexico. Even Maria said it would be no surprise if something was after him. They messed around with Santeria and played with dark magic. Frank was there to look in on Ruby's house but also to run errands for her. She told my mom he stayed with her because he did not want to be at Ruby's house alone. He said he couldn't sleep because things were walking around the house at night, keeping him awake. Maria felt certain he just wanted her to cook and take care of him while he visited, but I think he was telling her the truth.

I found it odd when Maria told my mom Ruby was a nice girl once upon a time. She said she knew her in Mexico long ago. But sadly, she changed from the kind young girl she once knew. Maria expressed hope that Ruby would permanently return to Mexico. They all had an uneasy feeling when she was at the house across the street.

My mom said, "I saw the demon, or whatever it was. I saw it land on the tree, spin its head around slowly, and then stand up. He was tall and imposing. Before I could call out for Jack, it flew away. Something inside me warned me it was a demon. I was frozen and sweat started dripping off of me instantly. I know what I saw, but Jack dismissed it as my mind playing tricks on me. Do you think that sounds crazy?"

Maria shook her head. "I think you are right, but I believe in this type of stuff. I think it's too coincidental that you saw something. Frank and I…we both saw it too, and he was so frightened by it. Then your tree just died without warning. You're not crazy, no. Did you see the other thing chasing him?"

My mom put her hand on her head and said, "I didn't, but I got the distinct feeling it was angry, maybe even afraid. Was an angel chasing it?"

Maria paused. "No…I don't know what it was, but it was not an angel. I don't know what to call it. Maybe I'm wrong." Maria took a breath. "Whatever it was, the demon, entity, or whatever, ran away from it."

Later in the evening, my mom was waiting for Mia outside when my sister came home from work. I couldn't hear anything they were discussing, but my mom seemed very upset. I think she wanted to know a little more about the shit my sister was involved in, trying to figure out the cause of the visit of the devilish ghoul that killed our tree.

I think when my sister was hanging with the wrong kids at school and was experiencing depression, perhaps she was unwittingly flirting with the devil and skirting around the edges of the occult. I believe she was tiptoeing in the water to see what it was about but knowing she would never go swimming the whole time.

I couldn't hear their discussion, but I could see my sister was shaking her head no. Mia's body language was very defensive. My only guess is my mom suspected my sister opened a world up to our family that we didn't want anything to do with. Whatever my mom saw, it scared the shit out of her, and she wanted it stopped immediately. Of course, it wasn't Mia's fault, but Mia, too, had encountered a demon just before that night and told my mom about her devil-loving friends at school.

Later in the week, I was jumping on the trampoline with a school friend and he inquired about the tree. We used to climb on it all the time. He, too, was surprised to see it weakened and almost deformed-looking now.

"It's dead; my dad is cutting it down Sunday when he doesn't have to work," I explained to him.

He looked at the tree. "Well, let's go climb it for the last time!"

I agreed and we ran to the tree and started climbing. My friend jumped down before going too far up to tie his shoe. As I reached for the branch, I felt a familiar presence. I was distracted by the feeling as I reached and missed the branch. I fell onto the ground, and my hand went through a window that was propped up against the house. My dad was going to haul the old window off when he cut the tree down. Unfortunately for me, I fell through the window, shattering it before he had the chance to get rid of it.

I don't know why, but I was afraid of getting in trouble for breaking the window, so I began running around the outside of the house crying with blood squirting out of my wrist. My mom stopped me as I reached the front yard. She tried to calm me from crying and hollering.

As the chaos of the moment was smothering me, a calmness came over me and I knew. I looked at the brown house and I saw her. Ruby, the witch, was back home from Mexico and watching from her door. I knew the pain I felt gave her sick pleasure and she fed on my fear.

I became angry. I didn't blame her for my fall, but I did blame her for watching and enjoying my pain. I angrily dried my tears—I was seething—as my mom wrapped my wrist with her bandana while my dad went to get the car to take me to the hospital. I felt myself leave my body for the first time ever. I could see myself looking over at the witch house and yelling to her, "I'm fine! I don't care. I'm FINE!"

This was my first time directly confronting with her—the first time I ever laid eyes on her as she stepped out from behind the shadows of her door and onto the porch where I first saw her and not her shadow. She wanted me to see her. She wanted me to see she was smiling at my pain. She wanted me to know she was a beautiful witch, not just a shadow watching from the doorway. Not some fragile old lady.

Ruby, the witch. I memorized the curves of her face as she flashed a crooked smile at me. It was malicious and made her ugly to me. She didn't have any shoes on, just her bare feet on the porch. She sat down and slowly waved goodbye to me as my parents loaded me into the car. I scooted myself to the far window of the car and smiled back at her. I was, of course, being a smart-ass kid that was fed up with her antics. I rolled down my window and yelled, "No! I will not let you in!"

She knew. She knew, without a doubt, I was aware of her presence in my dreams and I was, in fact, finally standing up for myself. I believe she felt confronted. She knew I was angry with her. She enjoyed the games she was playing with me. Ruby accepted the challenge I unknowingly presented to her. She accepted that challenge with a great deal of pleasure.

My dad asked my mother to roll up my window and inquired if I hit my head very hard. Of course, my ravings didn't make any sense to them, but I knew—and that witch-bitch knew—my head was just fine. I had finally reached my breaking point with her.

I got thirteen ugly black stitches across my wrist that day. The gash went the entire way across my wrist. I knew the vindictive witch was going to love seeing my pain. I don't, even to this day, understand why someone would get pleasure from someone's pain.

I'll never understand cruel people. Well, I am no coward, and I sure as hell wasn't a coward as a kid. Unfortunately, I was a kid who didn't know any better, but I *should have* known better than to indulge a hateful—and very likely mentally unstable—woman. But, being the stupid kid I was, I gleefully showed off my stitches to my friends, bragging and showing off my wound. "It barely hurt!" I would brag and look over in her direction as a way to snub her. Obviously, it did hurt, and it was very ugly too.

As I laid in bed, I wondered why my nightmares stopped whenever Ruby was in Mexico. Was I out of sight, out of mind? Was I simply too far away? Was all this just my imagination? I would always try to figure out the crazy world I was tangled up in.

The next morning, I got a phone call from my school friend, Charlotte. She asked me to have a sleepover. I begged my mom because she never let me do sleepovers. It drove me crazy! I resented that she was so overprotective with me and felt my sister had a lot more freedom than I had. I finally persuaded her to allow me to stay the night since this was the last day of school and Charlotte was moving over the summer.

Charlotte and I had a good time talking and making fun of her older sisters, who were getting ready to go to an end-of-the-school-year dance. They were fixing their hair while bickering with each other, yelling at one another about hurrying up as they were running out of time to leave. They left out in a hurry, leaving makeup scattered around the rooms and bathrooms with clothes tossed around the floors.

I met her mom on the car ride but didn't see her much after arriving at their house. Her stepdad didn't come home until later in the evening. He introduced himself and told me I was such a cute little girl. I was really awkward with compliments, but I still smiled and told him thank you. He seemed to be very nice and tried engaging with us often throughout the evening. In fact, it was annoying that he kept barging in and constantly interrupting us.

Charlotte and I got into a bit of an argument about our teacher later in the evening. I liked her a great deal, and Charlotte was making fun of her, which really upset me. Silly little girl fights about a whole lot of nothing, as I look back on it all now.

Her mother came in and told us we needed to settle down for bed. She noticed that we were upset with one another and she sent me to her room. I thought she was mad at me and was going to call my mom, so I was quite upset, but then she told me to get in her bed and she opened the door to the bathroom. She stepped into the entry of the bathroom and began speaking to whom I could only guess was Charlotte's stepdad. "She is in the bed; she is sleeping with us tonight. I'm going to tell Charlotte to go to sleep and I will be back."

I was scared. I wasn't sure why I was being made to lay in their bed. Charlotte and I weren't that upset with each other, and I would much rather make up and not be made to stay in her parents' room, which felt very strange and uncomfortable for me.

As I laid in their bed, wondering why I was in trouble and when I would be allowed to leave the room, her mom came back. She took off her robe and laid next to me, scooting herself to the edge while rolling me more towards the middle of the bed. She laid on her side, then turned away from me, facing the wall. I laid on my back, wondering what I could say to be able to go back to Charlotte's room. I didn't want to sleep with her parents.

After a few minutes, the bathroom door opened, and Charlotte's stepfather stood there in his towel, looking at me and smiling. He had a hairy chest and dark hairy legs. I shut my eyes tightly. I felt so out of place and began feeling very scared. I never even slept in my own parents bed, so this was very unfamiliar and uneasy for me.

As Charlotte's stepdad approached, he began speaking to me, I assume to put me at ease. "There's that pretty girl. Are you sleeping in here tonight, sweetheart?"

My voice shook a little. "I think so." I looked in her mom's direction but she didn't budge. I knew she was awake, but she didn't turn around or say a single word. The light from the bathroom was really bright, and I could only see his silhouette as he began walking towards the bed, dropping his towel as he walked, exposing himself.

"Scoot a little closer towards me." He rubbed my leg; his hands felt so large on my small thigh. He took his penis into his hand and started stroking himself until his penis was erect. I was terrified and felt sick to my stomach.

As he began to scoot me to the edge of the bed, he began rubbing his rough heavy hands up and down my legs. I started crying; my legs were shaking. I could literally hear my heart beating in my ears as my throat felt like it was closing on me, and I couldn't seem to speak a word.

I finally mustered up the ability to mutter, "I just want to go home." He chuckled a little then grabbed my leg, pulled me closer, and placed my hand on his penis. I felt so afraid and sickened; I believe I left my body. I was watching myself from the corner of the room. I guess I was not responding to him; everything was in slow motion. He shook me and told me to look at him. I watched as I appeared to lay lifeless on his bed.

I went from watching in the corner to seeing what appeared to be my shadow coming back into my body and the mayhem became surreal again. Just then, there was a loud knocking on the door—a panic-knocking, almost. It was like whoever knocked at the door was about to blow through it. It was so loud it shook the windows upstairs.

I was terrified. I used the distraction as my way out of the hell I was about to endure. I jumped up and said, "That's my mom! I called her to pick me up." Of course, that was a lie, but I was able to think quickly to escape what would have been a horrible situation for me. I ran out of the room so fast that I practically flew across the house and down the stairs.

My stomach felt like it was in my throat. I could literally see my body get up and could feel my soul rejoin me. It happened so abruptly and was a creepy feeling—one I can't exactly explain. I never ran so fast in my entire life. I didn't know who or what would be standing there when I opened the front door, nor did I care. I just needed to remove myself from that dreadful situation.

As I flung the front door open, I didn't know what to expect. I knew it wasn't my mother. Strangely enough, no one was there. Did I hallucinate? I am not sure, but I do know that I ran very fast down the road with my bare feet, paying no attention to the pain of the gravel and rocks I scoured across as I began running home. I was so afraid; it didn't even phase me—not one bit. My heart was pounding. It was pitch black out, and I could only see the streetlights that dimly lit up the roads ahead of me. I was navigating a scary neighborhood late at night, all by myself. The frightful shadows of the trees, and only God knows what else lurking and watching me as I ran the streets alone. No one else around me, except for the shadows of the night. Dogs barking and howling as I ran so fast to make my escape.

I would always be plagued with nightmares about that evening. I would dream that I was slowly running with tears streaming down my face but not making a single sound. In this hellish nightmare, I was always that little girl running in fear. I was always in the distance watching myself in the darkness. I can't hear my cries in the dream. Not even a whimper. The only sound I can hear is my feet in the gravel and the dogs barking and howling as I ran home—five long blocks. I would always helplessly watch myself running and crying when I would have that dreadful nightmare.

The night this all happened, it seemed to take forever for me to reach my house. When I finally made it to my yard, I collapsed. I became very dizzy and practically crawled to our porch and sat on the first step, intentionally looking across the street. There was no one there, and I felt relieved.

Just then, Dulce and my sister came home and saw me sitting on the porch. I was sure they had been out drinking, since they were uncharacteristically laughing and falling over each other. Trust me; my parents would have shit kittens if they knew Mia was out underage drinking. Mia made me promise not to tell my parents she stayed out late with Dulce.

My sister asked why I was home, and I told her Charlotte and I were upset with each other. I told her I didn't want my mom and dad to know that I ran home. She was so upset with me, lecturing me about the dangers. I asked her to promise not to tell our parents. The last thing I wanted was for my mom to call Charlotte's mom, and trust me, if my dad knew what happened…I had no doubt my dad would kill Charlotte's stepdad, had he known what that pig was about to do to me.

The following day, Mia didn't feel well. I covered for her, naturally, saying I came home too, fibbing that we were both sick from a stomach virus. We never told on each other. We stuck up for one another. We were sisters and nothing could divide us. Before I died, we were so close and cared so much for one another's happiness. We had an unbreakable bond.

Chapter Four
Serendipity

I remember on my eleventh birthday; my mom made me my favorite cake. I loved yellow cake with milk chocolate frosting. Even though it was old-fashioned at that time, it was still my favorite. I didn't want a cake from a bakery. I wanted my mom to bake me the cake because hers was the best.

As my family was singing "Happy Birthday," I closed my eyes to make a wish. I knew what I wanted for my birthday, more than anything else. I wanted Ruby to go away. I wished for her to leave and stay away from me as I blew out the candles. I wished her away. Yes. I knew it wasn't going to happen, but that is what my heart wanted. Anytime she was in town, trouble for me followed, and I don't believe it was all by coincidence.

As her house across the street went up for sale a week later, I knew it was serendipitous, but I knew Ruby's ass was going far away, which was the highlight of my day. I assumed the witch would fly back to Mexico, and I prayed it would be far away from anyone so she couldn't cause harm. Good riddance to the old witch-bitch that she was.

That same week, Dulce came to stay next door but only for a short bit. She was the first female in her family to go to college, and she was so proud of herself—even if her father wasn't as impressed. I remember her telling my sister that her family didn't see a need for her to go to college. I was proud of her, even if they were not. I did find it strange she was going to pursue an education in psychology. Why didn't she ever fix her mentally unstable hex-ass aunt Ruby, I would wonder.

I found out nearly a month after Ruby departed that she was going home to care for her ailing mother, who was getting ready to pass. Apparently, Ruby wasn't taking it well. I don't know why, but it surprised me. She never struck me as a nurturer. Not even a little. I never associated Ruby with actually being a human. Strangely, I guess, as silly as it sounds, I thought she was more like a vampire—soulless, cold, immortal.

As a young girl, I wondered if Ruby possessed a magical gift and why she wasn't living a glamorous and beautiful life. I just dismissed it as she wasn't right in the head, maybe. Mean, evil, sinister, selfish, perhaps. If I were a witch, I would want a beautiful life. I would also bless those around me with an abundance of love and beauty.

*****

As my mother and Maria were talking one day, my mother's eyes began to well up with tears. She tried to share with Maria what was on her heart. "Jack..." her voice trailed off. "He is sick again, and the doctor's prognosis…well, isn't good."

Although I knew she meant my dad, I was a little baffled. He is sick again? To my knowledge, my dad had never been seriously sick before, so I found this comment odd. Listening to them talk was very upsetting. I knew, then, my mother had been keeping secrets from me.

I stood up and approached the two ladies to interrupt their whispers about my father. My mother took my hand, and we went to my dad's work truck. She laid the tailgate down and I hopped up onto it. I stood momentarily looking at her. I wanted to know and didn't want to know at the same time.

"So," she began. "A few years back, your dad had gotten very ill with a blood disorder. You were too young to know about it. We didn't tell you so you wouldn't be afraid." My mind flashed back to many instances of my parents coming home late after my dad's treatments. I never knew, of course, and was too young to even question what was going on.

I then remembered Mia crying in her room often. Then she sought happiness by hanging around other kids with problems and reading books about magic. All the things that weren't in her character started coming together in that instant for me.

My mom crossed her arms and put her head down, closing her

eyes. "Baby, your dad's disease is very aggressive, and the doctors are saying there isn't much they can do but try to keep him comfortable."

At that moment, I knew the doctors had given up on him, and it made me angry. I don't know if I was angry at her or the situation, but I was seething and internalizing my feelings, as usual. I had another thought about my sister. She must have felt angry when she found out my dad was sick the first time. I believe she was angry at God too. I suspect that's why she became interested in the dark books and skeevy friends. I think she took an interest in the tarot cards too, trying to figure out the future. Not hers but my dad's. She was always a daddy's girl. We both were. We adored our dad so much. Naturally, I wanted to see my dad, tell him I knew and hug him.

After my mom talked to me, I went into the house and leaned against the entryway door to the living room, watching my dad play a video game.

"Daddy's just about to rescue the princess. Want to watch?"

He and I loved playing video games together. I went to the foot of his chair and watched him finally conquer level eight. He was quite proud of himself. It's a nice memory I will forever preserve. I didn't ruin the moment by bringing up what I had just learned about his failing health.

Towards the end of my dad's life, he started seeing things—maybe because of the medication or perhaps he was between life and death. This frightened him. Also, though I cannot quite explain it, the house felt different. There was evil energy there—a sadness so heavy I could barely take a breath without inhaling a thick sense of dread.

In hindsight, I believe whatever was in the house with us was feeding off his fear of the unknown—dying and leaving his family behind. We all felt a presence. I believe it was Ruby lurking and watching in on my family somehow.

I remember the night my dad passed away. I had held his hand as he went to be with Jesus. I felt a slight squeeze on my hand as he was telling me it was time for him to go, and then...he left me.

It was a very difficult time for us when he passed from our world into the next. It breaks my heart to think he was afraid, and I hope he was at peace more than anything and felt no sadness or fear when he left us behind.

After my dad passed away, it was time for me to bury the last six months of his suffering. I filed it away like a nightmare tapping on my window, never letting it in. I chose to remember the little silly things that brought me joy when I thought of them, like my dad bringing me mints from his job. Those were so good, and I loved raiding his truck to get them. I remembered zoo trips we took.

And, oddly enough, I thought about little things I used to do to annoy him. I was actually an ace when it came to picking and button-pushing. One of my favorite things to do when he was in the recliner sleeping was gently run my fingernail softly on the underside of his foot to make him jump and use swear words. It always amused me because he would doze off in his chair after a long day of working in the hot sun. I would want to watch TV—something other than Barney Miller or Star Trek—so I would try to turn the channel, but my dad would stop the snoring and twitch long enough to tell me to put it back and assure me that he was only resting his eyes, even though he was snoring. Needless to say, I thought I was hot shit when I finally got my very own TV in my room. Those are the memories I choose to keep—not the suffering and pain or fear he may have endured during his passing away.

The little things he loved became so precious to me, and I will keep those to myself. But one thing I will share is that a yellow rose blooming in a field always brings me a smile. My dad loved yellow roses because they made him remember his mother. I never met her, but he would tell me about her sometimes. He told me she had a beautiful garden of yellow roses when he was growing up. I also thought about my dad when his favorite songs would come on the radio. Memories of him always had a way to fill my heart with sadness and happiness at the same time.

My sister and my mom took over raising me once my father passed to the next world. The house still felt very heavy with sadness. It's hard to explain, but even though I knew my daddy went to Heaven, it still felt like a dark presence was in the house. My mom and Mia felt it too, but we never spoke about it. I guess we coexisted and hoped it would go away. But I know we weren't imagining it; we weren't the only ones who sensed it.

My mom had gotten me a new computer desk. In the late nineties, computers were quite the thing, and they were bulky in size. I thought it was such a big deal to have one in my room. Well, the desk needed some assembly, so my sister had a friend named Adrian—though he preferred to be called Deon—come over to help.

He had occasionally come over to help my mom with things after my daddy died, but this was the first time I had met him. He seemed really nice and was good to my sister.

The evening Deon came over to assemble my desk, my mom and I were at the store to get a few things. Even though it was only seven-thirty, it was pretty dark outside. The lights already lit the streets.

When we pulled into the driveway, Deon was already outside, standing at the corner next to his car. He hurried over to us when we got out of the car, and he looked scared to death. I mean, he was trembling! He motioned my mom over and said, "You don't know me well, but trust me, I'm not crazy. I don't know what is going on at your house, but there is something in there. I am not going back in. I don't want you to go in either. Keep my tools; I don't need them." He gestured to the house and started shaking his head. He was so shaken he didn't even know what to do. "I was assembling the desk, and I thought I felt something breathing, so I turned to look but didn't see anything." His voice shook while he spoke. "I started working on the desk again, and I heard the breathing. I swear to God, when I looked up, it appeared that the walls were breathing. I heard them and then I saw them. The walls were breathing! I'm leaving, but I think you all should leave too; something is going on inside the house."

I'm not sure what it was in the house or what was going on, but it was a long night. My mom, Mia and I did hear breathing but only in my room. It was eerie, to say the least. We all piled in and slept with my mom that night, but we didn't leave our home. My mom said, "This is our house. Your dad's house. We aren't being chased away by anyone or anything." I was really afraid, so I would have been just fine leaving, but I knew she thought it best to stand our ground.

The next morning, my mom's mother showed up unexpectedly. This was a happy surprise, as she was going to stay with us for a while to help with the house and me now that Mom would start working again. I loved my granny. My family called me Lucy, but my granny usually called me by my legal name, Lucinda. The only times my mom and dad called me Lucinda were the times I knew I was in big trouble. You know when you're in big trouble when the legal name comes out, but to my granny, I was always Lucinda.

Granny was a pistol. Let me tell you, she wasn't a sweet nana that made homemade cookies. Don't get me wrong, she cooked and baked, but that lady talked some serious shit and had no qualms about saying exactly what she thought. I am pretty sure she and my mom made me the smart-ass "almost" teenager that I was. Granny had a quick wit and a smart mouth. She was from the South. What more could you expect?

The first thing Granny did when she arrived was open all the windows, light her sage, and begin cleansing the house. Finally, the house felt fresh again. I think the cleaning did wonders, and cleansing the space took all the negative energy out, along with the sadness and the stagnant feeling of despair.

One afternoon, I walked into my mom's room and noticed my granny was reading the Bible. OK, this was new. She very well may have been a believer, but she was certainly not a holier-than-thou type of lady.

"Lucy, tell me something. Do you believe in this, or do you think it's crap?"

That was unexpected. I sat down with her. "I believe in God, I guess, but we're not exactly on speaking terms."

She was surprised by my answer for some reason. "Why is that I wonder? Do you fault God for your daddy dying?"

I took a deep breath, debating if I should tell her or if she'd only try to talk to me about it and convince me otherwise. "I just haven't felt God before, and when I did pray, he said no, and that's really all I want to say about it, I guess." That was my way of hoping she wouldn't begin to lecture me on my salvation. I believed in God, but I was disappointed that he took my dad and wasn't ready to be reasoned with on the matter. I was just a kid. I had a long life ahead of me to get right with God; that's the way I'd seen it.

To my utmost surprise, she didn't lecture me at all. No. Instead, she scolded me. Go figure. She told me to follow her. We went to my room where she had found the books that once belonged to my sister and pulled them out from under the bed. They were still in the box, of course. She slid the box towards me.

"Do you believe in magic?" she inquired.

Honestly, at that time, I didn't know what to believe in terms of magic. I didn't read the books of my sister's that I had recovered. I didn't read the Bible. I didn't delve into anything, really. I did know there were evil people in the world, and I knew bad things happened to very good people. I guess I was a little unsure how or who decided the haves and the have nots. The lucky ones and the unlucky ones. Who got to be blessed and who was shit on.

I was worried she would be mad at me for having the books. Like, she would think I was some heathen or a goddamned devil worshiper. I wasn't either of those things! Certainly not a devil worshiper. I always knew that wasn't the way to go for sure. I could have shifted the blame of the books in the house onto my sister, but we didn't tattle on each other, and in all fairness, she did intend on throwing out the books to begin with. I had recovered them from the trash, so that was on me.

"Yeah, I got those at a garage sale. I thought they were just scary stories, but once I got them home, I noticed they were different from what I thought they would be. So yeah, we can burn them this weekend and dance around them like wild heathens if that's what you want to do," I said in a joking manner.

Granny laughed but gave me a look that said she knew I was lying. It was spooky the way Granny could always see right through me. I could never get away with a lie to her—not even a white lie.

My mom came in to see us but quickly excused herself to answer the phone as it began ringing off the hook in the next room. My granny was still looking at me, waiting for me to tell her I was lying about where I had gotten the books. I would have told her, but I figured it would lead to too many questions and implicate Mia in having the books in the house to begin with, so I said nothing.

My granny shook her head. "Lucinda, don't open doors you can't close, and never call upon something you can't banish."

I looked at her with some surprise. "What do you know about that?" I asked, never expecting her to really talk to me about the dark side of religion.

"You have to be careful. You never know someone's heart, and people don't always use special gifts for good; sometimes they use it for selfish reasons," she explained. I was intrigued. "Want me to tell you a story about a girl I knew named Heidi?"

As she inquired, I, of course wanted to be cheeky and act like a smart aleck. "Only if the story isn't going to bore me," I replied with a smart-ass grin on my face.

"Sit your ass down and let me tell you. I will keep it short and sweet for you. Heidi was a cute little girl I knew, who had something magical about her. There was a witch that was after her and wanted to hurt her. I had to keep sending her away to protect Heidi. Between Heidi and her sister, I was always having to send away demons and witches and, perhaps the evilest of all, pedophiles."

Our eyes met and locked on each other. She looked deep in my eyes, into my soul, and said to me, "Never summon entities you cannot control, and never let your guard down away from your soul."

I nodded and then she said to me, "And always, ALWAYS report a pedophile."

As I went to leave the room, she said, "There isn't anything lower than someone that would hurt an innocent child." I got chill bumps on me. I knew she knew about Charlotte's stepfather, but I couldn't understand how. I had never told a soul. I felt ashamed and scared, even though I had done nothing wrong. I was innocent back then and never experienced such evil at the hands of anyone—certainly not a parental figure I had been entrusted with by my very protective mother.

My sister's car crept in the driveway. I had so many questions, but my granny stood up and put her finger to her lips to silence me. "You can't conceal your secrets from me, baby. I run in the shadows too!" she exclaimed.

That was a little weird to me, honestly. I wanted to know what she knew, what she meant. Hell. Was she a witch too? Or like, some witch hunter? What did she see? I had so many more questions, but we were interrupted by my mom and Mia. I was most definitely going to talk to her about this when we were alone again.

At bedtime that night, my mind was racing. Had it been Granny who sent the knock that helped me escape my friend's perverted stepfather? Did she banish the demon that my sister conjured to meet her when she was so desperately miserable? Was it really Granny that would send Ruby away from me when I was facing challenging times with her being across the street from our family? Was she the reason the demon in the tree left so abruptly? If so, how did she do it and how did she know?

The door to my room slowly crept open, and the hall light glared at me as my granny walked in. Standing at the door, she softly laughed. "You are just not going to sleep tonight until you talk to me, are you?" She stepped closer to the foot of my bed. "Since you don't have school tomorrow, I guess we can talk a little about what's weighing on your mind." She sat on my bed, and I scooched over as she looked at me with a grin on her face.

I sat up and we just stared at each other. "Are you a witch, Granny?" I asked bluntly. I just wanted to know. To be honest, I kind of wanted her to be. Well, I wanted her to be a good witch that banished evil witches and demons and protected us.

"Sweet Lucy. You are as subtle as a smack upside the head." She laughed at me. "It's not as simple as a yes or no answer. You and I were born with gifts of magic, but it is a call you must choose to answer. You either embrace your gifts and work to strengthen them, or you ignore them. If you choose to ignore your gifts, you'll find that, as you grow older, you will dismiss your intuition, dumb it down, and eventually lose your abilities. I guess some people label those who possess these gifts as witches. So, yes. I suppose I am a witch if I have been blessed and practice my many gifts."

I nodded and stared at her, open-mouthed before she continued.

"In time, you may gain some of it, or you may lose it forever. It's up to you what you do with the magic that I know you have just like I had at your age. I just caution you, if you answer your call and build your gifts, it will complicate your life at times. Sometimes, your gifts will tempt you to use your abilities for selfishness. Once you enjoy the pleasures of indulging, you will catch yourself in a dark circle. This is called black magic. Dark magic." I nodded again. "You can unintentionally open your thoughts to demons and followers of the dark craft, and you don't want to do that. Use your ability for your protection. Use it to watch over your loved ones, but be cautious using it for other reasons, even when you are tempted and think it's just a little nudge. If it's for selfish gains, you will pay it back in some way. The devil will always make it look sexy and tempting to be selfish, but..." she paused and looked down at the floor. "Lucy, never eat the rotten apple."

"Why did they hang and stone all witches in America? Are all witches bad?" I asked. I didn't really know what else to say. How do you acknowledge the fact that your grandmother just confirmed she was a witch? Thankfully, I felt confident she was at least a good witch.

She took the time to explain it to me very simply. "There were a lot of superstitious and scared men during those days. Some that were accused didn't even practice the craft. Anyone who was different, or an enemy of the power at hand, was a target. Any person with land and no family to defend them was a target. Men, women and even children were punished for witchcraft. They would hang them or stone them after torturous imprisonment."

She motioned for me to follow her, and we walked into the kitchen. She reached into a drawer next to the stove and pulled out a box of matches. "In Europe, they knew the only way to truly banish the witch and anything possessing her was to burn her."

"Why would they burn her? That's so mean and terrible," I wondered.

"She becomes one with the flame. Take note that when you light the match, the flame doesn't have a shadow." Granny lit the match and held it next to the wall where the only silhouette was the matchstick. The flame didn't have a shadow. It was then that I knew the fact that my shadow could separate from my living body, and that my soul hid within my shadow and couldn't be seen by anyone else, meant I had a special kind of magic. Maybe I was a little witchy too and didn't even realize it.

My sister noticed the light on in my room, but I wasn't in there, so she found us in the kitchen. "What are you night owls doing up? Let's order some pizza. I'm starving."

My granny nodded. "Lucy, go wake your mom and see if she would like some!"

I was excited. A late night in our PJ's with pizza sounded pretty fun, and honestly, we needed a little fun. It had been too long since we enjoyed an evening together.

I knocked on my mom's door, but she didn't answer. I began opening the door and looked behind me when I heard my granny's voice. "Close your eyes." I did as she said and my heart skipped a beat. In my head, I heard my mom softly sobbing. My eyes jolted wide open. The vision was so clear, it was like I was in the room with her.

"Go to your mom quietly and sit with her. She is missing your daddy and feeling lost. Interrupt her sadness for a moment and let her hear her baby's voice."

My mom was in the ensuite bathroom, so I walked to it and quietly opened the door. Mom was sitting on the shower floor with the water cascading over her. "Mom, don't leave me." Such a strange thing to say, I know, but the words just flowed out of my mouth.

My mom stopped sobbing, stood up and turned the water off and poked her head out from behind the shower curtain. "What's wrong, baby?" I could hear the concern in her trembling voice. "I'm not going anywhere. What's wrong?"

"Come hang with us, Mom. Put on your PJ's for the pizza party."

She shook her head but then said, "OK. Give me a minute."

I waited for her outside her bedroom door then greeted her with the biggest and warmest hug when she came out.

We had a nice night eating pizza and talking. My sister gave us the latest grocery store gossip. She didn't particularly care for her manager, who seemed to be trying a little too hard to hang onto her youth. She was a bleached blonde sixty-something-year-old that wore tight short skirts and was, to my understanding, sleeping with the assistant store manager, who was a very tall Jamaican man. A very tall Jamaican, *married* man.

My sister shared with us that her manager, Nancy, was wearing her little black skirt and showing off her flabby thighs and her new tan she had been working on relentlessly in the tanning beds. Mia was such a hoot. No doubt she was talking shit only to cheer up my mother and trying to make her laugh.

"Nancy was squeezed into that itty bitty skirt. She looked like a busted can of biscuits."

Yes, it was a mean thing for her to say, but we laughed. I guess we felt justified somehow because we knew how mean Nancy was to her employees. She had a spiteful side to her, unfortunately. My sister bitched about her all the time.

"She has been tanning so much she looks like a damn piece of fried chicken," she cackled and we laughed. "Oh, Nancy is gonna get her ass kicked by Junior's wife if she isn't careful."

I don't know why, but when the laughter seized, I leaned forward and said, "Don't go to work tomorrow."

My sister looked at me and blew off my comment. Granny paused and put down her pizza. "Aren't you off tomorrow?" she pressed my sister.

"Yeah, I was supposed to work, but you asked me to take it off to take you to the doctor, so I switched days. I work Wednesday night now."

The mood shifted back, and my mind felt at ease knowing my sister wouldn't be at work. Something inside urged me to make sure my sister wouldn't be at work the following day. I had no idea why, just an ominous feeling I couldn't shake.

It was past midnight when we decided it was time to sleep. My mom had never let me stay up quite that late before. She was going to see me off to bed, but my granny offered to so my mom could get some rest.

Granny tucked me in and said, "Get some rest, Lucinda. We will spend some time talking tomorrow. Close off your mind and think about good things." I agreed, and as I laid my head to pray, my heart and mind were set at ease.

*****

I had a peaceful night's rest. In fact, I slept nearly until ten in the morning before my granny woke me.

"Get dressed and meet me out back on the deck. Your mom and sister are going to run errands before we go to my appointment, so let's talk about and practice your visioning."

I wasn't sure what that really meant but it sounded enticing. I got dressed and grabbed a banana off the bar and met Granny outside. She had a cup of hot water sitting on the table. I sat down and reached for a tea bag.

Granny said to do everything with a positive intent. She took the tea bag and placed it in the hot water then added more hot water to the cup. She dunked the tea bag in and out and took a teaspoon full of sugar. "May Lucy's mom, Kezziah, have a sweet day." She stirred the tea slowly and stopped, then began stirring it counterclockwise. "May her normal thoughts be positive. Banish all sadness from her day today. Let only positive conception take over her thoughts." My granny looked at me and said even the small simple things in life make it a ritual, so we should send blessings to those we love. "Simply stir clockwise for positive energy and speak it aloud. Counterclockwise for banishing negative energy and situations."

Then she shifted the subject. "Tell me what you saw. Why didn't you want your sister to go to work? What did you see, and what did you feel?"

"Well, it wasn't good, but I didn't see anything. I just felt afraid for her to go to work, but I don't know why."

My granny said to me, "You know we all have gifts. I don't think you are exactly psychic. I think you do have a gift, though; I think you are intuitive."

I didn't know what an intuitive was, but Granny explained it is someone that gets strong premonitions and feelings about a person or a situation. She advised me to follow it, even if it feels uncomfortable. She even went so far as to warn me to trust it and to trust myself over any words of another.

"Sometimes, people dismiss their intuition because it seems silly or they're afraid of hurting someone's feelings, and it gets them in trouble. Follow yours if you get a gut feeling about someone or a situation. Don't dismiss it," Granny made me promise. "There are a lot of dead women because they didn't want to be rude to a man that they didn't know. So, don't be afraid to hurt their feelings. You'll never see them again—or maybe you will, and they will know not to mess with you. Either way, you live. Trust your gut. I'm proud of you for putting yourself out there and making sure you voiced concerns over Mia going to work." She stood up and shifted her eyes back to me. "You're right; she doesn't need to go to work today and that's why I made sure she was taking the day off."

I didn't inquire what she knew, but it was more than what I felt. I am certain she knew my sister shouldn't go to work. I guess my granny was a witch by definition. She was magical and divine in her own way. She had the best heart of anyone I knew, and her words were always wise, always right.

After I knew my sister wasn't going to be at work, my next concern was my mom. When she was with us, she'd smile—maybe even laugh with us—but her eyes were so empty. She was grieving, no doubt, but I wanted her pain to subside. I wanted my mom to stop hurting so much. She worked a lot and basically was just going through the motions of each day. I couldn't stop thinking about her. I was a young girl then, but I was so unsettled about her relentless and overwhelming sadness.

My mom had lost her husband in her late forties. She used to be a stay-at-home mom, and now she was without her husband, working full time, taking care of her girls, and grieving in her spare time. Without me even asking, my granny knew what I was worried about.

She tried to assure me. "Baby, no, your mama is just missing your dad and is going through the natural stages of grief. She is only imagining being with him again. I've learned that grief is just like any other wound. It may heal, but when the wound is deep, the scar remains. Healing is a process like any other wound. There is a natural process. First, you stop the bleeding. Then, the wound scabs over. The less you pick at it, the faster it heals. Once it heals, the old wound isn't as visible, but it's still there. It may hurt, it may even still be visible. Unless you keep picking at it, the bleeding will stop and it will heal with time as most things do. Eventually you may not even notice the scar any longer, but you know it's just under the surface." She brushed my hair back away from my eyes. "What your mom, my baby, needs is our love and our support. Let me explain it this way. Try to think of death as temporary. When we die, we reunite with our loved ones and they are so excited to see you crossing over. You are no longer confined by your body. You can cross back and forth and see your loved ones on both sides, living and dead alike. You will someday be able to interact with your loved ones again once we leave the bodies that bound us to this world."

I really wish I would have asked her more questions on this topic. If I knew I would be dying, I absolutely would have asked more questions. I'm not sure if she really knew more or if she was just simply trying to comfort me about death, but now that I have died, I think she probably did know a few things on this subject matter.

Instead of inquiring, I let her continue talking to me about my mom. "Yes, your mom is sad and needs to be grounded and reminded of the love she has here. In her mind, she is standing in the middle of a storm, which she will have to weather until your daddy welcomes her to the other side when it's her time. Sunny days will come again with time," she explained. "She wants to be with your dad but it's not her turn. If you go when it's not your time—if you take it upon yourself to end your life—the trip isn't peaceful; it's mayhem, and your loved ones aren't waiting for you when you cross over. You will be in your own storm every day. Your mom fantasizes about being with your dad, but she can't bear the thought of leaving you and your sister behind. She loves you two young ladies more than she loves herself or anyone else, for that matter."

I knew what she meant. I knew my mom wanted to leave this life but she knew that would leave my sister and I alone. My mom would never do that. She was perfect in my eyes. We struggled without my dad. It was hard and took its toll financially and emotionally. I am thankful my granny came to stay; she distracted me from my sadness and relieved some of my mom's worries about working and leaving me home alone.

Later that night, while sitting on the recliner watching TV, I glanced over to the couch where my mom was laying, her head in my granny's lap and Granny playing with her hair. That made me smile. My mother being comforted and loved by her mom made my heart full. It was peaceful and happy.

Then, suddenly, chaos stormed in. My sister blew into the room and dropped to the floor, crying, "Oh my GOD!" She was panicked and almost convulsing.

My granny leaped to the floor and held her tight then met my eyes. "Tell me what's wrong?" I knew the question was to my sister, but it was almost meant for me too.

My sister wailed, "Two of my co-workers, Nancy and Bill, were stabbed to death at work. My supervisor, Chris, called and told me that someone went into the office and stabbed Nancy, then Bill walked in and confronted the man. The guy chased Bill down and started stabbing him as he ran through the store." She gulped. "He ran into the freezer and tried to lock it, but the man was too close behind him and opened the freezer and continued stabbing him until Bill was dead. He stabbed him over a dozen times." She sobbed and shrieked. "Chris, told me the store is closed today. He said blood is everywhere, and he was crying; it is a mess. I can't believe this. Bill was a nice older man, so kind and sweet. I don't know why this happened to him!" She was screaming in anger. "Why?" Then she looked at me and granny. "I was supposed to work tonight. He was there because I wasn't there."

My mother assured my sister it wasn't her fault. It was now my sister with her head in my mom's lap getting comforted. I went to my room and turned on the radio to avoid my own thoughts. I felt terrible for my sister and the pain she was feeling.

My granny entered the room, gently knocking on the door. "Surely you didn't see all that, did you?"

I turned my radio down. "No!" I was in disbelief. "I just had a bad feeling like Mia shouldn't go into work."

Granny shook her head. "Lucinda, we are not God. Even God doesn't interfere with people's free will. We can get feelings about people and situations and sometimes may even be wrong. Sometimes we pick up on feelings that are meaningless thoughts. It's all very subjective." I nodded, trying to take in what she was saying.

"Just because someone thinks about something doesn't always mean they will act on it. However," Granny continued, "If someone thinks something that they don't act on, you should still stay far away from that person. Sometimes the thought alone is enough to make them dangerous. Sadly, there are too many scary people in this world." Granny pulled her hair back into a ponytail. "I had the same feeling you did about her going to work. I asked her to switch days to take me to the doctor, and it may have been for no reason." She paused, but I didn't say anything. "I also had a bad feeling but couldn't put my finger on it. Probably because I never met the person that did it, but I kept having a nagging feeling about her going to work. Such heavy dread." Granny pulled me to her and embraced me. "You'll see as you get older, you'll learn more about how to tell a person's fantasy from their intent to actually do harm. It was only a gut feeling I had, nothing more. I wasn't able to differentiate between this person's thoughts and their intent. It could have been because the decision to actually kill the employees was a last-minute choice or even because someone else put him up to it. Perhaps it was a hard read because there were drugs involved. Many things can hinder your visions." She explained.

My sister ultimately left her job at the grocery store, finding it too painful to return. Between demons in the parking lot that crept into her mind anytime she worked after dark to the thought of her coworker's bloodstains smeared across the floor along the back aisles of the store as he was butchered to death, it was probably best for her to begin a new chapter in her life.

Mia got a new job and seemed to enjoy it a great deal. My mom got a promotion at work, and everyone was in good spirits. Yes, there were good days and bad days when we thought about my dad. However, as time passed, it was easier and easier to move about our days again.

Chapter Five
My Last Living Summer

The summer I spent with my granny was much-needed, since my dad was gone and my mom and sister were working and grieving.. working.. and grieving. I needed a little escape, and my granny was my happy place. I enjoyed having her with me.

It was the last summer I would have before I died. I guess it is why I have so many memories of it. Even after my passing, I hung on to those memories so tightly. I spent a lot of time with my granny. We worked on incantations, and I read books on spells. I still hadn't been sure if Granny was an actual witch or not; I only knew she played with clean magic. We wished spells of good fortune and happiness to my mom and sister—never anything hateful or malicious on anyone. I did read spell books just for entertainment, never for evil doings. I wasn't even curious about that nonsense. When I was a kid, I didn't think that way. Well, only about Ruby, but by that time, I rarely thought about her anymore.

Ruby wasn't a witch like my granny. It isn't good witch versus bad witch, no. It was more like clean magic—do no harm versus dismal, filthy magic, selfish and hateful magic. My granny would never delve into anything sinister. Granny wanted peace when it was her time to pass on to the next life.

My granny was also really into paranormal investigating, back before it was the cool, trendy thing to do. She and I would visit local haunted places together. We didn't bring equipment like you see today. We read tarot cards and crossed over entities that were lost and wanting help. I had been under the impression it was all just entertainment but there really was something to it. Granny knew what she was doing. She didn't need devices to communicate with the dead.

I remember when I told my sister what granny and I did, and she rolled her eyes at us. "I've never met a ghost. I've never read an obituary where someone's cause of death was listed as 'murdered by a ghost,'" she chuckled, and my granny laughed and jested with us.

"Well then, Lucy, looks like our job in crossing ghosts over has been working."

I don't think my sister was a non-believer in the afterlife. I think she put walls up after her demonic experience and would rather believe in nothing than to think about good and evil and death. Mia believed in God, and being a good person is how she would explain her faith to me.

Granny showed me how to exorcise diabolical entities and innocent spirits correctly. My mom would have been thoroughly pissed off had she known my granny and I were messing with paranormal stuff. I think my granny was so in tune with the next life she didn't think much of it.

Granny was really connected with the spiritual world. I think she knew I was too, and she was just simply preparing me—or at least teaching me to stay away from things that may lead me down a dark, dismal path. These days, any Becky that picks up sage from the local grocery store thinks they're a witch. I will be honest, there are probably more witches walking around than you may realize. However, there are way more "wanna-be" witches than actual witches.

Be careful of the craft you follow and the magic you work. Some practice white magic, some indulge in dark magic, and some are so afraid of their own magic they don't practice at all. My granny only practiced clean magic, which was similar to white magic, but I think white magic was for healers and healing.

Granny's magic wasn't always about a person's health but more about protection. She kept it clean—no harm to those she was protecting. She feared you could make things worse in the long run, even with clean magic. We practice the magic to protect our loved ones, but anytime you interfere with free will, it can change the chain of events. Sure, sometimes it helps, and sometimes it hurts. It can sometimes put the right people and situations in their path, and other times it can put the wrong people and circumstances in their wake. Granny said the best magic was no magic, so when you need to meddle, use caution and make sure the risk is worth it. She didn't like practicing magic in general. She enjoyed performing sweet spells and prayers to bless her loved ones. She also joked about being a petty witch.

While she practiced clean magic for protection, she occasionally would be upset with greedy or hateful people, but she never tried to punish them. In her own way, she would make things right and bless the ones they wronged instead. Passive-aggressive witch, maybe. But a bad witch? No way, never.

My granny was hilarious. I remember my sister asking her about love spells before when we would tell her we were working on my magic, and she said, "Well, baby, I never had to worry about that. That's for ugly women who aren't good in bed." Mia and my granny always joked like that; those girls were worse than dirty old men sometimes. I will spare you the locker room talk. I think my sister talked crazy to my granny for shock value and to get my granny flustered, but granny didn't care. My granny could talk shit with the best of them.

I recall that Granny wore black when we practiced magic. She preferred to dress in all black, especially when we were away from home and unsure of what we would encounter. I was very curious why she always insisted that we wear black.

"The black absorbs every color in the light spectrum. It protects and discards other auras and energies," she explained.

Of course, I naturally wanted to know about the black, pointed hats witches would stereotypically wear too.

"From my understanding, the hats started as more of a stigma against women selling during prohibition. The pointed hats let others know they had alcohol to sell, and these women threatened men during that time, so they started the nasty lie these women were witches. Sadly, some cultures were forced to wear pointy hats to show their religion, make them easy targets, and track them. Lots of history with the hats. But, as witches, we are used to people being intimidated by our magic. It's always the people without magic judging us for ours." She smiled at me. "I had a feeling you might ask me about witch hats today. I made you this." She handed me a very large black witch hat. The brim was huge. I put it on and my granny smiled. "You have a witch hat made by a real witch."

I learned so much that summer. I constantly delve back into my memories of what I learned that summer whenever I am at a crossroads. I wonder what a magical witch would do when I encounter a questionable situation. We always search for direction from a higher power, don't we?

My charming and witty granny passed along her infinite worldly wisdom to me, and I have the best memories of her. She told me to remember to be a woman in total control of herself. I think that's where I get my sarcastic bitchiness from.

It wasn't until she passed, and I was dwelling on our conversations, that I picked up on the acronym WITCH: Woman In Total Control of Herself. In other words, mind my temperament. I didn't have a quick temper, but I have always had a hot temper. It would take me a bit to get pissed off, but I was ready to take off my earrings and beat some ass once I was there. More than anything else, it also reminded me not to teeter on the line with the type of magic I practiced, which is more challenging than you would think. Temptation gets even the best of us.

My granny told me never to believe anything a grackle tells me. She ascertained a grackle would lie. "Crows you must watch out for. Crows will come to visit you. They usually appear when there is a transformation on the horizon. Pay attention to crows; they won't whisper lies like the grackle. Instead, the crow will warn you and alert you before a major spiritual shift. Believe a crow. Grackles will trick you because they desire a relationship with a realm beyond this one, but they lie and deceive. A witch doesn't ever trust a grackle; you can always believe a crow."

One of the best things my granny shared with me is that the moon will keep your secrets in confidence; she will never betray your secrets. There won't always be people around you that you can trust, but the moon, she is an enigma. You can tell her all your secrets, and she won't tell a soul.

I would sometimes see Granny sitting on the back porch, enjoying coffee in the early morning hours before the sun came out—the quiet and the beauty of the transition between dusk to dawn—listening to the sounds of the crickets chirping. No doubt, she was sharing her secrets with the moon.

One of the more somber lessons she schooled me on was when she told me, "Life can sometimes surprise us with lessons, and not all surprises are happy. We honestly have no control over most of the hard times we get dealt with—none of us. We are all just people living ordinary lives, whether or not we embrace our gifts. People get sick, and accidents can be unforeseeable, as free will is the strongest of all magic.

"We control many aspects of our lives. One decision causes another and another. Just remember that we are all energy. Someone else's choices can impact us too, and we don't think about their actions causing our consequences." She took a drink of her hot dandelion tea. "Also, the universe has a funny way of removing people that aren't meant for you. Those people will freely make decisions that will hurt you and sometimes will even try to break you, just don't let it," she warned.

"Take a breath. Recognize the difference between forgiving people and when the time has come for you to release them. Knowing when those people are not for you is empowering. Friends, co-workers, bosses, even lovers. Sometimes you will find yourself in the darkness after being betrayed by someone. Put yourself back together. You will build a stronger version of yourself after you've been broken. We all break sometimes. Try to avoid reading into people when you can. You don't want everyone's burdens and sins on your shoulders." She smiled at me lovingly. "I guess this is a lot for a young lady your age to understand. Well. Just know it isn't good to wish bad things on people. Keep your thoughts clean. Just know they will not live a happy life when they hurt you, when they are bad people. Happy people don't behave that way. Those who are negative and mean in their thoughts are not your people." I nodded and continued to listen intently, taking in everything Granny was teaching me.

"Remember what I said about a grackle? There is a reason they are referred to as a plague when a group of them is together. A plague is a big problem. Some people are like grackles. You will pick up on those behaviors and just move along. Remember, those are not your people. Remove yourself from them quickly. A plague can be deadly. The funny thing about grackles is, they always find a way to gravitate to one another.

"Some people are like crows. It is said when you see a crow, you are seeing a bird full of wisdom, even ancient wisdom. Crows are connected to the spiritual realm. They know so much because they are taught by their elders, and the wisdom is passed down and shared. Crows are smart. They solve puzzles and even hold funerals for their dead."

I don't know why I laughed, but it made me think of her schooling me in the art of magic. "Granny, are you saying I can call you an old crow?"

She laughed with me and said, "Only if I can call you a little witch! Crows also love to gossip and hold grudges, so don't piss off a crow." We chuckled, and as the moment passed, in a serious tone, she told me to be wary of the grackles that will come into my life or Mia's life because they want to have our natural gifts. Grackles so badly want to be crows.

*****

The summer was ending, and I would start high school soon. When my granny came to stay, I had only been a little girl. It's funny how time does fly by, and before you know it, you are no longer a little kid. I was very mature; I was practically magic, after all.

My mom poured herself into her girls. She never dated after my father passed away. She told me, "Growing old with someone is the natural cycle of life, but I don't want to meet an old man set in his ways, having to bend to make him happy. I will not have some man around my young daughters. It's just not important to me. You and Mia are all I need. When your dad passed away, he took that part of my heart with him. He will always have that part of my heart just for himself."

A part of me didn't want my mom to move on. Selfishly, I liked that she only wanted my daddy, but a part of me felt sad that she'd never be loved by another man for the many years she had left. One thing I always wondered was why my mom never talked to me like granny did. I would think that about Mia too. We never talked about religion or magic.

I am certain my mom really knew granny was teaching me magic. I knew the demon in the tree freaked my mom out something awful. I justified it to myself as, "it's clean magic, so it's OK." I always assumed my mom and my sister's encounters frightened them so much that anything like that was upsetting for them.

One day, after we came in from school shopping, a storm blew in from out of nowhere. We were running with bags from the car, and when we entered, we realized the lights in the house were out. We lit candles, and then the house felt eerie. We dried off and gathered in the living room.

Since it was only the early 90s, we didn't have smartphones, so we couldn't look up the weather or scroll through social media to occupy our time. We simply sat around and talked to one another. Mia had moved out the week before, but luckily she was with us that day to tell us some funny stories like she always did to lighten the mood. She was a big shit-talker but so funny.

She told us about the time she walked in on her roommate trying on her clothes. She thought it was the funniest thing at first, but she shared with us his truth. The conversation turned from funny to very serious. He couldn't be himself during that time. The world wasn't as understanding as accepting. She was heartbroken for him. He was a young, gay man pretending to be someone he wasn't.

Mia never told a soul to this day other than my mom, me, and granny. She felt safe with us because we would never judge him, think poorly of him, or tell anyone his secrets. She only told us to get it off her chest and maybe get some advice on how to assure him it was OK to be himself. "How terrible it must feel to be unable to tell anyone who you really are." Mia was the only friend he had that knew his secret. She felt protective of him. She loved his friendship and felt so sorry that he had to live in the shadows because of society.

My granny always had a way of helping us understand how someone may feel or the struggle they may face. "There has been a time when we have all been running in the shadows, and even though we have nothing to be ashamed of, we just don't want anyone to know.

We don't want to have to re-live it, or maybe we don't want to answer questions about it. Maybe we fear people would blame us for it. Like we control what happened to us or how we were born."

Maybe she was talking about my sister's roommate being born gay; maybe she was trying to make me feel OK about embracing my special gifts, intuition, and foresight. Even now, I hesitate to say "psychic abilities" for fear of somehow being associated with people that are frauds.

Really, in hindsight, perhaps she was trying to make sure I wasn't blaming myself for what happened a few years ago with Charlotte's stepdad. I thought about it sometimes, and it made me feel so mucky. My granny tried to comfort me. "We all have events or thoughts and secrets we try to suppress because some people won't understand and can't fathom experiences they don't share with us."

After we talked about Deon, the conversation took a turn I didn't expect, and it shook me. My sister told us she was still haunted by what happened to her coworker, Bill, who had been slain. "I think about it all the time. I was supposed to be there, not him. Maybe it could have been different if I had been there. Maybe it wouldn't have happened. Maybe I wouldn't have gone into the office to talk to Nancy when she was being robbed."

I chimed in. "Maybe you would have."

She nodded. "I feel like a nice man died because of my changing schedules. He had been so kindhearted to the ladies, a real gentleman." Her eyes welled up with the biggest tears I've ever seen—her beautiful, sad eyes. "It was his last day there; he was moving the following week. His little girls and his wife don't have him anymore. He is gone forever because I didn't work that day," Mia wept.

"Baby, it is not your fault, you didn't know, and you certainly didn't do it," my mother added as she hugged my sister and stroked her hair.

My sister loved having her hair played with, so this was my mom's way of providing her comfort. Mia smiled at her and continued to tell us about her slain coworker. "His little girl, Charlotte, would often come in with her mom to grocery shop after school. She was about Lucy's age. She greeted everyone who worked there."

I got a knot in my stomach just then. "Did Charlotte have long brown hair and freckles?" I inquired.

My sister wiped her tears with her sleeve. "Yeah, I think she was in your class around that time because she said she knew you when I asked her. Didn't you spend the night at her house once?"

Suddenly, I felt like I was slipping out of my body and had the feeling of pins and needles all over me. My granny quickly came to sit beside me, almost to snap me out of it. "Here, baby girl, come sit in my lap." I was about as big as she was, but I was still her baby. She kissed my forehead and whispered gently in my ear. "Never mind him. He was a predator, a monster, and Charlotte can sleep better at night without her stepfather, Bill in her house."

We looked at each other, and she drew me near her again, whispering, "He was her stepdaddy, but she didn't love him; he needed to go. It's OK. Monsters never change who they are."

The storm outside continued to howl, and the living room lights turned on while my mind processed what I had just heard. My eyes were still seeing spots as I tried to focus. My sister was emotionally drained after crying, shivering, and wanting a nice relaxing shower. Mom suddenly popped up and said she was going to change out of her damp clothes and put on a pot of coffee.

When it was only my granny and I in the room, I said, "Granny, since you have only practiced clean magic, you didn't have anything to do with Charlotte's stepdad, did you? I know you know what happened."

My granny shot me a look, confirming she did know what happened. I already knew she saw it and sent the knock for me to run away. Granny explained she provided the knock, but it was my free will and choice to have the courage to run away. If I hadn't gathered courage to run and face whatever consequences were on the other side of the door, my fate would have been to stay and my innocence shattered by Bill, who was seemingly nice to people but molested his stepdaughters in the home.

The girls live with their grandparents now and are much better off. They have gotten counseling and have come to terms with their turbulent childhoods. Sadly, their mother was complacent with what he was doing and turned a blind eye as he brought her daughters into their marriage bed.

"Did you have her mom killed?"

My granny shook her head. "I don't play with the devil's magic, baby. She went to jail. She isn't dead, but she is where she belongs. The girls got their courage when they were at church with their grandmother. They told their grandparents everything that evening. After that, the girls went to live with them. Their grandparents turned in their mother and her wicked husband. Bill being slaughtered was the best thing to have happened for those girls. He would have never stopped bothering them." The room fell silent. "I didn't send Bill in harm's way either." She defended herself from my coy accusation. I was very skeptical about this.

"Granny, you're always honest with me; please be honest with me now. Was it really just a fluke?"

"Lucinda, you know how you get your visions?" I nodded. "I didn't see anyone getting killed. I saw your sister at work that day, and then I had a flash of fear and panic. I didn't see why or what; I just had a vision followed by a demanding instinct that she shouldn't be there. Nothing more. I didn't know Bill worked there; I didn't send any harm his way," she assured me vehemently.

She promised me again she didn't do vengeful magic. She assured me things usually have a way of coming to us when we deserve it, good and bad alike. I think my warning was to protect Mia from harm and instead place someone in the way who was deserving of the consequence.

"Decisions we make have a trickle effect every day. What we choose sometimes affects other people. Maybe we thought about buying a lottery ticket and didn't, and the person behind us wins a million dollars off it instead because we didn't get it. So, sometimes consequences can be good for one person and unfortunate for another. It's just the way life goes. Sometimes you're the pigeon, and other times, you're the statue.

"His ill intentions were sent back to him. Sometimes that happens. Death is harsh, but perhaps in this case well deserved," she said. "Your relentless dwelling on the pain he caused you…well, call it kismet." She put her hand firmly on my shoulder. "The pain he caused those girls regularly…well, he earned himself a very uneasy death."

My granny again swore to me she would never use witchcraft to do harm. When you think of a witch, do you think of the innocent people, men, and women that were stoned and hanged? The poor souls in Europe were even burned to death. Well, my granny told me the real witches went unknown.

"Do you think the real witches would get caught by the nitwitted men that hunted them? No, most witches were caught and burned by other witches—witches that were trying to protect innocent people from witches that practiced evil, soul-stealing magic. The others that were tried as witches never practiced magic whatsoever."

She told me her great-grandmother fell into magic after enduring a lot of abuse and asked for help to get out of a dark situation. She shifted her vulnerabilities to a darker lord. "It's important for you to know about this. I want to clarify that we don't play with her kind of magic. It is far too dangerous. Self-serving magic is a slippery slope."

I interrupted her. "We don't do black magic."

She nodded, affirming what I said. "A sorcerer skirts around the consciousness of men," she added.

Through stories of her ancestors, she gathered that her family was never accused of witchcraft, but to throw off their would-be accusers and the power of suggestion, they, in turn, had innocent people accused. That was upsetting for her. Pointing fingers at innocent people to save their own reputations—their own lives.

Her family is not clean; our family line is not clean. Sadly, some of them turned over innocence to protect themselves, but she made the conscious decision at a young age that she would only practice the magic of protection and good. She believes in God, her Creator. Is that a weird thing, to worship God and consider yourself a witch? Or is it weird to assume witches are evil and worship Satan?

Of course, there are selfish motives in their craft. They're people, after all. Hell, there are unhappy and even selfish people in every religion, aren't there? My granny practiced clean magic, but to be honest, I could see a razor-thin difference between one magic to another. She manipulated people to have a good day through her manifesting. I guess I didn't see a huge difference, manipulation is manipulation but I wasn't about to tell her that.

"Well, I didn't exactly have to." She seemed to read my thoughts. "I think you know how I feel. You know good and well there is a difference between me wanting your mother to have a good day or giving you an opportunity to escape a predator. It's much different than me having someone thrown in jail or even killed for being a cheater or thief. You know the difference, and you must be really careful justifying yourself. Grey magic can easily lead to dark magic. If you don't want demons lurking around your home and causing loved ones to fall ill and hurt the ones you love most, you will stay away from dark magic. There are always consequences, and sometimes you will be tempted to make deals with the devil that you can't undo.

"Never, ever conjure something you cannot banish. I have told you this before. Remember, you will bear the burden of all the repercussions you immerse yourself into." She shot a fierce look at me. "This is a warning you need to take seriously. I won't always be here to guide you." I knew she was right. Very bluntly, she let me know. "The devil always gets what is due to him. Owe him nothing."

I thought a lot about what she said, and she was right. It is a slippery slope. I always made it a point to remember that it is easy to blur the lines between what is right and what we want. You can find a way to justify anything you do if you try hard enough, I guess. Justifying an action doesn't make it right, though.

My granny and I kept practicing our magic and had so much fun working in the garden, stirring potions while sending good intentions to my mom and sister, and hearing about their days when Mia would come over and see us. When my mom came home from work, she was in good spirits, but the house always seemed to make her a little sad. So many happy memories—they haunted her. Could she ever truly be happy again?

We toyed with the idea of moving, but my mom didn't want to let go. This was the home her babies grew up in—a life she spent with my dad. Oddly enough, the bad things were here too. Sadness my sister experienced. The suffering my daddy endured, passing away right in the house. The terror I would have when falling asleep in front of the windows in our living room when I was younger. The witch that used to haunt me and my dreams. We all possessed mixed emotions. The good and the bad. The sugary sweet, along with decaying and rotten memories that will forever linger in our thoughts. The house held onto both.

Chapter Six
Premonitions of Magic

The more I connected to my magic, the more experiences I had that morphed into strong premonitions. Weird, little things I would dream of would come to pass—little silly things, but sometimes serious things too.

I remember freaking my sister out pretty good. I woke from my dream one night and called her on the phone. She was half asleep, but I told her to check on her roommate. I knew how much she cared for him. She was so protective of him and his kindness. He was a handsome, tall black gay man, but that's not how she viewed him. She saw him as she should. Just a man—a man that was loving and kind. He was strong and beautiful and she loved him for who he was, not who he pretended to be. His name was Adrian Washington, "Deon" to his close friends. I only met him a few times. He was always welcome at our home, although after the experience he had while putting my desk together, he didn't come around much. Never again, actually.

Deon referred to my mom as "The mom he has who doesn't care that he is gay." Our mom always sent him homecooked meals and little things she would find he may enjoy home with Mia when she would come see us. I don't know if he came out to his family or if they suspected he was homosexual. He gave off the impression it wasn't an accepted lifestyle with his parents, so he was never really himself. He even tried to date ladies, but he swears we are all nuts. My sister would always fire back and tell him she thought gay men were really into nuts. They would pick and poke at each other. They really loved and valued one another.

When I woke from my dream and called Mia to insist that she check on him, she promised she would. Ten minutes or so passed by, and I hadn't heard back, so I called her once more. "Is Deon, OK?"

She sighed in annoyance. "Ugh, Lucy. I have work in two hours and stayed up until about an hour ago talking to him. He was upset with his mom. She called him some mean names when he talked to her earlier today. She hurt his feelings badly, but I think he's fine. Did he call y'all or something?"

I insisted again, "I had a really bad dream, and I am not hanging up until you check on him. I had a dream that he tried to kill himself."

My sister fumbled around. "Lucy...fine. Hold on."

As it turns out, my dream—my vision—was spot on. The accuracy was uncanny. Deon was hospitalized for overdosing. He did, in fact, try to take his life, sadly, for being gay and shunned by his family, for hating his thoughts and fantasies as well as being made fun of by so-called friends at work that were gossiping about him. I want to tell you Deon had a happy ending with his family and that they learned a lesson, but I would be lying to you if I did. We were the only family that showed up for him. But Deon did get his happily ever after. We would tease, "Leave it to Deon to go to the hospital and meet a handsome doctor and live his happily ever after."

His family hated that his lover was white almost as much as they hated the fact it was a man. Deon lived a life that he deserved; he was loved and found his own way. He and Dr. Lowe ended up moving to the other side of Dallas together. They were part of a community that was accepting of their lifestyle and celebrated their love for one another. They would eventually move on and leave Texas in their rearview mirror and share a beautiful life together.

My sister and I talked about my visions at great lengths—what I saw and how it made me feel. I think it intrigued her and frightened her at the same time. We never talked about it with my mom or dad when he was alive. My sister got a kick out of it when we were younger.

I remember when I was quite young—maybe about two years before my father passed away—Mia and I were with her friends at a Mexican café close to our home. We had an asshole waiter, who, for an unknown reason, seemed put out as soon as we walked through the door. He curled his lip into a snarl and had a poor attitude.

At one point, I leaned over to my sister and said, "Watch, he is about to trip up the steps." I circled my index finger and we laughed as she shook her head to dismiss me and continued talking with her friends.

To her surprise, as the waiter approached, he stumbled up the last step before reaching our table, sure enough spilling our drinks all over himself and the floor. We quickly jumped up to assist him with the clean-up, and his disposition towards us instantaneously changed.

"Thank you for the help. I am sorry I was shitty when you came in," he said.

His apology was really unnecessary; we were young and annoying girls, so he probably assumed we were going to be high maintenance and leave a shitty little tip. My sister and her friends hadn't taken his scathing dirty looks too seriously when we all went into the restaurant anyway.

Mia was a little perplexed about what happened, and as soon as we were home, she followed me into my room where we were alone. "So, coincidence?" she inquired, brows raised.

I shrugged and laughed. "I just had a flash in my mind that he was going to trip. I promise I didn't know he was going to spill drinks on himself. I didn't make him do it," I reassured her.

Mia laughed and shrugged it off, dismissing it as a coincidental accident. She was heading out of my room but stopped and turned to me. "If you could whirl your little finger to make sure I get out of my history test tomorrow, I would be down for that. I haven't studied."

I smirked and made a circular motion with my finger. We laughed and she rolled her eyes at me and left my room. From the hallway, she jokingly said, "I'm going to go ahead and study now, just in case that didn't work." She had the cutest wit about her. This was before my dad passed away. Thinking back on it now, she stopped being playful like that for a long time after he died.

The following afternoon, when my sister got home from school, I could see she was preoccupied with her own thoughts. She went straight into her own room and turned her music up annoyingly loud. She didn't even speak to me or my mom, which was really out of character for her.

I knocked at her door and she yelled, "Give me a minute to myself, damn!"

I was really perturbed by her rudeness. As I turned away to leave, a chill went down my body, and the hair on my arms stood up. I knew somehow my sister was frightened of me. I closed my eyes to take a deep breath and had a vision of my sister sitting in class and hearing that her teacher passed away. I only hoped it wasn't true. Later, after it sank in, she admitted she had guilt pour over her. I knew she blamed herself. I could tell she definitely blamed me.

When it was time for dinner, Mia finally left her room once my dad called for her, and I was waiting for her. I know it added to the creepy factor, but I *wasn't* creepy. "A misfortunate event is all it was," I quipped.

She pulled me aside and asked, "What was?"

I shrugged. "You didn't have to take your test because your teacher had an aneurysm."

Mia grabbed my shoulders. "Lu, I didn't tell you my teacher died. I don't even know how she died. Did you..." Her voice trailed away.

"NO! No way!" I cried. "I only joked with you, and when you yelled at me for going to your room, I had a feeling that something happened to your teacher. I didn't know she died! I don't even know what that means, aneurysm. It was like I heard something in my head say that to me. I heard in a strange whisper, *Her teacher had an aneurysm.*"

She ignored me and we went to eat dinner. At the table, my sister kept to herself, clearly bothered. I started feeling upset with her. Did she actually think I would wish bad things on people or had any power or influence whatsoever over them?

Later, I approached her again. "So?"

She looked at me. "I used to laugh at little things you would say, and when they came true it would always freak me out. Seriously." She shook her head but continued. "But I think you have a gift of feeling and seeing things. Just be careful. Maybe even ignore it so it goes away. I heard Granny say that's what mom did before, so maybe you can do that too."

In hindsight, perhaps ignoring it would have been better. Maybe if

I had, I wouldn't have piqued Ruby's interest in me. I developed the habit of shaking off my visions and intuition. I think that's why I never saw my dad getting sick or dying back then. I stopped seeing things for a while. It wasn't until my granny stayed with us that I started opening myself back up. I guess I left the door cracked, and it didn't take much for my gifts to resurface again.

Thinking back to my granny coming to stay with us, I can't help but wonder if her purpose was also to help me get my gifts back. Just like any skill and ability, we lose them if we don't practice or believe in ourselves. I think granny protected me from a pedophile and my sister from a demon, but I didn't know, at the time, she had banished Ruby away from me too.

When she began working magic with me, I confided in her. "Granny, I keep having dreams about you by my old tree that I used to play in."

She asked, "The demon tree?"

I was surprised she knew, and I quipped back, "YEAH!! You are standing by that tree and looking into the sky, shouting, 'Go away! GO AWAY!' so loud that you don't even sound like yourself."

"You were dreaming about a ritual I performed. I was sending the demon monster in the tree away—the same demon your mother saw that scared her. It was never sent to possess anyone, if you want to know the truth." That really freaked me out. "Your little friend across the way."

My eyes widened at her confession. "A demon was after Ruby!?" It shouldn't have made me feel happy, but I won't lie, it did. I wanted her to reap what she sowed.

Granny stopped my excitement. "Not exactly. Ruby conjured the demon. She took a baby goat and began consuming it as she conjured it. The goat was her sacrifice to Satan. She was up to something, but what, I don't know." That scared the shit out of me.

The next morning, I woke up and was ready to talk. I made my tea with intent, stirring it for today to be a good day for my mom like I did every morning since my granny showed me how.

I went to wake Granny, but she was already outside, sitting on the porch. I sat with her in silence. Then she spoke. "I was much like you when I was your age. Curious. Magical. Afraid. My mom was a witch—a real practicing witch—who was beautiful and smart. But she was consumed with it; had an unhealthy fascination with it. She was far more talented in her craft than I will ever be, that's for certain. My dad turned a blind eye; he benefited from her knowledge. Financially, especially. But he opposed her teaching me and my brother's magic. So, she taught us in secret.

"We played with magic, but she didn't ever get to teach me everything she knew. She passed the warnings to me about dark magic as I passed to you. When my mother died, it was unexpected. She and my father died in an accident. I dreamed about it the night before it happened, and when I woke up, it had already came to pass. There wasn't anything I could do," Granny explained.

"Your mom never had the gifts we have. She had intuition, of course, but she constantly dismissed it. Trust me, I tested her throughout her life, but she never did have the natural gifts you and I do. I don't know if she got that from my dad or her dad, but she just never had them. I never talked to her about it much. People that don't have the natural aptitude for—let's call it what it is—witchcraft. They don't get it. They can't comprehend the visions, the experience of leaving your body, the feelings you can't shake.

"People are encouraged at a young age to ignore it. It isn't real; it's a coincidence when you have feelings. You know, Mia has done that to you many times, dismissing your visions and dismissing you. She was like your mother, maybe a bit curious about it but never had natural gifts—not like we do. Your gifts didn't even make her jealous; they actually scared her. The unknown frightens her.

"I told you never to do anything with selfish or ill intent, right?" I nodded. "I have a confession," she said. "I didn't know how to deal with the demon. I could banish the witch after she did harm to your dad. She made him sick to send him away. With him gone it would make it easier to hurt you.. to hurt you girls. With Jack out of the way, you all were alone and vulnerable. She never saw me, though. If there was one important thing my mom taught me, it was how to run and hide in the shadows. I'm pretty good at that. You, too, have been able to leave your body and cast yourself into a shadow. You need more practice. Work on leaving and moving about the house, blending and bending with the shadows, and you will strengthen and sharpen that ability.

"Ruby never saw me, not once. I watched her gorge on an innocent goat, making her sacrifice to send a demon to take you. What she didn't know was that I fed the goat that morning, and as she gorged her sacrifice, it made her deathly sick. She consumed the rotting body of a goat that I poisoned. I had no choice; I knew she would inevitably kill the goat. This way, he felt no pain and was unaware of what was happening.

"She was unsure what happened to her but feared she was dying, and as she traveled home to Mexico, she was enraged. Santeria failed her. Her dark magic didn't succeed, and she only wondered what she missed in her ritual. Ruby dwelled on her defeat. She still hasn't figured out what happened. Unfortunately for her, the poison she consumed crippled her. She couldn't get around like she used to."

I listened to Granny and thought Ruby got exactly what she deserved. I had no sympathy. My only sadness was for the goat. As bad as it sounds, it did make me feel elated that she was beat at her own game. No telling what she wanted to do to me had her plan succeeded. I was so thankful to my granny. Her story then followed with a stern warning.

"Ruby is very much alive. You stay on her mind, and as you get older; she sees your gifts and it is very enticing to her. I must be honest with you, Lucinda. I didn't know how to stop the demon on my own. My mother passed before I learned anything about that. I don't even know if there was a way to stop it through witching. The only person I know that had the capabilities…well, she has passed away, but I know she did it before, so it's possible I'm just uncertain how she did it."

Granny and I sat there for a few minutes, both lost in our own thoughts. I loved that she was teaching me so much, but it was pretty overwhelming. I think Granny knew that; that's why she gave me time to think before continuing.

"When I was your sister's age, I met a lady, and we became great friends. I later found that I was drawn to her because of my magic. I then became part of her coven. We would get together and do spells;

it was our girls' night out, I suppose. She was the most powerful witch I had ever known and quite lovely, beautiful in appearance and had the best heart of anyone I've known. She cared for others as if they were her own family. We called her, Topaz. She was the grand priestess of the group. She practiced all magic and was not only the teacher of the coven but also the witch master. Topaz took me in and worked with me a bit. She read to me and spoke to me about my family. I knew about my grandkids before they were even born," Granny explained to me as she hugged me.

"Topaz took me under her wing and really taught me much about white magic. I remember her taking me into her practicing room." Granny reached into her bag and pulled out a book. It wasn't a beautiful, cool-looking book; it was very heavy and old. As she thumbed through it, I noticed only about a fourth of the book was in English. "Topaz and her family were from Europe. As far as witches go, she was the shit. I think she probably even scared the devil. That bitch was a force. She gave me this book for protection. Now I'm giving it to you."

Part of me thought it was cool to have something so powerful and special given to me. The other part wondered why granny wanted to pass it along to me. "You need to work on this to keep yourself protected; work on your shadow casting so no one can see you or your work. Keep the other books you have under your bed too. Read them. Learn them. Be ready; Ruby will be watching for you—her sacrifice, her rival. However she sees you, you are a threat or a conquest. Be prepared."

"Granny, I like you protecting me, sending demons away and tricking a witch to eat a sick goat. What kind of witch actually wants to hurt an animal or a person anyway?"

My granny agreed and laughed with me. "A bitch that got what she had coming and now can't even get up to go take a shit on her own now." In all seriousness, she continued. "My body is tired, and I need you to be ready because I need my rest."

Mia took me to the movies later that day. We had a great time together; it was perfect. Later, as we walked up to the porch, we heard my mom crying and screaming for help. The neighbors started to rush over as we went into the house. To our horror, we watched as my grandmother passed away.

My heart was, once again, torn into pieces, reminding me of the wounded heart I had—that we all had—when my dad passed away. My granny was gone, and once more, I felt utterly alone. I never saw her passing in my visions. I guess I wouldn't see her passing since she ran in the shadows. I should have known when we talked and she passed her book of sorcery to me that she was, in her own way, preparing me for when she wouldn't be here to protect and guide me any longer. I tucked that book away. Away from the others so no one would ever find it.

Chapter Seven
Shadow Work

Days and weeks came to pass. I didn't do my shadow work, nor did I crack the book open, not once. It wasn't the same without my granny. I didn't care about magic or the craft anymore. I just led a normal teenage life at that point—a quintessential teenage girl who started noticing boys and preferred spending time talking on the phone and just doing the normal teenager life.

I neglected every warning my granny passed to me. In fact, I packed the book away with other keepsakes I had of her. I even packed away her photo of her and the gang of friends, her coven. I was surprised that the group consisted of two male witches. I guess when I think of witches, I stereotype a coven with a group of women.

My granny explained that the reason Topaz had a sundry group diversifies the teachings and makes the coven even stronger with the array of magic. Granny told me the reason they called her Topaz was because, like the gem, she represented strength and wisdom. Topaz was a strong witch; she could read minds—even the minds of witches. She read every old script of magic—witchcraft, voodoo, hoodoo. She practiced crafts of countries like Chile, South Africa, Philippines, Haiti, Mexico, Romania, Saudi and of course a number of small towns all over Europe. Topaz read every book and script; she knew of spells and potions from every practice it seemed. Yes, even Santeria.

My granny said Topaz enjoyed reading the Bible most of all. That surprised me, but Granny said the book of Psalms is a book in the Bible that also has spells. "Isn't a prayer similar to a spell? Making a wish, sending vibes?" She went on to tell me how Topaz would read the minds of witch doctors and medicine men, priests and rabbis.

Topaz was a force of nature. She banished demons and devoured them. My granny told me when Topaz was after a demon, they prayed for help because she would shake the gates of Hell to claim their souls to forever banish. Even Satan would hide deeper in the pits of Hell when Topaz would work her magic to summon his misfit of demons trespassing the earth to wreak havoc on innocent souls.

When I saw pictures of Granny in her youth, I observed how attractive she was and could see where my mother got her beauty. They favored each other so much; I always thought Mia looked like my mother. I was surprised to see my granny so young when I looked at the photos. Mia looked so much like granny too. My mom and Mia were little versions of my granny; it made me smile. They had her beauty, but I had her magic. I missed her. She had been like a second mom and best friend to me when I needed someone after my daddy passed—especially after being harassed by a witch who hated me.

Granny had been very intuitive and would pick up on visions of things to come and things that have been, but she didn't possess the strong abilities as her mentor, Topaz. In fact, she credits her gifts to being as strong as they were from Topaz helping her to open her third eye and sharpening her senses. She told me there were more than six senses.

I carefully packed the photos away, putting them with my book. Ruby was gone. I had no need for this stuff. Occasionally, I still had feelings and visions, but I ignored them often, thinking it would be better to lose my magic than to sharpen it. I was experiencing fewer and fewer visions after my granny passed away. I think it was easier to dismiss them and hope for a more normal life.

The last vision I recall having before I died was a dream—a familiar dream. I was at the pond again. I couldn't see or hear anything beyond that, but I took it as a warning. When I woke up, I felt frustrated. I knew I had ignored my gifts for so long that I couldn't see what I was supposed to.

I let my gifts get rusty. So, I knew it was time to start working on my shadow work and visioning again. I needed to know what my warning was. My greatest fear was Ruby coming into my life again, especially since I did not heed my granny's warning to practice my magic. So basically, I knew I just needed to keep my mind closed from Ruby. She had no need to come back now, especially after she sold the house across the street after she fell ill.

The old lady that now lived in the house that haunted me for years was peculiar herself. She had old-fashioned gray and white hair and was a little overweight. I remember she would always wear a dress with pantyhose and shoes and walk everywhere. No matter how hot and humid the Texas heat was, she wore pantyhose. I always wondered where she was going, often seeing her walk up and down the street. I wasn't sure if she was lonely or bored. She kept to herself. She wasn't unfriendly but was very unapproachable, giving off a little unwelcoming energy. I dismissed it as she was just someone that didn't want to be bothered. This made her the perfect neighbor compared to Ruby.

I remember thinking vampires needed to be invited in when I was just a little girl. I saw it in a movie. My granny told me Ruby would tap on my window asking to come in simply to toy with my mind. She said Ruby might have been probing to see if I could hear her and feel her when she would come to my window, wanting to see if I would let her in without a fight, without questioning. Ruby could have possibly been able to freely move about the house had she been in it before. Thankfully, she had never been invited into our home.

Ruby had been meditating and letting her spirit drift over to the house to see what I was doing. Granny knew Ruby sensed I had gifts and was either intrigued by the gifts or she was threatened by me and wanted to harm me to consume my magic.

All of these memories flooded back to me as I stayed in the shadows and watched my sister finish packing up my room and missing her dead little sister. I roamed the house reminiscing. Missing my life.

As she was putting away my things, she felt very uneasy. Mia thought she heard breathing, and it made her instantly afraid. She remembered Deon being fearful of the house and insisting we leave that one evening. Mia was glad mom was finally selling and ready to finally put this chapter of her life behind her after all these years. Avoiding my room out of sadness. It seemed as though the bad memories outweighed the happier memories.

Once my sister packed the last bits of my life away in boxes, I could tell she felt relieved and exhausted. She waited for her husband to meet her there to load the boxes. As he entered the house, I had a weird feeling he was about to trip, and sure enough, he did. He fell and crashed down hard, spilling his drink on himself. Ironically, that moment made my sister think of me and the time we witnessed the waiter spilling drinks on himself. She laughed. "Are you OK, klutz?"

Her husband laughed and went to wash his hands. "I guess. Damn, I just got that drink." He hugged my sister, getting her wet from the spilled drink as well. As he entered my room, he held my sister tight around her waist. "I'm sorry, Mia." He gave her the sweetest forehead kiss. I could tell Mia was truly happy and that gave me a sense of peace and satisfaction.

As they were beginning to load up, I had two fears. The first one was that I would be stuck here in our old house alone. The second one, I would leave again and miss seeing my mom and my sister while they lived. As I was in my purgatory, I didn't see my dad or granny. I was utterly alone without memory, just in a void while time passed me by. I didn't want that again.

However, I knew how to latch on. I read enough on how they do it—spirits, even demons—but I didn't know what I was. I mean, I wasn't a demon—I knew that much at least—but I wasn't sure what you'd call me. A ghost, a living dead girl.

I only heard of evil spirits latching on because they are problematic, and it is quite a task to exorcise them out of your body and away from your soul. Your soul is the most precious attribute you possess after all. Latching on can be a risky process. Demonic entities usually latch on, but only when the host is vulnerable. They can latch on to pretty much anything, even objects too. Typically, demons possess people that are susceptible. If they are able to do so, they will inhabit a body for the intent of taking over the body, weakening the person physically, making them sick, and even driving them mentally ill because they are so overwhelmed with the severe anxiety and illness, depending on the strength and intent of the entity. Once they succeed in consuming their victim, they will consume their soul. At minimum, they have fed enough energy to grow stronger.

This is not what I was going to do. I simply wanted to latch onto something so that I could still be with my family. I knew as soon as I saw the Lucy doll my granny made in my likeness that would be my target. I was afraid of latching onto the doll at first. What if they put the doll in a box and store it away and I'm trapped there for eternity—kind of like being confined to a coffin when you die? That scared me because in my current state, I had my senses about me, and knowing I am trapped would be a frightful thought. I would not be able to see anyone or be able to transition from the living world back to my dead world. Being confined to a doll in a box would be the worst thing, but it was a chance I would take to be around my mom again. Oh, how I missed her. I would rather see my mom for one day than to be in a void, waiting. I guess I would be in a conscious void if I was placed in the box. I weighed my options as my sister held onto the doll. I didn't feel like she would lock this part of me away.

My mom and Jacob came back to the house and the four of them stood in my room. It was quiet. My sister held the doll up and smiled. "Do you want to take this with you, Mom, or should I pack it away?"

My mom looked at the doll. "My goodness, Granny even painted the little fleck." Her smile faded as a tear surfaced into her eye. "No," she said with a shaky voice. "You keep it or put it away. I think it will make me too sad to look at it every day."

My sister agreed. "I will keep the doll. It reminds me of her and Granny."

I knew once she said she would keep it, I wouldn't be tucked away like a demon trapped in a dybbuk box. I latched onto the doll as my sister held it, and instantly, I felt that I relinquished control. I started to feel panic and anxiety, which was not expected. Don't worry, I wasn't going to terrorize people like *Chucky*. My intent was to only be with my family, and I didn't intend to stay long, and that's the truth. I just wanted to be around them again, even if just for a day.

The car ride to my sister's house was well over an hour. We left the big city of Dallas and headed to a small town just west of Fort Worth. The car ride was somber; everyone was tired. My new home was in the closet at my sister's house, apparently.

At Mia's house, I was placed gently on the top shelf. Perhaps I didn't think this through. I felt I had a better view when I was nothing but my soul—a shadow upon a wall. I was surprised that it really worked, for some reason, and pleased I was able to accomplish the task of leaving my childhood home and reuniting with my sister and my mother once again.

Everyone loaded up and went to my mom's new place, which wasn't too far from Mia's home. They spent time helping our mom get set up for her first night. She insisted on staying in her new house rather than staying at Mia's that evening. Mia and her adorable son, Jacob didn't stay more than an hour since he needed to be put to bed and her husband, Tyler stayed behind to finish setting up a few more furniture pieces.

It wasn't a couple of hours into the evening that my sister woke up to use the bathroom, and immediately after, she curled up on the floor, sweating profusely. Tyler was asleep next to her, but she didn't want to wake him. She was ill and tried throwing up very quietly. I could see her up close now somehow. I was no longer confined to my doll. She pulled a towel down to the floor to lay her head on but had to pull herself back up to the toilet when her stomach felt sick.

Her husband, Tyler, eventually came in to check on her, as he had been getting ready for work and noticed Mia was not in bed. He helped her up, and she told him she was sick all night and didn't want to wake him, so she slept on the bathroom floor. "I have no idea what got into me last night. I was so sick. I had a terrible dream and woke up sicker than I've ever been."

Tyler lifted her up and helped her into bed. He got her crackers and Ginger-Ale to nurse her stomach before he got ready. His kind and gentle manner was really something special, and I loved that he loved my sister so much.

He placed a cool rag on her head. "You may have eaten something that didn't agree with you. You also had an exceptionally difficult day yesterday. Stress could have been a culprit too. You need to see if Lily has any openings to see her this week to talk through how you're feeling if you need professional advice, baby."

Mia sat up a bit. "I am feeling better right now, but maybe I will go see her. The dream was so real and upsetting. I know you need to get to work, but I want to tell you about it tonight."

Her husband sat on the bed. "Tell me. I can be late. What upset you so bad?"

"I had a dream that I was running and saw a hole in the ground. It was kind of like a rectangle and filled with dark green water. I gave it no thought whatsoever and randomly jumped into the hole, swimming towards the bottom. As I swam, many doll parts began floating past me and bubbling up to the top. I kept hearing laughter." She paused for a moment before continuing. "It was mean laughter, not happy laughter. I woke up sick to my stomach. Physically sick. I associated the rectangular hole with Lucy's grave. My baby sister is still in the watery grave somewhere. They just gave up looking for my baby sister, and she has been in the cold water all this time." Mia was sobbing like a baby by this point. "Were the doll parts representing her limbs coming apart from being in the water for so long? Why didn't I just dive in and help? Tyler, I didn't go to the park with her that day. If I would have gone, she never would have fallen in."

Tyler, comforting my sister, said, "Babe, accidents happen. It certainly wasn't anyone's fault. If divers couldn't recover her, there was no way you could have. Listen to me, listen…" He pulled her close to him. "Darling, yesterday was emotional and stressful; of course you don't feel well. You had a nightmare. You need to take a breath and go see your mom. You and Jacob should take her to lunch and then help her get settled into her new place. This will be a bittersweet day for her also, I imagine. Maybe call Lily on your way out there and at least talk to her. She will probably be able to make you feel better."

Mia wasn't upset that she couldn't be there to rescue my lifeless body from the pond. She was so guilty and sad for not going to the park with me that day. In her mind, she wondered if I would never have drowned if she had gone. "Lily will analyze my dream as you have and offer me a prescription. I don't need anything. I just need to shake the feeling of my nightmare. It was so upsetting." Mia got up and prepared for the day.

Before leaving the house to go see our mom, Mia held the little Lucy doll and thought of me and her nightmare. She sat on the edge of her empty bathtub and began speaking to me. "I didn't go to the park with you because I was tired from working and came over to check on mom because she kept having bad dreams. So I stayed up late with her. She blames herself, but it was really because I was too fucking tired to go with you that you fell in and drowned. I'm sorry I was too shitty to get up and spend time with you."

Naturally, I wanted to comfort her. It wasn't anyone's fault, just a misfortune I found myself in. She screamed out loud suddenly. "WHY???!!"

Her little boy came running in, so frightened, and she grabbed him, holding him close with his racing heart against her.

"Comfort him; you scared him and he doesn't understand." I said out loud, but of course no one could hear my thoughts…until...she did. My sister popped up. "Did you hear that, Jacob?"

The frightened little boy stood up. Looking at my sister with his big, brown M&M eyes, he said, "No ma'am." He stood there staring at her. "Can we go to MiMi's?"

My sister tucked my doll away, and as she left I was able to follow along with her. She sat in her car for a good ten minutes before starting it. I could tell she was feeling sick again. As she headed out to see my mom, she dialed Lily, her best friend that was also an amazing therapist. Mia made plans to see her the following week at her office, since she worked tomorrow, and Lily was not feeling well. Apparently, her friend was struggling with morning sickness from her pregnancy, but Lily hadn't told anyone she was pregnant yet. Mia set her appointment to visit with her. She always felt better after she visited Lily, who was also her therapist—very textbook and logical.

My mom was sitting on her new front porch when we drove up. Evidently, my mom had taken up smoking. My sister and Jacob approached her, and Jacob was so excited to see her, giving her a huge bear hug. I could tell they were really close. He was such a precious boy with chubby little cheeks; he was absolutely adorable.

"So, you're smoking now?" Mia waved away the smoke.

"Sit down, Mia. I have to tell you something." My mom's hands were shaking. "I stayed up putting things together last night. I was pretty tired and didn't get much sleep. I had a dream about mom and Lucy. Lucy wasn't like she was when she passed away; she was an adult like what she would be today." She put her cigarette out. "It was so real. As I was getting closer to Lucy, Granny stopped me and said, 'Lucinda isn't dead, she is trapped.' I couldn't even sleep after that."

Mia hugged her to comfort her but did not share her own dream. She did offer the same consolation Tyler gave to her after her dream. My mom wasn't having it.

"Listen to me. There is a reason I had that dream. They never found her," my mom insisted in a very upset tone.

Mia added, "Mom, the pond was so big. It fed into the Trinity River. They couldn't find her because of the depth. There are also alligators in the river."

Mia should have never said that to Mom. It was as if she crushed any little glimmer of hope she had. But Mia knew she needed our mom to stop living a fantasy that I was alive somewhere, just lost. My mom knew that wasn't the case, but she often daydreamed about it. Since I was never recovered from the water, she would daydream that I would be found one day, like with amnesia or something.

They stopped talking about me and ordered a pizza then worked on unpacking my mom into her new place. Mom was living now closer to Mia and felt she had a nice little fresh start. Tyler came over later to finish helping. He stayed late into the evening, assembling furniture, just as he did the night before on my mom's first night. The house was coming together nicely. My sister was wrapping up to get home since she had to work the next day.

My mom asked if Jacob could stay the night, and my sister agreed, even though she seemed a bit nervous about leaving him. Mia must have been feeling overwhelmed because she still felt ill from the previous night. My mom even noticed her pale color and clammy skin.

"I must be fighting off a tummy bug, or maybe it was what I ate yesterday, but I've been feeling puny and probably do need to get rest before I have to go back to work tomorrow."

My mom figured Mia was feeling engulfed with so many memories. "Get some rest. Having Jacob with me will help me stay busy while I unpack so I don't dwell and feel…" Her voice trembled and Mia stood and hugged her tight.

"OK, Mom, I know. You're the strongest woman I know."

Jacob, of course, had to wedge in and get his hugs in on his MiMi too. Jacob adored my mom almost as much as she revered him.

Tyler stayed through some of the night helping my mother finish setting up for two nights in a row. When he came home, he found my sister, once again, on the floor, sicker than a dog. Mia felt nauseated and was experiencing bad stomach aches. She said she felt dizzy and stumbled and fumbled around the bedroom before making her way into the bedroom. She assumed her allergies left her congested and threw off her equilibrium, causing her to stagger around the room. Being sick and dehydrated certainly didn't help.

The next morning, she felt a little better, and she and Tyler enjoyed time together before work. She even seemed happier. When she called to check in on Jacob, our mom said they were making breakfast.

I really wanted to be with my mom and spend some time with her now that my sister was feeling better. I wasn't quite sure how to do it—how to stay with my mom. It seemed like I was following my sister, but it was completely by accident. I wasn't intentionally doing so. I guess it's better than being stuck in a doll by myself all day in her closet or left in limbo alone and unaware of my existence.

Chapter Eight
In A World Full of Grackles— Be a Crow

Let me tell you a little about Mia and her life while I was living between worlds.

Mia was a manager for a bank and really enjoyed her job. Being a manager was a hassle and tiring at times, though—especially with catty women who acted like they were still in high school.

I instantly didn't care for a couple of the girls at the bank she worked for. They were grackles. I could see a few of them for what they were straight away when they were in her branch for a meeting. I didn't like them one bit. Luckily, my sister didn't care for them either. She had a small circle of friends and only regarded the ladies at the bank as co-workers, with the exception of two or three of them. Luckily, in her office, there was only one grackle that she had to deal with. I miss hearing her talking shit about people; she did it with such humor and wit. She wasn't a bully, by any means, but she was good at spotting people that were fakes and talked shit accordingly.

The worst one was my sister's assistant, Doris. She gave me weird vibes. Doris was overweight and sloppy in appearance. She was strikingly tall for a woman. She had caked-on 1980's blue eyeshadow and wore Barbie pink glitter lipstick like an eleven-year-old girl. As she would come into Mia's office, she would ask silly questions, looking for lame excuses to go in and talk to Mia, knowing she was actually busy and working. For example, one day, Doris walked into Mia's office, eating a bag of powdered donuts, the powder sticking to her tacky lip gloss. She asked Mia how to lose weight and lavished my sister with compliments. While they were true, she was clearly sucking up to the boss. My sister graciously accepted the compliments and continued to work on her loans. Doris stood there as she pounded her bag of powdered donuts.

I found myself laughing. "Tell this chick to stop knocking down a bag of donuts for starters if she really wants to lose weight."

It was almost as if Mia heard me, because she then looked at Doris and said, "Donuts in moderation would be a good start if you are serious about losing weight." Doris laughed as my sister teased her. My sister was much kinder to her than she should have been.

Doris was the epitome of a grackle. I picked up on that instantly. A goulash of visions flooded me with dark secrets hiding in her past. She often knocked at my sister's office door to tattle on another employee. I never liked girls in school like that and certainly didn't like grown ass women that behaved that way. My sister was professional with her, but I could tell she would get annoyed with Doris smiling at everyone's face all while trying to get them in trouble behind their backs.

I think my sister had a lot of compassion for her initially, but as time went on, and the more she was around Doris, she saw her for the grackle that she is. Mia eventually stopped overlooking Doris' hateful ways. She held a soft spot in her heart for Doris but kept her at arm's length just in case. Doris was manipulative and an obsessively jealous woman, so she trusted Doris like you would trust a fart after being sick.

Then there was Jenny, her teller, who was nice enough if you could overlook the fact that she was a pathological liar and chronic adulterer. I hated that on certain people, I could pick up on vibes and visions like that immediately. It wasn't on everyone, but some people I could read like an open book. Jenny was one of those who was an easy read. She was an easy…everything, if you know what I mean. Nonetheless, my sister adored her and, truth be told, she really was good at her job and worked hard for my sister. My sister didn't care about Jenny's personal flaws. She just needed her to work and be nice to customers.

Doris, however, constantly betrayed Jenny to make sure she would never threaten her job as my sister's assistant. She knew when Jenny would tell her innocent little lies, and, being the type of woman Doris was, she would always point out the inconsistencies in one story, the contradictions in others. Doris constantly pointed out other employees' miniscule mistakes to ensure Mia wouldn't feel confident in them.

My sister's lead teller, Kimmy, was plain vanilla. I'm pretty sure vanilla was her favorite flavor. Some days, if she was feeling really edgy and wild, she would throw on a little blush cardigan over her vanilla "Little House on the Prairie" dress. She was exceptionally conservative. She was kind but lacked common sense. She was so uptight and old-fashioned it was almost shocking.

I wondered why my sister enjoyed her job so much. Her assistant, Doris, was a basket case. Jenny was a compulsive liar, but she was only twenty- two and had plenty of time to mature. Kimmy was crabby and a wee bit stuck up for the most part. The men that worked with her in the branch were lenders, which means they spent most of the time out golfing and pretending to work. They stayed out of her hair; they made money for the bank, so I guess you could say they were by far her favorite employees.

But, Mia was very important as a manager of a large banking branch, so during the time she helped our mom pack and move, she'd go into work early to get caught up.

One morning, my sister was working on a loan she was prepping for underwriting and one of the girls that worked there kept interrupting her. I could feel my sister's annoyance. I thought she was pretty nice and had a lot more patience than I probably would have.

Finally, she decided to take a break and use the ladies' room. As Mia made her way through the bank lobby, talking with her employees, she began feeling sick and shaky. She probably needed to go to the doctor or go home, but she wasn't the kind of person that went home for every little thing. Mia was certainly not the type of employee to miss work either. She would rather work through feeling badly than to go home and wallow in it anyway.

There was a sudden knock on the restroom door. It was an employee letting Mia know one of her customers pulled into the parking lot and would probably be coming into the office to see her since Mia had been out a lot lately. Mia sighed. Poor thing couldn't even use the restroom in peace!

My sister walked into the lobby and greeted one of the worker's from the corporate office, who came in to do routine maintenance at the branch. The worker was in his mid-fifties and was obsessed with wax museums. It was very odd, actually. He began talking about his recent trip to the wax museum, and Mia just laughed as she didn't know how to really talk to this strange fella.

"You are the only person I know that loves to go to the wax museum all of the time without children!" Mia teased.

Mia then became agitated as she had a glimpse in his mind as if she was reading his thoughts. He kept thinking about wanting to leave to go do a 'bump of cocaine' when he left. He was supposedly clean after years of drug abuse, but his conversation about museums fell into the background as his thoughts were louder than his words. Mia didn't know how to cope with the thoughts she was able to overhear in his mind and wanted nothing more than to break away from the conversation.

Finally, Mia had a reprieve. She noticed her favorite customer, Trina, was the customer waiting to see her, and Mia was relieved that someone came to pull her away so she could collect herself. It was then I realized her customers are what she loved about her job.

Trina was a black woman with beautiful, flawless skin. She had luscious lips along with a big smile and lots of perfect white teeth. Trina was a very hard-working woman and sweet-natured, but make no mistake about it, she was also a double barrel pistol when she needed to be. She wasn't one to take shit from anyone, except maybe her son. He had lost his wife, and she didn't speak her mind to him as much as she normally would. He changed, withdrawing a bit, and she tried to pull back so he could find his way again.

Trina was older than my sister, but they made fast friends and spoke to each other several times a week, chatting during banking hours and outside of the office as well. Trina enjoyed her visits so much she would drive out of her way to bank there just to talk to Mia. I could easily see that she was a crow—family-oriented and loving—but she also possessed very strong protective instincts.

I read Trina, inadvertently. She had her own trauma as a child. Her mother was abused by Trina's father, who beat her and cheated on her mom often. He physically abused Trina, too. Trina's mother was protective of Trina and finally reached her breaking point. One evening, her dad came home drunk, ready to beat on the ladies as he always did after his binge drinking. Trina's eye was swollen shut from the beating he had given her the night before. Trina's mother decided it was time for this mess to stop. Trina didn't have a granny like I had to send him away, so Trina's mom had to roll up her sleeves and take matters into her own hands. She boiled a large pot of water, added three hefty bags of sugar into the boiling water, and stirred as it thickened. As soon as Trina's dad staggered into the house, already hollering, she threw the scalding mixture at him. It seeped deep into his skin as he screamed in agony. Her mother added the sugar so it would stick to him as it penetrated deep into his skin.

Trina was placed in foster care after her mother went to jail, and she was shoveled around from home to home until she aged out of foster care. Everything she has achieved and accomplished was from hard work and dedication in order to provide a good life for her son.

"Well hey, sugar. I came to see you the other day, but they said you took a vacation day."

They greeted each other with a big hug and walked into my sister's office. My sister took a deep breath and said, "Moving my mom."

Trina smiled. "Girl, I know you're tired. You *look* tired."

My sister laughed. "That's a polite way of telling someone they look like shit."

She and Trina laughed, and suddenly, I had another weird flash before me. It was almost as if I was *with* Trina. I guess I captured a glimpse into what she was thinking about or a memory. I am not sure exactly why or what triggered my vision. I saw a woman named Mabel, a heavyset older black woman who wore her hair slicked back and had a slight gap between her two front teeth.

Mia suddenly had a nagging feeling to inquire of this Mabel. I know Mia was worried she would look foolish to inquire who Mabel was, but she felt she had to. "OK, really random question but does the name Mabel mean anything to you?"

Trina's smile immediately dropped. She stared at Mia, waiting for her to speak. Mia immediately regretted the inquiry and even felt a little foolish.

"Have I ever told you I don't trust that bitch?" Trina asked. "This bitch watches my grandbaby sometimes while Anthony works."

Trina's son, Anthony, had a young son with his wife who had passed away when Michael was a baby. Anthony began seeing another woman about a year ago, and they paid her mother to watch Anthony's son, Michael, since she was home during the day anyway. Trina worked full time at a retail chain as a district manager and couldn't watch Michael, although she wanted to.

"Have I ever told you I don't trust that bitch?" Trina asked again. Mia assured her she hadn't ever talked to her about Mabel before. "I can tell Michael doesn't like her and she acts nice to him, but she just gives me a funny feeling when she is around. He won't go to her; he turns away from her." Trina seemed to get agitated as she spoke about Mabel.

My sister asked about the little food iron painted up like a hamburger with the little seeds and pickle slices on it, and Trina seemed puzzled. I was puzzled too. How was Mia seeing the visions I was seeing? She never had that ability before; not when I was alive, anyway.

Trina was quiet for a brief moment. "Girl, Mabel picked that up from me at the garage sale last weekend at Anthony's house. Did I tell you about that?"

Trina did not tell Mia about that hamburger grille. I could see what happened and wondered if Mia could see what happened too. I began wondering if Mia had psychic abilities. There was no way her asking about Mabel and then about the iron was a coincidence.

Mia took a breath. "OK. I'm going to tell you something that will sound strange to you, I'm sure. It just popped into my head. I asked about Mabel because she was thinking about when Michael burned his little fingers on the grille." Trina leaned forward, listening to her with intent. Mia continued. "Mabel was in another room and heard your grandbaby scream out and cry, and she paused and smiled because she immediately knew he burned his fingers on the food grille that was next to him on the table. She got sick satisfaction out of it. She let him burn his fingers as she finished folding the towels she took out of the dryer."

This woman was no doubt a grackle, preying on a smaller,

defenseless child; it is sickening.

"Mabel slowly walked in and looked at him with his blistering fingers. She called him a dumbass fucking kid and jerked him up but didn't do anything to soothe his burning fingers. She is a cruel bitch," Mia confided in Trina. I guess it was a lot for her to process or she was just thinking my sister was crazy. "Ask Anthony to look for another sitter immediately and tell him your concerns."

Trina told Mia she has all but begged Anthony not to let Michael go over there, but after he burned off most of the skin from his little fingers that weekend, it just confirmed that Mabel wasn't watching him close enough. "I saw her pick up that grille and she had a cold smirk as she stared at it. I found it strange. I should have hit that bitch upside the head with it," Trina stated, with anger in her voice. "I feel like…like she was having a flashback thinking about my baby burning his little fingers on the iron."

My sister tried to keep her composure. I could tell she was shaken by her vision and the fact there was a possibility she was correct. Trina added, "I'm going over there and fuck this bitch up."

My sister was able to calm her. "There is another way. Get her ass locked up. Set her up. Put cameras up and don't tell her about it. Send that bitch to jail."

Trina agreed with my sister's idea. "I like that idea, but I need to make sure she doesn't hurt my baby. I will kill a bitch." Trina instantly thought about her mother and how she took action into her own hands. After that, she was thrown in jail for doing so. Trina thought it would be a better idea to involve the police.

"Do you not find what I told you strange?" Mia inquired.

Trina shrugged. "A little, and yet I believe you. I just know in my gut that what you're saying is true." They sat there looking at each other.

"Well, let's make sure." My sister gave Trina the number of one of her customers who worked for a security company. She told Trina to have Anthony keep quiet, not telling anyone—not his girlfriend or anyone else—about the cameras. Certainly Mabel's daughter would tip her off if they were recording her.

Mia recommended that Trina talk to Anthony about her concerns with Mabel. Explain her fears but express the importance that he has to keep it quiet and must watch from his laptop from down the street so he is close by just in case she is really being mean to him.

Trina meant business. Boom! Security cameras were up and running the next morning. My sister and Trina had hoped they were wrong and paranoid, but let's just say by the end of the week, Mabel was in custody for child abuse. They saw on tape where this cruel monster would put his little nose in his underwear when Michael accidentally soiled himself and started smacking him as if she was potty training a dog or something. She was terrible to him, and luckily for her, the cops beat Anthony to the house as he watched from his job that was two blocks away from his home. Mia was relieved Trina found justice and Michael was safe.

Mia had her first real experience with psychic abilities, and the fact that she was correct really bothered her and felt uncomfortable for her. Now more than ever she needed to talk to Lily to help her gain a reasonable explanation for this wild and unfamiliar experience.

Mia felt so blessed to have our mom stay with her for a few nights to help with Jacob while Tyler went to see his mom, who was sick in the hospital in Kansas. It was a relief to leave him with someone she trusted, who would never hurt Jacob.

Our mom stayed with Jacob so my sister could go to the doctor for her stomach pains and await blood tests. I know it worried my mom because of my dad getting sick and passing away at such a young age. My sister was constantly feeling sick lately, having terrible stomach pains for far too long. This was very concerning for our mom. She worried about Mia's health so much; it was all she could think about.

Mia also had her appointment with her therapist the same day. While my sister got ready for her appointment with Lily, my mom was playing with Jacob. I wanted to stay with them, but I felt protective of Mia, and I seemed to follow along with her. It was almost like I had become her shadow, attaching to her instead of my doll. I was always with her; I wanted to be with my sister.

Jacob didn't like to nap in my sister's room. He said he was scared of a shadow in the corner. I'm almost certain he could see me. I think my sister knew he could sense me; she hadn't said it out loud to anyone, but she sensed me too. I think she was too afraid to admit it out loud because in her mind she thought it sounded crazy. She certainly didn't want to upset my mom by mentioning something like that to her.

Interestingly enough, my family had a strong connection to the spirit world, and yet Tyler was closed-minded about it. In fact, the experiences he has had, he minimized. He had experiences at my mom's house—hearing footsteps and laughter that seemed to frighten him. He no longer acknowledged it after being removed from the situation.

My sister finally arrived to see Lily. Mia liked talking to Lily as a friend, but when Mia saw Lily as Dr. Roth at her office, it was a different dynamic. The setting is professional, and Lily ceases being the best friend, instead becoming the therapist she trusts and confides in.

As soon as Mia entered Dr. Roth's office, she was greeted with a warm hug from her. "I'm sorry I couldn't get you in last week. My schedule was packed already, and I was feeling terrible. Bad migraines."

My sister's embrace changed with Lily; she withdrew and stepped away. My suspicion was that she saw the vision I saw. Mia sat on the chair across from Lily then held her thumb up to her mouth and tapped her nail against her teeth.

Dr. Roth just looked at her and smiled. "Mia?"

My sister cleared her throat. "Lily, are you feeling OK?" This was my sister's way of letting her friend know they were speaking now as friends and not as doctor/patient. Mia could tell Lily wasn't herself.

Lily took a deep breath and then another. "This is your hour, Mia. What's going on, babe?"

Mia would see Lily anytime she had a flair-up. She faulted herself for my death for years and carried that burden on her shoulders. Lily assumed her moving my mom is why Mia needed to talk to her, the trauma, no doubt, giving her a hard week. My sister kept having the dream night after night of jumping into the hole filled with water and doll parts, and it was overwhelming for her.

"OK," Mia proceeded. "You already know I beat myself up about what happened to Lucy. I probably wouldn't be here talking to you about those feelings today, but to be honest…I think I'm losing my mind. I keep having visions of things. I will think they aren't true, and then I find out that they are exactly true. Plus the weird dream I continue to have is very upsetting to me. I think it makes me sick."

Dr. Roth inquired for examples in which my sister proceeded to tell her about Trina, and then she told her about Doris. Well. The annoying grackle always brags about her husband and family. Truth be told, they are far from perfect. Dr. Roth said most people overcompensate when they are unhappy or they know the faults of their family but they have an image and put on a facade.

Mia nodded but continued. "I get that, but her husband is a slow talking country boy—think Sling Blade. His name is Bruce. He works for a recycling company, and he is the epitome of redneck—a real roughneck guy. He has the tattoos, the big truck, the boots; everything to fit the stereotype of a roughneck country boy. He started bringing the coworker who he was training into the bank. His co-worker is a short tatted-up guy named Jerry. They were wearing cowboy hats and talking all macho. They had some Broke Back Mountain shit going on there. All the while, Doris talks about how faithful he is, he never looks at other women, blah, blah, blah. I had a vision while talking to them. I believe her; he probably never looked or thought about other women." Mia took a breath. "Well, on my lunch hour, I drove out there and confirmed what I would see when they came into the bank together.

"I didn't tell Doris; she wouldn't believe me anyway. She has a tracking app on his phone to know where he is at all times, not suspecting that he, of all guys, would be slobbing knobs." She snickered, making a crude comment to ease the uncomfortableness about what she was sharing with Lily.

"Like everyone else in her life, Bruce resented Doris and her controlling ways. She tracked him to keep close tabs on him. Not close enough, apparently." Lily's eyes widened as Mia told her about his affair with Jerry. "Doris was constantly mad at him and nagged him over every little thing. Especially money. He couldn't spend money on his parents or things around the house, but she would always spend money on her own parents. When he would spend money, even to feed his horses and dogs, she would get upset. She would be pissed if she knew he had a running joke about her with his lover, Jerry.

"They would laugh at her saying she would get real pissed if she knew he spent more money on his horse than his cow. Jerry called her a cow, not only because of her obesity but just her slow moving, lazy ways in general. They're mean-spirited about her behind her back as if what they're doing isn't terrible enough."

Lily interrupted. "Really, seems like he isn't with her for love or happiness but maybe out of obligation or convenience. Sounds like he is unhappy. A very unstable family dynamic."

Mia nodded. "Very unstable. She raises Bruce's niece, and she is basically an escort. The niece worked as a hostess at a restaurant, hoping to meet a man with money so she could trap him. Doris has boasted about it. The girl was barely seventeen when Doris let her move out and into an apartment with a coworker that was openly an escort that she met at the restaurant. Doris was perfectly happy with this seventeen-year-old dating an old ass man because he had money. I never understood that. You are going to sleep with an old man who has money? Why? He isn't giving you all his money. Their niece was accepting gifts to put out and she and Doris and even Bruce were all so impressed by a Michael "Gors" knockoff handbag she received as a gift." Mia rambled on. "I guess her coochie wasn't worth a Gucci."

Lily laughed and began coughing from her water going down the wrong way when she took a drink. "No doubt Doris has family issues. You probably picked up on her husband's homosexual tendencies, even with him trying his best to mask it. As far as the niece, she talks about her at work?"

"Yeah, not to me, but I can hear them chatter about it while I work in my office. She's a terrible mother figure, and her niece just found out she is now pregnant by one of these losers and he doesn't know it yet." Mia looked at Lily. "She is trying to find her lucky lotto ticket: child support. She will keep looking for someone to leach onto. She plans to trap someone into a family. As long as she thinks they have money to support her, she's interested in them." Mia rolled her eyes and shook her head. "Doris and her *motherly* advice. She encourages her to get pregnant and it disgusts me."

Dr. Roth/Lily, asked, "You saw this in a vision?"

Mia laughed. "OK, Lily...Dr. Roth. Ever since I left my mom's house in Dallas, I have felt like Lucy has been with me in my thoughts constantly. I never had gifts before, but I know my granny did, and honestly, Lucy did too. I used to dismiss it all as a coincidence when she would have visions and feelings. I even think in Lucy's voice now."

I realized what was going on at this point after hearing Mia, but I didn't exactly know what to do about it.

Mia continued. "I was right about what I told you with Trina. I never knew about Mabel or anything about someone babysitting her grandson, Michael." Dr. Roth started to interrupt her, but Mia spoke. "There was also something else…something smaller than the experience with Trina. I went to see the CEO, Mr. Shaw, at his office which I rarely go to." Mia looked down at the ground as she spoke. "I immediately was picking up on strange vibes, but then something really weird happened. As he was rambling on, I saw someone out of the corner of my eye. It was an apparition of sorts, I guess—like a lady, maybe. She was shorter than me in stature and had brown hair. The shadow passed through as quickly as it appeared.

"Initially, I thought it could be his mother that passed away a few years back, but she appeared young. I dismissed the feeling, and the apparition that passed from my right shoulder through the other side of the bank president again. I was so distracted by this; I can't even tell you what my boss was saying. At this point, I was nodding along and smiling.

"Midway through the conversation, I felt the presence again. She started telling me she wanted to pass along a message about her passing. I pushed her away in my thoughts, thinking there was no way in hell I would pass him a message. He would think I was nuts and tell everyone and pretty much ridicule me. He would never believe what I would say, so in my mind, I shut the request down and closed myself off to the possibility of passing a message along. I am not about to be Ode Mae Brown passing messages from ghosts!" she laughed.

"She was so insistent about telling me things so he would trust me, she was wanting to talk about her accident. I tried to ignore her but she was so persistent. I had her in one ear, all while trying to listen and interact with the boss.

"Luckily, he loved to talk, and I was a pretty good listener. While he and I talked, she was telling me to tell him about her trophies so he would believe me. She went on about their childhood home. I think she kept providing details so he would have to believe me. I couldn't wait to get the hell out of his office. My anxiety was through the roof. I was about to have a nervous breakdown, I believe." Mia had a nervous laugh about the situation, but I know it was troublesome for her. "And Lily, I hope I'm wrong, but you keep telling me you were having migraines, but -" Mia stopped short and the two locked eyes.

"You're a witch!" Lily laughed and then she began to cry.

Mia hugged her. "You miscarried?" Mia saw exactly what I did. I was now convinced that when I see visions, Mia sees them too, and I wasn't sure what to do with that or how to remedy it for her.

"I had a miscarriage last week, and I'm not ready to tell people. Can you tell me what you saw?" Lily asked Mia. My sister paused before asking who wanted to know—Lily or Dr. Roth.

Lily stood up. "Let's go across the street and grab a drink and finish talking. Dr. Roth and Lily both need a smoke and a drink," Lily said, joking to ease the intense emotion she was experiencing.

As they ordered their drinks and began to visit, Mia explained that she wasn't reading everyone. "It's inconsistent. Like, when I was getting a massage yesterday, I could hear what she was thinking the entire time. It was the most stressful massage I ever received. It didn't happen again until I went to the doctor and I saw a vision of his dog dying earlier that day. He was upset and wanted to get home to bury the dog that he placed in a storage bin in his garage, but when the nurse came in, nothing. No visions going on with her at all. Do you think I'm losing it or what?"

Lily, on her third drink, shook her head. "No. I know you think I'm closed off, but I know there are things that can't be explained. Clairvoyance is when people can see things; clairaudience is where you hear things and feel things. Claircognizance is when you just know things. What is it you think you experience?"

"I'm not sure. Maybe a combination. My granny told me my sister was gifted, and her gifts were growing with age; but, as you know, Lucy passed away. My granny, I think, had all of these special gifts—based on what my mom told me, anyway. She was always worried she would teach Lucy stuff and felt it complicated life and the element of surprise life offers, so she didn't want Lucy having gifts or learning about her gifts. I don't think Mom has cared too much about the surprises life has had for our family. Before this past week, other than normal intuition, I don't think I had any real gifts, and to be honest, I think they're making me paranoid and nuts. I feel sick all the time. I'm not myself, Lil." Mia put her hands to her face.

"I'm writing you a prescription so you can get some rest, and I want you to meet a colleague of mine. Can you meet me again tomorrow around three? She and I were scheduled to meet, but I think she would be helpful in this situation," Lily suggested. "She has a little bit of experience with this, whereas I don't. Her name is Dr. Flowers. I will fill her in tomorrow before you arrive, and we'll see what ideas she has to help you with your experiences." Lily filled out a prescription for Mia.

"You carry that prescription pad around with you for crazy people emergencies?" Mia joked. "Want to talk, Lily, about your loss?" Mia asked in a serious tone.

Lily sighed. "I was only seven weeks along. I get that I lost the baby early, but I'm still so heartbroken." Lily cried and Mia hugged her.

"You're worried because this is your second one," Mia said. Lily cried even harder because, aside from her husband, she hadn't told anyone that she lost a pregnancy six months prior.

I had a vision and Mia did too. "Look, I want you to go see another doctor, because you have uterine abnormalities, and your doctor isn't looking for anything right now. I think because miscarriages are so common, he isn't thinking anything is wrong. I don't want you to go through another loss. Will you try another doctor?"

Lily wiped away her tears. "I miscarried a few months ago. We were set to make a surprise announcement the next day with Duke, saying he was going to be a big brother." Duke was their dog that she treated like her first baby. "We had a little sign that he was going to be sitting beside with the announcement on it. In a way, I'm glad we did not announce it; less questions to answer and less hugs and sympathy from people. Just like this pregnancy, I only told my husband, our parents, my big brother and now my bestie." She nudged my sister with her shoulder. "I promise to see a specialist before trying again. I can't put me and Max through the disappointment again. Really sucks."

On the way home, my sister stopped to get her prescription. She was mulling over the events of the day and turned the radio from a low volume to off. "Lucy, are you in here with me?" I was a little stunned that she asked. I think she was in denial that it was even a possibility.

She requested again: "Lucy, if you are here with me, please tell me or turn on the radio or something."

To be honest, not only did I not answer, but I also did not try to turn up the radio. I wanted to think about her inquiry. What would it mean if she could hear me and what would happen next?

What could I do to make my sister feel better physically and mentally? Would acknowledging her make this all the worse? By now it was obvious that I was the reason she felt sickly. I was the reason for the visioning she was experiencing, and I wanted things to be easier for her. I knew I was the reason, but I denied it. I didn't want to be the cause of any pain or negativity. I needed to find a way to exit.

My plan was to, once again, leave my mom and sister alone to recover and move on from their loss. They deserved happiness and normalcy. I just needed to figure out…try to remember how to detach myself from the doll or my sister. I fear I accidentally attached to *her* when I stepped outside of the confinements of my doll.

I didn't want to be sent to the void again, but I regretted attaching to Mia and making her feel sick and upset. I had no right to tag along and bring the memories that haunted them the most along during the move. The last thing I'd ever do is hurt them all over again. I just wanted to spend time with them and see my nephew, never anticipating there would be a downside for them. Truthfully, rather than being in limbo, or being silent with my family, I would rather have made it to the other side of the ocean. I would prefer to be at peace and to be in a euphoric state—to be in Heaven and not what I can only consider purgatory. I never would have fathomed my sister feeling sick or experiencing anything that would cause her additional stress or uneasiness in any way.

So, I stayed quiet. My sister continued her drive back home to see my mom and her son. It was much later than she planned to get back.

She didn't intend on stopping for drinks with Lily and getting a prescription filled. As she sat at the red light, she yawned; she was already so tired, and I knew she still wasn't feeling well.

While we were still sitting at the red light in the dark, a hauntingly eerie feeling came over us both. The light remained red for a long time; no other cars were coming from other directions, and the streetlights were dimmed and subtly flickering. My sister considered cautiously proceeding through the red light. By now, she assumed something was off with the timers.

Before she had an opportunity to go through the red light, a large SUV pulled up beside her in the left lane. It was black with dark-tinted windows. I had a bad feeling but couldn't see inside the suspicious vehicle. To my surprise, my sister spoke to me again. "Don't look at it. It's him." She reached over to turn her radio up to play it off like she wasn't afraid and didn't know it was him.

The light remained red. Mia's hand trembled as she flipped through each station, making sure she kept her eyes locked on the radio. Each channel was static, but she continued flipping; there was nothing but loud static on each channel. Still, sitting at the light with no other cars in sight, no one else was around it seemed.

My sister's cell phone rang. It said Tyler, but she just stared at the phone. She was afraid of what would be on the other end if she answered, so she didn't pick up the call. She made the decision to proceed through the light and prayed the SUV wouldn't follow her through. I could see the hair standing up on her arms, little blonde peach fuzz on her goosebumps.

I began to feel angry that something was upsetting her and making her feel scared. I didn't look to see what it was. I listened to my big sister. I was pretty sure it was a demon that she saw when she was in high school. I picked up on it briefly, but now she was intently trying to think about almost anything else.

Just as my sister got the nerve to run the light, it changed to green, and the SUV continued to sit there as she left. She looked into her rearview mirror and didn't see the SUV anymore. Mia grabbed her phone; her hand was shaking and she called Tyler. As she spoke to him, she never mentioned anything about what she just experienced. I think she was afraid he would think she was overly paranoid.

Tyler was concerned about her being out late. He called because he wanted to make sure she was OK. He said he had a weird feeling and just wanted to check in. That didn't make her feel any better. My sister assured him she was OK. Tyler was very close to his mom, and Mia knew he had more important things to focus on. She didn't want Ty to be any more upset than she could tell he already was.

My sister saw a well-lit gas station, and it was pretty busy with customers, so she felt safe. She needed to get gas and knew she wouldn't want to mess with it in the morning. She pulled up to the gas pump and finished her call with Tyler. She then called my mom and told her she was ten minutes away from home and was getting gas.

My mom and Jacob were waiting for her. Mia was anxious to get home and put her sweet boy to bed. My sister finished her call and stepped out to get gas. As she was finishing, the radio volume seemed to turn up again and the static was loud—obnoxiously loud. Mia leaned in to shut off the radio, and I saw him coming before she did. As she stood up, a Hispanic man was behind her. He was close to her height, heavyset with thick black hair and wearing work clothes like he had been outside working all day, almost like an automotive uniform or something. He just stared at her. She asked if he needed anything as her eyes scoured the parking lot, making sure there were plenty of witnesses to see if he harmed her. He looked at her, saying nothing. As she was getting ready to leave, he spoke with a thick accent. "Your eyes…you have familiar eyes," he said.

Mia dismissed his comment. She wasn't sure if he was giving her an awkward compliment. But, to be honest, he had familiar eyes too. I recognized him from somewhere but couldn't place where I'd seen him. It was a very unsettling feeling for me. My sister was already pretty drained and her mind was still on the SUV. She was haunted by it.

Later, when she finally laid down for bed, Mia took her Xanax. She was calm, relaxed and felt better. I didn't sleep; I was always up, moving about the house. My mom was at Mia's still. Our mom was just there, relaxing and reading a book, completely at peace, and my nephew was in bed with his night light on. Our mom decided to just stay the night since she would be babysitting Jacob early the next morning. I liked her being there.

The house felt calm, peaceful. I saw a box of my stuff next to my doll. I hoped my sister was ready to box me up and pack me back away. This was for the best; I didn't want to be disruptive.

My sister woke up around three-fifteen again and looked into the corner of the room. "I see you; I see you, baby." She then jumped out of bed, crying, then went into the bathroom. No question she was sick again. She sobbed quietly, wiping her eyes until they were raw on the outer corners. I had to figure out how to leave.

I remember reading how ghosts or entities attach, but how to un-attach is what I needed to know how to do. I couldn't exactly pick up a book or look it up online. I was trapped. If it wasn't for my presence making my sister sick, or no longer being herself, being trapped with my mom and sister wouldn't be so bad.

Mia got herself pulled together for work the next day. She spent time with my mom and Jacob, but neither were quite themselves. My mom told Mia she didn't sleep well; she kept the reason to herself, but I imagine she felt my energy or maybe just felt so far away from home. I watched Mia sleep most of the night. That probably seems creepy, but you have no idea how much I wanted to hug my sister again.

Chapter Nine
Long Heels Red Bottoms

It was difficult being in my situation; I was completely helpless. I wanted to go and leave them in peace, but I felt trapped. I remember when my granny and I used to investigate the afterlife. They were just spirits that were stuck, needing to be crossed over. I need someone to cross me over. I hoped for that now. I got myself stuck, but now I needed help to get unstuck in a world I no longer belonged to.

My sister went to work that morning even though she wasn't feeling well. She was nice to her employees and customers and helped with transactions, making the usual chit-chat and small talk. She really seemed to enjoy her job. She was always put together nicely and very professional., wearing fashionable dresses and attire. I noticed she especially loved her beautiful heels with bright red bottoms. I guess a sexy pair of Louboutin heels will make any woman feel better. At least look the part, even if you are a little tired and not quite yourself. They were her signature heels. We grew up with modest means, so it was refreshing to see her so elegant and successful, living her life in a way we never dreamed of as young kids.

My sister finally left work for the day and I was glad. Doris was on my last nerve. She was a cry-ass over every little thing. She would tattle to my sister about Jenny while pretending to be Jenny's entrusted friend. I suppose there is a grackle like Doris in every workplace. Jenny was a decently smart young lady. I hoped she would finally clue in that Doris was not her friend, not her ally. Sometimes your so-called friends are your biggest foes, I suppose.

When Mia arrived to see Lily, she was a bit early, so she sent a message to Lily and said she would be waiting in her car whenever she was ready. Lily met her in the parking lot and got in the car with Mia. "Hey, I wanted to talk with you before meeting Dr. Flowers. I worried about you all night," Lily said with deep concern.

Lily smiled. "Did the medication help you rest?"

Mia took in a deep breath and exhaled slowly. "On the way home last night, I had a feeling Lucy was in the car with me. Remember I told you when I was a teenager I was going through a miserable time, and I thought I experienced a demon? I know you don't think so, but I did. I saw him, well…I felt him last night in the car beside me. I know in my bones he was there. I don't know why, but I think it's because I visited my mom's house when we were packing away everything. Stirring up old memories, I found demonology books that I thought were trashed under my little sister's bed. Do you think I am imagining it, reading more into what happened?"

Lily thought about it. "That's possible. You could be -"

My sister interrupted. "There was a man at the gas station that approached me after that happened. When he came up to me, I felt afraid, of course. It was late, and I was alone; being approached by a strange guy is always a little unsettling. It was what he said that upset me the most, I guess. He told me my eyes were familiar to him. I locked eyes with him briefly, but I never got a vision. It wasn't until I was asleep that I had a nightmare. It was him beside a bridge, looking at something in the water and laughing. I...I couldn't see what it was, but my initial thought was that maybe it was Lucy, but I never saw her in my dream," Mia said as she continued to share her feelings. "The most upsetting thing to me in my dream was he was fishing *me* out of the water and looking into *my* eyes and laughing. When he pulled me out, I was shivering. When I breathed, I was making a barking, gasping sound. He didn't help me. He looked at me and told me I had beautiful eyes.

"He threw me in a car, and the next thing I remember was being in some place like an old church." Mia paused to take a breath before continuing to tell Lily of her nightmare. "There were people there and he straddled me. My clothes were wet. He put his hands around my neck, then yelled in Spanish and began choking me with his hands tight around my neck. I woke up coughing. It was so real and it scared me."

It was then it occurred to me. Maybe I was here for a reason. Sadly, I realized that in my sister's dream, it wasn't her that was pulled from the water; it was *me*. Her familiar eyes were *my* eyes that he looked into when he was taking life from me. I remember now, I guess. I was close to death in the water before being pulled out. Perhaps he was the reason I never made it to the other side of the ocean. He pulled me from my death only to kill me all over again. But why? I was confused but knew I was right in my assumptions.

Lily, comforting my sister, said, "I told you before that you blame yourself for what happened to Lucy, but it wasn't your fault. Not at all. You're feeling guilty all over again because you opened old wounds, packing her room away. It's time to let the old wounds heal."

I realized Lily was trying to comfort my sister, but she wasn't explaining the dreams; she simply glossed over the nightmare my sister had. Mia reiterated her guilt once again. "I was supposed to be there with her, and instead, I told her to go alone with her friend and that I would take her for pizza later. I was so tired; I wanted to sleep and get my car cleaned. If I had just gone with her, she would still be here today. No question in my mind she would be here!" Mia cried.

Lily made a disagreeing head shake. They had been friends for so long and could tell each other anything. Lily had started as a customer where my sister worked, and they became close over the years. Then Mia became Lily's client. She had gotten counseling over the years to cope with the sadness she had carried over my death, but no one was as effective at helping her cope as Lily was. My mom would never get counseling. It was a generational thing, but she preferred coping on her own. I did too when I was alive. I guess I was like my mother about that type of thing.

Lily was a wonderful therapist. Sometimes she would help my sister through hypnosis, which was probably the most significant breakthrough for my sister—bringing feelings to the surface, getting help dealing with and coping with the emotions, sorting through memories, and focusing on the positives of the life I had before it was cut short.

Lily didn't want to keep Dr. Flowers waiting. "Let's talk to Dr. Flowers. She is probably waiting for us already. We can finish talking about this later, OK? Is that OK?"

Mia and Lily walked into her office building. They were quiet on the elevator ride; I'm sure Lily was dissecting the nightmare Mia shared. I know I was. I know now why they never found me; they never recovered me because I was removed from the water by a man I had never met. Mia's nightmare is what actually happened to me.

My recurring nightmares as a young lady were always of a witch tapping on windows or the rippling pond calling me to enter. Mia now had frequent nightmares of jumping into a small hole in the ground with doll parts floating upwards; doll's arms and legs bubbling to the top. Now she was dreaming of a *familiar* man that was pulling her from the water. She began experiencing my life in her nightmares. I believe this started because I was attached to her and hoped over time it would go away.

I have no idea why that man, who I didn't even know, pulled me from the water if it wasn't to help me. Why bring me to a remote dark place with others around him but not to a hospital to help me? Why look into my eyes and choke the life out of me? Why not just let me drown? Why all of the trouble?

Then, I had a realization—a dark and frightening revelation. He saw me and rescued me, only to kidnap me. Perhaps my bad luck that day was worse than I realized. Helping me only to murder me. What sense did that make? I couldn't fathom the explanation, and I don't know why I couldn't see anything beyond me going into the water. My only memory was that of me attempting to cross over.

I feel that my crossing over was disrupted not by my turning back to see my mom and sister like I initially thought, but I believe now my crossing was disrupted by this strange ogre of a man pulling me from the dark, murky green water, saving me from drowning.

I could see now; it hit me like a flash. I now remembered! This man, along with another man that was helping him, plucked me out of the cold and bleak waters. They pulled me out as I lay unconscious, my body still in the process of drowning and dying. They expelled the water from my lungs, and I was unaware and oblivious to them rescuing me, only to remove and kill me all over again. I was mulling over the scene in my mind. Indeed, it was a crime scene. I could have been saved, but my falling in only to be pulled out by this man was all a ploy, I believe. Mia couldn't see what I saw just then, but it was her nightmare that unlocked that terrible memory of mine. It was an intense and dark memory—a jarring memory that I thought best to keep to myself—for now, anyway.

We entered Lily's office. No Dr. Flowers; she briefly stepped out to make a phone call. When Dr. Flowers finally returned to Lily's office, Mia and Lily were both sitting down. They were both taking a quiet moment as they gathered their thoughts. She was a petite Hispanic lady with long hair dressed very casually in Capri slacks and a pretty blouse. I immediately recognized her scent, sweet demeanor, and wonderful smile. Dulce Ramirez. Apparently, Flowers now.

My sister was so distraught it took her a minute to realize the familiar smile. Dulce recognized Mia immediately. "I know those beautiful eyes!" Dulce shouted with enthusiasm. The embrace was warm and surprising; neither of them expected to see one another and certainly not under these circumstances.

"Flowers?" my sister asked. "I'm so proud of you! I have thought about you many times over the years."

Dulce flashed her amazing smile. "Thank you. I made my family proud with a degree and disappointed them by not marrying a Mexican man. Can't make your family too happy, or they come to expect it, so you gotta give them something to be disappointed with from time to time." They laughed.

I believe Dulce got pleasure from annoying her dad. Her dad basically shipped her off while he was with his new family so she didn't feel too bad about disappointing him. Dulce cared about her own happiness, as she should.

Dulce always knew she wanted to help people. Perhaps because she always felt like she was a burden, being shuffled from house to house, staying with people that loved her but never made her feel wanted. Except for Maria, I know she was the one that worked to help put Dulce through college. Dulce always had a loving heart, and she deserved better than what her family gave her. She did find love, and she deserved it.

As they shared with Lily that they knew each other from growing up together, the cold realization came over Dulce like a shiver down her spine. Dulce was frozen and choked back tears as she said, "Lucy??"

My sister's emotions took over as tears flooded her eyes and streamed down her cheeks, which confirmed my death to Dulce.

Lily was taken aback. "I am surprised you two know each other! That's a huge coincidence. I am so sorry I had no idea, or I wouldn't have used someone you knew. I am sorry I feel like I violated your privacy."

My sister immediately let Lily know it was no problem. "You couldn't have known, and it's fine. I am fine with Dulce knowing!" She looked at her with a gracious smile. "Well, Dr. Flowers, did Lily tell you I'm possibly losing my damn mind too?"

Both Lily and Dulce reassured Mia that she wasn't losing her mind. They assured her it was trauma, explaining that she had made tremendous progress with my death over the years. Mia really had a major setback after going to my mom's house to move her and nothing more. They could help her.

That very well may have been it, but truth be told, I believe it was my fault for inviting myself back into their world again. A dead girl, trying to cling to a life she would never be able to live again. I was ready to let go; I needed to give my family peace again, and I desired to cross over to see my dad and granny. The irony of it all is that Granny would know what to do.

I should have read more and practiced the magic like she asked me to. I don't believe she knew this would happen to me, but I think she somehow knew I needed to strengthen my gifts. It was too late, but I clearly have my regrets now that I had gotten myself stuck.

Lily continued reassuring my sister and tried to comfort her while she was blaming herself. "You know, in almost every accident, someone can look for a way to place the blame on themselves or onto someone else. Sure, almost anyone can say, "if only they weren't coming to see me" or "if only I didn't ask them to run that errand," if only, if only. I've told you this a hundred times. You must forgive yourself." Lily demanded. Lily's lecturing Mia made me think of when granny was talking to me about free will and the example of the lottery ticket. Every choice can be over analyzed, I guess.

Dr. Flowers cut in, changing the subject. "How are your parents? Are they coping better than you? Are they able to provide you comfort and support?" Lily's eyes widened as she shook her head as if to say don't ask. My sister brought Dulce up to speed about my dad's death shortly after she left the neighborhood for school.

Mia explained the haunted feelings in the house after he left. She told her all about my granny coming to help my mom through things. She told her about the passing of my granny in the house. She shared with her the terrible time we went through after losing them both. Her phone went off twice, both times it was Tyler. He was missing my sister and Jacob. His mother passed away, so he was flying home the following afternoon before he'd need to head back to Kansas for the funeral. My sister cut the meeting with the ladies short.

They didn't get too far into the weeds with the ailments my sister was experiencing physically and mentally, but the ladies agreed to meet again the following week. Mia provided Dulce with her number. They thought they could get together soon to catch up. I really think Dulce, while trying to keep her professionalism, took my death harder than she let on. I could tell she felt upset that Maria didn't tell her, but I think Maria wanted Dulce to focus on school and stay away from Ruby's clutches.

Lily hugged my sister goodbye, and Mia whispered in her ear, "I had a vision when we were leaving my car." Lily pulled back. Mia said, "How do you like the new doctor that you saw this morning?"

Lily slowly shook her head and smiled. "You should really consider changing your profession from banker to psychic!" They both laughed.

My sister quipped back. "Ugh, if only it worked that way! I would be crazy in my penthouse in Beverly Hills."

Dulce was puzzled by the joke and Lily said, "I'll fill you in. If it's OK with Mia, I will go through my notes with you in more detail so you will be up to speed when we get back together again. Will that be fine, Mia?"

"I think that will be perfect, that way I don't have to fill in the gaps. Talking about it and telling my story over and over again is in itself exhausting. Painful." Mia hugged both ladies goodbye. "I am heading home before it gets dark and the boogeyman slides up next to me again." She said it jokingly, but I knew she wasn't kidding.

"Boogeyman?" Dulce raised her eyebrows.

Mia giggled. "Fill her in for me! I am going to see Mom and Jacob. I will see you, ladies, next week."

"Mia!" Lily stopped her. "Tell Ty I am sorry about his mom, and please let me know where I can send flowers."

Mia smiled and agreed as she left. As *we* left. The whole way home, my sister looked in her rearview mirror. Paranoid, I guess, but with good reason.

My sister spent time with Jacob, and I sat with my mom as she read while sitting on the couch with her legs propped up. When Mom took her readers off, I swear she looked at me as I was in the corner of the room. As my sister tucked her son into bed, she passed through the living room. Mia kissed my mom on the forehead and walked to her room. It was as if I was drawn to my sister and unknowingly began to follow.

"Honey," my mom called out to my sister. "I found some books. Some I think you were supposed to get rid of, and some your granny was writing in." My sister came back to sit on the couch. "I don't have any interest in your demon books; I'd like those thrown out. After I read your granny's journals and finish going through these photo albums, you can put these in storage," she said to Mia as she scooted closer to our mom. My sister took the stacks of demonology and dark craft books and told my mom she would get rid of them.

As Mia walked into her room, she envisioned me reading the books when I was younger. She wasn't sure if it was a real vision or if she imagined it out of fear. Once again, she worried that she brought negative energy around our family and me. She also feared she would see the dark energy around the house again because she brought these books into her home. She was going to take them to work the following day to shred and discard the books for good. I got the feeling she was perturbed they were still around.

My sister took the pills Lily prescribed for her. They calmed her nerves but didn't seem to help her with the severe stomach pains, which have now also turned into excruciating muscle aches, unfortunately. As my sister lay sleeping, she stirred around, not feeling well again. Her son was standing at the end of the bed as she woke. She got up to check on him.

"I had a dream that Aunt Lucy was asking me to open the door for her. I went to the door, and MiMi stopped me and told me to go lay down and never open the door without you or Daddy. Can you go let Aunt Lucy in?"

My sister scooped him up and put him in her bed. "Daddy will be home tomorrow. Let's get some good rest tonight. Aunt Lucy is in Heaven with Papa. Never, never open the door without me. Only Mommy, Daddy, and MiMi open the doors around here." She kissed his head and snuggled with him. Snuggling with Jacob probably made her feel better than any prescription she could ever get from Lily.

I must admit, I was concerned that he was dreaming I was knocking on the door. I was already in the house. I didn't get a good feeling about the dream. Truthfully, it upset me because I remember when I was a little girl and was tormented by nightmares of a witch knocking on the door, begging me to bring her into my home. A witch was luring me into a pond. The memories horrified me. Dead and still taunted by a witch that hated me. Surely, she would be dead by now, I would wonder.

My sister overslept for work the next day, so she had to quickly get ready, so she wouldn't be late for her meetings. She accidentally left the books behind, which she realized as she pulled into the parking lot. Late to Mia was arriving after 7:30 in the morning, apparently. She was an early bird and liked to get her mornings started before other employees began showing up.

The bank branch wasn't yet opened, but she had quite a bit to work on since she left early for her therapist visit the day before. She wanted to prepare before her manager, and one of her co-workers who worked in the next town arrived that day. Sophie was a fellow manager that would come in for their business review every quarter with Mia and their boss, Thomas.

My sister absolutely adored Sophie. They had become much more than co-workers; they became very good friends. Sophie was beautiful and funny and a fashionista like my sister. They bonded over their love of labels, and the friendship blossomed from there.

Sophie was closer to my age if I was still living. Maybe Mia saw some of the same attributes in her that she imagined I would have at that age. She was young and had no real family anymore. Mia mentored her professionally but also cared about her on a personal level too. Mia took Sophie into her life and loved her and felt compassion for her. Sophie was successful; without a family, she still put herself through school and achieved great things on her own.

Chapter Ten
She Bewitched Him

Sophie was a go-getter, young in her career, and obnoxiously motivated. She was a single lady with no children, but she yearned for those things eventually. She worked out often and was naturally beautiful. I do believe with her being such a small-framed woman to have endowments like hers she probably had some renovations done. If not, she needs to thank her parents for a body like that.

My sister usually enjoyed her business visits with Sophie and her boss. They would usually visit one on one with him before going to lunch, and then they would have a joint meeting, going over expectations for the following quarterly meeting. My sister hoped the day would go quickly as she was anxious to see Tyler. She hated sleeping without him and missed him very much.

My sister's boss arrived a little early, which made her happy. She figured he would be able to get out of her hair a little sooner than normal if they got an early start. Doris and Jenny got in a little early, and my sister was in no mood to deal with Doris. She was such a nut job ever since her niece told her she was now pregnant. She cyber-stalked the baby daddy frequently, keeping tabs on his assets, hoping her niece fell into a gold mine and that she could somehow personally benefit too.

My sister's boss was in his early fifties. He was a silver fox, very handsome and quietly charming in his own reserved way, with beautiful eyes and an innocent smile. My sister enjoyed picking on him more than anything. He didn't get her sarcasm; he took everything so literally. He was pretty uptight and very by the book.

Thomas was married to a strange lady. She tried too hard to be prim and proper. She was odd. Maybe he saw it, and maybe he liked that, but to say she was a bit much was an understatement. Mia always tried to avoid her at company functions. Both he and his wife were very religious. I am pretty sure that's the only reason they were together. They probably thought a divorce would damn them to Hell or something. Regardless, they seemed more like friends than people in a romantic relationship—at least from the outside looking in.

My sister teased him and talked to him as friends—yet always keeping things on a professional level—but she sometimes felt a little judged by him and did her best to avoid being lectured about her shortcomings where faith was involved.

The meeting finally ended. It was the dullest meeting I could imagine. To say it could have been an email is an understatement. As they headed down the steps, Jenny announced, "Devil wears Prada just pulled up!" Everyone obviously enjoyed it when Sophie came but also liked giving her a hard time. Everyone except Doris. Miserable as she was, she tried her best to dislike everyone that spent time with Mia. Sophie dressed beautifully, and, truthfully, she was stunning. When she walked into a room, her beauty and confidence would set the room on fire.

I will say, though, Sophie cussed like a sailor and didn't hold back with her opinions. I immediately liked her! As soon as she entered the bank lobby, she noticed Doris holding her phone in her lap with her head down and eyes locked on the screen. Sophie knew, as most did, that Doris was a snitch on the other co-workers, especially for being on their phones instead of working. Doris was working hard surfing through her social media.

She would always do the very things she would correct another employee for doing. Doris always was looking down at her phone in her lap, thinking no one knew what she was doing. Everyone knew. The employees resented that Doris' was such a hypocrite.

Sophie took note of the other employees observing, knowing what a hypocrite she was. Sophie smugly inquired, "Praying, Doris? AMEN!" Sophie's smart-ass way of calling her out for being on her phone, with her head bowed down, looking at her lap. Mia always bitched to Sophie about Doris calling everyone out for being on theirs, even though my sister didn't care about people being on their phones if customers didn't see and they got their jobs done. Mia would tell Doris it was fine and she didn't need to know, but Doris still pointed it out as if to imply the other girls didn't work hard.

Sophie strutted across the lobby with her fiery red hair, hazel eyes and a dazzling smile. All you could see when she smiled were beautiful white teeth. Sophie was in a flattering pale yellow dress and six-inch heels. Not much was left to the imagination. While it was professional, it showed off her assets quite nicely. With curves like hers, everyone took notice quickly.

My sister's boss, although married and holier-than-thou, clearly enjoyed seeing Sophie as well. His eyes lit up and he had a little giddiness to his voice and couldn't help but smile when she walked in. Sophie was no fool. Of course she knew their boss enjoyed looking at her. I'm 100% certain she used that to her advantage. In fact, I'm pretty sure she was the favorite based on the embrace he gave to her in the lobby.

My sister and Sophie chatted briefly before Thomas ushered Sophie away for their meeting. Mia was still hoping to dip out of work before six so she could spend time with Tyler. My sister got a call from her doctor's office and hugged Sophie before she went off to her meeting with Thomas.

Luckily, my sister's lab results came back good. They were still confused by her symptoms. Mia was relieved her lab tests were normal, but she was hoping to have some answers before leaving to go out of town for a funeral. She was still sick on and off and didn't want to have a bad experience while on an airplane. Her stomach pains were causing her to develop bad anxiety.

My sister began working her loan pipeline and paused, placing her index finger over her left eye, which began to twitch. She started having a vision, and so did I—small glimpses and words being exchanged. The visions are glimpses, not exactly like seeing them in real-time or watching a movie.

As Sophie was upstairs with Thomas working on their review, more was going on than met the eye. Sophie was flirting with Thomas. As she was a natural flirt, friendly to everyone, I am certain—and I know Mia was certain—that her flirtation with Thomas wasn't completely innocent. I think she wanted him. It became evident she was just as smitten with him as Thomas appeared to be with her.

My sister was having small glances of Thomas watching Sophie. He was daydreaming of her. Sophie interrupted his day dreaming by kicking off her heels and sitting on the conference room table in front of Thomas. Sophie paused to see his reaction, and he didn't object. She did it in a playful way to gauge his interest in her.

To Sophie's surprise, he rolled his chair back, welcoming it. He was wearing his "Jake from State Farm" khakis. He was so conservative; seeing him welcome the advances was shocking. In fact, he was excited to have Sophie sitting on the table in front of him, her long legs straddling both sides of his legs as he sat in his chair.

He slid his hand along her legs and gently caressed her thighs with his strong, sexy hands. He shook his head. "I'm married." Sophie wanted him and knew she could never put him in a position of cheating on his wife. Not only would she not want to hurt his wife, but she also wouldn't want to put him through the guilt of cheating on his wife and hurting him. She couldn't hurt his family like that, yet she still wanted to be selfish.

Mia got up to interrupt the meeting, as she just knew something wasn't right. As she stood up and began to step out of her office, Mia had a customer needing to visit her. She went back into her office to sit with her as the customer pulled out a stack of files. My sister was agitated because she wanted to interfere with the nonsense brewing upstairs and remained distracted.

Mia had a strong suspicion that Sophie was blurring the line between flirtation and being sexual. With Mia having glimpses of Thomas' thoughts of Sophie, Mia feared it would ultimately end up with Sophie getting hurt, either personally or professionally. Perhaps both. Sure enough, Mia faulted Sophie for her actions, but she didn't want to see Sophie hurt over a bad decision. Had Mia known the flirtation between Thomas and Sophie had been escalating for months, she would never have left the two of them alone; she just didn't know they were skirting along the edges of adultery.

As Thomas' hands drifted to Sophie's inner thigh, she stopped him and got down from the table. "You're right; you're married, and I am not going to fuck you," she said. "But you can look at me." She turned and sat on his lap as he slowly unzipped the back of her dress. His hand was trembling; he was so nervous but excited at the same time.

Thomas unzipped her dress and she turned back to him and flashed her brilliant smile. Sophie stood up and slid her dress slowly down her body and onto the floor. His heart raced, watching her slowly undressing. He never imagined someone as beautiful as Sophie wanting him, lusting over him. She did; she wanted him more than she wanted anything before. After months of talking and spending time together, she had fallen in love with him. It snuck up on both of them.

Sophie took off her lace bra, exposing her large, perfect breasts. I'm certain she absolutely had some *improvements* done. Thomas hesitated momentarily, engulfed with nervousness, and then gently grabbed both of her breasts while looking into her eyes. He wanted to kiss her, but he didn't. He just sat there looking at her, holding her breasts in his hands. He gently rubbed her nipples, making them hard.

He wasn't sure what to do. This was not his typical behavior, not even with his wife. I'm pretty sure his children were likely conceived in the missionary position. Thomas knew it was wrong to be with her and he resisted. He removed his hands and told her once again that he was married and he was sorry he couldn't. Sophie felt stupid and covered her breasts by crossing her arms in front of her chest.

Thomas put his head into her lap, his warm breath against her bare thighs. "I'm just going to look." He proceeded to remove her tiny lace panties from her body. He gently rubbed his thumb along them. I guess you would still call them panties. They were a pair of tiny, nude sheer and lace thongs. They were so tiny, as he removed them from her petite body, his hands firmly cupped her perfectly round ass.

"You have an amazing body and your ass is perfect," Thomas said to her, knowing she would always get teased for her curvaceous butt. All the guys enjoyed looking at it, though, Thomas included.

Sophie turned around so he could get a better view. He smacked her butt and she looked back over her shoulder surprised and laughed. "I have a bubble butt!" she giggled with a slight shyness that surprised him.

He laughed. "I know. I've always loved that about you. Your ass is voluptuous. I want to bite it!"

Her eyes grew big as she would never have expected uptight Thomas to say something like that. It was out of character for him. Naturally, the way he craved Sophie was out of character. He was bewitched by her. Bewitched by her beauty and her humor. He was attracted to her essence, her soul. What neither of them realized, I could sense that their souls were very old friends.

Sophie got back onto the table and laid back as he looked at her naked body, rubbing his hands along her sides and her firm, tight stomach. She opened her legs wide as he looked at her. He spread her legs even wider, and then wider still so he could get a good look at her, all of her. He then ran his hand softly along her stomach making her get goosebumps. His touch made her tremble and moan quietly as she bit her lip.

He wanted nothing more than to kiss her stomach, but the truth was he desired to lick kiss all over her. In fact, he never wanted anything more. He salivated just imagining it, which he did on a regular basis. He never yearned for anything or anyone the way he did Sophie. Not even his own wife. He stopped himself short of fulfilling all of his desires. He was proud of himself and angry at himself at the same time. He was angry for desiring her, and on some level he even resented her for it. He would never admit it to himself but he resented his wife and marriage that restrained him from having a taste of something he thought about every day, all day. Thomas and Sophie wanted each other, but they knew nothing could come of it. It was more than just a physical attraction at this point in their relationship.

They connected with each other. There was a spark, a kind of magic between them that they couldn't deny. They couldn't shake it no matter how much they tried to put one another out of their minds. There was this infatuation, this desire, these urges that haunted them.

Instead of touching Sophie, he guided her hand to touch herself. He wanted to watch her play with herself. It was dripping wet and he wanted nothing more than to taste her. She rubbed herself, gently as he lustfully watched. She quietly moaned, placing her left hand over her mouth so it was barely audible.

Thomas' penis was throbbing hard and all he could think about was fucking Sophie. It took every bit of will power he had not to take his dick out and fuck her hard right there on the conference room table. Instead, he took her finger and licked it, getting her finger wet with his saliva and then he stuck it inside of her. He helped her play with herself, making her quietly moan his name.

Thomas leaned closer to her so he could smell her. His mouth watered. He wanted to taste her and it took every ounce of restraint not to indulge himself. Thomas took her fingers and had her rub herself and then he put them up to her lips. She licked her finger and smiled at him. "I taste like a juicy, salty peach." He pulled her into his lap. He was so hard as he pressed himself against her naked body. He was so horny he could barely control himself. Thomas pressed himself against her and she pressed back on him as she began rubbing herself all over him. Thomas wanted to start licking and sucking her tits, giving into his temptation. He was in awe of her beauty and thinking with his dick and not his brain.

Sophie is so sexy and he couldn't believe someone so desirable wanted him, he couldn't believe this was really happening. Her beauty was captivating and her body was perfect, but with that aside, there was something about her he couldn't resist. It was her. Her personality, her scent, their phone conversations, her good heart and smart mouth. He never knew someone like her would want him and he never anticipated he would want someone like her.

Suddenly, Sophie covered her breasts with her hands again. "We aren't doing this. I'm sorry; this is wrong. I don't know what I was thinking." Sophie was head over heels infatuated with Thomas, but she couldn't allow him to do something he would later torture himself over, they had already gone much too far. While she behaved poorly over Thomas, she actually was a kind person and this wasn't typical behavior for her. Thomas wanted to be talked into being with Sophie. Truth be told, she was a master in the art of manipulation to get her way and she could have very easily tipped the scale in her favor but she stopped.

Thomas knew if he gave in, he would have religious guilt that would constantly eat away at him. He knew he would beat himself up over the culpability of his actions. Sophie wouldn't admit it at the time, but she fell in love with a man she could never have and was heartbroken over it. She knew someone's husband, someone's dad, wasn't who she was supposed to be with, and her lapse in judgment embarrassed her, making her feel dirty and shamed.

"So you're teasing me?" Thomas asked.

Sophie laughed. To lighten the mood, she joked, "I'm a tease, not a slut."

He looked at her. He felt bad she would say that about herself. "I know how you feel about me, and I don't think of you as a slut. I think about you all day long, every night. I dream of you. I can't wait for the next day; I wait for you to text or call me. You're the best part of my day," he said to her. He was completely vulnerable at that moment.

Sophie wanted nothing more than to indulge her selfishness, but she didn't. She began getting dressed as Thomas watched her. She felt uncomfortable as he kept his eyes fixated on her the entire time.

Suddenly, my sister knocked on the door, interrupting the two. Mia knocked on the door like she was the damn police about to knock it down! It even took me by surprise and scared me, and I wasn't even doing anything to feel guilty about!

"Are you guys ready for lunch yet? You've been in there for a long time; I've tried reaching you both." My sister was texting and calling them both as she walked up the stairs to the conference room from her office. She certainly didn't want to see Thomas fumbling over Sophie with his moral superiority.

While she didn't think of Thomas in any way other than a boss and somewhat of a friend, she related to being a married woman and how she would feel if a younger, more attractive woman seduced her husband. From that standpoint, she resented the carelessness and selfishness of them both. She wasn't going to support it.

Mia wasn't sure what did or didn't happen, but she had a strong inkling something went on, and she was disappointed with them. Just texting and calling each other would be considered adultery to Mia. As Mia knocked on the door, Sophie quickly slipped on her high heels and sat back in her chair. Both of their hearts were beating through their chests. I'm certain they had forgotten where they were when they were so wrapped up skirting around the edges of infidelity that getting caught was far from their minds.

No matter how you want to dress it up, while there wasn't sex, what they did was wildly inappropriate and many would consider cheating just the same as if he did fuck her. Thomas betrayed his wife even though he stopped short of having sex with Sophie. The fact Sophie dominated his thoughts, even when he was with his wife, was upsetting enough.

I'm sure his wife got a lot of attention that night since he was horny and thinking of Sophie. He fantasized of her often, and in his life, he never wanted a woman more than the woman he could never have. It wasn't even that he just wanted something because it was intangible. He was just drawn to her from the first time he met her. Once he laid eyes on her, he instantly became fixated on Sophie.

Thomas and his hard dick waited at the table while he pretended to be on the phone as Sophie opened the door. Mia looked at Sophie. "Zip your dress the rest of the way and let's get going." My sister closed the door and proceeded downstairs. Sophie, panicking, said, "Do you think she heard us?" Thomas assured her there was no way; they were very quiet. They pulled themselves together and came down for lunch.

Thomas teased my sister. "I thought the boss said when the meeting was over!"

Mia wasn't in the mood for him pretending to be innocent. She wanted to tell him to stick his *'I'm the boss card'* up his ass and call his wife. Mia was pretty pissed off at both of them. "Oh, I think you and Sophie were close to being finished anyway, right?"

He looked at my sister, unsure of how to take the comment. He looked at another woman; he looked at her naked body, and yet he felt he didn't "technically" cheat. He justified it to himself so he wouldn't feel guilty. My sister was so perturbed with Thomas she wouldn't even look at his face. She was even angrier and more disappointed with Sophie. Her behavior was completely surprising and disappointing. This wasn't the Sophie she knew.

As they were all heading to lunch, Thomas suggested they all ride together, but my sister wanted to call my mom and Tyler as they drove to the restaurant, so she thought they could all take their own cars. She suggested that in case Thomas decided to head back to his office which was close to an hour and a half away which is what my sister hoped he would, she was really upset with both and didn't see a need to have an all-day meeting since there wasn't much content left to discuss.

She was a little surprised just how annoyed she really was. She was angry at her boss with his self-righteous, I'm a better Christian than you attitude. She was mad at him for his actions and hypocrisy. She was mad at her boss that would deliver speeches on being faithful to God. Sophie, a friend Mia adored and knew had a wonderful heart, infuriated her because she lusted after her boss, whom she had no right lusting after. Her annoyance was written all over her face.

While they were heading out to lunch, Thomas informed the ladies he still wanted to have the joint meeting after lunch. "Sophie, you can ride with me so Mia can call her husband," Thomas suggested. Mia felt this was just a ruse for him to get more alone time with Sophie. She knew he was trying to soak up all the time he could with her.

Of course, Sophie jumped all over that opportunity to have a few more moments with Thomas. Ten minutes ago Sophie was ready to jump on his dick, so of course she was happy to ride with him to the restaurant. Mia was a little put out but was done with their sneaking and flirtations by that point and just wanted to visit with her husband on the phone.

I think the thought of Thomas, who had been married almost twenty-nine years, being tempted by Sophie made her appreciate her own marriage and motivated her to be more attentive to Tyler. Mia would be devastated if he thought of another woman and wanted a woman more than her, the way Thomas wished to have Sophie more than his own wife.

As they arrived at the restaurant, they were immediately seated. As they reviewed the menu, Sophie continued flirting. Although she didn't think Mia knew what she was doing, I did, and Mia did too. "Mmm, peach pie. Do you guys like peaches?" She shot a sultry look at Thomas and smiled with a devilish grin.

He smiled ear to ear. "I love peaches. I think I will order two slices. Warm peach pie is one of my favorites, especially with cream on it. I could probably eat the whole pie," he said, looking at Sophie the entire time.

Mia didn't disappoint. "Thomas, you should have your wife bake you a peach pie tonight. Doesn't she like to bake? There is nothing like homemade pie."

Sophie quipped back, "Taste the pie here and see if you enjoy it more than your wife's pie." Her suggestion irritated Mia. Enough was enough already.

"Not to be tacky, but my wife's pie was never anything particularly special," Thomas said, still looking at Sophie as if he was worried she would be jealous or upset about his wife being brought up into the conversation.

Mia interjected. "Aw, don't say that; you love your wife and your family so much. How is your wife? She is so sweet. Will she be at the banquet next week?"

Thomas confirmed she would go to the banquet and the conversation turned to banking as he was agitated Mia brought up his wife. He could see Sophie shifting in her chair, clearly bothered thinking about him having a wife. The conversation was now focused on work. They now talked about goals and upcoming regulatory changes. I was so bored of the dull conversation that I could just die if I hadn't already. As they finished lunch, Thomas actually ordered a piece of peach pie. Mia was in a bad mood over it too. She watched him offer a bite to Sophie off his fork. Sophie indulged him by taking a slow bite, almost as if she was making out with the fork.

"Take the rest home to your wife and let's get going. I got a husband to get home to and I have a lot to do," Mia said in a sassy tone.

Thomas chuckled. "Wow, Mia is in a hurry today and a little spicy."

Mia stared at him. "It's salty. Not spicy."

Thomas finished his pie quickly and they were ready to head back to work.

Once they got back, the meeting was pretty short, and they wrapped up early. Thomas and Sophie were about to head out, but Mia asked Sophie to stay behind and visit. Doris was sitting at her desk. She got up and followed my sister into her office, as she needed to speak to her privately.

Sophie was waiting, making small talk with Mia's employees, while Doris spoke to my sister. Human Resources had called my sister while she was out at lunch and spoke to Doris about her refunds and a customer complaint against her. She was apparently paying her family members' overdraft fees when she wasn't even supposed to be accessing their accounts. That was the least of their concerns, though. HR began looking into Doris after receiving a big complaint about her. A customer's adult daughter called the corporate office when she noticed there were large amounts of funds missing from her mother's account that Doris opened for her only weeks prior. Doris processed the transactions, and it appeared she took the funds personally as they reviewed the bank cameras.

Doris began trying to explain that she "borrowed money" hoping to gain my sister's sympathy, but it fell on deaf ears. My sister wasn't interested in lame explanations for stealing and preying upon an elderly customer. Doris justified it by saying the elderly customer wouldn't need it and that she planned to pay the funds back as soon as she received her tax return.

Doris, the grackle, was taking advantage of the customer, stealing her money, thinking she wouldn't notice it missing. Doris swore that wasn't the case, but it was. It unequivocally was. She was like any other grackle preying on a vulnerable bird. No cares in the world if her own needs were satisfied.

My sister was appreciative of the heads up by Doris, even though she was just trying to smooth things over and gain my sister as an ally. My sister called Sophie into the office after excusing Doris. "What was that about?" Sophie was being nosy, of course. Mia filled her in, since they were both managers it wasn't a secret that my sister was going to have to terminate Doris for being a thief.

Doris was stealing from customers and stealing from the bank by waiving fees for her family. Apparently, she credited almost a thousand dollars when my sister was off those days to her mother's account, hoping no one would notice. She took almost seven thousand dollars from an elderly customer, which was even worse.

"See, this is why I can't even miss a day of work. Shit falls apart when I do," Mia said to Sophie.

Sophie laughed. "It isn't your fault Doris decided to steal. You know Krispy Kreme needs her donut money. I know that was mean, but every time I see her, she has a donut in her hand." Sophie continued. "I can't stand thieves. She stole from an old lady, wow! What a fucking bitch. She needs to be cunt punched." The ladies erupted into laughter.

"Before you leave, Sophie, I need to tell you something. Unsolicited advice; do with it what you will." Mia began her lecture. "Whatever you are feeling and whatever is going on with Thomas, just stop! You are used to winning, and you won't win in this situation. You can't win. No matter what, you both lose already." Sophie shifted in her chair. "If you win and sleep with him, and let's say he leaves his wife, think about something. The kids are not that much younger than you. You would be resented. Besides, his wife loves him and won't allow it to be easy. He will break an oath that he takes seriously—something he has preached to me for years of knowing him. Trust me, the guilt will be a problem." Sophie said nothing, just listened to my sister. "If you sleep with him, and he stays with his wife, you'll resent him, then it will be a messy situation at work too, throwing away your career you love so much! You can't win in this battle. Neither situation will satisfy you. Stop before you can't turn back. You can't un-fuck someone you fuck, so just pull back and withdraw yourself from the situation."

Sophie, though frustrated, agreed. "You're right, Mia. UGH!! I hate this. He is such a dork anyway. He's older than me and most certainly unavailable. I am not a shitty person. What was I even thinking? All of his attention just felt so —"

"Any man will give you that attention. You don't need an unavailable man to complicate your life."

Sophie agreed with my sister. She already knew it, but Mia saying it just confirmed it by saying it out loud. "Besides, you told me before you like your hair pulled and your ass slapped. I can't imagine Thomas doing either of those things," Mia joked, trying to make Sophie crack a smile.

Sophie smiled and laughed. "I bet he's never had his dick sucked good anyway! I give the best blow jobs; he would have lost his mind. I would have fucked that son of a bitch so hard he would have gone insane," Sophie said and she and Mia laughed so hard.

Remember, I warned you about her mouth.

"I really love his beard. Every time we are in a meeting, I think about sitting on it and rubbing my...*you know* all over it," Sophie said with a smile, and she laughed so hard, but she was not joking. Mia made a shocked face and said, "too much information." Sophie would definitely have sat on Thomas' face if he was not married to *Saint Teresa.* That's what they called his wife. She too was holier and better than everyone else. At least, that's how she acted.

Sophie made light of the situation. "His son just turned twenty-four, a younger version of Thomas." They laughed. "I'm at the age where I can fuck him or his daddy." She was so wrapped up in Thomas, I don't think she had any interest in anyone other than him, but she joked that she could just be his daughter-in-law instead.

Mia threw a pen at her in a playful way. "He's only twenty-four; he barely got hair on his peaches." She laughed and motioned goodbye to Sophie. "Get out of here, hoe. I gotta call corporate and see when I can get rid of that basket case out there." She motioned towards Doris' desk in the lobby.

"She did it to her own sour ass," Sophie said as she picked up her bag.

"Yeah, but also, I've been manifesting her out of my life. She isn't a good person, so maybe this is my fault too for imagining her out of my life," Mia joked.

My sister was able to get rid of Doris. She didn't like firing her, but it was a necessary part of her job. She cut the dead weight. She used to feel sorry for Doris, but the closer she got to her, the more Doris started revealing her true self, and her manipulative, hateful ways. Doris was lucky the bank and the customer weren't going to press charges.

She definitely deserves jail time, in my opinion. Sure, Mia wished her away, but it was Doris' own actions that got her fired. I do have to wonder if my sister wishing her away had anything to do with her getting caught or if she would have been caught anyway. My sister had a tender heart and felt sorry for Doris even though it was apparent that not only was she a liar and two-faced, but she was also a thief and deserved what she got. Probably even more.

*****

On her drive home, Mia was feeling excited to see Tyler. She was longing to be with her husband and make love to him. Sadly, she had to pull over to the side of the road when she felt sick. I hated her feeling so bad. I don't know if it was me making her sick or the stress of the day. I'm sure she also wished for an uncomplicated life—no visioning, no intense emotions, just an ordinarily normal life she longed to have again.

Once Mia finally reached the house, my mother had a delicious meal prepared, and she was greeted by the handsomest boy you will ever see!

"Mama, I drew you this picture!" Jacob held the picture up to show Mia. It was my sister holding him. He actually did a great job.

"Look at this natural talent! Great job, bud. I love it!!" Mia hugged Jacob tightly. I never knew little boys could be so sweet. He was very kind and well-mannered.

They had dinner, and my sister put the picture on the refrigerator, then cleaned up before Tyler arrived. After her shower, she began packing for the funeral. Mia looked out of the window, seeing a storm blowing in, and feared it would delay Tyler getting home to see Jacob before it got so late in the evening.

When Mia took a break, she found our mom in the kitchen with Jacob, who was drawing more pictures. Mom smiled at Mia and said, "Jacob is pretty creative. He is good at drawing, isn't he?" Mia nodded and peered at the latest drawing.

Mom was standing at the refrigerator, looking at the drawing Mia had put up. She looked confused and asked, "Who is holding him in this one?"

Mia laughed. "It's me and Jacob."

My mom took it off the refrigerator. "I guess it is you. It looked a lot like Lucy to me, so I thought he was drawing your sister."

Mia looked closely, clearing her throat. "Jacob, baby, who is this with you? Mommy?"

He nodded his head.

Mia smiled. "See, MiMi? It's Jacob and Mommy."

Jacob shook his head. "It's Mommy and Aunt Lucy. It's '*boff*' of y'all," he said.

Mia and Mom looked at each other and my mom picked Jacob up. "When you get back in town, I want to go put some of these things in storage, and I want you to read some things in your granny's journaling book and see what you think," she told Mia while hugging Jacob.

Mia promised they would do that, but she feared the emotional toll of reading it all. She decided to take the journals with her on the plane. Even though it was a short flight, she wanted to read them since she suspected the smaller plane wouldn't have a TV to watch to kill time, but also to appease our mother.

"Mia, babe, I think Tyler is here in his Uber. Poor guy. I think he is waiting for the rain to pass; they're just sitting there," my mom called out.

"I'll take an umbrella out to him." Mia had the umbrella in her hand but stood in the doorway, her eyes fixated on the black SUV sitting in her driveway. Mia felt unease—almost fear—as it reminded her of the black SUV that waited alongside her at the red light only days earlier.

As my sister began to shut the door, Tyler opened the back door to the SUV and ran to the door, getting drenched while carrying his small bag into the house. "Holy shit, that rain is cold. Oh, baby, I missed you!" He leaned in to kiss Mia so he wouldn't drip on her. Her heart was racing. The black SUV remained there with the lights on.

As the SUV backed down the driveway, my sister could see the streetlight reflecting in, and she felt a sense of relief. Apparently, now she was fearful of all black SUV's. She didn't feel like it was him or it, but the black SUV certainly made her think of "it." She was so glad to see Tyler again she quickly dismissed her initial concern.

* * * * *

The next morning after breakfast, Tyler was putting their bags into the car. They decided to drive to the airport instead of taking an Uber. "Mia, Jacob, Mom," he called out. "Look at this." He pointed to the window of Jacob's room. There were layers upon layers of leaves stuck to the window. "How in the heck did these leaves get stuck like that?"

They thought it was funny, but I didn't; I found it eerie. Mia found it all too familiar as well. She had a flashback to when my dad found the humor in leaves stuck to only my window, and she remembered finding it strange that it upset me.

As they left, my mom reassured her that Jacob would be OK and that she needed to comfort her husband during his time of mourning. My sister was never close to Tyler's mom; she was probably a loving mom to Tyler growing up, but I don't think she was one to put her kids first as my mom did. I just had the impression Mia wasn't a big fan of his mother, but she felt an obligation to go and support her husband, of course.

My mom had given Jacob my Lucy doll to put in his room. My sister took notice as she was leaving for the day, and for some reason, it spooked her. While she didn't think the doll was haunted or evil, she wondered if bringing it or the books had something to do with her visions or even her feeling so sick lately.

"Mom, I was keeping this doll safe and preserving it as a memory of Lucy's."

My mom stepped back and looked at her skeptically. "No. You are afraid the doll is bad luck because you started feeling sick after we brought it here. Don't think that way. Your granny made this doll for Lucy, and she loved Lucy. This is not a voodoo doll or anything that should make you feel worried for Jacob to have it. He asked me for it because he thinks it protects him." My mom took the doll from Jacob and placed it on a shelf. "Here, now, Jacob, let's leave Lucy's doll here in your room, but let's keep her nice and clean."

Jacob agreed then his brow furrowed. "The doll doesn't protect me, MiMi. That shadow over there protects me." He pointed to the corner of his room. My sister was upset; she didn't dismiss it as easily as my mother did.

Mia still had the demonology and spell books and placed them in the trunk of her car. "What are these?" Tyler inquired.

"I had these when I was a teenager and found them at my mom's when we were packing. I don't know why, but I think Lucy or my granny was reading them or saving them. Hopefully, anyway. That would be really creepy if they just found their way back into the house."

She said it as a joke, but that prospect frightened her even more than me bringing the books back into the house.

My sister was having a mild anxiety attack. She wasn't normally afraid of flying, but her nerves had been on edge more than usual. Once they got to the airport, she started doing some work on her laptop. Tyler rubbed her neck as she worked. It was time to start boarding the plane, and Mia called again to check on Jacob. After my mom assured her, Tyler assured her that Jacob would be fine.

Watching my sister work on her laptop and texting on her cell phone was very unusual since none of those things existed before I died. Yet, the thing is, I already understood what they were, what they did, and it wasn't strange to me. The world went on without me, growing and changing.

Chapter Eleven
Lurking in the Shadows

As my sister's plane took off, something strange happened to me. I ceased to be with her. I don't exactly know why, but I found myself trapped, only this time, I wasn't in limbo. I had a cognizant awareness of myself. I was in a memory, watching myself run barefoot, and I felt fear. I was running so far and fast with tears streaming down my face. I was watching my younger self relive the memory of my escape from Charlotte's house. I knew how it would play out. I knew I had gotten home safely, yet I didn't know why I felt so nervous and afraid. I watched myself over and over again.

As I observed myself reaching the front yard, suddenly I would find myself once again running the street with the dark shadows lurking. Leaving Charlotte's house and being so afraid was terrifying. I wanted to help the younger me; I felt so sad for her…me. I had been running in the bleak contours that lined the streets on my way home, afraid Bill would get in his car and find me that night, and that panicked me. It was almost as scary as the darkness and looming shadows while the howls of animals seemed to be just as afraid as I was.

I had nightmares as a child after it happened, but this felt different somehow. I felt as if it was really still happening to me. I was watching myself and feeling the same fears and emotions I had that very night in my gut and deep into my soul.

As I reached the front lawn, I found myself at the beginning of the nightmare. It was like I was stuck in one of the worst memories. I was in a nightmare that haunted me, only it wasn't a nightmare. I couldn't help but wonder if it some kind of punishment. I lived a good life; I was young and innocent and couldn't understand as I didn't feel I was due any sort of punishment.

*****

My sister and Tyler returned from the funeral of his mother. They were both so excited about seeing Jacob and my mom. Jacob was showered with hugs and forehead kisses as soon as they returned home. The only difference was I wasn't there to see them anymore. All of this was happening without me, yet I was aware it was happening. It wasn't like when I was in limbo before. I saw glimpses of my future as I died, but from that point, until my sister began packing my room at our childhood home, I had no memory. What I was experiencing now was new to me.

The silver lining in my being away and stuck in this nightmare was that my sister started feeling better now that I wasn't attached to her. She noticed that she didn't feel or see anything—visions—with anyone she encountered while she was away. I think this made her happy. There was a small part of her, though, that felt unhappy. It was as if she felt a sense of grief—like she knew I was no longer with her. Once again, she felt a void and was uncertain I was OK.

The next morning, she went to work and began a new week, although her weeks were habitually the same in many aspects of her job. The best thing about that day was that Doris wasn't there to tattle and annoy her with unnecessary interruptions. It was refreshing. She didn't realize how much of a negative energy Doris had brought to the workplace until she was gone.

Mia had an uneventful morning, which was much needed for her, and later she met Lily for lunch. They made small talk about the funeral and chatted about the food.

"Well, tell me what you see. Any visions?" Lily asked, biting into a mozzarella stick.

My sister told her she couldn't see anything anymore, no more visions, and it sounded like she was a little disappointed. She smiled and shifted the conversation back to Lily as Lily took the queue. Mia wasn't in the mood to navigate the discussion just yet.

Lily updated Mia on her recent OBGYN visit. "I talked to the new doctor about my miscarriages and she ran tests. She said the good news is I can get pregnant and feels confident we can make a few changes and get myself ready to try again. We are going to get lab results next week and hopefully be able to start trying again soon." Lily was so excited. She mourned her miscarriages, and she didn't want to put herself or her husband through the turmoil of another loss. It was hard for him but devastating for her. Lily wanted a child so badly and hoped to have the experience of carrying the baby herself before trying adoption. My sister was so happy that Lily got positive feedback.

Lily circled the conversation back to my sister again. "So, no more visions. How are you feeling?" Lily asked, testing the waters to see if Mia felt like discussing it.

Mia shrugged and set down her fork. "You know, I feel fine. I feel better; I don't feel sick. I stopped taking my Xanax, and I'm sleeping fine again," Mia said. "But, to be honest, I kind of have been feeling sad. I feel like something is missing from me now." My sister's phone began ringing. She answered and talked for a few minutes. "That was Dulce," Mia told Lily after she ended the call. "She wants to get together and visit before we meet again on Wednesday and catch up."

Lily smiled. "She is really a terrific lady. She and I met a few years ago at a seminar. We work with each other quite a bit. She consults with me for hypnosis sessions with some of her clients, and I refer some of my clients who are experiencing religious or spiritual situations to her since she has so much more knowledge and experience with her education and personal life."

They chatted a little more while eating lunch, then said their goodbyes, and Mia went back to her office. Later, after leaving work, Mia picked Jacob up from preschool then stopped to see our mom.

MiMi had a little tricycle for Jacob, and they let him ride around the block while they walked and talked behind him. "Have you been feeling better?" Mom asked Mia.

She held our mom's hand. "I have been feeling like my old self again," Mia answered. "But I've still been feeling sad."

There was a brief silence, with only Jacob's tricycle wheels screeching on the sidewalk. My mom asked, "You didn't get to read granny's journal, did you?"

"Oh, no. Tyler was very edgy, and we talked a lot about his mom and the funeral and childhood memories while we were gone. I am sorry. I didn't get a chance, but I plan to finish them again soon," Mia assured her.

The next day, Mia got a call from Sophie while on her way to work. "Girl, we have the banquet this weekend, and I don't have a date. It just crept up on me. I was so busy playing grab-ass with Thomas that I didn't even try to get a damn date. The fuck!! He's going to be there with his weird wife, and he's going to see me fucking alone!"

My sister laughed. "I forgot about the banquet this weekend. Do we really need to go? You've been to one, you've been to them all."

Sophie was insistent, "No bitch, you're going or it will be weird if not. I have a cute dress and need Thomas to see me in it. Let him see what he can't have!"

Mia rolled her eyes. "Just forget him. Who cares about him?" Mia continued. "Let him look at his wife and don't give him the satisfaction. He can go pound sand." Mia was so over Thomas and Sophie's drama.

"Well, truth be told, he doesn't know it, but it's the last time he will see me, and I want to look fabulous. Maybe it's wrong, but I do. I want to look great; I'm going to be indifferent with him moving forward."

Mia was confused. "What do you mean?"

"I'm moving on." Sophie held her cell phone up to see who was calling her other line. "Thomas called me twice in an hour. I think he knows something is up. I've withdrawn from talking to him since our meeting. He keeps calling me about "work" stuff, but he can't understand why I'm being aloof when we talk. I only take some calls, and he can't stand me not giving him attention," Sophie shared.

Mia was surprised and proud of Sophie for not pursuing her affection for Thomas. She suspected Sophie was having Daddy issues, perhaps. She lost her father when she was younger in an accident, not having many memories of him. Thomas was her boss; she listened to his advice, he mentored her, he was attractive, and she loved that he was a man of faith. Those qualities appealed to her. Perhaps the qualities she loved, such as being a good family man, were also challenging. Sophie was competitive and felt she could get him to give in to their temptations, but Mia was right. No matter what, she would lose, so she figured she would forfeit for once in her life and let him have the point.

"What do you mean you won't see him after Saturday? You're moving on? Are you quitting?"

Sophie nodded happily. "It's bittersweet. I'll miss you so much, but I'm taking a position on the other side of Dallas, almost two hours away from where I live now. I'm moving and starting over. I need some distance. I think I need to be in a big city and try something new."

Mia seemed a little surprised. "OK, but don't let him be the reason you pick up and move your whole life. Work for another bank, but don't leave home."

Sophie thought about it. "This is really a good opportunity for me, and if I had family here, I wouldn't consider it. I really do want to go, and it's not because of him. He is the reason I passed on this opportunity two months ago, but when they called me again, I jumped on it. You're right, Mia; I can't win with him, and I need to move on. I'm far enough away where I won't cross paths with him but close enough where you and I can still see each other!!"

Mia was excited for Sophie but selfishly sad because she knew once Sophie left, they would probably stay in touch, but as with all things, they would talk less and less—especially since they would now be working for different banks. Mia worried her relationship with Sophie would be like the one she had with her best friend, Deon. They had been so close, but after he married his husband and moved to Colorado, she only visited with him through his posts on social media.

Mia also knew that after Sophie quit and moved on, Thomas would be in a funk. He became a Sophie junkie, texting her all day and frequently calling her on video phone at work to see her. Of course, he never reached out to her when he was home in the evenings and on weekends. During those times, he was busy being "husband of the year." Except, of course, when he scanned her social media, looking at her pictures. Looking at her eyes and her brilliant smile. The separation was going to be a good thing for his marriage, but he wouldn't like it, and he wouldn't welcome the resignation.

*****

On Wednesday morning, Mia had to reschedule her lunch date with Dulce and her appointment a week to the following Tuesday.

Jacob fell off the slide at school and bumped his head, so Mia left work to take him to the doctor. He did get two small stitches on the back of his noggin, but he was OK.

My mom went to see them once they arrived home. "MiMi, I bumped my head, and it bleeded all over my shirt," Jacob told my mother.

She looked at the wound. "You got a battle scar now, don't ya?"

He nodded his head and asked us, "Do you 'member when Aunt Lucy fell off that tree and she bleeded?"

Both my mom and sister were shocked. "Did you tell him about your sister falling out of the tree?"

"No, never," Mia assured my mom. "How did you know Aunt Lucy fell out of a tree?" Jacob shrugged his shoulders.

"Mia, have you read the journals yet? Granny talks about her visit with us when Daddy died, and I want to know what you think about it. I wonder if maybe she was writing it for us to read."

My sister confessed she still hadn't read the journals yet. She was honestly putting it off and avoiding it. Now that she was feeling better, she let our mom know she would begin reading. She was trying to take a little break from the emotions, as she was still feeling overwhelmed.

Our mom informed Mia that she had been reading a lot, but she feared another journal was packed away or thrown out unless Granny just stopped writing. The last month of her living with us when she was visiting was unaccounted for in her journal. She was still in good health, in good spirits, it seemed odd that she just stopped writing when it appeared that she had been working on her journal and referenced the books of magic under Lucy's bed.

Mia thought it was possible that Granny stopped writing but also promised they would finish unpacking on the next nice weekend. They were supposed to go to storage and go back through my boxes just to make sure there wasn't another journal somewhere.

Mia made that suggestion knowing it would buy her time to mentally prepare herself to go back through my belongings, most of which sat in storage until they decided what to keep, donate or discard, but truthfully, I don't think either one was ready to let go of much of anything belonging to me. I was so loved—so fortunate for these two ladies—that it broke my heart they still mourned over my passing to this day.

Had they known I was now trapped in a nightmare of one of the most traumatizing events of my childhood, they would be beside themselves with grief for me. No longer was I with them. I was held captive in a dream state, dealing with fear and trauma. I had no idea how it came to be. It just happened without warning. When I was in that state of mind, I was in a living nightmare.

As I was watching myself and experiencing the torment of reliving the very real nightmare I experienced when I was an innocent girl, I realized my younger, living self was looking quickly up and off to the right, and that's when the tears would really start flowing. The dogs went berserk around this time too. It was as if *she* saw something that was even more frightening than Bill that night.

I don't recall seeing anything the night I made my escape from Bill, but I do remember looking over to see what the dogs were howling about. Perhaps I unknowingly saw something, and it's been locked away in the back of my mind. Perhaps I didn't see anything that dreadful night, and whatever was now watching me running and afraid is new in the memory I appeared stuck inside of. I do remember the howls of the dogs that night, but now they appeared so incited with anger I was so afraid they were going to come over the fence and attack me. They appeared more agitated than the night I ran from Bill. I noticed as I began moving about that I was a shadow, and as I moved about, I got a better view of myself. I got closer and closer to me. It was like navigating your own dream. In my case, I was navigating my nightmare.

*****

When Saturday arrived, Mia prepared herself for the banquet. Tyler was already dressed and looking handsome as always. Mia dressed and not only could Tyler not keep his eyes off her, but he also had a hard time keeping his hands off her too. My mom asked Jacob if he wanted a brother or sister because his daddy looked like he was trying for one. Mia thought it was funny, but even funnier was that Jacob made it clear that he didn't want a brother or sister. Jacob enjoyed having the attention for himself. I do wish he had cousins to play with, but my sister made sure he did go to a good preschool so he was able to interact with other children his age.

Upon arriving to the banquet, Tyler bumped Mia as Sophie entered in with a young man. "Oh goodness!" Mia said and bumped Tyler back. "Keep your eyes on your own paper." He laughed, and they walked over to greet Sophie.

"DAAAAAAAYUM girl!" Mia teased. She pulled her to the side. "You bitch, look at you. You're wrong for this!" Mia laughed. "You look stunning, so beautiful." Sophie did look beautiful, and her dress hugged her body as if it were painted on her.

Thomas was staring as the two girls were talking. "I'm pretty sure Thomas sprayed his pants when you walked in, Sophie. His wife seems to be taking notice of him noticing you too," Mia jested.

Sophie smirked. "I can't wait to quit Monday."

Mia just replied with, "So, who is this guy with you? He's pretty good-looking."

Sophie shook her head. "Girl, he's just a friend. He is good-looking but will talk to you for hours about computers and Star Wars. He is one of those. There is no interest there at all. We are only friends."

Mr. Shaw, the CEO of the bank, took to the floor and danced with his charming wife. He then took notice of Sophie and went to chat with her. She was very charismatic and everyone naturally gravitated to her. Sophie and her date danced and had a nice time. Mia and Tyler danced and laughed at Thomas. It was obvious Thomas was watching Sophie. Even Tyler noticed, so I am certain everyone else did too.

There was a girl who worked for the company that was attending the banquet and it was someone Mia and Sophie absolutely couldn't stand. Initially, they were nice to her, but straight away she was rude to them. Her name was Lin, and she thought she was much prettier than she actually was. She was tall, but she had a strong, masculine jawline. Lin would tan so much she had the coloring of an Oompa Loompa. Her hair was bleached so blonde that Sophie would call her 'Dog the Bounty Hunter.' *Dog* for short. Her bleached-out hair was so dry you definitely would need to be careful if you lit a match around her hair. Her smile looked like she was smelling a fart with her mouth open if you can imagine.

Lin hated any woman she was intimidated by. She was manly tall and had rock hard fake tits and bleached hair, so she looked easy. She had big implants and a flat pancake ass. She dressed like a cheap whore, so she got attention and she often would mistake that attention for being pretty.

After a bit too much to drink, Sophie pointed her out to Mia. Lin was constantly looking over and staring at them. "What's her problem? Why is she so obsessed with us?" Sophie asked, laughing.

Lin walked over to speak to Thomas and put her hand on his shoulder. You could tell Thomas had no interest in her—he didn't even glance at her while she was talking to him. Thomas kept talking to the guys around him, and Lin couldn't stand it.

Being the attention-starved slut that she was, she kept getting closer to Thomas, looking for his attention. I suppose she was seeking attention from the boss. Her date was nearby but didn't give her much attention; he was too busy looking at Sophie. Just like Thomas would. All eyes seemed to be on her that night. Mia was every bit as pretty, but she was very married and carried herself more reservedly than Sophie.

Lin was a bit of an alcoholic; an angry one at that. She started bickering with her date and being loud and obnoxious after a few drinks. Sophie pointed it out to my sister. "Lin is stepping up her plea for attention; she is ready to make a scene now."

Mia walked closer to Sophie, leaning into her ear. "I hope that slut trips and falls." My sister spun her finger around, making her think of me. It made her think of the waiter when I spun my finger, and he fell.

The girls laughed and began to walk away, and then it happened. Lin was walking past the girls, and she tripped and fell, hollering, pissed about it. Once my sister and Sophie saw she wasn't hurt, they erupted into laughter. "You're a witch, Mia!"

They laughed and finished the evening dancing and having a nice time. The last banquet they would attend together. Sophie would be quitting on Monday; walking away from a job she enjoyed to self-protect. She was tired of having a broken heart.

*****

The rest of the weekend was uneventful. For them anyway. I am living a nightmare now—day in and day out. As I navigate through a stale memory of mine, I am able to navigate among the shadows of the night. I begin to step further and further away from myself and darker into the shadows. I was in my nightmare, not with my sister, yet I was perfectly aware of everything happening in her life somehow still.

In my living nightmare, I worked up the courage to investigate the howling of the hounds and the mysteries of the trees that shaded the streets. I didn't know what I would find, but I wasn't scared anymore. I was constantly there, so I had to figure out why. It wasn't curiosity; it was really a sense of hope. I was ready to find out what caught my attention, scaring the younger me, making me cry and run even faster with my bare feet along the roads' sharp gravel. I hoped to figure out why I was there once again, in my nightmare.

Not many things are worse than being dead and eternally trapped, reliving one of your worst days, and I hoped this wasn't going to be the case for me. Losing my dad was probably my hardest day, but luckily, I wasn't alone in coping with the loss. Arguably I could feel the day I died was one of my worst days, but truth be told, I had a good day that day. Up until I went into the water, it was an uneventful day.

Almost being raped by a childhood friend's stepfather, Bill was probably the scariest day of my life, and now I keep reliving running away from him for whatever reason.

When I died, I don't remember much after going into the water. As my brain was dying, I remember drifting in the ocean and experiencing my loved ones before finding myself back at my mom's when she found out I had died. That was also very hard, but I was already dead by that time. I suspect this was where I was stuck because it was one of my dark days, and I experienced it all alone, and here I am once again. I'm alone with myself, and I am feeling helpless.

My sister woke up Saturday night to the storm they expected to roll in. The thunder barged in aggressively. Mia couldn't sleep a wink. She was lying in bed listening to Tyler snore through the crashing sounds of the thunder. She quietly exited the room to tiptoe to look over Jacob, who was peacefully sleeping. As the lightning peered through the blinds in his room, it lit the room brightly and she noticed my doll on his shelf. My sister thought about getting me when storms would roll through when we were younger. She hoped I wasn't alone and afraid of the storms still. She still thought of me as just a little lost girl, though she knew I was dead. It was easier to think of me as lost.

Mia went to the guest room where my mom stayed when she visited. She sat on the bed and took notice of the journals on the nightstand next to the bed, so she picked it up and flipped through it. My granny began her journaling as she was preparing for her visit to our home after our dad passed away. Straight away, Granny talked about Topaz practicing magic with her.

My mom and sister probably didn't know who Topaz was, but I knew. Granny used to credit Topaz with helping her learn the secrets of magic. She said Topaz could even bend the rules of magic. She joked and referenced Peter in the Bible handing the keys to Heaven over to her if she had asked him to. She was very persuasive and powerful with her knowledge of magic.

My sister began reading through the first journal, and before she knew it, it was time to settle down to prepare for another workday, despite her lack of sleep.

Mia glammed up for work, got Jacob ready for pre-school and saw her husband off for the day. She slipped the journal into her bag for work. After dropping Jacob off she called our mother.

"Hey, Mom, I started reading the journals." My mom listened. "Who is Ruby?"

My mom wasn't sure, but she thought it was the Hispanic lady that lived across the street many years ago, although she couldn't be positive as to who granny was referring to in the journal. Our mom asked what my sister thought of the journal. "Do you think the journal was like a diary, or do you think Granny was kinda just jotting down thoughts and passing down stories?"

"I don't know. I have only read a portion of it and wondered who Ruby was. I kind of agree with you; maybe it was that lady that lived across the street from us." My sister pulled into the drug store parking lot so she could talk to our mom without navigating heavy traffic.

"Have you read the part about the doll yet?" Mom asked, but Mia hadn't gotten that far along.

Suddenly, Mia was startled as a man appeared at her passenger side window and knocked on it loudly.

"What was that?" My mom seemed afraid; the knock was loud enough to frighten her.

The man stood on the curb, looking at my sister through the windshield straight into the car. Mia had an unsettling feeling. The sun blinded her, so she couldn't get a good look at his face. She began backing out but stopped when she heard him question her. "Who is Ruby?" She pulled back into the parking spot and locked eyes with the strange man. She instantly recognized him from the gas station the preceding week. She really wasn't sure what to make of it. He couldn't have heard her ask about Ruby; she was driving when she asked my mom. She just sat there in the car. She was partially backed out of the parking space, just staring at the man.

Finally, another car pulled up and honked to get her attention. She snapped out of her daze and pulled out, leaving the parking lot.

"What in the world is going on?" my mom asked in a worried voice.

Mia didn't want my mom to worry, so she tried to ease her mind. "Everything is fine. I just hadn't read the journal all the way through, so I wanted to see if you knew who Granny was referring to." Mia was careful not to say the name "Ruby" again.

*****

While Mia was dealing with that, I still lived in my purgatory. As I approached the tree line, I felt an unsettling feeling. I hid deeper into the shadows so I would go undetected by whatever was up there. It was a darker shadow; blacker than any shadow I'd seen before and massive in size. It was watching me—the living me, not the dead me, the frightened little girl running from the worst kind of predator: the human predator that would hurt a child for their own selfish urges.

I approached this *being* closer but still couldn't see beyond a shadow. Perhaps whatever it was, was nothing more than just a dark mass. It caught the attention of my living self and stirred the dogs, causing them to bark and howl, almost in a way they would get upset or protective when a predator would be, impeding on their territory. I was in a perpetual state of fear and uncertainty both as a living girl and a living dead girl.

I had to figure out a way to confront the being or a way out of this horrible, horrible memory. I felt sorry for my younger self; even worse, I couldn't help her. I couldn't help myself, a frightened little girl. I couldn't ease my own fears. I was so scared and panicking, lurking in the shadows and reliving my own personal hell.

Chapter Twelve
A New Beginning

As Mia began her day at work, she got a call from Sophie. "Happy Monday, bitch. I sent my notice over to Mr. Shaw and Thomas." Sophie read the notice to Mia.

"This makes me sad, Sophie. I just hate that you're leaving, though I think time and distance will put Thomas out of your head. Maybe you will find a single man that really enjoys peach pie!" They giggled like teen girls. Sophie was embarrassed by her behavior.

Mia was saddened by the realization that Sophie was really leaving. She wasn't so sure Thomas was worth picking up and moving away. Mia wanted Sophie to work at another bank but not necessarily out of town. Mia liked having her friend close enough to meet for lunch and chat with her. She would miss Sophie. Sophie felt like a little sister in many ways. Sophie felt a lot like a little sister Mia had once upon a time.

Mia was supposed to be working, but she read through the journals of my granny. She read page after page when her friend, Trina, entered her office. Trina stood at the entry of the door with a big smile on her face. She leaned onto the door frame.

"That bitch got sentenced to thirteen months yesterday. I wanted her to get longer, but I'm happy she will be locked up and have a record now. Thirteen months isn't enough, but I am relieved she will serve time." Mia was happy that an abuser was put away. They hugged in celebration. Trina was curious about how Mia knew, and Mia tried to explain it again. Now that time had passed, Trina began being curious about how Mia could know things about Mabel.

"It sounds crazy, but it was just a fluke, I guess. I feel better now, no more visions or feelings anymore. I experienced it for a short while, but it disappeared as quickly as it happened," Mia tried to explain to Trina but worried about the skepticism.

"Mia, are you psychic or...?" Trina was curious.

Mia nodded slowly, thinking about how she should answer. "I do believe in that stuff. I don't know how someone can believe in miracles and God but then don't believe in our own abilities. My granny and little sister had strange connections and abilities, but I never had those gifts."

Trina confessed she, too, believed in things bigger than what we can know and explain. They left the subject at that and got on with the day.

A few hours later, Mia wrapped up her workday. She was going to finish the journal since she encountered too many interruptions at work. She didn't have much down time while working like she sometimes would get to enjoy. My mom called Mia, just chatting with her, and asked if she was still feeling better, which, thankfully, Mia was finally back to feeling like her old self again. It was a relief to Mia to be back to her familiar self.

Mia and my mom spoke on the phone a bit before our mother inquired about the journals Mia was supposed to read. Our mom was beginning to get flustered that Mia was putting off reading them as she was quite anxious to discuss the journals and wanted Mia to prioritize them now that she was feeling better.

The journals referenced my granny needing to help the family when my dad passed away. She dreamed of my dad experiencing fear and seeing entities passing through the house that frightened him, which disturbed my mother and made her sad. Granny went on about Ruby sending her observers, her onlookers, to the house but never mentioning who or what they were watching. She referenced protecting the family and working magic with me before it was too late for her. I know this was really unsettling for my mom, since I died in a cold pond shortly after my granny passed away. Mia hadn't gotten that far along; otherwise, I knew it would upset her too. My mom was bothered by this so much and wanted to talk to Mia about her thoughts on what granny had written. Our mom felt as if granny didn't warn her about watching me closer and protecting me more. She didn't take into account how depressed and fragile she was after losing her husband and the fact that she wouldn't have listened to Granny about something like that anyway. She definitely had her walls up, and Granny did what she could to protect me. She saved me from Bill, sent Ruby away, and tried to keep me from the deathly waters.

The day at the pond when the divers went in like it was yesterday. Thinking that the journals were written and left to them as a warning that went ignored and unread was upsetting. Mia often thought about me being in the cold pond, especially at night. She hated to think of me in a watery grave, scared and by myself. Mia often would think about her baby sister going into the bone-chilling water. It was very disturbing for her, and it crept into her mind frequently. When Mia would think of the cold water filling my lungs, along with the pain and fear I was experiencing, it was maddening for her, and she would try her best to cope but had to seek help to keep her sanity.

Mia and my mom spoke until Mia reached the preschool to get Jacob then headed to the restaurant where they were meeting Tyler. My mom didn't want to go since she just got settled in; she was overly exhausted and wanted to get some rest. She wanted to spend time relaxing, but she also wanted Mia and Tyler to have a good evening together since they have had an overly stressful time as of late.

Mia and Tyler relaxed and took a brain break from both of their recent stresses. Tyler was going to be working from home the rest of the week and spending time with Jacob. They enjoyed spending time together; Tyler was a good husband and father. Mia had a lovely family, and I loved that for her.

The next morning, Mia got to work early. She wanted to have peace and quiet as she worked on the outline of everything she encountered over the last two weeks for Dr. Flowers and Lily so she could discuss it with them. At this point, she wanted people that were not emotionally connected to the situation to give unbiased feedback of what she was encountering. Mia worked on her list up until employees began to arrive.

Her teller, Kimmy, was walking through the lobby to see my sister as she wrapped up her timeline and notes. She lightly tapped on the door. "Did Doris tell you her brother was getting out of prison in a couple of days?"

Mia was completely unaware that Doris' brother was even in jail, although she wasn't surprised. The only thing Mia recalled about her siblings was Doris complaining about her sister. She was constantly calling her younger sister a pill popper. Mia didn't ever even recall Doris referring to her sister by name. Doris didn't talk about her family too often, but Mia was completely surprised she even had a brother. "I haven't spoken to Doris since she left, to be honest. I never followed her on social media, so I don't stay in contact with her at all anymore," Mia explained.

In actuality, Doris was bitter after her termination and blocked Mia from social media. Mia rarely got on social media, so she didn't even realize and certainly didn't care. Sometimes people will block you from their lives, and that's OK because sometimes you just need to let the trash take itself out. Doris removed Mia from social media thinking she was ghosting her or somehow getting back at Mia. It's just funny because Mia never had any intent on ever speaking to her again anyway. In fact, Mia manifested Doris away from her after finding out the kind of person she really was. Doris is a grackle; she is not Mia's kind of person. Mia didn't like people that could steal from an elderly person.

All the while, Doris was angry at Mia for firing her, but it was in reality, her own thieving actions that caused her to get fired. Doris knew it was her own fault, but in her twisted mind she expected Mia to protect her. She felt Mia should throw herself on the sword to safeguard Doris' job. Lofty expectations for someone that was a subpar employee.

Kimmy lingered around Mia's office. She wanted to share further information she knew about Doris' brother. Kimmy continued. "I hate that he is getting out of jail. I know that sounds bad, but my uncle was a court reporter in Dallas, and he said that was one of the most brutal crimes he ever sat through. I never even knew she was his sister until she was posting about it on her page. It's a small world.

"Doris is celebrating his release saying justice is served because he was young and on drugs. She said he should not have had to spend so much of his life in jail, even though it was a brutal crime and he was too young to realize the consequences of his actions." Kimmy shrugged. "He killed two people and laughed about it with friends, who later turned him in. He even knew the lady that he killed. She was his mom's good friend, so he knew she would be at work and had access to the cash because she was the manager at the store."

Mia tried to comfort Kimmy. "Well. From Doris' point of view, she is happy that her brother is being set free. I don't know the details of the crime, but I am sure she has missed her brother and isn't thinking about how the families of the victims are feeling. Doris has tunnel vision; she is only thinking about being glad her brother is going to be set free. Just don't read the posts about it so you don't get yourself upset."

Kimmy agreed with my sister. "My uncle is also posting about it too. He is angry about him getting out early. He is angry this guy killed his mom's friend and chased down and butchered a man he never met before at the store. He even urinated on the guy after he killed him. Just a sick, sick murderer." Kimmy's recounting of the events piqued Mia's interest as it seemed too familiar.

Kimmy gave Mia Doris' brother's name, and after her morning conference call, Mia began to research him a bit further. Sure enough, yes, it was Doris' brother that killed Nancy and butchered Bill to death. Mia had no idea what Bill did to me the night I ran home in the late evening hours. As far as Mia knew, Bill was a nice guy—just a coworker that took her shift so she could go to the doctor with my granny that fateful Wednesday that Nancy and Bill were slain by a low-life thug.

Mia became busy with work and didn't think any more about Doris' brother. Later, however, Kimmy once again appeared at the door to see my sister. Mia didn't really have time for chit-chat, but Kimmy invited herself in to have a seat. "We've been slow today, so I've been reading about Doris' brother again. I hope that's OK."

My sister wasn't bothered. "As long as your tasks are handled and you're taking care of customers, I don't care what you do in your downtime," Mia assured her. It was much different than having Doris micromanage their time while she was constantly sitting on her own cell phone and not working.

"Her brother said it was his mom and oldest sister's idea to rob and kill Nancy. According to the reporting, he claimed they told him to rob Nancy at work. They told him where to get the money and told him to shoot her because she would easily recognize him and he would go to jail."

Mia looked up from her computer. "Doris and her mother told him to rob and kill?" Mia hoped that wasn't the truth, but at the same time, she wouldn't put it past her and wondered if that was the truth or just what her brother said to save himself. Doris' brother was barely eighteen; he was a thug, and mentally, he was a little slow. Of course there was a possibility someone put him up to the crime. Mia comforted Kimmy, but at the same time, she felt as appalled and as uneasy about Doris and her brother as Kimmy appeared to.

Life has a funny way of working out, I guess. Bill was a child abuser; Charlotte's mom was a child abuser by allowing unfathomable things to happen to her children. In the end, he got slaughtered and she got jailed. The girls lived a happier life as a result of those earthly devils being removed from their lives. The girls all have their own families now.

Thankfully, they didn't carry and start generational curses of inappropriate relations. From that aspect, I couldn't be sad for Bill. I can't feel sorry for a monster that roams the earth in human flesh. He lacked empathy and self-control. Bill was the worst kind of predator. Humans can be the scariest thing on this planet. His wife, complicit in the molestation, wasn't any better than Bill.

Undoubtedly, Bill was a monster hiding behind a smile that manipulated people into thinking he was a nice person. Sadly, when Bill was fifteen, he molested his little sister too. She ended up hanging herself just to get away from him and his father. I can't be sad for someone like that. Eventually, everyone will get what they deserve. If justice isn't served in this life, it will be served in the next. One way or another, we all get what we deserve.

Nancy was slain over three hundred and twenty-one dollars. She had an affair with a married man, but did that warrant death? No, and it was unfair. She befriended the wrong person with a daughter and son that were drugging, thieving murderers, apparently. Makes you wonder about the company you keep. Doris was annoying and a tattler, but who would guess she was also a thief and would encourage her brother to rob and even kill a family friend? She was a grackle. It's sad to think you can work with someone and never really be able to fathom what they're capable of.

Mia cautioned Kimmy to keep the information she learned to herself. Jenny was easily manipulated by Doris and, for some reason, allowed herself to be controlled by her. Jenny was impressionable, and although Doris talked a lot of shit about her, Jenny had no idea Doris was her worst enemy. A friend that would mislead you and manipulate you isn't really a friend.

Out of the blue, Thomas called for Mia at her desk. "Why did Sophie quit?"

My sister knew he was fishing to see what she knew, hoping Sophie never told Mia anything about the flirtation between the two of them. Of course, Mia didn't want to get in the middle of it at all. She had no interest in being shunned by Thomas for knowing their dirty little secret. After all, Thomas had a goody-two-shoes image to uphold.

Mia was also a little surprised he called her to ask and not just call Sophie. Sophie left him, and he took it personally, so he would never reach out to her now. Mia sent Sophie a text. Thomas is on the phone asking me why you are quitting??!!

Sophie responded back. "He hasn't reached out to me at all, not even to acknowledge my resignation. Tell him to eat a dick!" No doubt, her anger stemmed from a bruised ego along with a hurt heart.

Mia wasn't sure what to say other than to let Thomas know Sophie had an opportunity to work in a bank where she could also sell investments, something she wouldn't be able to do at this bank.

"Have you not asked her about it? She's really excited. You should call her," Mia suggested, knowing he would never. He, too, had a bruised ego now that he knew she was leaving him and moving on without him. Mia knew that he was not happy. He would miss her; she was the part of his day he enjoyed the most, though Thomas would never admit it—not even to himself. He was glad to have his wife as a fallback. She was his comfortable place, but he knew the excitement he felt for Sophie would be something he would miss. Thomas had fallen in love with Sophie and knew, without a doubt, she loved him too. He couldn't offer her what they both wanted, so she was leaving him. He resented her for moving on without him. She was brave like that. Sophie was a wild card and picking up and starting all over again didn't scare her.

Sophie leaving did scare Thomas. He knew she would eventually find and fall in love with someone else, which was upsetting. He was comforted by knowing he had the solace of his wife. Sadly, he would never feel the love and curiosity that he did for Sophie. He was eaten up with regret about not being able to give her what they both wanted. Mia changed the topic and began making small talk, chatting about random things. Before getting off the phone, Thomas told Mia the story of how the sun could never be with the moon, but the sun loved the moon so much that he died slowly each night just to let her shine and breathe, Mia knew Sophie wasn't the only one hurting over their separation. Maybe that was his way of telling Mia he loved Sophie. Maybe he wanted her to know; maybe he wanted her to tell Sophie she really meant more to him than she could ever know. She was the moon, and he would admire it each night, thinking of her.

Mia's relationship with Thomas changed after her finding out about him and Sophie, but she still cared about him and didn't want him to be hurt either. Mia knew her idea of Thomas being a perfect husband was an illusion, and it did upset her because she wanted her own husband to be the perfect husband too, if that even exists. Knowing Thomas could have feelings for someone else made her feel Tyler could too, and she didn't like that thought. Thomas probably was a pretty good husband, but Thomas was human.

Thomas had been tempted; I guess it could happen to any of us. Mia just thought Thomas was above desires and urges, but he was just like any other man, any other person. We are all capable of missteps and we all deserve forgiveness, but it doesn't mean we are entitled to absolution from the people we hurt and betray.

Thomas was her boss, and Mia had respected him up until then, at least. She loved Sophie, but she sympathized with the wife, feeling like they made a fool of her. There she was, on social media posting photos of her and the husband she put on a pedestal. He was a good husband in the respect he was a good dad, provider, and even faithful—faithful up until he met someone that woke up something inside of him that he had never felt before.

At the end of the day, Mia wrapped up her work and got ready to see Lily and Dulce. She packed her notes into her bag and headed out the door. Jenny was at her desk and walked Mia out to the car. "Hey, probably nothing, but when we were closing last night, there was a man in the drive-thru asking for your name. 'The girl with the eyes,' he said." Jenny laughed. "I mean, don't we all have eyes?"

Mia was concerned and felt certain she already knew who it was. She hoped she was wrong, but she knew. "Did you tell him my name?"

Jenny shrugged. "I gave him your business card."

Mia didn't scold Jenny; she probably did the right thing as far as being an employee was concerned. For all she knew, he was a customer or potential customer.

"Do you recall what he was driving?"

"Yes, he was just in, like, an older truck. If he comes back, I will get the license plate. I just thought it was weird he called you 'the girl with the eyes.' Like, maybe he meant because you have pretty eyes, but we had a good laugh about it."

Mia went to her appointment to see the girls. She was looking forward to discussing things with the girls but also dreaded talking about it because it was exhausting. She wished she had a chance to talk to Dulce before the meeting to fill in some of the holes, but Lily did bring her up to speed while Mia was at the funeral of Tyler's mom. Mia laid it all out for them, explaining what she experienced after leaving my mom's, rehashing her visions and talking about how she felt sick. She told them about the demon she saw in the limo, then again after leaving Lily's office. She knew the demon was lurking in the SUV. Mia also mentioned the man that she has had encounters with who seems to be following her and commenting on her eyes.

The meeting ran well beyond an hour, and Lily was taking notes and asking questions, but Dulce remained quiet. She was processing everything she was hearing; it was undoubtedly a lot to take in. "I need to get going to see Ty and Jacob," Mia said. She was exhausted. The discussion was emotionally draining for her.

"Dulce, sorry, Dr. Flowers, did you have any questions for Mia?

You've not said much," Dr. Roth said.

"Ever since our meeting last week, I keep dreaming of crows. They are circling a…" she hesitated. "You said Lucy drowned in a pond, and I keep dreaming of crows circling the pond. It wakes me up. I don't feel upset. I just feel like…" her voice trailed off. "I feel like it's a message."

She went on to talk about crows and their symbolism around warnings and death. "We are all friends here. Can I just ask...Why didn't you watch Lucy? I told you not to trust her!"

Mia was taken aback. "Are you blaming me for what happened to Lucy?" Mia paused. "My granny mentioned Ruby in her journals." Mia started pulling out the journals. "I knew the name was familiar but couldn't place it. I had almost forgotten about her."

"Can I make us each a copy of these journals?" Lily asked.

"Of course. I can't even get through them. I just feel so sad reading the accounting of the summer before Lucy died. I guess I just need to make myself sit down and just do it," Mia said in an exasperated tone.

"I'm not blaming you. I'm sorry. I didn't mean that at all. I'm just worried Ruby had something to do with Lucy. It doesn't make sense she would go into the pond. Were her friends going in? She just jumped in?" Dulce asked before continuing. "Ruby was always watching Lucy. Always. She was obsessed with your sister." Dulce clasped her hands together. "I'm a psychologist and an educated woman. I don't want you to judge me." She looked at Dr. Roth. "The lady I lived with, Ruby, was a witch. She practiced Santeria. She sacrificed small animals in her backyard when I was inside the house. She was very much active within a cult. I was scared to sleep there," Dulce confided. "I could feel her watching me. I would dream of Lucy, and I know it was because Ruby was casting spells against her. In fact, I believe Ruby was glad when I went away so I couldn't warn anyone against her cunning thoughts. She said someone was blocking her from seeing Lucy, and I think she thought I was practicing protection spells for Lucy, but I wasn't. I never practiced any kind of magic."

The others nodded and waited until she continued.

"I am Catholic, but I was raised around the dark church. In fact, that's why I would stay with Maria next door to you. She got me into church and sent me away to live with some of her church family when I went to school. She knew Ruby was deep into Santeria. She was a sinister woman. Maria would call her, 'Diabla and Puta.'" Dulce laughed nervously. "She controlled and sabotaged people in her own family."

Lily sat down beside Mia and her phone started ringing. It was Tyler. Mia told him she would be home before seven, and he told her not to rush. He and Jacob were just checking in. They were going to grab McDonald's on their way home. "I will just grab myself something on the way, but I will still message you when I leave here." Mia always let Tyler know when to expect her now. Being followed really shook her up.

"Sorry, Dulce, please continue. I didn't want Tyler to worry, and I wanted to make sure Jacob was OK!" Mia put her phone away.

"I completely understand!" Dulce continued. "Maria used to tell me Ruby had Frank come to Texas from Mexico, but she didn't know why. I think, in hindsight, it was to abduct Lucy. Ruby always commented how there was something special about her."

"Remember me telling you Ruby would always talk about how much money Lucy would sell for in Mexico?" Dulce asked Mia.

Mia's eyes shifted. "I do now that you mention it. That guy, Frank, didn't stay long, though. He left soon after arriving, right?"

"He was scared off. He said there was a demon in the tree watching him—the demon your mom saw that killed your tree. At least that's what Maria told me when I saw her at church."

"Maria said Frank thought possibly his ex sent something after him, but Maria also mentioned Frank somehow pissed Ruby off the very night he saw a demon. He claimed it was an ex-girlfriend sending something after him, but Maria thought he said that to her not to further anger Ruby. It was as if Frank always thought Ruby was listening to him. Maria said he was so frightened. He asked Maria to pray over him, so she did. She gave him her rosary and he left to return to Mexico."

"I don't like talking about the day Lucy died," Mia began. "I was exhausted. I was supposed to go with her to the park with her little friend, Chris, and his little sister. I didn't go, and I should have. Chris always babysat his little sister, Lisa, and Lucy asked me to go with them. I told her I would, but the day of, I was so tired I just wanted to sleep before I ran errands for the day. Lucy and Chris had been best friends since they were six years old and always liked walking to the park to hang out.

"Lucy went to say hi to some of her little friends on the swings, and while she was gone, Cathy, Chris' mom, met him to get his little sister. They met at the park that day because Cathy was supposed to have a photographer take pictures of the little girl. The park had a lot of beautiful scenery. Before the day Lucy died, I had never been to that part of the park. I never knew there was a pond that fed into the local river. At least, it did back then, anyway.

"Lucy was completely unaware that Cathy was picking Lisa up. As she approached Chris, he was crouched down, reaching his hand into the pond with panic on his face. He told her that 'she fell in the water.' He explained to us later that his sister Lisa's baby doll fell into the water when he was slinging his backpack up from the ground. When he told Lucy she fell into the water, he was referring to the doll and before he could finish explaining his sister's doll fell in, Lucy jumped into the water. Chris said he initially laughed because he knew Lucy jumped to the conclusion his sister fell in, but it was only her baby doll."

The ladies all sat quietly, Dulce choking back tears because she had never heard the story of my passing away before then. Mia comforted her. "He said Lucy never came back up, and he was too scared to go in. He couldn't swim, so he started calling for help after a few minutes. They never found her. They only recovered the doll. It was floating under a bridge about a mile and a half away from where Lucy went into the water looking for the little girl."

The room fell quiet.

Mia put her handbag onto her shoulder. "I think I just want to go home now," she said.

"Let's all walk down to your car together," Lily said. "Can we all agree to read the journals before we meet again next week?" Dulce promised, and they all agreed to meet next Wednesday. They would end up meeting before then, unofficially anyway.

As the ladies went home and went about their evening, I was still in my never-ending nightmare. I was trying to grasp why I couldn't get close enough to the being watching me from up high in the tree. I was trying to go undetected, though I didn't feel afraid anymore. I was tired, too tired to be afraid. When I was about to step into the light, I hesitated. I didn't want to scare or disrupt myself; I was so young and so afraid that night.

Although I was still trapped in my dream state, it was very real. I was now in the moment that I feared so much. The fear, the crying, I was so scared that night. The *being,* the towering shadow in the tree, just watched me running down the street, over and over again and again. It lurked and watched ever so quietly.

I began creeping towards the street to get a better view when the shadow in the tree seemed to take notice suddenly. I felt afraid again. The fear was paralyzing. The only thing I could think of being worse than being dead was being in some state of purgatory, being trapped in this living nightmare. Even scarier than that, I guess, would be getting dragged into Hell, which is what washed over me in that instant.

I stood still. I watched my younger self pass by, once again running scared. I saw myself noticing the shadow with a frightened look on my face. The shadow in the tree was just watching me—the girl not paying attention to the smidgen of my shadow now nearing the edge of the street.

The shadow on the edge of the street jarred me into a memory of my granny. Suddenly, I had an epiphany. I now had a better understanding of why I was in my living nightmare. My granny talked to me about casting shadows when I told her about my out-of-body experiences, and then I knew. At least, I hoped so.

Chapter Thirteen
Bending Magic

There was a book that contained a lot of information regarding demonology I had thumbed through when I was younger. When I showed Granny a photo in the book, she explained that Topaz shared how when those practicing hard magic cast spells against your soul, they make a pact with Satan.

As I flipped through the dark book, I noticed a shadow that appeared to be hiding. I saw this shadow drawn many times throughout this book, and I was puzzled. It reminded me of my out-of-body experiences because my shadows were away from me—watching me. A powerful witch, an enchantress, wrote the book and crafted the illustrations, taking a lot of time with the information and details she passed along with great care.

When I pointed to the various drawings with hidden shadows, Granny explained the meaning. "When someone wants to sacrifice your soul, you can't just hide your body; you have to hide your soul."

Granny told me I had more magic in me than most people my age, which really surprised me. My granny told me I could do this: hide my soul when I was being hunted. She said not everyone had the gifts to bend magic in such a way, but I could. She told me my gifts made me special and enticing, so guarding my soul was the most important thing I could do. She told me my soul would retreat and hide when something was after it, even without me being aware. She said this could happen in my sleep, for example.

I don't know if that was true or if she was just trying to make me feel special. She always wanted to build me up and make me feel good about myself. She was like that with my mom and sister too. Honestly, she was like that in general. She wanted people to feel good about themselves.

Granny told me something that was probably the best piece of advice. "Sometimes you have to reach in and save yourself." She told me she could tell me about my gifts, but I would have to create my own magic to save myself when the time came. "The only hero we can rely on is ourselves. Be your own hero," she would say, but she would also remind me to accept help when help was needed.

I knew it was time to rescue myself; I just needed to figure out what to do. Did I want to step out of the shadows and let the being that stalked me see me so I could try to outrun it, or did I want to confront the being in the tree and be prepared to battle it? Something in me urged me to be patient. I knew neither was the right way, not right now, anyway. I just had to figure out an exit plan without drawing attention to myself hiding within the shadows.

* * * * *

The following day, Mia read the rest of the first journal and learned that Granny felt called to teach me the art of bending magic. She wrote about Topaz predicting my abilities and warned it would make me a prime target to sacrifice to Satan if I ever crossed paths with someone exceptionally strong within the occult. There are so few witches that possess their own natural gifts and magic because, over generations of not embracing gifts, people lost their own supernatural gifts; finding someone with such abilities was highly coveted. "You say witch like it's a bad thing. I say witch like they are enchanted and skilled." Granny wrote.

This created more questions for Mia than it did answers or directions. Granny mentioned that no one would have understood or believed her when she lived if she had discussed such things. Being closed-minded and afraid of the unknown could be why I fell prey after my granny crossed over after her death.

Mia went about her workday, rehashing the details of the journal over and over in her head—magic incantations, shadow work. It bothered Mia that granny was telling me this stuff as a little girl, but she understood it was how she tried to protect me.

Mia realized she had the mysterious books in her trunk still. She intended on shredding them a while ago, but after going out of town, they were out of sight, out of mind. She wondered if she should keep the books and read those too. She remembered how they appeared mysteriously and thought, perhaps, they had been intended to be read to protect our family. She remembered the book had information about demonic possession and exorcisms. She recalled being unable to sleep when she was younger because the subject matter frightened her. Even thinking of it reminded her of seeing the demon in the parking lot when she was a teenager.

Mia decided to go out to the car and get the books to bring inside. As she exited the bank lobby, she noticed the man she had encountered twice before and had come looking for her at the bank when she was gone for the day. Mia made the decision not to be afraid of him but to go ahead and confront him finally. It was time to address him head-on.

Before she had an opportunity to speak, he leaned up against her car. "Good afternoon, Mia." His accent was thick, and it was apparent to her that English was his second language, although his English was very good.

Mia approached him, but she kept a good distance away. On her car key ring, she had a key to the bank branch, and she placed the key between her fingers, preparing to protect herself if needed. He laughed. "You won't need that. I'm not here to hurt you." She wasn't going to be fooled by his words, so she remained prepared for action if she needed to defend herself. He stood up straight. "You have familiar eyes. Your eyes are like a lady I know. Her name is Ruby."

Mia didn't like that he was bringing up Ruby. She knew Ruby certainly didn't have the same beautiful eyes as Lucy or her, so his statement was just to rattle her. After revisiting the journals and talking to Dulce, she feared and hated Ruby. "Isn't Ruby dead by now?" she quipped as she paused to think that maybe, perhaps, he referred to another lady named Ruby and not the witch that lived across from us.

Mia saw Ruby briefly when she went to see Dulce years ago and recalled Ruby being a shorter Mexican lady with dark eyes. Her eyes were so dark. You couldn't see her pupil. It was as if her pupil consumed her entire eye. Mia remembered her eyes being so dark and soulless. Mia remembered being afraid of looking at Ruby because of her eyes, which stayed with her.

The man snickered at her. "No, no, Ruby lives, and she has your eyes," he snickered. Something deep inside her whispered. "You need to read. Ruby is looking for her, and she will find her, and Lucy will need to be ready to fight."

Chills ran through Mia, and she felt like she was about to pass out. The mysterious man left, saying nothing more. Mia stood next to her car in shock. She unlocked her car, climbed in, and sat down. She was breathing heavily, very upset, and felt like she was hyperventilating. She couldn't catch a breath in her lungs. She dialed Tyler as her hands were trembling; she could barely make the call.

When Tyler picked up, she told him about the man, what he said, and how it frightened her. He listened and tried to support her but couldn't understand. He was more concerned about her safety and urged her to contact security to ensure they kept an eye on the parking lot when she was leaving for the day.

Mia started to call our mom, but she didn't want to upset or cause her worry and concern, so she didn't. She called Dulce. Dulce would understand, and Dulce knew Ruby, so she wanted to see what she made of everything. Dulce didn't initially answer, so she started to put her phone away when Dulce finally called her back.

Before Mia could explain what had just happened to her, Dulce asked if she could meet at the park so they could chat, which they did. Dulce read through some of the journals Mia left the last time they all met with Lily and whipped out her childhood diary. I had forgotten about her always writing in her diary. She was always on Maria's porch scribbling in her diary and drawing.

"I read through some of the journals and combed through them all night," Dulce said. Mia felt a little guilty as she procrastinated reading the journals and dreaded getting upset by reading Granny's long-lost words. Dulce also made copies of her own diary and notes. "These were things I wrote about as I observed Ruby when I lived there and why I left. I was hidden from Ruby. Ruby wanted me to lure Lucy away from your family, but I didn't know then. Maria figured out Ruby was up to something and sent me far away for my protection. Maybe even for your and Lucy's protection too." She turned over her journal to Mia. "I don't think she was looking to sell Lucy." Dulce cleared her throat. "Listen, you're not going to like this, and I don't want to anger you. In my opinion, as your friend, not a therapist, I believe Ruby had the intent to hurt Lucy. My opinion, and it's just my opinion."

Dulce kept prolonged telling my sister what was on her mind. She was worried my sister wouldn't believe her or would lash out and get angry. "Spit it out already, Dulce. I won't be upset with you; just be honest with me. What are you thinking?"

Dulce exhaled slowly. "Mia, what happened to Lucy may very well have been because of Ruby. After the journals and going back through my diaries, I figured out she was planning to use Lucy to..." She was still hesitant. "I think Ruby was hoping to use Lucy as a sacrifice."

Mia didn't say anything. She just handed over one of the books she had to Dulce. She gave her the one on demonic possession. "I really feel like Lucy possibly read this book. It talks about possession. Lucy isn't a demon, but could she have been the reason I was sick and had visions, dreams, and crazy feelings? I think Lucy was attached to me somehow when I left our old house. In one journal I began reading, Granny writes about her doll being her salvation."

Mia went on to explain. "Lucy had gifts when she was a young girl. I ignored her gifts when I was younger; it freaked me out, honestly. Lucy saved a friend of mine when he thought of suicide; she had a vision. It was accurate, and I credit her for saving him." Dulce listened intently. "After I took her Lucy doll that my granny made and some of her stuff from her old room into her house, things changed," Mia explained. "Even my son Jacob started having dreams about her and people at the door, which worries me."

Dulce nodded. "I don't think Lucy possessed you; she isn't a demon. A demon has never been human, so they desire to inhibit a body and overtake the soul. I don't think that was what was going on with you. I wonder, though..." Dulce trailed off, thinking. "Perhaps she was with you, and her presence was overpowering. Maybe she did attach to you accidentally. I think that's possible, and on some level, you knew and were able to pick up on things she was able to perceive."

"What do you think about us getting together tomorrow? Read what I gave you. I will read this book, at least some of it; it's pretty big," she laughed. "I want to go through Lucy's stuff in your house and develop a game plan. If she was with you, where is she now, and is she OK?" Dulce worried.

* * * * *

Around two in the morning, Dulce got a call that woke her up. "Dulce, Lucy is hiding in the shadows."

Dulce was half asleep, and as she stood up, she felt lightheaded and loopy. "Hold on," she whispered. She crept out of her room so she didn't wake her husband up as he was sleeping and loudly snoring. "OK, what?" Dulce asked.

"I read the journals," Mia whispered. "Lucy was having out-of-body experiences and visions; my granny was trying to teach her to control and how to...I don't know, like, navigate her magic. They read on how to hide your soul when being hunted."

"Being hunted by who?" Dulce asked, but she already suspected she knew the answer to her own question.

"My Granny was told by a good friend of hers that was magical, and I assume psychic, to protect Lucy once her father passed away. This friend was named Topaz. She warned my Granny that Lucy would be in trouble and wanted to pass along books for Lucy to be prepared to protect herself."

"Topaz gave my granny books that would help her train Lucy. I believe Granny worked a spell from one of the books and sent Ruby away to Mexico to protect Lucy, according to the journal." Dulce was quiet on the other end of the phone. "Is this crazy?"

"It is, but I believe you. Did you read my diary?" Dulce inquired.

"No, I haven't. I've just been reading the journals from my grandmother."

Dulce went into her home office and rolled out her chair. "I used to see a shadow roll across to your house, going from Lucy's room then back to the living room window. It upset me, so I went to the living room and saw Ruby laying on the floor with a candle and salt around her." Mia gasped. "Ruby's eyes were rolled back into her head, and she was making a gurgling sound as if she was in a deep trance of some kind. I started to wake her, but something inside me told me to go back to my room. I watched the shadow creep back over from your house from my window. I heard her erupt with laughter. It didn't sound like her; she sounded so evil. It was bone-chilling." Dulce felt frightened just talking about it. "I quickly jumped into my bed and pretended to be sleeping. Ruby creaked the door open and asked me what I wanted. She knew I was only pretending to be asleep. She shut the door and told me to stay out of her way, and I swear when I heard her laugh, it wasn't just her. There were almost, like, more people with her laughing at me. Like inside of her." Dulce told Mia this, putting herself out there as someone educated in psychology and not one to indulge in religion and fear about the spiritual realm. They began talking and putting the pieces together.

Dulce experienced the occult firsthand. Maria sent Dulce away after that night. Dulce didn't share the details of what happened; she didn't have to. Maria was sitting on her porch and saw the shadow lurking and crawling back to Ruby's house. Right after Dulce left, another visitor arrived. Granny arrived at our house, and Maria saw her blessing it. She knew us girls would be safe. She also knew Granny was strong. Ruby left shortly after Granny arrived.

Ruby's mother fell ill, and the timing was suspicious. Ruby had no idea, but she was sent away from me with intent. Granny needed time with me to work on magic without me being distracted by Ruby and her hatred of me. I wonder if, after Granny passed, had I worked on my spells and skills as she told me to, I would be alive today.

I let my guard down. If I had kept my word to granny and if I had stayed focused on the magic, perhaps, I wouldn't have been scared of that evil witch anymore. Maybe I wouldn't have drowned in a cold pond. Make no mistake about it, the baby doll going into the pond, was not a simple misunderstanding. I believe now that it was very calculated.

I now realize in my living nightmare that I unintentionally placed myself into my worst memory. My fight or flight sense kicked in without my realizing it, and I found myself squatting down in the shadows. I didn't expect whatever was looking for me to search me out in that memory. My soul was hiding.

Typically, when you want to escape, you go into a happy memory, a special event. If you ever find yourself being hunted by a predator after your soul, that's the first place they will stalk you. Granny told me to always hide in a miserable feeling, they won't look there, and if they do, they can't see you if you are hiding and running in the shadows. I placed myself there, into the shadows where I was a little girl running and afraid. No one else did. I unknowingly went into self-protection mode.

I knew I needed to leave so my sister would stop feeling sick, but I also somehow knew it was time to go. The demon at the light that night we left Dr. Roth's office was summoned to look for me. When my sister stirred me and my belongings, something else awakened too. Something heavy and ominous.

There was something exceptionally dark and familiar to Mia too. It was trying to listen to her thoughts at that traffic light, but she knew what it was, so she didn't let her mind wander. Mia only focused on the traffic light. Once again, the demon was put out and found her to be a waste of time as it tried to scour her thoughts. She was a waste of its time, just as she was the first time it was sent to her many years ago.

Mia thought she called the demon into her life, but in fact he was called to her. Ruby was very much alive and well. She thought I was a dead girl; she thought I had a lost soul and Mia was the key to finding me. She owed Satan my soul that she promised him long ago. Ruby didn't practice white magic; she practiced more than black magic. Ruby had given herself so much to Satan that she did his bidding. She wanted to be the right hand of the devil. She invited the demons in—welcomed them, even. I wonder if perhaps she suffered from serious mental illness, surely one would have to have something wrong with them to live their life the way she did. No simple pleasures in life, just always conniving, vengeful and hate-filled.

The first time the demon came to Mia was when she was a teen, almost a young woman. Mia was convinced she summoned the demon by reading books and going through normal teenage rebellion, but her visit had nothing to do with why the demon came to observe her. Ruby removed my dad from the home, our protector. His illness, the darkness that fell over our house was Ruby setting the stage for things to come.

Ruby never saw my granny, but my granny saw her. Ruby was able to hide from being seen for a while, but the more she desired me, the more she stepped into the light, and my granny saw her and cast her away. The demon came to my sister and then to my mother, killing the tree in our backyard. He was stalking them; they were in grave danger. We all were.

Thankfully, a white witch came and saved them. She came to save me too, and she trusted me, but I let her down. I allowed a black magic witch and her demons to win all because I wanted to be a normal teenager. I put it off and avoided magic, and because I did, dark magic destroyed my life as I knew it.

Soon after Mia ended her call to Dulce, she went to check on Jacob and saw him sleeping peacefully. Mia suddenly had a weird feeling creeping up on her as if she was being followed around the house. She shook it off, dismissing the feeling and fear she was experiencing. Just in case she was wrong and something was following her, she crawled back into bed with Tyler, moving up close to him like a scared five-year-old seeking protection from their parents. She finally fell asleep.

The next morning, she woke to find a text message on her phone from her good friend and now former coworker, Sophie. She was in her new place and sent Mia a photo of her boxes. Mia replied, I'm not helping you unpack without pizza and wine. Sophie smiled and replied with a photo of a bottle of their favorite wine.

Sophie found a place she was extremely excited about; at a time when leaving made her feel a little sad. She had a realization of how little her life actually was without anyone in it. Mia called Sophie that morning, right after her conference call ended with Thomas. Sophie didn't have to work out her notice since she was going to a competing bank so she wasn't a part of the calls anymore. There were about twenty people on the call, and Thomas made a point to mention that he and his wife are going on vacation next week, so he would be canceling that week's conference call. Mia knew he hoped that would find its way back to Sophie. He was bitter and wanted to cause her to feel upset.

Thomas was also sure to casually mention that he and his wife would be going on vacation in South Carolina to hunt down a nice spot for a vacation home. Mia figured he wanted Sophie to know that he and his wife were buying a vacation home and going to South Carolina to hurt her. Sophie always said it was her dream to move back to South Carolina where she grew up as a child and had shared that with him and Mia both a number of times.

Mia knew it was almost as if he was trying to one-up Sophie now. Like some strange revenge. Thomas was not one to usually talk about things like that on a business call; he was very private. So much so, up until he met Sophie, he wasn't even open to his wife about intimate conversations like he was with Sophie. Something inside him was awakened when he met her, and he couldn't seem to break free of her.

Mia did not mention a peep about it to Sophie as she suspected Thomas hoped she would. They talked and visited, but not once did Mia mention it to her. Not only did she want to protect Sophie's heart, but she also didn't want the situation to be harder for either one of them. The truth was, Thomas was just hurting too. Sophie just picked up and left him behind after he formed a strong bond with her. Thomas knew he would never hear from her again, and he was hostile thinking about it, and he was managing that realization day by day.

Sophie respected him for staying in his marriage. She respected his commitment even though she knew it was obligatory. She was thankful, at least, that she wasn't in a dull marriage. She wouldn't want to be stuck in a relationship where she had to hide behind Bible scriptures as a way to make her feel better about being in a marriage that had run its course. She would rather be by herself than be in a flat marriage without passion.

Sophie asked how dull the weekly call was and Mia confirmed it was as pointless as usual. Sophie just wanted to bring up the topic to complain about Thomas. The call was just an excuse to bring him up to vent about him. "That son of a bitch never even acknowledged my leaving," Sophie told Mia. ". He just began interviewing people around here for my position but wouldn't even solicit my input or anything. I never realized how little he respected me. He hired this one dude in town that no one else would hire because he's dull and has bad breath. It seriously smells like he ate the butthole out of a buzzard. Good luck to my ex-employees and customers catching wind of that," Sophie spat resentfully.

"He didn't say goodbye because he couldn't show you that he cares for you. He was and is ignoring you like you mean nothing to him, and here's the deal. If you don't reach out to him, you'll never hear from him again. Just know if it was as real for him as it was for you, he will still think about you every day. He will think about things he wants to tell you, and you won't be there for him." Sophie listened to my sister's words. "He doesn't win, either. Neither of you win in this situation. Just remember, the first person to speak loses. Just let him go. Each passing day will get easier and easier; time will lessen the pain."

Sophie knew Mia was right. Truth be told, Sophie loved him enough to leave him alone and hoped he and his wife could once again ignite their passion.

Mia abruptly ended the phone call with Sophie when she saw Lily and Dulce walk through the bank lobby. The ladies saw Mia getting off the phone as they approached her office, closing the door quietly behind them.

"Mia! Years ago, Maria told me Frank was scared away when he was staying with her, and this morning, it hit me. Ruby sent Frank when she was away in Mexico," Dulce said without saying "hello." Mia shook her head, trying to understand. "Maria said he left because he saw something in the tree and it scared him. She said she never saw a man his age act so frightened, almost like a little boy. He was so scared he left early that morning. He said something was chasing a demon, and it really shook him up.

"As soon as he arrived in town, he settled in and almost immediately started asking a lot of questions about the girls next door. Maria laughed and assumed at the time he was only asking out of his curiosity about seeing the pretty girl next door,—you, of course, because Lucy was too young back then. I started thinking about that conversation, and then it hit me today. I think he was there to watch, take or even hurt Lucy at Ruby's command." Dulce was rambling on about her suspicion. "I think Frank came to get Lucy because Ruby had a strong hold on him. He wasn't her son, but he treated Ruby like a superior. Ruby had to leave to be with her mom—a mom that she didn't have a particularly close relationship with, yet she still would leave when her mother would fall sick. I think she had her eyes on Lucy but needed someone close to do her bidding against her since she had to leave. I think maybe anytime she got close to taking Lucy, something would come up, almost like there was a protection spell keeping Ruby from getting your sister. I think Frank was sent to retrieve her, if you want to know the truth. I think Ruby figured it out when she was heading to Mexico. I don't know why I think that, but I really do," Dulce intensely explained.

"Dulce, do you think we are getting too far off track with this? Doesn't this all seem a little...I don't know, wild?" Lily asked, the voice of reason, the Doctor of Psychology.

"I'm not being crazy about this, Lily! I have grown up around this. Mia isn't wrong, and I'm not wrong." Dulce was very defensive. She looked at my sister. "Mia, I didn't want to get into this with you on the phone last night, but a few days ago, I spoke to Maria on the phone. I am always very careful not to ask her about Ruby. In fact, both of us are always careful not to speak of her. Maria told me about your mom recently moving away. She started to tell me about Lucy, something she had avoided telling me when I was younger. She said she was afraid I would come back to see y'all and she wanted me to stay away while Ruby was there. After years past, she just didn't want to tell me and upset me because she hid it from me. She felt guilty but something kept nagging at her to tell me. She was surprised when I told her I knew already. I told her you and I reconnected recently. Maria told me after your family moved, she started seeing weird things going on over there. She swore when the house was empty, she'd see things walking around and get a bad feeling about it; she was really upset by it all." Dulce shared.

"Did you know the new family that moved in recently had a priest come to the house not once but twice because they've been having negative experiences there?" Before Mia could even answer, Dulce continued, hyped up and full of energy. "I asked Maria about Frank and if she hears from him anymore. She said she never heard from Frank again after he stayed briefly that summer. She mailed me this, it just arrived this morning." Dulce pulled out an envelope and opened it. It was a photo. "Maria gave me this picture of Frank she came across when she was getting ready for her garage sale; it's old. She saved it just in case Frank ever came back for his stuff. It was left in his small duffle bag that he left behind on the lawn the morning he abruptly departed the area. Did you ever notice him watching you or watching Lucy?"

Mia took the picture from Dulce's hand. She looked at it and then held it even closer. "I am a thousand percent sure this is the man that has come up to me and talked to me. He's the guy that talked to me about my eyes."

Dulce took the picture back. "You're sure? Do you think he recognized you from when you were younger?"

Mia shook her head. "I've never seen him before. I saw his truck parked at Maria's house, but never once did I see him. If he saw me, it would have been too far away, and he couldn't have been close enough to see my eyes," Mia explained.

"Do you think he saw Lucy?" Dulce asked.

Lily was quick to chime in. "You always said you and your sister had the same eyes with the unique fleck of green."

Mia shrugged, "Yeah, but I doubt that he would've been that close to her. There is no way to really know, I guess." Mia wondered if he could've crossed paths with me without her knowing about it.

Chapter Fourteen
A Living Nightmare

As I grew tired of lurking in the shadows, I decided to reach in and save myself, just as Granny told me to before. As I watched myself run to the edge of my yard, I stepped back away from my living self in my nightmare before the nightmare once again started over. This time, I pressed forward and snuck into the house, still hiding and skirting along the lurking shadows. I watched from my sister's bedroom window as my worst memory replayed outside, knowing something outside was watching me.

I found my way back into my bedroom. As I navigated, I was careful to stay low and in the shadows to try to stay in hiding. There, in my room, I found the books I had hidden away under my bed. I found the chapter I needed within seconds of opening the book. I suddenly was reading how to navigate from the dead world to the living world. Once you go to Heaven or Hell, you can no longer move about unless you are an angel or a demon of sorts—but I was neither. I was a lost, living dead girl that was still living through glimpses of her sister's life now.

As I read through the book, I felt I understood how to bring myself back to the living world again and out of this nightmare. I now knew I needed to find my way back to the doll. The doll my granny painted and sent me that was identical to me. She made this doll as a portal for me. It was made in my likeness, just as the book instructed.

I shut the book and noticed the author of the book was Topaz Morning. I instantly knew, without a doubt, that this book was written by the same Topaz that Granny knew and worked with her to strengthen her own magic. Now I felt a greater sense of empowerment.

I knew this would work. I felt Topaz, and possibly Granny, knew I was going to be overtaken and I'd have to save myself.

I left my terrible childhood memory. I couldn't take my younger self with me. I couldn't change the memory; I had to leave the little frightened version of myself behind. I was able to escape to the living world by bending the rules of magic, only this time, I wasn't a scared little girl anymore. As I attached myself to the doll, I transitioned from the nightmare and back into the present living world once again. I knew this time to stay with the doll to not affect anyone.

It was a gift of books my sister had discarded that would come to aid me and rescue me. A stack of books I pulled out of the trash and safeguarded for reasons that were unknown to me then. At the time, I kept them as a safety net against a mean old witch. A safety net that allowed me to pull myself from the shadows.

I found myself in a familiar place; it was Jacob's room. He was playing trucks, and he brought so much happiness to me after so much sadness and confusion I had been experiencing. Strangely, I felt we weren't alone anymore.

Suddenly, an ominous feeling presented itself in the room. Jacob began talking as if he had an imaginary friend with him, but it wasn't imaginary. I remained undetected by whatever entered the room. I felt frightened for Jacob and felt I had to somehow protect him.

My brother-in-law entered the room. "Who are you talking to, Jay?" Jacob stopped playing with his trucks and told his daddy he was playing with Iikin and Mann. Tyler brushed it off as imaginary friends as he picked Jacob up to see Mia, who had just pulled into the driveway.

The air had been sucked out of the room. I knew the ominous feelings were entities that had no reason to be in the house. The same dark feeling that haunted my childhood home now lingered inside Mia's home, and it frightened me. I felt scared for my sister and her beautiful family she loves so much.

As Mia entered the house, she felt heavy feelings too. Mia introduced Dulce to her husband and son. Tyler and Jacob then greeted Lily with a warm hug as she entered the house. Dulce suddenly pulled Mia aside by her arm. "Ouch, you're hurting me!" Mia quipped. Dulce whispered, "Something isn't right in your house."

Mia looked at her and motioned everyone outside. "What's going on, Tyler? Something feels weird in the house."

Lily sighed. "OK, even I thought so too. The hairs on the back of my neck stood up as soon as I walked in."

Tyler would normally dismiss such suggestions, but even he seemed concerned. "I was hanging my jacket up, and I felt something watching me, so I went to check on Jacob. He was talking to his imaginary friends,"

Jacob chimed in. "Iikin and Mann aren't my friends. They said they hate me." Jacob's sweet voice trembled.

"Iikin and Mann?" Dulce asked, looking over to Mia. "Are they -"

Lily interrupted. "Jacob, how long have you been seeing these guys that aren't your friends?"

He paused to think. "Yesterday. Today they came just a while ago when I was playing with my Tonkas."

Mia added, "I never felt that way in the house before; have you, Tyler?" He shook his head no.

"Iikin and Mann are two demons; I'm certain of it," Dulce said. "I don't know how, but I just know they are, and they're looking for Lucy—or maybe they want Jacob. You need to stay out of the house until we get this place cleansed, or they won't leave until they get what they're after." She was very persuasive in her demand. Dulce had been around demons before and she experienced their negative energy. She felt it many times when she was younger. She lived with Ruby, after all. At the time, she didn't know that was what she was hearing and feeling. It wasn't until she was heavily involved in church that she realized exactly what was happening around Ruby's home.

"These aren't ghosts needing to be crossed over; these are demons, and they will start trying to harm you or claim you as theirs," Dulce explained to the group.

Mia asked, "Do you know of a good priest?"

Dulce was thinking as Jacob pointed to the window. It was almost like he could see the demons inside the house.

Mia was startled, "Don't look, Jacob. Tyler, you and Jacob go to my mom's, and I will go in and pack us an overnight bag. Don't mention the details to my mom this would scare her too much."

Tyler began to argue, but Mia insisted, and the girls promised to stay and go in with her.

"A priest would need approval from the Catholic Church, but I know someone that may be able to help. Lily, you know who I am talking about. The girl from the gym, she may know someone or she may be able to help." Dulce suggested

Lily paused. "Oh. Yes! I don't know if she does that, but I'm sure she would know someone who would be able to help."

Mia sighed. "OK, let's talk about this tomorrow. Let's not talk about anything or even think about it when we are inside. Let's get in, grab clothing and some personal items for the next day or two, and get out."

The girls stayed quiet for a moment, looking at the house as they felt afraid to enter. Then…

"Let's do this!" Lily exclaimed.

Before they could enter, Tyler stopped them, insisting on staying with Mia. He was worried about letting her go into the house again, so he had her wait in the car with Jacob while he went into the house. The ladies went with Mia to her car as Tyler went into the house. He caught a glimpse of the Lucy doll out of the corner of his eye but didn't want to draw attention to it. He had a weird feeling about the doll and he felt strangely protective of it. He wanted to bring the doll but was too afraid to show it had any importance or significance. So he left it on the shelf. He left me on the shelf in Jacob's room with demons rummaging through the house.

As Tyler came out, he took Jacob with him so Mia could follow in her car.

Mia hugged Lily tightly. "Call me tomorrow after you talk to the girl at your gym. Let's try to get this all figured out." Lily had a nervous laugh about her. "This is a lot to take in," she said.

When Mia went to hug her, Dulce joked, "She's soft, Mia. She never grew up with crazy shit like we did!"

These ladies were what Granny called crows. They were loyal friends to Mia, trustworthy, and they were good to my sister. Even Lily, who was a skeptic, opened her mind and got out of her comfort zone to help my sister.

I stayed behind; I didn't latch on. I didn't hide. I sat in plain sight inside a doll in my likeness, created just for me. Granny knew I'd need to hide; she knew, despite her best efforts, I'd need help safeguarding my soul. After her passing, I would still be in danger. The doll was the way she could still protect me. Creating the doll, telling me of my magic, was her way of trying to save me. She couldn't protect me from the free will of others, she couldn't save my living body, but she could help teach me to save my soul.

*****

The next morning, when Mia arrived at work, she was greeted by Jenny and Kimmy who were high-strung and anxious to see her. "Doris caught her husband cheating!" Jenny blurted out as soon as Mia entered the bank. Mia, of course, wasn't the least bit surprised since she saw it firsthand. She also wasn't interested in the gossip, although she was listening as she worked. She was being nice to the girls as they were so shocked and excited to give her the big scoop. Kimmy explained that Doris went through the messages on Bruce's phone, and she was determined to figure out if he was having an affair because he was always wanting to sleep in the recliner instead of with her. She saw messages from Jasper. Bruce insisted Jasper was in love with him, but he was straight, and Jasper was blackmailing him to be his lover. He said Jasper threatened to lie and tell people at work and in town that Bruce was his boyfriend, so he had to be with him.

Kimmy and Jenny were sitting there waiting for Mia to have a big reaction.

"Wow, that's too bad!" Mia said. "I feel sad for her that she was deceived like that."

Jenny laughed. "Well, she called me last night telling me about it, and the craziest part is she feels bad for Bruce." Mia looked up, puzzled. Jenny continued. "Yeah, Bruce basically claims to be in a gay relationship out of being blackmailed."

Kimmy asked Mia's opinion, and although Mia was certain that wasn't the case, she put an end to the gossip and told them to let Doris figure out her own way to handle it. Mia knew Doris and her family were the types of people not to get involved with.

The day was long for Mia; she didn't work much but instead read through some of the journals again, reading as much as she could from the books. Our mom called to check in with her and let her know Jacob was having a good day. She asked Mia about the house blessing. I think it reminded her a lot of when Dad passed, and Granny came in to cleanse our house, which seemed heavy with sadness and dark energy. Mom teased, making sure Mia knew not to haunt her new house. Mia worried about exposing my mom to anything wicked. Lord knows my mom has certainly been through enough heartache and misfortune to last a lifetime. Mia didn't want to put any stress or burdens on our mother.

Mia and Tyler met the ladies at the house after work. They introduced them to Charlie. Charlie was an expert paranormal investigator and owner of, *Witching Hour Paranormal Investigations.* She asked us to do a walk-through with her quietly as she assessed the situation. Charlie wanted to get a good grasp on what was afoot in the house. She walked through, and instantly I felt her presence. She entered Jacob's room and looked around then wandered from room to room. She finally sat down in the living room, asking everyone to sit with her.

"This is what I am picking up. No demons are here, but something evil has been in your home. I feel like possibly two, maybe three evil spirits or demons."

Mia looked at Dulce and Lily. "I didn't tell Charlie anything other than we wanted her to do a walk-through and possibly investigate," Lily quickly said to set their mind at ease. She wanted them to feel confident in the message they were receiving from Charlie.

Charlie continued. "Mia, when you brought something into the house, is that when you started feeling different?" Mia nodded. "I feel a presence of a female," Charlie said as Mia nodded again. "Was it a doll?" Mia was shocked and didn't realize by this point tears were streaming down her cheeks. "Who was the female that passed away? A sister?" Charlie asked. Everyone was amazed, and Mia felt hopeful.

"Yes, my sister passed away, but it's been many years. I recently brought the doll back from my mom's when she moved closer to me," Mia explained. Tyler and Dulce sat quietly, stoic, as they listened intently.

"What I'm getting is a lot of energy from the doll. I believe your sister was or is attached to this doll." Charlie looked at Mia. "She was somehow connected to you before too. Fairly recently, in fact. You've even experienced a little bit of her…magic. Even after she has unattached from you, you carry a little piece of her now," Charlie explained.

Mia explained her sickness and her visions after leaving the old house. Charlie listened intently. "I feel like your sister was with you, but something called her away. I feel as if she was being sought after, so she hid. I've never had the ability to read or hear things before, but your sister is here and I feel very strongly she is wanting you to know this. I also feel there are demons seeking her out. It's weird to say that to you, but it's a feeling that has a strong hold on me," Charlie explained.

"The demons were looking for her?" Mia was worried. She worried about me all over again.

"Well, they were sent to look for her. There's something bigger going on here. I don't have much experience with séances, but I feel your sister needs help."

Tyler seemed uneasy. "I thought you weren't supposed to disturb the dead?"

"I get your concern, and I agree with you. This is not something I would normally suggest. I just get the feeling Lucy is not at peace. She needs help crossing over, but I get the feeling she needs to communicate before doing so. One thing about the dead is you don't have to visit them. When they need to or want to, they will come to visit you," Charlie replied.

Charlie set her paranormal detection equipment up, which was much more sophisticated these days compared to when Granny and I dabbled in investigating the dead. As the evening drew near, everyone seemed very nervous. "Relax. We are just looking for answers to help your sister and to help you all get back to normal again." Charlie had a very calm and relaxed demeanor, setting Mia at ease.

Mia told her about my unexpected passing but didn't go into the emotional toll it left on her. She explained that she now believes my granny was worried about me when I was living and tried to pass along incantations and spells to help me. Dulce shared what she knew about Ruby and how she feared she used dark magic against me when I was a young, innocent kid. The ladies listened with great angst. Lily sat quietly, being supportive but not understanding the gravity of the situation. It was all very raw to her. Never in her life had she engaged in any such thing.

"I have this recorder that should pick up any activity around the house," Charlie said as she held up a piece of equipment." Lily laughed and Charlie asked, "Did you think I was going to break out a Ouija board?! There's been some advances in paranormal communication since the Ouija board." Charlie said laughing as she took the time and explained how the equipment worked and tempered their expectations. She hoped I would be able to communicate something, maybe a word or two or even a hint to point them in the right direction of what to do. Charlie's fear was that everyone would be disappointed; sometimes you can go for hours and days in an investigation and you don't get anything documented. Sometimes you get something but nothing impressive. Communicating with the dead isn't an exact science.

As soon as Charlie called on me, I could feel myself lift from the doll. It was an exhilarating experience. I felt her ability to reach me was as if I was alive again. It was the first time since death I ever felt this alive. Communicating with her came very easy to me.

"I'm here."

While I expected it to fall on deaf ears, the equipment didn't fail. It mimicked my words, and it was then that it was finally confirmed to my sister that I really was there. Mia felt joyous and saddened at the same time. I was careful to navigate away from them. I didn't want to accidentally attach myself and cause anyone any harm through illness or sixth sense abilities again.

"Baby, it's Mia. Can you hear me?" Mia called out, forgetting Charlie was leading the communication. "I'm here, Mia. I am sorry for upsetting you." As soon as I communicated with her, she felt a lump in her throat that burned as she tried to hold her tears back.

Charlie cut in. "Mia, I will set a time for you and your mom to visit with Lucy if you would like before we cross her over. Would you like that?" Mia nodded yes.

"I can't leave," I answered unsolicited.

"Tell me why," Charlie demanded.

There was silence and then static going through the airwaves. I felt so drained communicating through the device; so tired, the way you would feel winded after blowing up a lot of balloons, one after another and another and another, without taking a break in between.

Charlie knew there was a small window to be able to reach me before I would tire out too much and not be able to communicate, so she wanted to make sure she was able to guide the conversation in a productive way and not just the "I love you," and "I miss you's." Charlie was delightfully surprised with the success they had received from the communication with me up to that point. She knew my spirit was strong.

Before Charlie could ask anything else of me, I took over the conversation. "The man that's been coming around—the one that commented about your eyes. He's the same one you dreamed about. I remember him," I said. I started feeling different. It was almost the same sensation you would have after standing up too fast after you've been sitting down. I felt it was time to tell Mia what I knew, but my energy went from low to completely depleted suddenly.

"Who is he?!" Mia insisted, taking over as interviewer again. She was seeking confirmation for what she already suspected.

There was nothing. I couldn't speak. I felt like I was fading but feared I was fading into the darkness of limbo this time. I made it a conscious effort not to let it happen, hanging on but not using my energy to speak. It took all my vitality to just stay present.

Charlie called on me again and several times before she gave up. "Perhaps we can try again tomorrow," Charlie said as she began packing up when I was suddenly able to communicate once more. I had to tell them what I recalled. I just had to tell my sister what I know really happened.

"He took me out of the water, just like you dreamed about, but it was me. It's what happened to me. He was only saving me for something else. I woke up in some kind of church," I began.

Mia and Tyler grasped hands. Tyler was literally shaking.

I didn't share this with them, but I died in that church. My body died but my soul slipped away from the church before Ruby could consume it. Immediately after my death, I watched my mom and sister in our house and at the pond, and I stuck around until my soul knew it was about to be found. My mom's praying for me to be found safe inadvertently kept demons and wickedness away from our home. When my mother had the realization too much time had passed for me to still be living, her prayers turned to rage. That is when the hedge of protection left our home and my soul became vulnerable. It was then my soul tucked itself away for over a decade asleep, void of consciousness.

Mia was livid. "He killed her. I'm going to kill that son of a bitch!" she spat frantically. She jumped to her feet. Her rage gave me a boost of energy, and somehow, I was able to feed off of her emotions.

"Mia, it *was* Frank, and you must stay away from him. He is searching for me. The two beasts that were here were sent to look for me. Jacob can see and hear them too. Keep that man and the demons away from here. Keep me away from Jacob for his own safety," I pleaded.

Charlie listened to my pleas. "I want to take Lucy home with me. I can protect her and keep her out of your home if they come to look for her. I want to keep her away from your son as well. We can communicate with her at my house," Charlie suggested.

"You're not afraid of your house getting haunted?" Lily asked without even thinking about the insensitivity of the question. "Sorry," she said, hanging her head.

"Actually, not at all. I do so much of this, and it wouldn't be the first time I've been followed home." Charlie smiled. "I'm not related to you in any way, so I don't believe anything will look for you there," Charlie said to me, and then assured Mia, "I don't anticipate they will look for her with me. I will safeguard her."

Mia and Tyler agreed. Mia decided that maybe they would hold off on telling the details to our mom for now. She also thought it was best to hold off on having her and my mom contact me until they were more clear as to what was going on with me. Mia had a lot to process—especially after learning it was Frank who rescued me from the water, only to choke the life back out of me, and all for Ruby.

"Lucy, you are not bound by this doll. You are not bound by the limitations of this world. I want to keep helping you communicate with Mia, and we want to help you figure out what we can do to get you where you belong. Would you like to come with me, Lucy?" Charlie asked.

I weighed the options, but it was an easy decision. I didn't want Ruby's devils hunting for me around my family. I didn't want to disturb my mom or Mia's life any more than I already had. I certainly didn't want anything to hurt Jacob. He was innocent and so special to my family. "Take me with you. Leave my Lucy doll here with my sister," I insisted.

Charlie paused momentarily then nodded her head and smiled. "Lucy is a smart one. She wants to leave the doll in case she needs to bring herself back here. This doll is her portal back to her family."

Mia didn't fully understand but was curious. "Will she be able to come back to the doll instantly? If we leave it with Jacob, in his room, will the demons know or..." She was concerned for Jacob, understandably so.

"No, they don't know about the doll. Granny made it so I wouldn't be found," I answered, and Mia put her head back and placed her hands over her eyes as she gathered her thoughts.

"I feel like this is all a very weird dream," she said.

I left with Charlie that night. Something about her energy was familiar and safe to me. Charlie asked me to save my energy and try to gather my thoughts to try to recall what happened to me when I died. At this stage, they were doing a murder investigation along with a paranormal investigation.

Mia and Tyler kept quiet around my mom regarding what was happening with me. They feared it would upset her, and they didn't even know what the next steps would even be at this point. Mia and her husband took advantage of the quietness of the house. They were both so emotionally drained from the day's events that they didn't even speak about it.

* * * * *

The following day, my sister woke at 3:45 in the morning. The room was freezing cold. She scooted closer to Tyler to feel the warmth of his body heat, and suddenly, she saw something out of the corner of her eye. A "pins and needles" sensation pulsed through her body when she saw a large, black mass at the edge of their bed. There was chaos and fear associated with the entity. She felt it was possibly a demon and was afraid. Mia wouldn't look at it; she quickly closed her eyes, not even looking in that direction. She then shook Tyler to wake him.

"Tyler," she whispered. "Tyler, something is looking at us from the foot of the bed."

"Shhh," he said. "I saw it; it's been there all night. Just ignore it." Mia was even more terrified. They didn't go back to sleep; they just kept their eyes closed until daylight presented itself.

Later that morning when they were in the kitchen, the house finally felt normal again. Tyler explained to Mia that before bed, he was flipping through the book my mom was reading here one day and he came across a page that caught his eye. A passage instructed to not feed into it with fear or confrontation if an entity appears before you. So, he ignored it.

Tyler never met me but felt a sense of loss and wanted me to find peace. He feared the supernatural and was afraid of death and the unknown, so Mia was surprised he delved into the books and participated in trying to reach me. Tyler saw it as a way of protecting Jacob but also helping Mia finally make peace with my death and finding the closure she and my mother have yearned for.

*****

When I was hiding with Charlie, she told me she wouldn't ask me questions. She explained she wanted me to rest and save my energy for our *next* séance, and, though she would talk to me, she didn't want a response. She talked to me a lot. She was a beautiful young woman. Charlie had dark hair with caramel skin and twinkling brown eyes with touches of sweet shades of honey. She was kind and thoughtful in everything she did.

She read the journals and the books Mia gave her. They set a date to meet again, to talk to me, so she wanted me to simply stay present and make sure I wouldn't slip beyond this world; she wanted me to rest easy. No looking in on family, no worrying. Meditation, I guess you would call it. She talked to me, I think, to make sure I stayed in the moment with her. I learned a lot about her and liked her very much.

Charlie loved the thrill of "ghost hunting" and the paranormal. She lost her dad at a young age; he was crushed at work, which was exceptionally traumatic for her. She had a hard time letting go and accepting her father's demise, so she became interested in the supernatural. She was a daddy's girl growing up, she was even named after him. His name was Charles, so they named her Charlie. She said she never had special abilities—natural abilities like I did—when she was younger but has learned to open herself up to the world beyond our own. She developed abilities with hard work but they were lower on the spectrum of psychic or gifted so she was quite surprised when she was able to pick up on my feelings so strongly at Mia's house.

Charlie's eyes glitzed with curiosity and optimism. Her smile was inviting, and she could easily disarm anyone when she flashed her smile at them. She could ease their worry and make anyone feel comfortable. Even the dead, apparently.

Chapter Fifteen
The Genesis

During the first few weeks, as she opened herself up spiritually, Charlie told me her anxiety went through the roof. She would wake up with her heart racing, upset stomach, and eerie nightmares that terrified her. She almost gave up until she figured that was too easy, and she was not one to ever give in and give up. She was too stubborn, so she learned to deal with it. Charlie trained herself to anticipate the anxiety and bad dreams, and she learned to help her mind cope. For someone that was so young, she was tough and unapologetically herself.

She was also very into her job. Charlie helped with police investigations occasionally and was quite successful and helpful when it came to cold cases that needed a new direction. The detectives in the local area would often call Charlie for assistance. She was also a bit of a history buff, and in addition to her investigations company, she owned several ghost touring companies around the country. The companies paired the town's history with *tales* of the souls that haunted the towns to the present day. She was a real go-getter and very successful.

Charlie put a lot into studying the journals and books to prepare for the séance. She took it very seriously. After Charlie read the books, she admitted this was well beyond her realm of experience; she was a believer in the afterlife but was utterly afraid of magic and associated all magic, including white magic, as devilish. However, she was open-minded and determined to help me cross over and remove the demons from my family, especially Jacob. She worried that with his age and innocence, he was susceptible to evilness. I was worried, too. I worried Jacob was like me, seeing and hearing things. The dreams he had were too familiar, and they haunted me.

Charlie reached out to my sister and let her know that she and Dulce would be heading back to our old neighborhood. They were going to visit with Maria. Charlie was hoping to uncover some more information on Ruby. Who was she? Why was she so ungodly and wicked? They invited Mia, but she was wary about going there. Mia didn't want to stir the demons back up by talking about Ruby with Maria and Dulce. She wanted peace around her home and her son.

Charlie communicated with me on the plan to meet Maria; she spoke to me just as if she was talking to a friend. She insisted I continue saving my energy and keep my mind clear of the past as best as possible.

Charlie went to my sister's the following morning and cleansed the house. She salted the window seals, going from room to room, saying prayers and chants. The house felt clean to Charlie, but there could be no guarantees. Charlie feared these intruders stalking Mia and invading her home were far more powerful than anything a ghost hunter could guard against.

Mia felt something was better than nothing. Charlie warned Mia this was by no means absolute protection. If they have another visit, simply ignore the monsters; they do indeed feed off fear. At the same time, be cautious and safeguard Jacob. Charlie set up lovely crosses around the house.

"Jacob, if you see Mann, if you see Iikin, promise me you will slowly get up and go wake your mom and dad," Charlie instructed.

"They told me they hate my mom and me," Jacob said, making a sad face.

Mia was worried and upset about the situation they were all in. Charlie hugged Jacob. "They are ugly and hateful; you are a magnificent young man. They are strangers and are mean and hate everyone, so don't let that upset you." Jacob embraced Charlie with a hug and vivacious smile.

Mia sat with Charlie, looking for reassurance that the demons wouldn't enter their home again. "The good thing is, Lucy is in my home, and if they are looking for her, she is not here, and she isn't with you, so they may give up coming to your home or be called off the chase altogether. Their lurking hasn't turned up anything other than suspicion that Lucy is hiding and being guarded by you. Your mother hasn't been bothered, so it seems as if they sensed her when she was attached to you."

Charlie continued. "My real question is, after all of these years of her being dead...why now? Why are they searching for her soul now? She surfaced, and somehow, they knew. What do they want with her? I need answers, and Dulce and I are going to Dallas to see Maria to see if she can provide them. If not answers, maybe at least a little direction for us."

On the drive to Dallas, Charlie and Dulce exchanged stories of their childhoods. They talked about their losses and heartbreaks. They shared their triumphs and seemed to bond with one another. As they got closer to our old neighborhood, Dulce kept touching her chest as they spoke—a light tapping.

"You have anxiety," Charlie told Dulce.

Dulce shrugged her shoulders. "Yes. I just caught myself too. I feel very apprehensive and nervous, and I keep reasoning with myself that I shouldn't be worried, but I do still feel very anxious," Dulce said, laughing it off as if it were nothing. But Charlie could see the old memories still haunted Dulce, even as an adult—even as an educated woman. She feared the mysteries of her past.

As they arrived in the old neighborhood, Maria was waiting on her front porch. She was excited to see Dulce again. After Dulce moved, she never returned out of fear until recently. She would call Maria to check on her and visit. They would see each other occasionally, but never at Maria's house. Maria knew the old place spooked Dulce, and they never spoke about it, but Maria knew Dulce didn't want to go back to scary memories. Maria didn't want that for her either.

Maria was so proud of Dulce and felt partially responsible for her success. Maria moved to America when she was a young woman. She and her husband worked hard and were fortunate to inherit money from her family. Her father came to America with very little. He worked in kitchens, eventually opening his own restaurant, and then two, and soon had five successful restaurants. He saved most of his earnings for his children throughout his years of hard work. Maria took some of her money and invested it in Dulce's education. She also knew if she hadn't rescued her from Ruby, she would be dead or tainted with Satanic beliefs and an evil heart like Ruby.

Maria lit candles and prayed when Dulce and Charlie entered her home. I believe she did this, asking for the protection of God. She hoped their conversation would stay tucked away and unrevealed to anything or anyone seeking information on the Santeria witch, Ruby. Maria didn't waste much time; it was as if she knew time was of the essence, and as a believer in God, she knew the evil was very real. Maria knew to dismiss the mysteries of the dark world would be like dismissing God himself. Something was brewing; she felt it.

"I have never talked to many people about this. I knew Ruby when we were just girls. When we were back in Mexico, she used to babysit me when my parents worked. Ruby's mother was a nice lady, so kind and hard-working. She worked from sunup to sundown. Her husband got sick unexpectedly and passed away, so Ruby's mom began working many jobs to make ends meet. The lady she worked for during the day, Ramona, was not kind. She was very scary. Ruby's mom was desperate for work, and Ramona paid her twice as much as she could have earned working for anyone else in town. There were whispers around town that Ramona was a devil worshiper. Some would even say she was the devil himself. It was said she would summon the dark lord and cast against anyone that was her enemy. Vindictive. Hateful. Cruel. People did their best to stay out of her way.

"Ramona was an old, old lady, blind in her left eye, and her right eye was a lazy eye with a gray haze upon it, so her appearance alone was frightening, especially for children. I never saw her, but Ruby told me about her. Ruby was uncomfortable around Ramona and dreaded going with her mother to her house.

"My parents also had a bad feeling about Ramona. They safeguarded me and my brother from her, keeping us away from her and her property. They were credulous people who would never even speak her name in our home and were careful not to even refer to her."

Dulce and Charlie sipped their tea and listened intently, almost as if they were being told a ghost story. Charlie had Maria's permission to record the conversation. Although, Maria was a bit nervous about it.

Charlie wanted to document the conversation along with the investigation.

Maria continued with what she knew of Ruby. "Ruby's mother cleaned and cooked for Ramona, but she feared her. She had no choice; she needed work, and times were very hard in Mexico especially, back then. Her mother hurt her shoulder after a fall, so Ruby would come on the days she needed to do deep cleaning. Ruby's mother would tell my mom that Ramona watched Ruby if she brought Ruby along to help her clean. She wouldn't smile, she wouldn't engage with her, just watched her with a cold and stoic face," Maria explained.

"I cannot recall Ruby's mother's name so many years ago, but she was such a pleasant woman. I can, however, still remember Ramona's name. I can never forget her; even without seeing her, she scared me. My parents were afraid of her too. Ruby's mom and my parents, along with the rest of the town, thought Ramona was an evil witch.

"Once Ruby's mother's suspicions grew stronger, she stopped letting Ruby go with her to clean. She became very afraid she angered Ramona further by not allowing Ruby to come to the house anymore. I'll tell you what happened, but it's hard for me. I never told anyone. I've thought about it many times but never spoke of it aloud, it still frightens me."

Then, she very reluctantly began to share a horrific memory. "Ruby's mom came to my mom and my father, pleading for help. They spoke secretly, leaving my brother and me out so we wouldn't know what they were talking about. I do remember my dad sketching. Being a curious child, I went into the drawer where he placed his sketch. For some reason, he was sketching a secret room.

"My father and uncles went to Ruby's house, and they constructed a room under the back porch steps. The sketch looked like a safe room with crosses and rosaries. I can still picture the sketch in my mind, but I never saw the actual room. My father made a safe space to hide Ruby away at night. He and his two brothers built it in two days. Ruby's mom seemed to be in a hurry to get the room built.

"My mother told me, oh, so many years after this all happened, that Ruby's mom was dreaming of Ramona looking for Ruby almost every night. She felt haunted. Ruby's mother told my parents she dreamed about a witch in her house. They all knew it was, somehow, Ramona, hovering about the house, looking in on Ruby perhaps. Ruby's mother could feel the chill in the air and the heaviness of something sinister in the home.

"It was as if it was a bad dream. She felt the cold air and heard hissing and gasping for breath. Her mom knew Ramona was somehow visiting their home. Ramona knew the layout of the house; after all, it was hers. Ramona rented the home to Ruby's parents many years back, so she had been in the home many, many times before.

"Ramona began asking her mother to bring her daughter with her once she stopped bringing Ruby. Ruby's mother insisted she was busy with school and helping her keep the house clean at home. This displeased Ramona. She knew they were keeping Ruby away from her because she practiced witchcraft. Ramona knew people were afraid of her. She fed on the fear. She didn't care if they thought she was scary and evil; she loved that they all feared her so much and fed off their hatred." Maria sipped her tea, closed her eyes, and sat quietly for a moment. Silence filled Maria's house.

"Ruby's mom asked my dad to build a secret room that could shield Ruby while she slept. If Ramona didn't know about the room or had never been invited into that room, she thought maybe she couldn't enter without an invitation. It was something she heard long ago. Perhaps an old tale that may or may not have even been true, I heard that with vampires, but I don't know.. maybe witches too. Ruby's mother just felt Ramona could roam their house freely, knowing the layout and she was able to let her spirit roam since it was her home after all. Her mother wanted to move but had to save money to be able to do to. Ruby liked the room her mother had built for her. It was a safe space, but young Ruby soon made a mistake. When Ruby walked to my class to pick me up from school, she told my teacher about the new room. She thought of the room as her own quiet space that all teenagers would enjoy and thought it was so cool because it was tucked away under the stairs outside. Somehow, that conversation fell on the ears of Ramona. Once she knew about the secret room, Ruby was no longer safe. I believe the secret room actually even provoked Ramona."

Tapping the table with her fingers, Maria continued. "Ruby's mother had a nightmare that very night. At that time, she had no idea Ruby told anyone about the room. It was meant to be a secret, and only my family knew besides Ruby's mother and, of course, Ruby. She urged Ruby not to tell anyone, but like most teenagers Ruby didn't listen to her mother. The adults all knew not to speak of the room to anyone.

"That night, her mother woke up frantic, drenched in sweat. She was so wet it was as if she just stepped out of the shower. She ran around the house—including the safe room—screaming for Ruby and even checked outside, but Ruby wasn't to be found.

"I will never forget. Ruby's mother showed up at our house close to four in the morning. I climbed out of bed, and my brother and I stood in the hallway quietly listening; we were both terrified. Ruby's mom was frantic. I had never heard anyone so panicked. She was asking if Ruby had come to our house but was told Ruby hadn't been by. My parents saw my brother and me and approached us, asking if we saw Ruby. My mom even checked in our room.

"I told them Ruby seemed fine when she picked me up from school. She talked about how much she liked her new room, and she told me it had a comfortable bed, and she loved her hideaway room. She was happy about it and told my teacher too. Her mother sat down as if she was about to faint. Looking at my mom and uttering, 'she spoke of the room. I told her never to speak of it.' She kept repeating that over and over again. I explained to the adults Ruby was just excited about the room and didn't think she had to keep it a secret from me.

"My mother listened intently as Ruby's mother spoke of her nightmare, waking her to find a missing Ruby. She said she had a dream and could see a shadow of a witch; she somehow just knew it was a witch, she knew it was something evil and mean. She explained to my mother the witch lurked around the house and crept outside the back porch. In her dream, she heard cackling and growling that was so ferocious. She even said she tried crying out to Jesus but was paralyzed and couldn't speak. There were no words, nothing would come out of her mouth.

"Her mother said she saw a silhouette pass by with evil laughter and then instantly saw another, smaller shadow following behind her.

Both shadows appeared to merge and vanish. She told my mom how scary and real the nightmare was, then she stepped outside to wait for my dad to get dressed to help her look for Ruby.

"They went to Ramona's first. My dad told my mother she didn't even wait for him to stop the car; she jumped out while it was still rolling and ran up the porch steps, falling several times. She banged on the door, but no one answered. My dad kicked the door down, and when they entered Ramona's kitchen, they found her slumped over, dead with blood on her face from something she just consumed."

Maria looked at us before she continued sharing the story of Ramona. "She must have known she was dying. She had written instructions to have her body burned within three days of her death and her ashes scattered among the trees in the back of her property. My dad said she couldn't have been dead for too long because the candles were still burning and Ramona wasn't yet cold to the touch. She had just consumed an animal as there were animal parts in her kitchen next to bloody knives." Charlie flinched as Maria described the bloody mess left behind by Ramona."

"They called for the police, but Ruby's mother didn't wait with my father. He told her to take his truck and continue to look for Ruby, and he would send the police to look for her, too, once they arrived at Ramona's. Luckily, Ruby was found asleep in her room. She wasn't in her safe room, just her bedroom. Her mother wondered if, after the nightmare, she just missed Ruby, but she was screaming for her. Her mother knew she would have certainly woken a sleeping Ruby if she was in the house. She hadn't understood how she would have missed her. She was certain she checked the bedroom, but after so much panic and rushing around, she couldn't be certain.

"Ramona left Ruby and her mother money and homes, including this one across the street over there." Maria pointed across the way at the old brown house.

"My parents left this one for me, and well, Ramona left that one for Ruby, I guess. My family had no idea Ramona owned that property. Strange coincidence I suppose." Maria laughed and shook her head. "It was in Ruby's mother's name until Ruby was an adult, at least that's my understanding." Maria explained.

"Ruby and her mother weren't very close after the night Ruby went missing. Only a few days after Ramona's passing, Ruby's mother had a stroke and became quadriplegic, no longer able to walk or speak. She was so young; it was such a shame.

"Ruby's aunt moved in and helped take care of her, for a little while anyway. Ruby's aunt became afraid of her. She wasn't the young lady she used to be. Ruby's aunt thought her to be wicked and mean. She accused Ruby of being mean to her mother, which surprised me because growing up, Ruby loved her mom so much.

"I didn't see Ruby again for many years. Her eyes, once so innocent and mesmerizing, seemed dead the last time I looked into them. Her smile and laughter, once so contagious, was no more. She was not the young lady I knew as a child. She had bad energy. She wouldn't come over because of my silly *superstitions,* and she hated my crosses and my faith, so I only added more to keep her further away. She was not the happy girl I knew in Mexico.

"She also didn't like Dulce." Maria gave a sad look to Dulce. "I think was because Dulce was protective of Lucy across the way. At least Dulce stayed out of Ruby's way," she explained to Charlie, who was very interested in the history Maria was sharing with her.

Dulce chimed in and explained to Charlie that she came to live with Ruby when her father remarried. "My dad knew Ruby and her family for many years. He was working on Ruby's house across the way when she offered to let me stay there. Once my dad got remarried after my mom passed away, I didn't want to move away with his new family. I wanted to stay in Texas since I grew up here. Ruby said she could use the help around the house," Dulce explained.

Ruby always hated me, so I'd often find myself here with Maria. As soon as I met Maria, she treated me like family and welcomed me with open arms. I wish my dad would have known Maria so I could have just lived with her instead." Dulce gently and lovingly embraced Maria's hand. "Your home was always my safe haven," Dulce explained. "I came here and escaped from the nightmares Ruby would put upon me. To escape the dirty looks and the many cold nights that I woke to growls and screeching in the next room."

Maria hung her head low with sadness. "Ruby was never the same after the night Ramona died. Then Ruby's mother had a stroke shortly after that. It was hell," Maria explained. "Ruby changed. Ramona passed her fortune along to Ruby's mom and Ruby, which helped financially, especially after her mom's stroke. Ruby kept to herself and turned down offers to help her with her mother. My parents offered help to her around the house and yard, but their offers would go ignored. It was very strange. My parents kept my brother and me away from Ruby after that. She seemed very bitter and not herself anymore."

As Charlie and Dulce were getting ready to leave Maria's, Dulce expressed her concern. "I think Ruby was possessed somehow." Based on what they heard, Charlie and Dulce *both* suspected it was a real possibility.

When they walked out of Maria's house, Charlie looked next door at my childhood home, giving it a once over, looking at the living room window that the witch would tap on to taunt me. She glanced at the bedroom window that was once covered with layers upon layers of leaves caked on by a witch who had been toying with me. Finally, as they rounded the corner, Charlie looked into the backyard that used to dawn a beautiful Oak tree but was now a small, barely visible stump after being killed by a demon and cut down to the ground.

In the car, Charlie and Dulce were quiet as they decompressed. After about half an hour, Charlie pulled over to get gas, and when she got back into the car, she asked Dulce if she read the books written by Topaz. Dulce hadn't read them. At that point, she had only read my granny's journals and quickly flipped through some of the books. She was most mesmerized by the art drawn in the books.

Charlie pulled over down the road from Dulce's house. Dulce took off her seatbelt and looked at Charlie. Both sat quietly. "I can tell your wheels are spinning; what are you thinking?" Dulce asked.

"When did Ruby disappear or die?" Charlie asked. "I started to ask Maria, but I was so enthralled in her account of Ruby's childhood, I didn't get to it."

Dulce confirmed Ruby did go missing, and it wasn't until years later Maria found out Ruby died and left properties and money to some friend of hers or something. Maria didn't tell Dulce much more than that, and at the time, Dulce wasn't interested in asking questions.

"It's a shame that Ruby seemed to hate Maria in their adult life. Maria didn't bring it up, but I think she was really heartbroken when Ruby changed. As a little girl, Maria cherished her so much," Dulce shared. "Maria said there was so much death when I left the neighborhood. Animals were dying, missing and diseased. The neighborhood felt haunted or cursed somehow. I think that is another reason she wanted me to stay away from the area.

"Initially, I found it upsetting that Maria never mentioned a word to me about Lucy dying when I was younger. I know she assumed I would come back to see Mia and get sucked into whatever was going on there. Truth is, I probably would have.

"I spoke with Maria many times over the years, and she never mentioned it and that bothered me but I guess I can understand her concerns and fears. I stayed away from the old neighborhood. I admit, I tried to forget it. I guess I feel guilty too, like I also abandoned Lucy. I had been so protective of her and felt a strong sense of duty to her. She was really something special, and I took my first chance to get away and leave everyone behind. I feel at fault for her passing too," Dulce admitted as she was getting choked up.

Charlie consoled Dulce, assuring her that my death wasn't Dulce's fault. "Maybe it wasn't really Maria.. maybe Ruby sent you away. Maybe you were willed away from Lucy so that you couldn't save her," Charlie suggested. "OK, I'm just thinking out loud. I need to get my thoughts in order." She said.

Dulce reached into her bag and grabbed a pen and paper to take notes. Charlie giggled. "Take notes in your spiral, old-school." They both laughed. "I am going to record my initial thoughts on my recorder, and we can add more as we think of things. I'd like to get organized this weekend before we meet with Lucy and her family." Charlie explained.

Then Charlie became serious and said, "I think Lucy's grandma knew about Ruby from this Topaz chick—maybe even years before Mia and Lucy were even born, as absurd as that may sound. I think these books were written and existed simply to safeguard Lucy and maybe even Mia from the devil's right hand. Hear me out." Charlie knew what she was chewing on seemed very wild and unimaginable. "I find it strange that these books that were sent, written by their grandma's good friend, a high priestess of a coven, were an accident or coincidence. I think these books were actually designed to help Lucy hide from Ruby, even after death. I don't think it's by chance that Topaz wrote these books, divulging secrets of underground magic, things most witches don't even know about.

"With every secret on bending the rules of magic, she reminded the intent of bending magic was for protection only, not for selfish reasons. Once you expose yourself to darkness, you're vulnerable to Satan. She cautioned that probably a hundred times throughout the books." Charlie explained.

"In her books, Topaz speaks about bending magic and hiding your soul in the shadows from demons, witches and those transforming into earthly devils. I believe she somehow knew how to hang on and navigate beyond death. Topaz referenced letting go, making peace and crossing over when it was your time to go. She also warned about doing it when it was safe to cross over."

Dulce wasn't resistant at all. Something in the pit of her stomach knew what she was hearing was the truth. "Wow! Wouldn't that be something to know and have that power? It would be so tempting to turn to dark magic if you never had a moral compass or a conscience, especially if it were glamorized or even forced upon you," Dulce said. And, at that moment, I think she felt pity for Ruby.

Charlie continued. "In the last book I read, *The Golden Book of Sorcery,* she talks about the undead living among us. She calls them Havacavters. Topaz explains that when a witch practices devil worship, she can sell her soul to live forever IF she is strong and her soul is strong enough—at least as strong as a demon. She can sell her soul to Satan, but the price is owing him the souls of each person she overtakes as well, damning them both for eternity—snatching souls to become more powerful, more godlike. A soldier for Satan when the time to end the world is upon us.

"The Havacavter begins as a dominant witch grows strong and Satan moves him or her to his front lines. The witch jumps from body to body as they age or get sickly, all while trading the strong souls to Hell to build *his* army. They trade in young, vulnerable souls, enlightened souls to Satan. The innocent souls, well, they have to be old enough to be aware but young enough to be vulnerable.

"The book says twelve years to sixteen is the prime age to overtake the innocent person. The stronger the aura, the more gifted the soul, the more enticing it is for Satan. He has some but very little interest in ordinary souls. They must have strong attributes and strong connections to God or earth. He covets power and innocence. He wants to smother those with good souls out before the *Rapture.*" She sighed.

"Well, that's what the book says. Once Lucifer agrees, a demon inhabits the witch for each soul they take. The witch is willfully possessed by the demonic, no longer with a human soul. She trades her old or ill body with a healthy one, taking their soul and becoming more powerful. The only time a witch that inhabits another person's healthy body will leave that body for another is when they *have* to. If they are forced out. They will even jump into an unhealthy body if it is vulnerable. It will only be temporary until they find another healthy, strong host to occupy.

According to the books, they sell themselves for an eternity to Satan, damning themselves and the souls they overtake for a new body to walk the earth, wreaking havoc."

"I think Ramona took Ruby, and you do, too. Don't you?" Charlie asked.

Dulce was, once again, tapping her chest nervously. "I'm afraid to talk about this," Dulce admitted. "Ramona took Ruby and damned her innocence." A single tear streamed down her cheek. "Ruby killed Lucy to inhabit her body and promised her soul to fucking Satan, didn't she?!"

"I believe so, but Lucy—with help from an enchantress and her magical granny—slipped between Ruby's fingers. Lucy's been hiding. Hiding and running from a deviant witch. Dulce, we must help her continue to hide her soul and figure out what to do."

Charlie dropped Dulce at her home, meeting her husband only briefly before heading out to see Mia on her way home to share with her what she learned. As Charlie pulled up to Mia's house, she saw Mia and Tyler's cars were gone. However, there was an unfamiliar car in the driveway. Jacob was outside with an older lady; it was our mom. Charlie approached and introduced herself. Our mom explained she was watching Jacob while Mia and Tyler were helping a friend move.

Once Charlie got back to her house, she instantly knew something wasn't right. She sat in her car and waited in the driveway. Charlie debated what to do as the hairs on the back of her neck stood up. She swallowed her fear; she knew she would have to go inside eventually.

Charlie decided she would not succumb to fear and feel unwelcome or afraid in her home, so she headed towards the door. She was much too headstrong to leave out of fear, and I admired that about her. It reminded me of my mom at the time Deon ran out of our old house in fear. My mom didn't ever leave her own home out of fear of the unknown. She stood her ground.

Tucking her fear deep inside, Charlie stepped into the house, holding a cross; she was quite unconventional. She purposefully left the recordings and the books in the back of her Jeep for safekeeping.

Inside the house, Charlie spoke loudly. "I am addressing you demons and Satan himself. Get the fuck out of my house. I carry favor with God, and you have no authority to be here. You have no power in my home. Get the fuck out!"

The presence lingered and an undeniable stench of sulfur began to fill the air. "You are not welcome in my home. You are not scaring me," Charlie continued. She was panicking but did her best to show calmness in the situation.

Charlie glanced into the mirror in her living room and quickly turned around, looking at the back wall. She was screaming, "GET THE FUCK OUT OF MY HOME IN THE LORD'S NAME!" However, she was having a difficult time getting the words out of her mouth. The words were slurring and coming out slowly, but she managed to keep repeating for the monsters to leave her home and commanded them to do so in the name and the power of the Lord. She was compelling and relentless, continuing to slur and push the words out of her mouth.

Then, the dark forces left abruptly. I was relieved because I wasn't sure if I would be able to stay below the surface of the light much longer and feared they would soon apprehend me for Ruby. It had been odd for me to hear Charlie cuss and use the power of God in the same sentence. Charlie was really something. She was very unique and quite a badass in my opinion.

Once the fog lifted, she told me, "I am not a witch; I am not like you or your grandmother with gifts of magic and sorcery, but I do have my black girl magic." She quipped. "Those evil fucks are not about to push me out of feeling safe in my home. Not today and not any day."

I loved that about her. She was a strong woman. I was very thankful we had Charlie's help.

Chapter Sixteen
The Onlookers

Charlie explained to me what she knew—or at least what she thought. "Lucy, they are searching for you, babe. Your soul was promised to Satan by Ruby. They will continue to hunt you. We must figure out our next steps." I remained quietly in the shadows, listening. Charlie continued. "I am copying the tapes tonight of Maria's stories and the thoughts I have on the matter, then taking them to Mia and Lily, so we can be on the same page."

Charlie was excellent at keeping me informed about what they were doing. I think she was trying to reassure me she had a plan to help me. This was by far the biggest investigation she was ever tasked with as a paranormal investigator. "I think I know my next steps but need to revisit the books and journals. I must get this right. I will read the books aloud and record those, too, so you can also hear those along with the information from Maria. You need to know what to do when the time is right," Charlie said calmly and very matter-of- fact.

I wish I had kept my promise to Granny before she died. I just thought there was time, no urgency. Ruby left to take care of her mother. She had stopped bothering me, and I guess I wasn't even thinking of her or afraid anymore. I had been a foolish girl. I failed my granny once and wasn't going to fail her again. I was no longer a child. I was dead, but I was wise and ready to fight and compete against evil for my soul.

Charlie cleansed her house, the sage filling the rooms, and she opened the windows, the fresh air breezing through the house, releasing the smell of rotting Hell. Charlie cleared the space of evil that lingered behind.

When she opened her front living room window, she spotted an SUV with blacked-out windows parked at the curb across the street. Charlie recalled Mia telling her of the demon she saw when she was younger and then again when we left Lily's. She knew they were watching because they needed to find me. I could feel the sense of desperation that lingered in the house. Charlie knew what was in the SUV and suspected this was no ordinary demon; this was something more. This demon was referred to as the observer or the on-looker in the book written by Topaz that Charlie had read. It watched and hunted for Satan.

This demon has belonged to Satan for centuries; another fallen angel. Like Satan, he fell from Heaven, then chose Satan to be his black angel, acting as Satan's unworldly slave after selling his soul for power and rank. His ego had gotten so big, and he wanted to topple the hierarchy in Heaven, so he was cast out. Sometimes, the trash really does take itself out.

Charlie knew profanities and yelling could provoke it, so she knew she needed to be better prepared next time. She did feel fear but didn't want to expose herself and her vulnerabilities to it. She wouldn't back down. The SUV's window began to slowly lower. I know it wanted to scare her and intimidate her, but Charlie looked on without flinching. Then she grabbed her Bible off the shelf nearby.

Oddly, Charlie began speaking Topaz's words and incantations while holding the Bible close to her. Her voice grew louder and louder, and once again, somehow, Topaz's words rattled the gates of Hell. The SUV abruptly pulled away from the curb.

Clearly shaken, Charlie said the Lord's prayer, then she said to me, "They're not getting your soul, Lucy. Topaz's books and your granny's journals are going to guide us, and we will save your soul." Charlie had so much commitment in her voice.

The tapes were recorded that evening into the early hours of the following morning by Charlie, who then dropped them off to my sister, Dulce and Lily that afternoon.

As the week drew close to an end, it was finally my time to speak once Charlie called upon me. My sister still didn't tell my mom about contacting me, worried that my mother would be upset, but Charlie knew something must be done to save my soul from the underworld. She believed in everything written by Topaz and Granny. This gave me relief and peace of mind that she could really help me cross over successfully.

Lily and Dulce listened to the tapes together. Lily was afraid and really didn't want to attend the séance they were planning on Saturday. I hate calling it that. I don't know why, but that's exactly what it was: a séance for the living dead girl who had become a nuisance and burden to her family, once again causing hurt and sadness.

I was sick of it all and ready to put it behind me, regardless of the price I would have to pay. I wanted to go to Heaven but feared it would be impossible now. The best I could hope for would be purgatory, which is where I believe I had been before coming back to the living world. I feared if they failed in their attempt to help me cross over, I would be doomed and would spend eternity in Hell, forced to fight on the wrong side of the war of *Revelations.*

Lily confessed to Dulce she had been using antidepressants since everything started. She and her husband weren't trying to get pregnant again at this point, due to her high stress level. It was all my fault and I hated it; it was so unfair to everyone. A part of me wanted to give up, give in.

Lily shared that she too now has been having dreams of crows flying toward her, and after a recent dream, she woke up and her yard was flooded with crows so much, so she felt afraid. "Crows in my yard by the hundreds appeared, cawing in the middle of the night. My neighbor across the street even called me out of fear and asked me about it."

Dulce reminded her that crows signified transformation, and warnings. Granny spoke of crows in her journals, just as she spoke of crows and grackles to me once upon a time. "I don't think the crows are intended to scare you. They're signifying the impending battle of what is on the horizon—your dreams, the crows showing up. I think they are being sent to prepare you." Dulce zipped her jacket and smiled at Lily. "Don't come if you're afraid but know that I've had similar dreams. I am ready for this battle—ready to help Mia and her family so Lucy can have the peaceful transition into Heaven that she deserves.

Mia will understand if you don't want to join us. Besides, Ruby will only feed off your fear."

Lily sat quietly then smiled at Dulce. "Fuck the devil! I may be high on Xanax, but I will be there!! I will be there for my best friend and her little sister."

Dulce laughed. "Hey, bitch, I thought I was your bestie." The ladies giggled and hugged.

Before the séance, Charlie and I arrived at Mia's house early. My mom was there to pick up Jacob, sitting on the couch next to Charlie.

"I see on your Jeep that you're a paranormal investigator. Are you here because of Jacob seeing things?"

Mia came and sat down beside them before our mother could begin her inquisition. "What do you mean, Mom?" she asked, worrying about what my mom may have heard from Jacob. Although they'd been careful and quiet, she wanted to make sure Jacob hadn't saw or overheard anything new.

"Jacob told me about the man-dogs, as he calls them, in his room. He was upset because they told him they hate him and they asked if he wanted to see Aunt Lucy in Hell. He said you knew, Mia," my mom said gruffly.

My mom was pissed because Mia hadn't told my mom that Jacob was seeing things or afraid. It would terrify her; it was terrifying to even think about it. Tyler and Mia lied; they told her they were fumigating the house and that's why they stayed with her the day the demons were in Jacob's room. Our mom figured out that wasn't the truth; their house was heavy with negativity. It felt familiar. It felt like our childhood home after our dad passed away. "Jacob is staying with me; I hope you all will undo whatever has happened here," my mom said, giving them a warning. She looked Mia in her eyes then backed off her strong stance. She was always vulnerable when looking into Mia's eyes. My eyes. *Our* eyes. A part of me was always there when she looked at Mia.

"Yes, ma'am. I'm here to get rid of them for good," Charlie chimed in, breaking the weird tension consuming the room.

My mom then asked, "Will you be able to help Lucy cross over? I think she came with us when I moved away, and I worry she needs help crossing back over. Please tell her I love her." Before Charlie could speak, my mother went on. "The weird thing is, I lived in our house, her childhood home, for years and years after she passed away and was always so sad because I could never feel her. I feel her more now than I have in any of those years." I swear my mom looked in my direction, as I was tucked into the shadows as I followed along with Charlie to Mia's house. It was almost as if she could feel my presence.

"I hope you can cross Lucy over peacefully; my mom knew how to do that stuff, but I never had that ability, or at least never wanted that knowledge, I guess," our mom explained to Charlie. "I feel Lucy sometimes, and I think she can't get to Heaven. She was a lot like my mom. They both had the ability to see things and cast innocent spells, but my mom grew up with other people who taught her and helped her skills. Lucy had some natural gifts, but she never had anyone like her granny did that could really teach her and guide her understanding of magic. Her granny worked with her a little bit one summer before she passed away. It was innocent, but I still didn't like it. My Lucy was naturally gifted and had powerful visions. She was so receptive to the afterlife. If only she could have seen and prevented her drowning. I never encouraged her gifts. I hoped they would just go away, to be honest." My mom's chin quivered and her broken heart hurt me. I wanted nothing more than to hug her and never let her go.

My mom touched Mia's hands. "We never had gifts like Granny and Lucy, but I think Jacob does, and we need to protect him. I have a bad feeling. I'm glad Charlie is here to help. We need to send whatever is bothering Jacob far away." Mia nodded in agreement. Our mom looked at Charlie and pleaded, "Please see if you can contact Lucy and find out if she needs help. Please make sure my baby is okay." My mom took a deep breath, looking so sad. "If you contact her...I'd also like to know where her remains are so we can lay her body to rest. Maybe that's why her spirit is restless," she said. I could tell the words haunted her and washed over her with sadness as she thought about my remains being trapped in a swamp like pond or even scattered about the wildlife and discarded like trash somewhere.

As my mom and Jacob left, I was paralyzed with sadness. It was apparent my mom had really been thinking and worrying about me even still. Even after my death, she worried for me. She took Jacob to his room to gather a few things and left to take him to her house.

My sister and Charlie began going room to room to prepare, when suddenly, the doorbell rang…and rang. To my sister's surprise, it was Sophie.

Mia turned to Charlie. "It's my good friend. I wasn't expecting her." Mia went to the door and opened it.

"I have been calling you all morning!" Sophie said in an excitable voice. "I need to talk to you!" Sophie entered the house and then noticed Charlie. "Oh, my gosh. I am so sorry. I didn't realize you had company. I saw the Jeep parked at the curb but thought maybe that was for the house across the street." Sophie paused and looked out of the glass door slowly. "Paranormal?" she questioned. "Are you, like, a Ghostbuster?" Sophie asked, being cheeky but also being serious.

Mia looked at Sophie and smirked. "This is my good friend, Charlie. Charlie, meet my good friend, Sophie." The ladies shook hands, politely greeting one another.

"I'm sorry to intrude. I was just so upset and needed someone to talk to," Sophie said. She was hesitant to talk about it in front of Charlie.

"Girl, Charlie knows all my dirt, and she is not judgmental, so you can dish to her too; she doesn't care." Mia said, and they laughed.

Mia set a cup of coffee down before Sophie. "I'm worried I made a mistake moving and taking this other job that I start on Monday. I met my new boss at my office to get my keys and meet the employees. When I was getting ready to leave, my manager called me over to meet one of our largest depositors at the bank, a lady named Lacy. She was so gorgeous and elegant. She was wearing red Louboutin heels, and I thought of you. But…there was just something about her—very glamorous yet cold and distant. I was intimidated by her, but at the same time drawn to her. She was probably about my age and she has a successful real estate company and an elite customer." Sophie sipped on her coffee and looked at my sister with a serious expression.

"She looked through me and said '*I know you and the company you keep*.'" She was rude and my boss seemed as uncomfortable during the introduction as I did. It was strange how familiar she seemed. The crazy part is her eyes. They were just like yours, Mia! Odd as it may be, she seemed like…well, you in some peculiar way!" Sophie exclaimed.

Charlie excused herself and went to the next room and I felt I was supposed to follow and so I did. Charlie said to me, "Lucy, I need to protect you at all costs, and I am concerned your presence will throw off the investigation. I don't know what it is about Sophie's customer, but I want to eliminate my suspicion and concern. Please, please stay here for now and hide away in case we have visitors again." I stayed away as Charlie went back into the living room.

Mia looked at Charlie with concern. Charlie's suspicions of Lacy were *my* suspicions of Lacy. Mia's suspicion too. Something about that seemed too uncomfortable and off. Could it be that Lacy's hostile treatment of Sophie was because she felt her connection to Mia? I don't believe in coincidences. Neither did Charlie nor Mia at this point. "Well." Charlie said. Mia looked at her. "Let's see if we can get a peek at this Lacy chick." Sophie stood up, ready to take the ladies to her new side of town now.

As they exited the house, Mia turned to Charlie. "Could it be possible?"

Charlie assured her, "Seems crazy, but we are about to find out."

Dulce then called from her office and said, "Hey, something's brewing."

Charlie nodded. "Yeah, something definitely is. We are about to go to North Dallas; you in?"

Dulce looked at her calendar. "I have a seminar I was supposed to attend but let me see if I can get out of it." Dulce hung up and called Lily to cancel their attendance of the seminar before texting Mia saying she would be joining.

"Pile in with us, Sophie!" Mia said.

The three of them loaded into Mia's silver SUV and headed out to pick up Dulce, and to their surprise, Lily joined.

"This is turning into a big field trip!" Sophie said jokingly. Charlie looked into the rearview mirror.

Mia chimed in. "Ladies, Sophie is my good friend." They made their introductions before Mia shared with the crew: "Sophie doesn't know anything about the project we are working on."

Sophie looked left and right. "Well, someone fill me in," she said. The car ride became quiet.

"Someone fill *me* in on what's in Dallas!" Lily added to the conversation.

Dulce began by explaining the wild experiences Mia had been undergoing since moving our mom. She spoke of the visions, being followed, the books and journals. Not one time did Sophie interrupt; she listened intently. Mia assumed Sophie was regretting joining them and found it to all be a bunch of malarky, but Sophie believed every word of it. "I know Mia well enough to know she is a sharp, sophisticated woman, so if she believes, I believe without question," Sophie explained to the ladies.

Charlie filled the ladies in on Sophie's encounters with the lady, Lacy. Lily sighed. "Mia, you sure have many ladies that love and support you."

Mia smiled. "I sure do love y'all."

Charlie added, "Your granny would say you have a lot of good crows in your life. A murder of crows."

Dulce laughed. "You're right, Charlie. That's what a group of crows is called. A murder. Maybe we should name our gang."

They all laughed; it seemed the joking was relieving the stress and worry each one felt.

As they pulled into the real estate office parking lot owned by Lacy, Sophie immediately leaned to the front seat and shook Mia.

"I see her," Mia said solemnly. She turned to Dulce, who was sitting in the back.

Dulce had tears welling up in her eyes. "What's going on? That's Lucy, isn't it?" Dulce asked Mia.

Sophie piped up. "No, that's Lacy. Oh…" She realized Mia and Dulce felt that Lacy was, in fact, me. At least my body, I suppose.

Mia just sat there, frozen. "That's my baby sister." She sat there quietly. "I'm going to confront her." Mia took off her seatbelt and put her hair into a ponytail, taking off her earrings. She was preparing to get physical if need be. She was pissed that someone was living what should have been my life!

"Sit tight. I need you all to be cool," Charlie said, then turned to face everyone. "We aren't up against a woman. We aren't up against a basic witch casting a spell against you or me. She's much more than that. I just want to walk past her and engage her." Charlie slid the recorder she used in ghost hunting into her jacket pocket. "Let's see what she has to say." She placed a trinket around her neck. It was similar to a rosary and had something that looked like an evil eye on the end next to the cross. "My all-seeing eye." She pointed to the trinket. It looked eerily similar to the one granny sometimes wore, but it wasn't the same one. "I did the guarding ritual in Topaz's book using this trinket I made like the book instructed to protect me. Now, cross your fingers and toes that I performed the ritual correctly."

Everyone playfully laughed and crossed their fingers. At this point, they were willing to go out on a limb—except Mia. She didn't laugh; she was locked in on Lacy.

Charlie looked at Mia and handed her a specially blessed trinket identical to hers. "I will be right back. Now, duck down so you aren't seen."

Charlie walked across the parking lot briskly so she could engage with Lacy before she reached her car. "Hi! I'm sorry to bother you, but my husband and I were looking for houses, and I was told you were the lady to see!"

Lacy unlocked her car, placing her handbag into the back seat. "I don't show houses, but you can go inside and set an appointment with any of the agents; they're all wonderful." Lacy smiled.

Charlie just stared at her. "Sorry to stare. You're just so beautiful, Lucy," Charlie said with intent. She got a surprising reaction.

"Thank you." She didn't correct Charlie.

They stared at each other. "OK, I'm going to set an appointment inside. It was nice talking to you, *Lucy*," Charlie said again, hoping for a reaction by calling her by my name instead of calling her Lacy.

Lacy watched as Charlie walked away then shot a look over to the SUV, but she couldn't see in. Perhaps it was the sun blocking her sight, but I believe it was the trinket working its magic.

"I'm about to shit my pants!" Lily said, her stomach going wild with nerves. The girls wanted to laugh, but they were too afraid to move.

Charlie went inside the building, asked for Lacy's business card and a few other agents, and then exited, catching Lacy's attention once again.

Lacy got into her car and left. Charlie hurried over to Mia's SUV and Mia slid out of the driver's seat so Charlie could drive. As they pulled away, she said, "No one get up. I need to stay back so she doesn't get the license plate." Charlie explained. Mia said, "I don't have a front plate on, so you have to keep her in front of you."

No sooner than they started driving than Mia got a bad and all too familiar feeling. "Charlie, look to your right. Do you see anything unusual?" Mia asked as she was still on the floorboard of the passenger seat hiding.

Charlie casually looked to her right, then looked forward, keeping her composure. "I see it. I see. I see." It was that same blacked-out SUV. Charlie immediately turned to the left, drove down the road, and pulled into a church parking lot, where she saw a towering, tall man walking to his car.

The blacked-out SUV drove slowly past them, not turning into the church behind them. Charlie wanted to be safe but also give the illusion that she was going to the church as planned, and not because of the SUV following. Charlie walked toward the church as the SUV proceeded past.

"Can I help you?" the man turned away from his car, looking at Charlie. She thought he had a kind smile, and she could see the kindness in his eyes. He was an older gentleman, but he had a naive innocence about him.

"I felt I was being followed, so I stopped here. I'm sorry. I'm leaving," Charlie said in an apologetic tone.

The man nodded. "Smart lady. This is a good place to come to be saved," he jested. "I will walk you to your car." And he did. Before Charlie got in, he asked her, "Can we pray together? I feel very strongly that I need to pray with you. For you."

Charlie touched her heart. "Please do; that would mean a lot to me."

They prayed together. It was a beautiful moment. The man explained that he was the pastor of the church and was supposed to be gone hours ago, but for some reason, he felt the need to stay and wait. For what, he wasn't sure of, but now he knew. The pastor pointed to Mia's SUV. "I am praying for all of you." He somehow knew the others were hiding. "Protect yourselves and proceed with extreme carefulness and caution," he warned. As Charlie opened the car door and got in, he leaned forward. "Don't be alarmed, but I think you're right. There appears to be a black SUV waiting for you at the end of the road. Maybe I'm wrong, but go to the right instead, and if it turns to follow you, please call the police," he pleaded. "I will follow you and that SUV if it begins pursuing you." It was as if the pastor knew something sinister was in that SUV. He felt something was off about the situation—more than just some weirdo following Charlie and the ladies.

Lily sat up. "Here is my card; it has my cell phone on it in case you need to call us when we head out." The pastor accepted the business card from Lily and she quickly hunkered back down on the floor. They knew Lacy had the SUV follow, so they remained hiding out of view, as if that would help.

The SUV that was waiting for them did, in fact, turn around as soon as they headed out. It wondered who she was and why she was snooping around. It was most definitely lingering and waiting for Charlie to leave the church.

Mia felt worried that the driver of the SUV knew Mia was with Charlie. She was afraid of provoking the driver. She knew it was the demon. This demon that she had anguished over for years now was once again back in her life.

The SUV stayed on Charlie's tail for a while and she hurriedly pulled off the shoulder on an old country road.

"I'm calling the cops," Sophie said, her hand shaking while holding her phone.

"No," Charlie demanded. "Hold on for a minute." To everyone's surprise, she placed the SUV in park and jumped out. Dulce followed.

The kindhearted pastor followed and parked behind the black SUV, then climbed out, holding his Bible. "This is no man we are dealing with," he explained to Charlie and Dulce. He began to pray aloud. The girls felt afraid while the SUV revved its engine in a threatening manner.

Then, without a second thought, Mia leaped out and walked briskly to the SUV. Everyone was stunned and afraid for her. They gave no hesitation in following Mia. After all, they were a murder of crows.

Mia put her hand on the glass and dragged it from top to bottom, saying, "I'm not afraid of you. You are not disrupting my life anymore." Suddenly, Mia felt dizzy and stumbled as if disoriented. She felt like she would pass out or vomit and instantly regretted the confrontation.

Charlie and Dulce hurried over and supported Mia, one on each side of her to hold her up.

Then, Lily surprised everyone. Once afraid and timid, she was now bold and ready to swing at whatever was in there. She was very protective of Mia and confronted the devilish ghoul. "Leave her alone. You have no authority over her. You are nothing to us!" she yelled to the unmarked SUV. The pastor stepped forward next to Lily, still praying.

Sophie gained courage and whipped open the back door of Mia's Suburban, her adrenaline pumping and heart racing. Without thinking, she went to open the passenger side door of the SUV. "Get the FUCK —" she stopped short and slammed the door shut, stepping away. Then she ran around to the other side to the others, saying, "Let's get out of here." Sophie was trembling.

Everyone hurried back to Mia's vehicle and climbed in. The pastor followed and said, "This is far beyond my scope. Whatever you have provoked, you need to stop engaging in it. I'm worried for you."

Charlie thanked him and assured him that they were fine. She told him she appreciated him and asked him to continue praying.

"You leave. I will stay here, and if the SUV begins to follow, I will call 9-1-1, then I will call you and let you know. Drive safely; be careful and please take this seriously. I believe this is a warning," he said.

Charlie sped off, and everyone was quiet. The only sound that could be heard was the tires on the pavement. The SUV didn't follow this time. The pastor stayed behind, praying.

"Now what?" Mia asked.

Charlie didn't answer, but she did change the subject to a lighter note. “OK, that pastor was a good-looking older man.” The girls laughed.

“He sure was,” Dulce agreed.

The car ride was still intense, even after Charlie’s attempt at humor to relieve the tension. She tried again to ease their minds and calm their fears. “Lily, Sophie…y’all were about to beat some devil ass.” Everyone laughed except Sophie, who simply stared ahead.

She finally spoke. “When I opened the door, it smelled of death, decaying and rotting. You never forget the smell. When I was a little girl, I found a large dog that had passed away in the back of the park near some trees. As soon as I opened the door to the SUV, the smell of spoiled flesh came over me, like that decaying dog at the park I encountered years ago. You never forget the smell of death. The only thing I saw was a young girl with wet, muddy, gray, decomposing flesh. She looked at me, her eyes sparkling blue with the green fleck. It was Lucy; I know it was Lucy, and then she faded away.”

“It was a trick,” Charlie said, matter-of-fact. “A mean, disgusting trick to play with your mind so you would tell Mia. It wants to upset Mia.”

Lily comforted Sophie, who was doing her best to hold back her tears. She began to counsel and comfort her.

“Always the therapist,” Dulce quipped.

“I didn’t see anyone in the driver’s seat, though. It was like the SUV was driving itself. It just doesn’t make sense.” Sophie was puzzled and shaken by what she had witnessed.

“Sophie, you have a long drive back home; it’s late. You are welcome to stay with me if you don’t want to go home,” Mia offered.

Sophie appreciated the offer but really wanted to go home and relax in her own space after such a stressful day. A part of her was also a little afraid to stay at Mia’s.

“Tomorrow, we will be working on communicating with Lucy. You are welcome to join us. I understand if it is too much and too hard for you, but you’re my girl, and if you want to be there, you should be.” Mia extended the invite to Sophie, who had been so brave and unexpectedly defensive of Mia. So much so that she was willing to scrap with a demon for her.

"I will be there!" Sophie exclaimed without hesitation. "This has definitely been a hectic day. A lot to take in, but I will be there tomorrow. I promise."

Charlie and the ladies lit a candle and did a small ceremony, ensuring no unwanted spirits would follow them to their homes. "Tomorrow is the big day. We need our rest; we need to clear our minds." Charlie set the expectations. "I will prepare us. You all eat, get some rest, and be prepared for anything tomorrow. Expect nothing; be open-minded. Pray," Charlie instructed.

When everyone went home, Charlie showered and relaxed only briefly before getting to work, preparing for the next day. Lily and Dulce also researched and worked; Charlie needed their expertise. Mia rested. She went to see our mom and Jacob. There was a large part of her that wanted to put this behind her, and an even bigger part that wanted to help her baby sister find peace. The thought of me dying was hard enough. She couldn't stand knowing my soul might be sold to Satan. She could not let that happen.

The night was long. Everyone was anxious. A restful night would be out of the question for all. Each of the ladies woke throughout the night with anxiety, pounding hearts, and racing minds.

Mia's husband, Tyler, was very supportive of Mia and she felt guilty. Tyler just lost his mother, and he should have been able to focus on his own grief but found himself taking care of Mia and her needs. His love for her was admirable, really. He was her rock, her safety net. I am so thankful she and my mom had Tyler to lean on. He was something special.

Chapter Seventeen
The Bridge

Tyler left the morning of the séance to take Jacob and our mom to breakfast. When he arrived at my mom's house, Jacob ran to him and gave him the biggest hug. I'm sure Jacob was missing Tyler and Mia. There was no doubt our mom was good to him, but Jacob felt homesick.

My mom told Tyler she witnessed Jacob spinning his finger around, and she was perplexed, as it appeared like he was moving the leaves around outside. It freaked her out.

"Let's keep this to ourselves. Mia has a lot going on right now, and that will worry her," Tyler suggested. "If you see him doing it again, let me know, and we will go from there."

"You don't believe me?" my mother asked.

Tyler sighed. "No, I do believe you; that's the problem." They watched as Jacob played and became uncomfortable, as he would close his eyes as they flickered intensely and laughed.

In the meantime, Charlie was pulling her braids into a ponytail, getting ready to help me cross the bridge into the next life by stating her intentions aloud and also praying. Normally, Charlie was very calm and cool, but she was nervous and on edge this morning.

She gathered the journals and books she had been pouring over and picked up my Lucy doll she brought home with her to cleanse to ensure my safety if I needed to go to it for my protection. "What a beautiful little girl you were." Charlie was good about speaking to me, but I do think she felt a little silly at times, essentially feeling like she was speaking to herself. She knew I was there but made it clear she wanted me not to communicate in any way so I would have energy. I didn't feel any different than usual.

"You were robbed of your youth and tormented by a witch. You were robbed of years of living your life. You deserved more. I won't fail you. I can't give you your life back. I wish I could; you deserve it. I vow to keep Ramona, Ruby, Lacy—whatever she is—from harming another child and stealing away their innocence," Charlie swore to me.

She took this very personally. A ghost hunter turned witch hunter. A young woman that tragically lost her dad and opened herself up to the otherworldly beings in hopes of contacting her daddy again someday.

The séance was to be held at Charlie's for a couple of reasons. Mia didn't want to conjure anything that could linger around Jacob. Charlie didn't want me to unintentionally latch on to Mia, causing her to become ill. She also feared if I latched on, Mia would become a target again.

Charlie wanted to control the environment; she didn't want any portals to be at Mia's house. Since Mia has had encounters with the demon on a few occasions now, Charlie has been very careful in keeping dark entities away from her home and her family. If something stayed behind with Charlie, she knew how to cleanse and protect her home. Even if Charlie was fearful, she was strong-minded enough not to give in to her fear. She spent her life learning about the afterlife and investigating. This is what she knew.

On Mia's way to the séance, she received a call from Trina. "I have missed you at work, it's not like you to miss work, and I'm worried about you." Mia asked about Michael and Anthony, making small talk. "I feel I need to see you. Something inside me is telling me to come to see you," Trina explained.

"If I tell you something, will you promise me you won't think I'm crazy?" Mia asked. "Well, I already think you're a little crazy. If you weren't, you'd be ordinary and dull." Trina had her own way of setting Mia at ease. "Meet me for coffee."

Mia and Trina got together at a local coffee shop and visited. Mia was looking forward to getting together with Trina to hug her neck and see how she was doing. Even with everything going on, she would still wonder about Trina and her grandson, Michael. Mia knew how much Trina loved her grandbaby, and she was curious how he was doing now that Mabel wasn't around him and hurting him anymore.

It was normal chit-chat at first. Trina worried Mia was going to leave the bank, and that's really the only reason she still would drive that far for her banking. Mia assured her she just had some personal things going on. Trina told her that Michael had been doing so well and thanked her for giving her the push she needed with Mabel.

Anthony ended his relationship with her daughter, Aja. It was too complicated after that; he didn't trust her and felt differently after she would justify or defend her mother. Mia listened and hoped to dodge the questions she knew were lingering in Trina's mind. Not that she didn't want Trina to know, just that a small part of her knew when she explained it out loud, it made her sound really off, and talking about it seemed to exhaust her. She didn't want to admit it, but she was also paranoid that something was listening to her.

"So, you say you're not psychic, yet you know things. Tell me what's going on, I adore you and would never, ever judge you." Trina reassured Mia again.

Mia explained everything to Trina, pretty much everything from A-Z. No doubt it was a lot to take in—especially if someone never had supernatural experiences before. To Mia's surprise, Trina was not only supportive but very understanding.

"I want to go with you if you need support," Trina kindly offered.

Mia didn't see the harm in having Trina there but wanted to reach out to Charlie first to see if it would create an issue. "I want you to know it's actually not like playing with a Ouija board." Mia warned Trina of the seriousness of the evening events.

Trina understood, and truthfully, she was nervous about attending but felt compelled to go. Mia had been on her mind a lot and felt she was in danger. Trina wanted to partner with Mia and help her through whatever she was battling.

Mia sent a message to Charlie asking about Trina attending. Charlie was surprised someone wanted to come; it wasn't exactly going to be a fun event. It would be a taxing and stressful evening. Charlie wanted to make sure Mia really emphasized this with Trina. Trina needed to understand the risks and the consequences of getting herself involved in the situation.

Mia explained that Charlie was an afterlife specialist and has had many successes in contacting the dead throughout her career. For some reason, I was easy to contact. Mia warned Trina about the demon she encountered and Trina listened. She wasn't skeptical like Mia expected. In fact, Trina told her that her grandparents were very gifted, and she believed very much in spirituality and, yes, ghosts. She shared with Mia that she grew up with a little house ghost at her grandparents.

Her family joked about it, it was harmless, but they all encountered little things here and there. They even named their little house ghost guest, Marlin. Well, Trina's grandmother named him. Trina was always an avid churchgoer.

"I am going to head out to my mom's and see Jacob and take him a few toys on my way to Charlie's. Here's Charlie's address," Mia said as she texted Trina the address. "Be there around five. We will start at about seven, but I'd like you to meet Charlie and everyone else." Trina hugged her, and Mia headed out.

Mia got a call from Trina as soon as she pulled out of the parking lot and onto the highway. She assumed Trina was already backing out and not wanting to go to Charlie's, and she wouldn't blame her. It was a big deal; nothing to play around about. "Hello, my darling?" Mia answered.

Trina was talking in a low tone, just hovering above a whisper. "I am following you. Go to the police station at the next exit." Mia wasn't sure what Trina said and asked her to repeat herself. Trina urged her again to pull over and into the police station. "There is someone in your backseat!" Trina exclaimed.

Mia subtly looked into the rearview mirror, unable to see anything, but took Trina's warning seriously. She exited and went straight into the parking lot of the police station. Trina followed and parked close to Mia. Two police officers came out of the building and approached Mia's car; one had their gun pulled. Mia's heart was pounding, not realizing Trina had called the police for help.

One officer opened Mia's door while the other held his gun on the back passenger door. Mia slowly got out. "I didn't see anyone back there," Mia told the officer, but Trina insisted. "I saw someone, and they laid down quickly."

The officer opened the door, and no one was there, but he pulled back quickly and cupped his nose with his arm. "What was in your back seat, ma'am?!" he asked passionately, appearing concerned.

Mia walked over to the officer. "Nothing, sir." When she neared the open door of the vehicle, she made a gagging sound and covered her nose. "Oh my gosh, what the fuck is that smell?" The other office came near to investigate.

They all had the same look on their faces. "Something dead or rotten has been in this vehicle. Did you hit something or move something lately?" the officer inquired.

"Nothing. I didn't smell anything when I was driving. I don't understand," Mia stated. The police officers seemed skeptical, which upset Mia and Trina.

"OK, well, I know I saw something back there when she was driving and followed her here. It's hot outside; maybe that's the reason the car smells funky when you turn it off," Trina stated.

The police talked among themselves.

"Do we have a problem here?" Mia asked.

"No, ma'am, you seem to be good to go. Get that car looked at, though. Something smells awful in there," the police said in a skeptical tone while the other officer began scribbling down her license plate.

The younger officer approached Mia and Trina. "Here's my info. If you ladies need anything, call me." He moved closer to Mia. "Please don't take this the wrong way, but there's something familiar about you. Do I know you?" He inquired.

She took off her sunglasses. "I'm sorry, but I don't believe so."

He nodded and stepped back. "You have beautiful eyes. I feel like I've seen them before. Maybe in a dream or something." He laughed. Mia took his card and smiled. "I promise I'm not flirting with you. I know it probably seemed that way, and for that, I'm sorry. I am sincere with what I said. Do you have family out this way? I feel like I've met you before." he pressed further.

Mia shook her head. "Sorry, I would have remembered you." He was strikingly tall and handsome. He also had an unusual scar along his cheekbone that she felt certain she would recall.

"Sorry, girl," Trina said and shot the officers a nasty look. Mia walked to Trina's car.

"My friend smelled death in another car that was following us just the other day. I realize this sounds crazy, but I think it means there was a demon in the car. I think. I don't know. I'm worried about getting you mixed up in this. Maybe you shouldn't come tonight," Mia suggested.

"I'm going. I'm already involved. I will be there with you," Trina responded firmly.

Mia arrived at our mom's house and was already feeling exhausted from the mental and emotional strain of the morning. She hugged Jacob tightly before leaving to head to Charlie's.

"Mommy, you are stinky," Jacob said as he backed away from her.

Our mom got closer to Mia. "Is that you? I thought maybe Jacob was tooting after eating all those eggs this morning," she joked. But she suddenly stepped away quickly almost as if she was frightened. She motioned to Tyler, and after he got closer, he also stepped back.

"Are you feeling, OK?" Tyler asked, wondering if maybe Mia had a stomach bug as the stench of sulfur filled the air.

"I feel fine, and I didn't crop dust you. I don't have gas," Mia defended herself, kind of laughing at the fact that they were politely suggesting she was tooting and not feeling well.

Before she could even tell them about the smell in the car earlier, Jacob spoke up. "Don't worry, mamma, it's just Mann. He stinks like that sometimes."

Mia felt the blood rush out of her head. "OK, baby. Love you. Mommy will shower and get this nasty, stinky funk off me."

My mom looked at Mia. "What are you doing? I feel like there's something you aren't telling me." She pulled Jacob to her as if she was safeguarding him.

"Mom, Tyler is going to stay here with you."

Tyler shook his head. "I need to be with you tonight," he insisted, knowing what the plan was and the risks involved.

Mia leaned in and hugged him, avoiding our mother's inquiry. I guess sometimes it's better not to answer questions that shouldn't be asked. Tyler squeezed Mia tight, and she smiled. "Stay with Jacob and my mom. I have Charlie and the ladies. I need you, but Jacob needs you more. I need you to protect our son," she pleaded.

Tyler understood but hesitated as Mia left him to head over to Charlie's house.

Before arriving at Charlie's, Mia called her and brought Charlie up to speed on the events of the day.

"We need to meet before you arrive," Charlie told Mia as she grabbed her keys. Then she said to me, "I will be back." She didn't give an explanation; she didn't have to. I had become very attuned with Charlie. The truth is, I admired her willingness to help me and my family. She wasn't born gifted, but she was open and diligent about studying to strengthen her knowledge of life after death.

Charlie hurried out, but for a split second, I thought she had come back because the door swung open. There was a weird vibe that filled the house. Another door opened and slammed as something was moving about the house very hastily. Another door opened and slammed, then another, opening and shutting without grace—just loud opening and closing as someone or something ran around the house.

Whispers filled the house. I couldn't make out the words; it was another language that was unrecognizable to me. It was unworldly. I felt afraid; I felt trapped.

I slid from the corner of the wall and back into my doll. I knew the doll was a safe place for me even though I feared forever being trapped inside of it. I felt confined and claustrophobic upon entering my Lucy doll.

In the meantime, Charlie met with Mia just around the corner of her home. The first thing Mia asked Charlie was if she smelled like death. "You smell fine to me. Whatever the smell was on you isn't lingering anymore," she commented as she smelled Mia's hair and shook her head, confused. "I wanted to meet to make sure nothing attached itself to you before you came over to my house since we will be calling Lucy to come out of the shadows. I think something was with you but passed through quickly," Charlie explained.

"I know in my gut something is hunting for Lucy in a panic today. I strongly believe something is running in circles, frantically searching for her soul. I have a strong sense and it feels like chaos," Mia said with frustration.

Charlie agreed. "I believe it's Ruby or her demon dogs. They are most likely panicking because they need her, so they don't want us to cross her over. They know we are aware of her, and they want her soul. I fear they know we are close to removing her and working on sending her to Heaven soon. I think they know my plan, and that's why they come to my house too." Charlie explained.

Dread fell over Mia. She called Tyler as she began her drive, following Charlie to her house. "How's Jacob and my mom?"

Tyler looked around the house. "They seem fine. Your mom is making Jacob a snack."

Mia was relieved. "OK, watch our boy," she pleaded again, and, of course, Tyler promised.

As soon as the call ended, another feeling of nervousness flushed over Mia. "Lucy!" she cried out.

Charlie was startled. "Let's go!" They bowed their heads, asking for protection, then Charlie held her trinket up to show Mia. "The protection of Topaz." She smiled.

Mia clutched her chest. "I left mine with Jacob when he told me Mann was at the house. I need him unseen by the demons."

Charlie nodded with understanding and agreement. She placed the trinket into Mia's pocket. "Keep this on you tonight. You need this more than anyone right now. Are you still up for this?" Charlie inquired, almost as if she, herself, was having doubts.

"Lucy needs me, and this time I will be there for her. This is all my fault. Her life was cut short because I didn't go. I didn't protect her."

Charlie smiled at her. "You are a badass sister, and none of this is your fault, but saving her soul is much more important than her earthly body." Charlie kissed her cheek. "Let's go save Lucy!"

As soon as they were in the driveway, Charlie and Mia could sense something off. "Stay here. We have visitors. They're suspecting something, and they're here. They're looking for Lucy," Charlie advised as she got out of her car. The strange thing is, Charlie wasn't a medium. She couldn't see the future, but she was now so in tune with me and my thoughts were as if she was riding the waves of my abilities. "I need to seal them out so they don't know what we will be doing later," Charlie said as she held her finger to her mouth so Mia wouldn't mention the plan. "Sit tight. Give me some time to check things out."

Charlie entered the house and began cleansing the space. Mia was shocked while watching from her car. It was almost like dark sweltering smoke was leaving the house, something you'd see after a fire. The smoke was thick and dense, so much so that Mia began to worry there was something smoldering in the house. Her nervousness was only heightened by what she watched. The smoke fled the house swiftly, and the air began to clear.

Mia received a call from Tyler. "Your mom is upset."

"What do you mean?" Mia asked, slightly trembling.

"Your mom thought she heard Jacob calling for her, so she went to his room. He was sitting with a blanket over his head, calling to her." Tyler took a gulp before he went on to explain. "When she took the blanket off, nothing was there. She said a horrific smell came out from the blanket, and she was taken aback. Jacob was in the closet and she opened the door. He was so frightened. Jacob told your mom that it wasn't him calling. He said they are mad because you won't tell them where Lucy is."

"They?" Mia whispered.

"Your mom said the room became cold quickly, so she grabbed Jacob out of the closet and ran outside on the patio to me. I went in, and the house had a strange vibe. We are going to go to our house. Your mom can stay with us. She was asking for you to come home. She is really freaking out."

Mia's fear turned to anger at those monsters who were toying with her mom and Jacob. "Yes, take mom and Jacob to our house. Charlie and I will be over to do a cleansing of her house tomorrow. We need to get this done tonight. We are going to keep chasing this thing in circles. It's only trying to distract us. I believe it knows we are up to something. I think it's panicking, searching for Lucy." Mia sighed. "Hopefully, nothing will happen at our house once you get there. Just please help me buy some time because I gotta get this done."

Tyler knew Mia was talking about needing to help me cross over, but she was paranoid about listening ears of the demons that were surrounding and closing in on my family pretty aggressively.

Mia was finally able to come into Charlie's house, and as soon as she did, I knew she could sense me—feel me. The other ladies arrived shortly after, and there was a sense of fear throughout the room.

Charlie continued to chant, cleansing the space. She added fresh salt around her home. She blessed the Lucy doll she had hidden away with me now hiding inside it once again. Silence filled the room. Charlie placed the journals and books into the center of the living room rug and neatly placed my soul doll on top with the trinket Topaz had promised would silence any unearthly entities that may be interested in my whereabouts.

Charlie read tarot cards and took notes. Everyone watched her diligently prepare the final touches. Using my granny's and Topaz's ways she learned through reading, she prepared for my séance. My granny would be proud.

Charlie finally looked up. "Shall we begin?" she inquired. She began by opening the communication by praying and asking for understanding and guidance. She needed help in the quest for salvation for my soul.

This was not fun or games for her or anyone else. Everyone took this seriously, and they all had a deafening calmness come over them as they prepared to reach me. This murder of crows that didn't know me was ready to protect me—prepared to help me because they all loved my sister so much.

"Lucy, you are safe with us. Please step out of the shadows and come forward," Charlie pleaded.

I didn't sense anything ominous, so I felt safe coming forward to speak to Charlie. I placed myself in the center, still near to my protective space. I was still a little reluctant to go too far away from my Lucy doll.

"Lucy, can you speak to me and tell me you're ok?"

I began to speak, but my voice was having difficulty carrying through. It was very hard to communicate and quite draining on me. I had been rested, but the stress and hiding were very hectic. I repeated "yes" over and over and could see how elated they were when my voice came through. Trina and Sophie looked terrified but also intrigued. The look on their faces was that of a scared child.

Charlie got into the séance. It was almost as if she was able to place herself into a state of mind that was completely open and free. She studied Topaz's books so thoroughly and took this night seriously, very determined to have success in crossing me over. This wasn't about her work as an investigator anymore. Charlie had become completely invested in helping me.

Before crossing me over, Charlie wanted to go through a series of events to get an understanding of my passing. By now, they all knew it was not an accidental drowning. The ladies believed something dark had lured me to my watery death but needed confirmation. The last thing she wanted to do, of course, was lead me into the arms of the witch, who sold her soul to the devil and hosted demons within her body.

"Take me into the water with you, Lucy. Step into me and let me see what you can see. Show me so I can help you," Charlie said.

I was too guarded; I didn't want to do that—the most vulnerable moment of my life, my death. I just couldn't go back there with a stranger. It was like I was a kid again, so full of fear. Mia knew; she knew I wouldn't want that. She said, "Charlie, she has been attached to me before. I can do this, if you guide us."

Charlie and Mia looked at each other with the same subtle smile.

"I didn't want to put you through the stress, but I hoped you would say that, Mia." Charlie told Mia to lay down, and she placed the blessed trinket and the Lucy doll on Mia's chest then kissed her forehead. I was instantly afraid the demons would be waiting in that memory for me but was assured by Charlie that the trinket would blind them from seeing us as we explored. "Open your third eye. Know nothing of our worldly restrictions."

Everyone locked hands and began praying to themselves as Charlie asked me to latch on to my sister again, this time on purpose. It was easy to do. Mia was an extension of me and wanted to be with me as I crawled back into the cold, murky water—a dreadfully sad moment but something I had to experience again so I could cross over peacefully.

Charlie cautioned Mia, "Do not interact with Lucy or anyone or anything you see, hear or feel. Do not grab attention or they may be able to see you and Lucy. You're just an observer, so you can help report what is happening to us as Lucy transcends the present and lays down in her young body to show you what is happening. You will know when to pull yourself out of this trance." Charlie took a breath, knowing if Mia failed, she and I would both be vulnerable in the dead world.

"Lucy, you will not move about as you die. When it is that time, you will join Mia above you, as she will be observing and talking to us through her with visions only. She will tell us what she sees; you cannot. You must not do anything different. This is only for us to gather information today," Charlie urged so we would not do anything that could jeopardize me or us. She looked at Lily. "OK, do your *thang,* girl."

Charlie and Lily coordinated the séance they had been preparing and working together. Once I was successfully attached to Mia, Lily would lead me through my nightmare—my reality of dying through hypnosis.

"Mia, your mind is at ease; you're drifting up above your body and can only see what Lucy will see. Your mind is not thinking of anything other than the words of Lucy's; you see and feel what she sees and feels." Lily's words began to echo and fade out as Mia was subconsciously in my world. Lily proceeded. "Lucy, you are in the water with Mia. She sees and feels what you see and feel. Show us."

Charlie and the ladies began breathing in deeply in sync, and the room fell to a somber rhythm. "Walk us through, Mia. Lucy must stay silent in the shadows."

It was quiet. Mia began to shiver and tears streamed down her eyes and onto the rug she lay on. Her lips were turning a shade of haunting blue, and her lips trembled as her teeth chattered. "I'm so cold."

Sophie pulled a blanket off the chair behind her to cover Mia, but Charlie held her hand up for her to stop. Sophie draped the blanket along her arm and her lap. She wanted to comfort Mia, but Charlie needed Mia to feel and see what I was going through without interference.

"Lucy was swimming upward to the surface but is being pulled and swept away. Leaves are swirling around her like a hurricane brewing in the pond. Lucy is swallowing water and leaves and trying to call out, but she can't. She sees a limb and reaches for it, just then spotting a man wearing a denim jacket. He pulls her out, and Lucy feels relieved. A gurgling noise comes from her mouth as water seeps out, and she is gasping for air. It sounds like a squeal as she is attempting to clear her airway. The man covers her mouth, almost as if he doesn't want anyone to hear her." Mia continued to shiver, and her tears flowed hard and fast as she watches this man throw me into the back of his truck.

"He is tossing her into the back cab of his truck. It's white and..." she pauses. "Frank and this man…they took Lucy. He looks younger, but this is him. It's the same son of a bitch!!" Mia was so loud, almost shouting at us."

Charlie was worried Mia's anger would carry over. She nudged Lily, who glanced at her and nodded.

"Mia, I'm going to pull you out if you get too emotional. Be calm for Lucy. Breathe," Lily urged.

Mia held in her rage and began speaking calmly again, although she couldn't keep her voice from shaking from emotion. "He's driving. Fire trucks and ambulances are passing us, heading to the park. Lucy keeps gasping in the back, just lying there, shivering. He has no interest in helping her. He's taking her away from help.

"He parks and gets out but it's really muddy, and he almost slips. There are other cars here. It looks like we are in an old building, an abandoned church. He's pulling her out of the truck. She is coughing, and he's mad that she can't stand up, and begins dragging her along the ground," Mia whimpered. "My baby sister."

Mia's breathing escalated. "Other men meet him and help her inside. It's dark and there are candles lit. Oh my God, these people are dressed normally, but it looks like... like a devil worship event or something." She began to shake uncontrollably. "Dulce, it is Ruby. They are helping her out of a wheelchair. She looks sick. She is talking to them in Spanish but I don't know what they are saying. They are laying her next to Lucy. They flip Lucy upside down and now she is throwing up water. He reaches into her mouth and starts clearing out gunk and a bunch of leaves, and now she's breathing on her own but appears to be in and out of consciousness." Mia paused. "She's crying for our mom now." My sister took a minute to pull herself together. "They are laying Ruby next to Lucy, and there appears to be gurgling and laughing coming from Ruby without her mouth being open. There are a lot of shadows appearing as if they are *her* shadows. It's eerie. I've never seen anything like this. They are all chanting and speaking in Spanish with murmurs of Latin. I don't know what's going on. There is a loud noise outside, and the door is opening.

"A young man just entered. I think I know him; he looks a bit familiar. He is standing there almost in shock. He asks what they are doing and tells them they are on private property. There is a growl that shakes the church, and he begins to back up. Before he has a chance to run off, Ruby calls for Frank to get him and put him with Lucy."

Dulce covered her mouth when Mia shared what she was seeing and experiencing with me. She knew Frank and his relationship over the years with Ruby. It was Frank that pulled me from the water. Dulce now knew without a doubt he didn't pull me from the water to save me; he pulled me from the water to take me to Ruby. Although the ladies felt this was who hurt me, Mia now seeing it and confirming it, really shook Dulce.

Mia continued. "The boy is about to turn and run, but another man steps into the doorway, and Frank grabs the boy. He is fighting aggressively, but they lay him next to Lucy and put a knife to him. Lucy sits up and tells the boy to run, but Frank moves the knife over to Lucy and tells her to shut up. The boy reaches for her, and as Frank shifts his weight to wrestle with Lucy, the boy escapes. He's running away, and another man takes off after him. Ruby is saying something to Frank and seems angry." Mia was sweating profusely. "High pitch growls and voices are echoing among the church walls. Lucy is trying to pry Frank's hands off her. Everyone is chanting something in Spanish. Frank tosses the knife aside, and now he is straddling her. There are noises I can't explain…not a dog howl but something louder, and it's scary. I don't know where it's coming from. It's almost like it's leaving Ruby's body. One after another, things are coming out of her." Mia was deep in the vision. Her heart was pounding so loudly, I could see Dulce was getting concerned from a medical perspective, but Lily was checking her pulse and keeping a close eye on Mia.

Mia's mind was racing with everything it was taking in. "This is intense. Lucy is moving her leg, rocking it back and forth. She's moving her head back and forth now, trying to stay awake. Frank is still on top of her. It looks like…yes, he's choking her. He's choking her hard now and looking her right in the face. Her eyes are bulging, and I can see the vessels burst in her eye. How can he do that to her? Oh my God. My poor baby." Mia was sobbing and trying to catch her breath. "Oh, my baby; I think she just died. I see something floating up towards me now. I'm certain it's Lucy. It's her soul. She's here with me," Mia said while sobbing. "Lucy is here with me, and we are watching. I think we should go."

Charlie asked Mia what they were doing. "They are doing a ritual. They are panicking, calling for Lucy and looking around. There are sounds and grunting. I can see shadows, and it appears they are going into Lucy's body, but Ruby keeps calling for her.

"I've seen different shadows; I smell sulfur. There is something weird going on. The chanting continues. They are wrapping Ruby into a blanket. Ruby's breathing is very shallow now, but she keeps calling out for Lucy.

"They are pouring something on her. Oh my gosh, it smells like gasoline and something else. OK. Frank is lighting a cigarette. They are all speaking in Spanish and I can't understand them. The man that took off after the boy just came back in. He doesn't have anyone with him; he's alone and has blood on him. I don't know, but I think he hurt the boy, or maybe killed him." Mia was flustered and angry, but she looked on. "Frank just put his cigarette out, and now they just set Ruby's body on fire. The smell and the smoke are overwhelming. They are sitting Lucy up now. I think they are about to burn her too. No, wait. Wait, she's starting to stand up. Lucy is speaking Spanish." Mia was puzzled. "She's talking, and OK, there is something else. Pull me out, Lily. Pull us out. Now, Lily," Mia pleaded, and Lily complied.

Mia rolled onto her side and then to her hands and knees. "They removed Ruby from her body and placed her into Lucy's body. Didn't they?" Mia asked. She was right. No, she wasn't asking to come into my house when I was a kid. She was asking to come and live inside of me and inhabit my body with me. That's exactly what Ruby and her demons, her workers, did.

Ruby had been aging and dying after she ingested the poisoned goat. Once a young, beautiful girl, Ruby's body was inhabited by a witch named Ramona. Ramona sold Ruby's soul to Satan; she grew her magic strong and bold. She had at least three demons that shared her body with her. Ramona invited them in and grew stronger within the occult. Ruby didn't willingly go with them. Ramona left her old feeble body, and she took over Ruby. She promised Ruby's soul to Satan, just as my soul was.

Ruby didn't know how to resist; she was young and unaware of such things existing. She certainly didn't know how to hide in the shadows. Ruby had the gift of seeing things into the future. She was never trained in her gifts. Instead, she would keep them to herself, dismissing them as Déjà vu. Ruby had so many wonderful qualities that she could have drawn on. Instead, Ruby was overtaken by Ramona, the evil witch.

Eventually, what was a sweet and kind young lady was consumed by Ramona entirely—the *Ruby* Maria once knew and loved didn't exist any longer. The two became one in her body. Ramona grew even stronger with every gifted soul she devoured.

The demons could come and go as they pleased. They were the strongest of all demons since they had access daily, feeding on a human with human emotions that never resisted them. They roamed about the earth without detection. The witch welcomed the demons as they drew her even closer to Satan. They didn't even make her feel sick anymore. They were an extension of her now. She was the whore of evil, letting them feast on her body so her soul could grow darker and closer to Satan.

The evil witch, Ramona, that overtook Ruby, had become close to becoming a Havacavter. She needed my soul to reach this dark achievement. Some occults get together to summon the devil. The evil witch had become so close to the devil that he would summon her. She was his slave. She was his mistress. She and the demons would interact with people and direct their souls away from good and God.

The evil witch, Ramona made a deal with the devil long ago to shelter his loyal demons so they could roam about and be his eyes and ears.

I thought of the time my granny told me, 'You can't undo dirty deals. Your soul is for keeps, and he always gets you in the end.' The witch had time to find me, she had never given up. She was always actively looking for me. She promised me to Satan and couldn't fail the *Beast.*

The only fear the evil witch had was that I crossed over and was in Heaven, but she could still sense me about the earth. If I made it to Heaven, she feared her soul would be called back to Hell where she would burn for all eternity, not moving about the earth and enjoying the life she knew. Therefore, she had an urgency to hunt down my roaming soul. The witch had to get me, or she would have an eternity of pain and sorrow never achieving her goal of becoming a Havacavter. Much like the pain and sorrow she bestowed upon those she would take and the families she would leave behind. I know if she had taken my soul and I lived in the body along with her, my family would have never known, just as Ruby's family didn't know.

Ruby's family saw her change and grow evil, but it was dismissed as mental illness and would have been for me as well. To think I would have been like that sickens me, especially because I believe Jacob would have been at risk around me, just as any other innocent, magical, wonderful child being sold to Satan for an eternity in Hell.

One day, Ruby would return to Hell, and she had to have the souls she swore to Satan or she would burn like any other sinner before her that sold their soul for cheap. The problem with the witch was she was strong, and she was here. Topaz could rattle the gates of Hell. She foresaw the witch wanting me before I was even born.

Topaz wrote books and worked with Granny on protecting me. She couldn't stay too long before her time to pass, otherwise she would be stuck in purgatory for eternity until *Revelations,* and so she and my granny did what they could to warn me and protect me against the evilness lurking around this earth, waiting for the battle on Judgment Day.

My mom disdained witchcraft and moved away with my sister and me when we were young kids. She felt creating distance from magic was my best protection. I'm sure she had no idea that eventually a witch would move across the street from us. My granny worked with me during the summer before I died. I didn't stick to it, and so here I am, dead and still being pursued by a cruel and evil witch. The witch infused her *souls* with demons. She was the highest priestess of the dark occult.

By this point, the evil witch was more evil and able than any dark magic witch or demon that has ever put a foot onto the earth, yearning to be Satan's darkest angel.

Witches are only human, so always keep that in perspective. Demons are evil beings that have never been human. They're evil and filled with hate. As scary as demons and demonic possession can be, remember, humans can defeat demons. It happens all the time, actually.

The only time you must worry is when a witch reaches a status so high that only angels can do battle against it. That time will come. Satan is always working on his army. When a witch swears themself and makes allegiance to the devil, he will give the witch tasks to complete, souls to consume or turn against God.

When a high priest or priestess reaches a high level in the occult, they begin losing their human qualities. The more souls they consume or commit to Satan and the more destruction they cause, and the more powerful they become, according to Topaz. They know nothing of love or kindness. They become everything you fear. They betray; they wreak havoc in all that they do. There are no boundaries or remorse.

Eventually, as they climb high enough in the occult, they lose all human form. Not many people know this. If they become high enough in the occult, they will have the ability to shed their human form and turn into an image of their father, Lucifer.

These demons and Havacavters will prepare until it is time for the end of the world. In that time, they will battle with the angels as they try to devour susceptible souls to spend eternity in Hell. This is their best punishment to God and his followers, consuming their loved ones. That is the goal of the Havacavter. When you see them in their devilish form, it will petrify you. They are evil and hideous, and their stench is the foulest smell you *can't* even imagine.

Chapter Eighteen
Shuffling Memories

What worried me the most was if Topaz could see I was in danger, and my granny tried to warn me, what now? If *they* could see it, what could the evil witch see? My sister had that same fear too. After seeing what she saw, she became paranoid more than ever about my fate, so much that I think she was close to a mental break from reality.

As soon as Mia recovered from the stress of being put under and going through my most disturbing memories, she felt jittery and on edge. She struggled to draw in a deep breath.

The doorbell rang unexpectedly, followed by a faint scratching at the door, and everyone was paralyzed with fear. I was so tired and immobilized; I don't think I could have run away if I tried. Hiding would be improbable in my current state. I was helpless after such an energy-draining event.

Charlie tucked the doll away, and the ladies broke from the circle. Mia was a hot mess, with perspiration pooling around her hairline, teetering, as it was close to sliding down her clammy face.

Dulce began gently blowing on her face as she pulled her hair back. "Everyone, be cool," Dulce pleaded as Charlie went to the door and flipped on the outside light. Charlie's body language immediately exhibited relief.

"Mia, it's your family." Charlie turned to Mia, but her legs felt wobbly, and she couldn't get to her feet on her own.

Charlie invited them in as Mia sat on the closest chair. "I'm not sure you should be here right now," Charlie said to Tyler with a frustrated look on her face.

"I didn't have a choice. Mia's mom was coming with or without me," he said in an equally annoyed tone. He knew my sister would be upset with them showing up with Jacob because of the importance of the evening and the risks associated with the séance. He tried calling to warn Mia, but the calls went unanswered.

The wind picked up quite a bit, and as they were entering the house, the gusts of wind began aggressively swinging the doors open and knocking plants over. Charlie felt alarmed—not so much worried about a storm as much as she was afraid of the nature of the storm. She prayed Topaz's shade of protection shielded them from the evil witch and her watchmen. She hoped their investigation into my death remained in the penumbra that only they could see.

Our mother stepped forward to where Mia was sitting on the couch, still feeling weak and sluggish from the undertaking she just experienced. Tyler held a sleeping Jacob in his arms near the front door. Mia looked up at my mom as she began kneeling and put her head in her lap. She let out soft whimpers and Mia stroked her hair. They didn't speak, only quietly consoled one another. Mia was still in shock over the events of the evening.

Our mom turned around and sat on the floor, then began to speak, but not just to Mia. She explained to the ladies sitting nearby, "I want you all to cross Lucy over." She looked at Mia and said, "I read Granny's journal, and I know why she tried to teach her protection spells. I shunned my mother for working magic, but Lucy actually needed the magic to save her. I failed Lucy." Before Mia could interject and place the blame on her own shoulders, my mother stopped her from speaking. "I never wanted to believe this. Until you experience supernatural events on your own, I guess most people resist it. It's intangible, and really, you have no control. It can be frightening." She was explaining her resistance to accepting witchcraft as a way of life. She was like her dad in that way. He, too, was fearful of witchcraft and magic. For many years, Granny laid down her broom for him, led a normal life, raised children, and merely dabbled in the craft from time to time.

"After reading the journals, listening to Jacob and our encounters with demons, I believe," my mother continued. "Charlie, I wanted you to hurry and cross Lucy over before they hunted her down, but I think they are watching us and will not stop haunting us until they get my baby. We can't let them find her. We are fighting for her not for the rest of her life but for eternity. My baby was such a good person; she doesn't deserve an eternity in fire."

Charlie nodded her head. "We have to cross her over, but we have to make sure she is safe."

Mia stood up, a little disoriented. She closed her eyes and sat back down. Mia was very in tune with me, as if she could read my thoughts and feelings somehow. Our souls were momentarily intertwined.

Our mother continued. "Lucy can't go until we lure the demons away from her body. Once the witch is no longer a threat, we can cross Lucy over. Then we will need to burn the evil witch. She's become too powerful to ignore. She's too vengeful to leave her be." My mother reached into her bag and pulled out the third journal from my granny.

Charlie's eyes lit up. "Is that another…?" My mom handed it over to her before she could inquire about it.

"I want to cross Lucy over. Granny and her mentor, Topaz, explain further. In a nutshell, if the witch, were to trap Lucy or Jacob…" my mother paused and looked at Tyler and Mia. "Topaz specifically mentions both my daughter and my eldest daughter's child," she said hesitantly.

How was Topaz able to see events and possibilities so far ahead? It's mind-boggling, really. Our mom seemed lost; her thoughts scrambled. "If the witch fails at abducting Lucy, she will fixate on Jacob and his gifts. He would be her next potential target. She says Mia's child will have some sparks of magic but not as strong as Lucy. Lucy is the main objective. Jacob is not nearly as gifted with visions and magic, but he does have some gifts that could be stronger if he had someone to work with and guide him like Lucy did. If Lucy slips through her fingers again, Jacob will be in grave danger, I'm afraid. The witch will have to get him before what magic he does have burns off.

"We have to go to war with her, or she won't stop, whether it's Lucy, Jacob or some other innocent with special gifts; they are all susceptible to her cruelty. Even if she does capture Lucy's soul, Jacob could still be her next victim. She has to have Lucy, though. She swore her to Satan, and she can't give up on her. She can't fail him. The witch can't let Satan see her fail. She has too much to prove and her own power to lose." Mom sat down next to Tyler and took Jacob from him. Jacob was sweaty and still sleeping very soundly.

"A war with her would mean a war against demons," Dulce said aloud.

Mia nodded, acknowledging the reality. "We will be in a war with the devil, so if you're not in, if you're not up for it, I understand, but we need to know now." Without hesitation, Charlie committed, followed by Dulce, Sophie and then Trina. Mia looked at Lily. "I know you have your own family you are trying to work on, and I get it."

Lily stood eye to eye with Mia. "I am with you each step of the way. Wild dogs or demons couldn't carry me away from you." The ladies embraced.

Suddenly, without warning, Mia passed out on the floor. They tried waking her. "We need to get her to the hospital," Dulce said, grabbing her keys.

Tyler picked Mia up and carried her to the car, then sped off to the hospital. Lily and Sophie took our mom and Jacob, following Tyler and Dulce.

"I will be there shortly. Let me tuck things away here, and I will join you." Charlie wanted to pause and make sure this wasn't a trick to get them out of the house, leaving my soul vulnerable.

She locked the books away and placed my doll and her trinkets into her bag for safekeeping. She took everything with her. "Please attach yourself to the doll. I can't leave you here after the events of the day."

I was weak, and I tried to attach but was unable to do so. Charlie waited for me. She called Lily and explained she was waiting but would be there as soon as possible. Then she began flipping through the journal as she gave me a little time to recharge and attach to my Lucy doll.

Mia began feeling better as they reached the hospital. "Let's just take you in to get looked at, just in case. Let's make sure you are OK since we are already here," Lily suggested.

The others sat in the emergency waiting room as Lily and Tyler put Mia in a wheelchair since she was still a bit weak in the knees. They rolled Mia into the elevator, and as soon as the door shut, it opened again. They closed the door, and it opened again. Tyler stepped out to see what was going on, and the lights began subtly flickering. "Maybe we shouldn't get on the elevator; there seems to be something funky going on," Tyler suggested.

As soon as he said that, the elevator door abruptly closed before he could reenter and started moving upwards with Lily and Mia, who felt unsure of what was going on.

Mia felt her hair moving, and when she looked up, she gasped at seeing her hair lifting towards the top of the elevator car. Her body was suddenly lifted into the air. She grabbed her hair, gathering it together and pulling it back down as she was levitated to the top of the elevator.

Lily was in shock as she watched the events unfolding. She grabbed onto Mia and pulled her back to the floor while screaming at the top of their lungs. Something was taunting Mia.

The elevator lights turned to an ugly fluorescent shade and then to a dark orange color. Something else grabbed at Mia's hair even harder to where it was now excruciatingly painful. It began slowly pulling her up again. Mia's feet lifted from the ground as she was being pulled completely away from the floor again. Lily was holding onto Mia's feet as the top of the elevator began to grow taller and taller while Mia floated to the top. Lily was still pulling on her legs, trying to bring her back to the ground, but her own body began to lift away from the floor too.

Suddenly, the elevator dinged and the doors opened at the same time. Mia and Lily both fell to the floor, almost as if whatever was pulling Mia suddenly dropped them. They fell pretty hard but were not seriously injured, just shaken up.

As they stood, a beautiful lady stepped to the entrance of the elevator. They recognized her instantly. "Lacy," Lily uttered.

Mia interrupted. "Or do you prefer Ramona? Ruby?"

Lacy knew Mia was aware of the game now. She cackled. "Did you see anything you liked tonight? Did you enjoy watching your sister die?" Lacy leaned into the elevator. "When you cross her over, I will get her. If you don't cross her over, I will find her. I always win, Mia. Shouldn't you be home with your little boy, *Mommy?*" Lacy was taunting and confrontational.

Mia stood strong, directly facing Lacy. Lily separated the two ladies. "Leave us alone, and we will leave you alone. Find someone else to haunt," Lily pleaded.

Lacy simply smiled. It was hard for Mia to see her sister's smile and her beautiful face, knowing it wasn't really her. It was my face and body but evil *souls* behind the eyes.

"You can't even have your husband's baby. You need to worry about your own life before meddling in someone else's."

Lacy's words stung Lily. Lily stepped outside the elevator and stood toe to toe with Lacy and the demons that consumed her body. At that time, Lily showed a side of her that no one had seen before.

"You need to be worried about your life; it's over. You're living someone else's life that you stole. You won't win; this is all temporary. You're done, Lacy. You will get what you deserve, bitch." Lily was shaking. She wanted to attack Lacy, but she knew it was a battle she wouldn't win.

Mia was standing but slouched a bit, as she was still weak. She could not fathom the words to express her anger and rage. In the pit of her stomach, she felt a great deal of fear growing stronger. She wasn't afraid for herself. She was afraid for Jacob. She was afraid for me.

"Lily, let's go. Lacy has work to do. She was outsmarted by a teenager years ago and still can't find her," Mia taunted. She knew she shouldn't provoke her, but she did and instantly regretted her words.

The ladies all stood face to face on the top floor. As the elevator doors opened Lacy stepped in. "Thank your granny and Topaz for that, Mia; they saved her, not you," Lacy quipped back. "If not for you being too lazy to go with little Lucy to the park, she wouldn't have died and fallen into a life between worlds." Lacy slowly waved good-bye.

The elevator doors shut, leaving Lily and Mia on the top floor, alone and at a loss for words.

The night was long. Mia finally got evaluated and was released after an IV and some meds to help her sleep. Everyone went home. Dulce called Charlie to tell her to rest and not head to the hospital. Instead, they would get together for lunch and decide when they would reschedule the bridge to cross me over. Mia was already headed home, and she was going to rest as Lacy's words replayed over and over again. No one slept well that night. In fact, they barely slept at all.

The next day at lunch, Mia and Lily told the other ladies about their encounter. They knew if they crossed me over, they would risk my soul being intercepted.

"Lacy. Ramona became Ruby, and now she has become Lacy. She has taken both of their bodies but only Ruby's soul, that we know of," Charlie clarified. "The demons lurk inside of her, but she needs Lucy's strong body to live. She needs her soul to become a Havacavter."

"She's not a Havacavter yet, thankfully. She would be unstoppable if she were one already," Mia said as she took out Topaz's books and placed them on the table. "There's a lot in here, but I am pretty sure I'm right." The ladies agreed. Ramona and Ruby's identities were now crammed into Lacy's body—my body. Their evil souls were in my body along with monstrous demons.

Charlie spoke up. "We need to come up with the next steps. I think I may know a way out for Lucy. I am working the details out. We will continue, business as usual, and plan to meet again on Saturday. If that works for you all. I need time to prepare, and to be honest, Lucy needs to rest. We can't risk crossing her over into the witch's clutches."

Mia nodded her head in agreement.

"My husband and I have breakfast planned with his mom and brother on Saturday morning, but I can be there after that," Dulce said.

Trina nodded and Lily did as well. They had no hesitation at all about joining.

Sophie took a deep breath. "I will be there too, of course."

Sophie dreaded the following day, Monday. Lacy was a big customer of the bank. She worried about her job and contemplated leaving the new job before she really even started. "How can I keep her from getting me fired or going into the bank?" Sophie asked, but she didn't really expect an answer. "I will be there, for sure. I just wish I added more value." Sophie held her hand out to Mia. They held hands for a moment and smiled at one another. "I guess worrying about my job just sounded really selfish and stupid provided what's really happening here." Sophie stated.

The ladies all felt a sense of togetherness. A bond that no witch—not even a Havacavter—could break.

*****

The week came, and for the most part, it was pretty quiet. Sophie worked at her new job without a sign of Lacy, to her surprise. Mia went to work, and she wasn't followed or harassed either. The only surprise she had was her boss, Thomas, showing up to see her unexpectedly. Mia worried a bit, knowing she'd had a lot of distractions, but she had also been using her vacation time to cope with the mess she'd had to sort through. She wasn't worried about getting fired, just worried she wasn't balancing her sales production in the midst of the chaos.

Mia sat at her desk as Thomas approached. "Are you going to quit and go work with your friend?" Thomas asked straight away when they entered her office. "Friend" said in bitterness as Sophie leaving him behind was apparent.

Mia laughed. "Not at all. I work here. I just have some personal things I am dealing with, that's all. I've been under a lot of stress."

Thomas seemed relieved. Mia asked if he missed Sophie, but he shrugged and dismissed her question. He probed Mia with questions about Sophie, never mentioning her name—missing her, loving her, wanting her more than he ever imagined possible. Missing Sophie would just be something for him to cope with, and in time, he only hoped it would become easier. Thomas prayed that, over time, he would think of her less and less and eventually not at all.

Thomas really wanted Sophie for more than just her physical beauty, but he knew himself enough to know it could never be. He would never be able to live with his guilt, so he just let her slip away. Thomas thought of her every day.

Thomas pushed his memories deep. Sophie would only have life to him now in those memories. Familiar songs and the smell of the perfume she would wear would trigger her familiarness to him, but he worried he would never see her or speak to her again. He knew he had to let her go, as their love only invited trouble in his marriage and his life.

For some reason, it was easier to break his and Sophie's heart than to break his vows and his family. It was respectable enough, but he would always wonder about her and the life they could have had together. Thomas thought he could get over her, but he never would.

Sophie felt that she wouldn't hear from him again. Deep inside, she would always hope she would. Disappointment would lurk in the back of her mind at the end of each passing day. She thought of him every day without fail. Sometimes, she would catch glimpses of his face in a crowd, but it was never him. Two broken hearts that would never fully heal from knowing each other. Sophie never loved a man in the way in which she loved Thomas.

Sophie would not ask Mia about him. Mia's words echoed in her mind. She assumed if she didn't reach out to him, she would never hear from him again. The way Sophie saw it was if she wasn't on his mind enough to hear from him, she wasn't putting herself out there for him. After all, she already stripped down and let him see everything about her. She exposed her body and heart to a man who wasn't hers.

At this point in her life, Sophie was tired of being the vulnerable one, and she was going to take what was left of her broken pride and walk away. Actually, she was exhausted from it all. She knew she would eventually find someone that would love her for her, but it wouldn't be someone else's husband.

As Thomas wrapped up his visit and left, Trina stopped by to see Mia. She brought Mia her favorite Starbie's drink and her grandson, Michael. Mia hugged Michael and gave him coloring pages. He was a happy little boy with big beautiful brown eyes and a sweet disposition.

"I love seeing my baby happy," Trina said. "Mabel had a heart attack last night." Trina had a small smirk on her face. Mia was surprised and Trina went on. "Karma is a…" She covered Michael's ears and mouthed the word, *bitch.*

Mia agreed as they chuckled. "All things done in the dark eventually come to light," Mia said and Trina agreed.

"I'm going to see Charlie tomorrow. I'm baking her a cake for her birthday. She told me it was her birthday when I told her me and Michael were celebrating ours together next month."

"Oh my gosh, I had no idea she had a birthday coming up. I will need to do something for her. I owe her so much," Mia said. "More than I can ever repay."

"Just come with me, and we will give her the cake," Trina offered.

Mia explained that she had met Charlie through Lily and Dulce. "They vaguely knew her through the gym but connected me to her with everything going on." Mia wildly gestured. "They thought she would be able to help me. She has been a Godsend to my life."

Trina and Mia planned for the other girls to surprise Charlie with balloons, cake, and small gifts of appreciation. Charlie was surprised and caught completely off guard. She was actually working on another investigation when they arrived. Charlie was always working and trying to bring closure to people who missed their loved ones.

"Is Lucy here?" Mia asked.

Charlie laughed. "Yes, and actually we are quite the team. She has been helpful with another investigation I'm working on. I need some of these visions your sister gets. I'd make a fortune!" she joked. At least, I think she was joking. Maybe she was a little serious.

Once everyone was leaving, Charlie thanked Trina for the delicious cake and explained how much it meant to her. Trina's car wouldn't start, so Mia waited with them as Trina's son headed over with Michael to fix her car. Luckily, she was only out of gas, so it was a simple fix. With the hectic week, Trina didn't think about stopping to get gas, I guess.

To Trina's delight, Anthony and Charlie exchanged flirtations with one another. Michael took up with Charlie right away. Of course, she was gorgeous, charming, and delightful to be around.

"I'm going to ask your friend out, Mom," Anthony stated, almost as if he were asking permission. "If you are Ok with that?"

Trina was more than OK with it; she respected Charlie and knew she was a special person. When Charlie agreed to go out with Anthony, it made Trina's heart full.

As we were all finally leaving, Mia went to see our mom and Jacob. When she pulled up to the house, our mom was pushing Jacob on the swing. They stepped away to talk quietly.

"Have you and that Charlie lady decided what to do next?" my mom asked.

"Charlie is working out details with my friend Lily before they get into what to expect with the rest of us. Charlie pours over and studies and cross references. She's very thorough, and she will help protect Lucy," Mia assured my mom.

There was a long awkward pause. My mom whispered to Mia softly, but it was inaudible.

"What? I didn't hear you." Mia asked my mom to speak up.

Our mom put her hand to her mouth and backed up a few steps further from Jacob. She grabbed Mia and looked her in the face. "I saw a lady that looked so much like Lucy today when I was picking Jacob up from Tyler at your house." My mom was very distracted by her thoughts about this lady, and she continued explaining to Mia. "She was coming out of the house that just sold across the street from you. I kept looking at her, thinking she looked like Lucy if Lucy had grown up. So tall and beautiful. I didn't realize I was staring at her; she so enthralled me. It's bothered me all day."

Mia had a gut-wrenching feeling that it was, in fact, Lacy, who was in Lucy's body. Our mom didn't know anything about Lacy at this point. They didn't tell her because they didn't think our mom could handle it, knowing it was my body being possessed—her baby, but not her baby.

Mia was worried about what my mom would do if she knew this lady was really Ruby, going by the name of Lacy now, after leaving her ailing body behind and taking over my body—a body now haunted by a witch and demons.

It chilled Mia to her bones and frightened her for Jacob's well-being thinking about Lacy moving in across the street from their home. Mia knew that, as unbelievable as it may sound, it would be devastating for my mom to know this. At last, it was time to divulge the truth and lay it all out on the table.

Tyler came over, and they sat down with mom and talked to her about it. She took it quite well; better than expected, which was a relief to Mia. Mom didn't cry; she just took it all in.

Our mom shared, "In the journals, Granny wrote that we could try to protect Lucy, but try as we may, it would all be unsuccessful. She was destined to do battle. I think now, Granny was right. This is why Lucy didn't cross over. She was being watched. They were waiting for her. Topaz told Granny this when I was pregnant with Lucy at a reading they had. She warned that good and evil would cross paths. The collision would impact our family personally. Granny wrote that Topaz warned that the demons will do battle with the crows."

Mia knew she was right. She agreed with what Granny had written. "I think we are meant to help Lucy when she goes up against this witch that covets her soul. She yearns to consume Lucy, and we can't and won't allow that to happen."

Mia called Charlie to let her know what our mom shared. "It is time and Lucy is ready to step out of the shadows," Charlie told Mia.

Charlie knew my running in the shadows was safe for me—a dark place but not scary or evil. It protected, strengthened, saved me all of my life and even protected my soul after death.

"After reading what your granny wrote about what Topaz told her, I believe we will be able to do it. It's going to get messy, worse than it has already been," Charlie stated.

Mia listened. "If it's true and she is my neighbor, she did this to try to upset and intimidate me. I'm going to strike first." Mia did just that when she arrived home. She paused when she noticed the big black SUV that had caused her anguish and stress parked in the driveway at the house across the street.

Mia went inside the house and flipped the oven on to bake that bitch across the street cookies in order to give her a proper welcome. Mia knew she wouldn't look her in the eyes, knowing it would weaken her anger because she would see me in Lacy's eyes. Mia knew those eyes were stolen but had to stand against the witch to protect my soul. Lacy wanted to become a Havacavter so badly. The battle was getting close, and it was dangerous for everyone involved.

Mia peeked out of the window and saw Lacy's shadow standing at the screen door, looking over at her house, much like she would look over at my house when she was Ruby.

Mia gave Jacob a cookie before dinner, which surprised him. "You eat this cookie. Mommy is going across the street. I will be right back and start dinner."

Jacob gleefully agreed and ate his cookie with a small glass of milk Mia had poured for him. Mia knew she should wait for Tyler, but she was so livid she didn't want to wait.

As Mia walked across the street with a big attitude and a plate full of cookies, Lacy was surprised at her boldness but assumed she didn't know she was now the house's occupant. She wasn't sure what the reason was, but she thought she would frighten Mia when she stepped into the doorway to greet her. Lacy felt excited, thinking she was about to shock and frighten Mia.

Lacy began to open the door, expecting to surprise Mia with a smug grin on her face. Instead, Mia flung open the door, taking Lacy off guard. "Hi, Lacy! I mean, Ruby…er, Ramona. Satan's whore, his flunky? What shall I call you? Cunt? Bitch? Here, I baked you some delicious cookies to enjoy." Lacy looked at Mia, lost for words. Mia continued. "I'm from Texas, so know this. If you or your demon dogs wander onto my property, I will get my gun out and blow your ass away. You won't be in my sister's body. You and your rotten ass souls will be explaining to your boss how my kid sister was more badass than you all are. She escaped and you couldn't even find a young girl in a game of hide and seek. So stay the fuck away or you'll get blown away." Mia threatened her with a tough-girl persona. She felt tough and confident.

Lacy stepped out onto the porch. "Watch how you talk to me. I'm not a witch; I'm THE witch." She looked at Mia with a big smirk on her face. "A good mom wouldn't leave her kid eating a cookie by himself. He could be choking. Call 9-1-1. Hurry!" She laughed.

She took a step closer to Mia. "Stay off my property or I will fuck your whole world up. Jacob could join us too, you know."

Mia leaped off the porch. She knew the threat from Lacy wasn't empty. Mia ran home to see Jacob was having a hard time getting his cookie down. Tyler came in to see him choking on the cookie and was able to help him get it dislodged. After Jacob was breathing fine again, Mia fell to the floor with relief and aggravation. Her feelings were very mixed up and confused. She felt no matter what she did, there was no beating Lacy. She had the lingering fear of something happening to her son, and as much as she loved me, she loved him more. She felt helpless once again and hated not having the answers to the next steps and hoped with all her heart that Charlie and Lily would figure out what to do before she had a nervous breakdown.

Mia was ready to put this behind her, get back to her life, and raise Jacob in a safe and loving environment. She knew once they got rid of Lacy once and for all, she would have a sense of security again. Once I crossed over, she would at least have the closure and peace in knowing I was OK and one day would be able to see me again, as I was a child before I died—before my body was taken from me.

To Dulce's surprise, the next morning at work, she had a patient show up without an appointment. Lily was waiting for her in the lobby. "Your receptionist told me your schedule was open until 10 a.m. Do you have time for me? I tried calling you, but your phone kept going to voicemail."

"I always have time for you, doll. My phone didn't charge all night, and I didn't realize it until I was getting ready for work. I figured I would charge it on the way in, and naturally, my charger is at my desk." She laughed at her misfortune. "Come on in, lay on my couch." She winked at Lily as they entered the office.

Lily threw her jacket on the chair and sat down. She put her hand on her desk. "This is serious, I see. Lay it on me," Dulce said. She put her hair into a bun and put her nerdy doctor glasses on.

Silence overtook the room for a minute. A few minutes passed before Lily gathered herself. "Last night, Max and I had a nice evening. We had dinner and a few glasses of wine. We showered, and we got ready to spend the evening together." Lily gave Dulce a knowing look. "I wore something sexy for him, and he was really excited. We were going to try to get pregnant, obviously. I was ovulating, and last night was the night." Dulce nodded and smiled, not knowing where Lily was going with her story. Lily pressed her lips together firmly as she paused to gather herself. "Well, OK, we were fucking, right?" Dulce's eyes widened and she tried not to laugh. Lily was usually polished and poised, not to mention very private about her love life with her husband. "It started great, and then something strange happened. I was on top of him, and he rolled me over and he started being really aggressive…" Lily's voice trailed off. "It was different and fun at first, and then he started hurting me. I asked him to be gentle, and he started laughing like he wanted to hurt me. I was getting really upset. He just kept going, thrusting hard, and it felt dirty to me. I felt violated. As he was climaxing, he looked me in the face and looked different. I became frightened. His eyes weren't green anymore; they were black and dilated. He didn't look like himself," Lily explained, her voice trembling so much Dulce could hardly make out what she was saying.

"When he got up from me, I saw a shadow leave out of him, the room became cold, and there was an unsettling feeling washing over me. I asked Max about it when he came back to bed and he acted as if he didn't know what I was talking about. He seemed agitated, and when I brought it up this morning, he acted like he didn't recall. He just said he only remembers feeling bad and getting sick this morning and not being able to fall back asleep until after four this morning."

Dulce sat there, trying to sort through what she just heard. As a doctor, she was trying to give Lily an answer from a medical perspective.

"Don't analyze me. We both know what I think it is. You're thinking it too," Lily said.

Dulce agreed. She called Charlie and asked if they could see her after finishing their workdays. Of course, Charlie was interested in visiting. "Something strange happened to Trina too. She called me upset this morning," Charlie explained.

Chapter Nineteen
A Murder of Crows

It was becoming more apparent that they needed to be on guard, as they were all feeling targeted, and it was terribly upsetting to them. Oddly enough, they didn't regret helping Mia. They just wanted to help me and prevent the witch from becoming a Havacavter. They knew it was now their duty to banish her along with the rotten entities that consumed her.

Charlie met everyone outside of her house and gave them full disclosure that she had just turned her investigating devices on so she could communicate with me to see if I was able to be helpful in the discussion. Mia was aware they were meeting, but she couldn't come over. Jacob had met his teacher, and she and Ty had dinner planned with our mom after. I think Mia really just needed a little normal time with her family too.

I so wanted to be there with my family, but I knew they needed some time together, and besides, I was safer with Charlie. She cleansed her house, following Topaz's rituals like clockwork. She was also frequently cleansing Mia's house and my mom's. From the sound of it, she would need to cleanse everyone's house after the experiences of late.

Charlie explained to me that Trina had gone through poltergeist experiences, things moving about the apartment and knocking sounds. Her doorbell rang at all hours of the night. She looked at her doorbell camera and saw black orbs and scary shadows come in and out of the apartment. Trina was bringing the video footage from her doorbell camera so Charlie could review it. She mentioned to the ladies that Trina was working and was a little perturbed she had zero sleep.

The ladies told Charlie about Lily's experience, and she felt the same way. I immediately had a vision, but it worried me to share it. Charlie specifically asked me to share if I had any thoughts or ideas. Lily directly asked me if I thought a demon had come into her home and possessed her husband. I confirmed. I saw exactly what happened, and it was true, her husband was possessed by a demon.

Charlie asked me to attach to her. She didn't want me to just tell her; she wanted to see what I saw when the shadow left Max. She knew it was risky, and it scared her a little bit. Now that the other ladies were at risk, she didn't have a choice. Charlie had to see firsthand what she was up against, as they were still trying to figure out not just how to save me but how to put the entities away for good.

Charlie knew they would have to lock away the demons to protect other people from harm. She also knew from Topaz's books and my granny's journals that they would have to burn the witch to keep anything else from occupying the vessel.

According to Topaz, a Havacavter always has a new soul and body to go into when it is time to shed its human ailments and enter a younger, healthier body. Ramona had her body, and Ruby's body burned, so their souls could never find their way back home. When our souls roam the earth, they are always drawn back to their homes.

Our souls always wants to return to its shell, home, and body. Some souls get lost; some do, in fact, have unfinished business, so they linger and roam the earth, such as me. You just have to be careful. You must stay away from your body. You'll be drawn to it. You don't want them to capture your soul, your essence. I had to stay away from Lacy for this reason; she snatched my body away from me.

I had my own plan. I remember when Granny told me sometimes that we have to reach in and save ourselves, and that's exactly what I needed to do. Charlie reading the books out loud to me as she formulated her plans, in turn, helped me to formulate my own plan. I needed to start fighting for my own soul. I wasn't a helpless little girl anymore. I was ready to fight my own battles, even if that meant giving up eternity to put the witch pursuing me to become a Havacavter where it belonged.

That witch wanted to be the whore of the devil. I was now ready to send her there so he and his demons could have her, since she was not welcomed in my body. It was mine and I was ready to take it back.

As I was attaching myself to Charlie, I sensed she began to feel poorly; she was overwhelmed. Understandably. Her breathing was erratic; her eyes were glazed over, even though she was speaking and appeared to be completely lucid, and she had a very hard time having me attached to her. She struggled much more than Mia. I don't know if it was because Mia was my sister or something else, but it was strange how much she struggled.

I started walking Charlie through the vision I had, and she was quiet. I could see a change in her immediately. Dulce and Lily both appeared to be alarmed with her eyes jumping around and the clamminess of her skin. Finally, she spoke up as I unattached myself from her.

"Phew, that was terrible. How did Mia do that nonstop? That was crazy." Charlie's equilibrium was off, and she had to lay down with her feet up. It was a solid twenty minutes before she could calm herself and share with Lily and Dulce what she was able to see through her vision. She struggled as Mia did, too.

The vision was narrow, and Charlie could see where, yes, in fact, her husband was himself when they were making love but was overtaken during the process. There was no right way to inform Lily that a demon stepped inside her husband as they were making love.

The lovemaking had turned into something more aggressive and cold, so Lily already suspected something was wrong immediately. She just wanted to be assured she was wrong and her imagination was running away with her. In the pit of her soul, his black eyes, the stoic face, the cold distance between them, she knew this wasn't her husband. Lily was making love to her husband but ended up getting fucked by a demon. She felt dirty and unclean. Charlie tried to see where the shadow was going, but it was instantly gone.

Lily wanted to see a priest. She could not cope, and there was no way to explain this to her husband. Not only would he not believe her, but he would also think her cheese slid off her cracker. He was very religious—and would in no way condone what Lily was partaking in with the ladies to help me. In fact, he wouldn't even believe her, so she kept the details to herself.

At this point, I had enough. I felt like I had my mind made up on how I wanted to deal with the witch, Lacy. I was ready to go up against her. I knew I had to be careful. If she overtook me, she would become a powerful soldier—a Havacavter. No matter what the cost was to me, I knew I couldn't allow that to happen.

Truth be told, it wasn't Mia's fault for not going with me to the park the day I died. It wasn't my mom's fault for not letting me learn the necessary protection spells. It wasn't Granny's fault for dying before she could do more to save me from a witch that hated me. It wasn't even my fault for being a teenager who felt a false sense of safety and security. My destiny was never to live a full life, and I accept that now.

I have finally forgiven myself for my misstep, and I am so thankful for a murder of crows putting their own lives in jeopardy to save my soul. But it was time to confront the bitch that made my life hell. I just had to be careful. My soul will naturally be drawn to my body, its home where it rightfully belongs. The last thing I would want to do is trap my soul in my body with Ramona, Ruby, the demons and God knows who or what other entity she has harbored inside my body and allow her to win the game that easily.

To my dismay, Charlie and the ladies received a call from Mia. She was on her way to the hospital. My biggest fear was our mom or Jacob being in harm's way. It was as if time stood still when Charlie was on the call with a frantic Mia. Although there was a sense of relief that my family was safe, I was saddened to hear Sophie was in surgery for an injury sustained by a car crash she was involved in overnight. It saddened me that she had been in the hospital, but she had no family, and they had to track down Mia, a friend.

As soon as Charlie hung up the call, she asked me what I saw. I felt panic as I began looking into Sophie's crash. I saw headlights coming the wrong way, but my vision was limited, and I figured out why. Charlie knew too. They were skirting around us in the way we were skirting around them. We couldn't see what Lacy and her demons were doing either, but we knew they were trying their best to pull me out of the shadows.

"Please attach to the doll. I am locking you away in protection, but we will be back. It is not safe for you to come out right now. This is clearly a trap being set for you. Probably for me too, but you are much more vulnerable. You're their target, babe," Charlie explained to me.

I couldn't risk it. I compromised with her instead. I would get in, but she had to take me to Mia's house just in case there was a situation with Charlie and I wouldn't remain locked away for eternity without anyone knowing and my family not having access to me.

I once again was in Mia's closet, tucked into a blessing box, and I felt very safe.

As I was tucked away to rest and prepare myself for crossing over, the ladies got ready to head out to the hospital to visit Sophie. It was tragic that she was targeted and hurt because she was trying to support Mia and help her help me. I was ready for this to end so none of these charming, beautiful women would be in harm's way.

Aside from Mia, these ladies never knew Sophie until she was unexpectedly drawn in after crossing paths with Lacy. Sophie could have turned and run away, but she stayed against her better judgment, faced her fear, and risked it all.

Apparently, after arriving at the hospital, everyone found out the injuries were much more serious than they expected. Sophie had unknowingly risked her life for me by placing herself in the middle of this situation. The funny thing is, Sophie had no regrets.

After twenty-four hours at the hospital and a little sleep deprivation, the ladies got some good news. Sophie was awake, but the doctor warned them she was talking crazy from her concussion and wasn't making sense. She did ask to see Mia. Sadly, Sophie had no one else. No parents, no siblings, no husband, no Thomas; only my sister. It was sad how someone so beautiful and fantastic could be alone in this crazy world.

Once Sophie could see the girls, they were all so sad to see her in pain. She had a concussion, bruised ribs, a broken wrist, bruises and cuts on her face, and a very concerning lump on her forehead. Thankfully, the doctors expected her to make a full recovery fairly quickly. Poor Sophie: she was banged up pretty good.

"The doctors said a wrong-way driver struck you on the freeway."

Mia inquired with concern but stopped short of telling Sophie the doctor told her the other driver wasn't doing well. The driver was texting, which they believe caused the confusion of getting onto the freeway in the wrong direction.

Sophie had a foul mouth, but she was soft-hearted and would have been beside herself if she knew someone was seriously injured, even if it was their fault. We all make mistakes; we are all just human, after all.

In the back of all our minds, we all wondered the same things. Was this really just a random accident? Was it something more? They all wondered if it was Lacy being the source of this assault against Sophie. They thought about it but didn't speak it out loud. It was just there, lingering in the back of their minds: Lacy, the demonic witch, and her sickening cruel-hearted games.

Sophie told the ladies she thinks the person that hit her left the scene because the doctor said they were unsure about the other person.

Dulce comforted Sophie. "We are so beyond thankful you are okay."

Lily added, "Yes! Sophie, we are all so relieved. It really could have been so much worse!"

Sophie felt good with the outpouring of love from the ladies—these wonderful crows that have become like a family when she didn't have one.

"There was something more," Sophie added. "I wasn't alone. When I was driving, a song came on the radio that made me think of Thomas." She rolled her eyes and shook her head. "Static came over the radio, an aggressive voice came through, broken and hard to understand, then clear as day said to me…" She looked around at everyone. "Do you think he is fucking his wife right now?"

Everyone just looked at each other. Sophie continued. "It was as if it wanted to upset me. I turned the radio down all the way and looked in the rearview mirror. I saw red glowing eyes and heard laughter that was deep and jarring. I kept my composure, though. I started to change lanes to get out of the car to see what was going on. I was honestly too afraid to stay in the car, so I slowed down as I changed lanes. Suddenly, I heard something ask me, 'Will your life flash before your eyes?' Bang! The next thing I know, I'm here. I am thankful that I slowed down or no telling what else would have happened."

It was obvious to everyone Sophie was upset about the accident and frustrated not being able to remember the details. "I didn't see any white lights, and my life didn't flash before my eyes. Fortunately, no gremlins came out to drag me to Hell, and no one tried to jump inside and live in my body." She joked, but the room fell silent. "Oh my gosh. I was trying to be humorous in this fucked up situation, and I am so sorry for saying that."

Mia didn't hold what Sophie said against her. I was always on Mia's mind. She could never be fully happy again until they could help me cross over. There would be small glimpses of happiness, but there was always my wrongful death and sadness hanging over her head. As my big sister, she felt a sense of obligation to help me find my way home. She knew my granny and daddy were probably worried for me and wanted me to be with them safely again.

Mia called home to talk to Tyler. He had Jacob in bed, and my mom and he played cards until she got home safely. It had gotten so late my mom decided to stay the night and watch Jacob, so he didn't have to go to preschool the next morning. That's what she said, but she was very curious about the lady living across the street, which was probably the bigger reason she wanted to stay. Our mom felt helplessly curious about her. She also wanted to be there to protect Jacob.

I was tucked away for my own protection. Mia and my mom wanted nothing more than to stay with me close by and talk to me, but their desires to reconnect with me were overruled by the fear they shared of losing me—not just in this life but in the next one as well. Especially with the new neighbor across the street.

While at the hospital, Mia caught a glance of Trina walking by, so she waved and called out to her.

Trina's face lit up and was quite surprised to see Mia at the hospital. "Did you know I was going to be up here?" Trina asked with an unsure look as she slowly approached Mia and hugged her.

"I'm here for Sophie. Isn't that why you're here too?" Mia asked.

Trina rubbed her eyes. "What happened to Sophie?"

Mia explained what happened and Sophie's car experience before having a car accident. Trina shook her head. "Girl, I told Charlie the bullshit that is going on with me too. Nothing like an accident, though, thank goodness."

Mia was so disappointed and upset that they were all being tormented by the witch. She had never hated anyone or anything before, but she hated Lacy.

"I will stop by to see Sophie; I am so sorry that happened to her. She is really a sweetheart," Trina said. "Girl, I'm here because Anthony called me to meet him up here. His ex-girlfriend, Aja, called him frantic and crying that her mom, Mabel, got very sick in jail and was transported over here. She's now on a ventilator after just having her heart attack recently. I don't think she's doing well. Getting what she deserves, as far as I am concerned. Anthony didn't want to come, but she was a screaming mess, and he felt obligated but didn't want to be alone with her. I guess he thinks she will use this as a reason to need his shoulder to cry on or something. My baby is with his other grandma tonight, so I can't stay too much longer." Trina shook her head and continued. "They better not let me in that room. I will unplug that bitch." Trina was completely serious. "I'm sure his ex will try to manipulate her way back into Anthony's life, and that's why I am here. Truth is, he is very into Charlie, but I just want to make sure she doesn't manipulate my son. He has no interest in her anymore; he's disgusted with her mom and that's all he can see when he looks at her. I just don't want him being foolish out of pity," Trina explained.

Mia smiled at her. "What a day."

They smiled and hugged each other, shaking their heads in awe of recent events. When they looked up, they saw Anthony coming out of Mabel's room and he caught sight of them.

Trina hugged him, and before she could say anything, Charlie, Dulce and Lily walked up to them. "We were just going to get coffee while Sophie was resting and didn't know there was a party in the hallway," Dulce laughed.

Anthony's eyes danced with delight when he saw Charlie. He hugged her and smelled her neck, making her giggle, and she gently pushed him away.

Bad timing was an understatement. As Anthony and Charlie were flirting in the hallway, Aja came out of her mother's room and saw them embracing. She was fuming with anger. Anthony seemingly lunged toward her to hold her back. "Who the hell are you?" she demanded, glaring at Charlie.

Charlie looked at her straight on, then her eyes darted to Anthony. She was completely taken aback, not knowing who this woman was and not knowing why Anthony was at the hospital to begin with.

Trina gently tugged on Charlie's shirt. "Come on, baby. Let's go get some coffee. She isn't relevant, so don't even worry about her."

Charlie got a little grin on her face and looked the ex-girlfriend in her eyes. "Don't slide up to me and think you're going to intimidate me," Charlie said with a wink.

Once they all reached the hospital café, they filled Charlie in on who the ex was and why she and Anthony were at the hospital. Charlie felt some regret about how she reacted and saddened by Aja's situation with her mother, remorse written on her face. Trina comforted her, explaining the kind of woman Mabel was and how she was cruel. Trina glanced at Mia, knowing Mia saw firsthand the kind of villain Mabel was.

"I would sometimes wonder why my baby boy was always so hungry when he would leave her house. She would not feed him all day and tease him by letting him smell the food she was eating. She sometimes put him in a cold tub to wake him up from his nap, and when he cried, she would pour it over his head…so much he could barely catch his breath. She was cruel and ugly to my baby," Trina explained, her voice shaking with anger and sorrow. She shared what happened after finding out more upsetting details during the trial. She continued. "That bitch let him hurt himself, it brought her joy to see him cry. She's an evil lady and she's sick. I'm not sorry if she dies. Not at all. There is nothing but hate for him in her heart. I don't like her daughter either. I'm glad Anthony dumped that bitch. She justified Mabel's behavior by trying to say she was upset that Anthony had a child that wasn't her daughter's. I'm sorry, but that child was a part of his life before her daughter, and if that was a problem, she shouldn't date men with a child or children. Anthony loved his wife so much before she passed, it was devastating. Michael is the only piece of her he has left to love on. He loves his baby," Trina explained to Charlie and the others. "Anthony is kindhearted and is only here for Aja out of obligation. Aja had no one else to lean on, so he is here, but he would rather not be."

The ladies drank their coffee, and Anthony stopped by to see Charlie, wanting to explain why he was there and assure her he felt nothing for his ex. He wanted to make sure Charlie wasn't upset. Charlie was indifferent. The situation made her uncomfortable, but she wasn't about to get overly emotional over some guy. That's just not the type of woman she is.

Our mom was home, playing with Jacob. They called Mia so she could talk to him. Tyler was on his way to get him and Mia was about to head home after she took Sophie a light snack and a Starbie's coffee. Sophie was still in a lot of pain, and her spirits were low with everything going on: a new job that she was already worried about and now she would be missing days due to being in the hospital.

Chapter Twenty
If Snakes Could Scream

Mia spent time with Sophie, getting her comfortable before she headed out. Sophie was still banged up pretty well, and even taking a breath was painful. Mia was there for her—taking care of her, comforting and supporting her.

As Sophie finally drifted off to sleep, Mia received a desperate phone call from Tyler. He was frantic and she was barely able to understand him. Tyler was always calm, so Mia instantly felt lightheaded and scared from his tone alone and hurried into the hospital hallway so she wouldn't disturb Sophie.

Jacob was attacked by two large black dogs. The dogs were dragging him around by his jacket, and he had several bites and was bleeding pretty badly.

None of us saw it coming. We were blindsided; the game had reached a new level. Lacy set her sights on Jacob and hurting my family further beyond just hunting for my soul.

Tyler told Mia the dogs were viciously growling, and it was as if they were communicating with each other. They weren't ordinary dogs; he knew something sinister was at hand, and so did Mia, who was crying and shaking, so angry and worried for her baby boy.

"Is Mom with you? I'm at the hospital and heading down to the emergency room!"

Tyler told Mia he was driving Jacob since they were close to the hospital, and he didn't want to wait for the ambulance. Mom was following. Tyler told her that to comfort her but left out the part where my mom ran in and got a shotgun to kill the dogs that attacked her baby while Tyler was wrestling them off. He also was bit and attacked by these hell hounds. Tyler had never seen my mom so calm and steady. He left my mom there with the two dead dogs as he hauled ass to get to the hospital but didn't want Mia to be concerned for our mom.

Our mom was fine. In fact, she called Charlie while she was at the hospital and asked her to meet her at Mia's house. Charlie excused herself quietly and left the ladies as she raced to meet my mom without anyone knowing, honoring her promise. Once she arrived, my mom explained the day's events to Charlie.

They then began talking about experiences mature people and babies have with the other side. It is true that older people sometimes get visits from death, including interactions with those who died before them. Older people nearing their end are on one spectrum, close to death. Babies and very young children are on the opposite spectrum, as they are young and just born into this world. Children also see death and loved ones; they just don't understand and cannot communicate what they are seeing or feeling. I think Jacob was a lot like me; he was still in tune with his abilities which is why I think he was a target for Lacy, just like I was in her crosshairs when I was alive she was still Ruby. Jacob was still young—too young to be taken, I believe—so there was still time to keep him safe from the evilness lingering around my family.

Charlie was upset and worried about Jacob. My mom went on about the events leading up to the vicious attack. "As I was sitting on the bench, talking to Tyler, I heard a whisper in my ear that warned that the dogs were demons and that they were coming. I believe it was the woman that worked magic with my mom; the woman called Topaz," my mom explained as Charlie took it in. "I met her as a child when my mom took me to see her, and I feel confident she was warning me to be alert. Stupid me, I sat there looking around, not seeing dogs and dismissing the warning. The next thing I know, the dogs appeared as if from nowhere.

"When I was a little girl, I kept having nightmares that a python was after me and wrapping itself around me. My mom took me to see Topaz because the recurring nightmares of this snake was too much for me. Topaz did a protection spell on me and told my mom and me that my former teacher from Peru was casting against me. I had apparently upset him when I told my mom he made me uncomfortable, and after she moved me out of his class, he grew angry.

"He didn't ever touch me, but he would always ask me inappropriate questions making me feel uneasy. My mom reported him, but times were really different back then. They never asked him about it, at least not to my knowledge. They just moved me out of his class.

"Topaz did a spell, and that very night, I had another dream about the python. It was even bigger; it could easily have devoured me. It was entering my room, slithering, very fast. Normally in my dreams, I could call out to my mom and see a strange shadow against the wall, and I would feel safe. This time, I couldn't call out for her, as the python began wrapping around me. Suddenly, I could feel the python became frightened as a domineering shadow cast upon the wall. The shadow was much larger than I had ever seen before. The shadow was intimidating, even to the python that promptly slithered away.

"A few nights after that, the python gathered the courage to come back to me again. The anger towards me outweighed its fear. I looked but I didn't see the shadow. I didn't run. I stood tall and grabbed the python by its tail. I felt in control and very powerful. It was strong and tried getting away from me as it raised itself, eye to eye with me. I knew without a doubt it was my teacher coming into my room, wanting to scare and intimidate me. He intended to kill me in my sleep, but it didn't work out for him. He too practiced a dark craft and was strong in the art of Satanism.

"I had him by his tail and was looking into his eyes, then I grabbed his head, squeezing hard. I could hear Topaz's voice whispering in the background, gradually growing louder. To this day, I can't tell you the language she was spouting; it was her angelic voice spewing words unknown to me. I could sense the fear of the python. It was so afraid and was scrambling to get away from me, but I was too powerful for it somehow.

"This snake, my teacher, wanted to get away. If snakes could scream, if snakes could cry, he would have. Snakes don't have that intellectual capability, but I know my teacher did. He regretted slithering into my dreams. He knew he was outmatched. The snake died in my hands.

"The next day at school, I learned about the teacher that was haunting me. He died in his sleep of a heart attack. My mom explained to me that Topaz was able to protect me while she lived, but I needed to practice my own protection. Once you cross over, it is very hard to get protection no matter how strong the white witch is on earth," my mom explained to Charlie.

My mom shared that before I was even born, Topaz warned my granny that her daughters, especially the youngest, would be susceptible to dark entities. My mom told Charlie that as she grew older, she denounced anything to do with it all. No witchcraft, no anything. She ignored the warnings and washed her hands of it, wanting it to just go away from her and her family. I believe she thought this would be how she could best protect me.

As time went on, and my mom grew older, she even dismissed it as silliness and coincidence. She was clearly wrong and began realizing it again when Mia had her experience in the parking lot at work and when she laid her own eyes on the entity that was in our tree that night when I was a kid. All the old feelings she had when she experienced it when she was just a kid herself came flooding back to her. The feelings frightened her so much, she felt like a scared child again.

Our mom became so distracted by my ailing dad, she didn't know or realize I was having my own problems, and she certainly wasn't aware Ruby was watching me and wanting my soul. She just didn't foresee me being chased by a witch. With everything going on with my dad, she was closed off to receiving warnings or messages from her mom and even Topaz.

Mom was burdened with guilt because she felt she should have heeded the warnings and protected me the way her mom protected her when she was a child. My mom regretted closing herself off, making her intuition unavailable to pick up on the fact that I needed help. That's why she now wants me to cross over so badly. She knows that my soul is still up for grabs, and I am being pursued even in death, and time was quickly winding down. She could feel it.

My mom continued. "Topaz explained in her books that if she put an eternal life spell on herself and lived a life beyond her immortal life, she would be stuck here on earth forever, roaming and not having peace. I think she served God in her own way. I think she was more than a white witch. Maybe her white magic was far more special and powerful than the dark side of magic.

"Some may say her magic was a sin, but I think it was her greatest gift from God. She was not a sinner but a protector. I wish she lived to protect Lucy, but I think she knew what would happen and helped us through her books, trying to guide us without interrupting our free will. Yes, she helped and gave us warnings, but she couldn't control the fact we would dismiss the cautions she shared. My mom isn't here to help me." My mom paused as she looked at Charlie.

"I'm here, though," my mom said confidently, taking Charlie by surprise. She reached beside her chair, pulled out a large, heavy box, and slid it to Charlie. Charlie was amazed by the beauty of the box. "Topaz made this and left it to me when she passed. I stored Lucy's baby keepsakes in this box. Topaz did a protection spell on Mia before she passed away. I acted like it was silly, but the truth is, I wanted her to do it. I wish she could have protected little Lucy, but she passed away before Lucy was born."

Charlie went to open the box, but my mom placed her hand on top of hers. "Don't let the demons out. It's a dybbuk box," my mom explained. "I removed Lucy's belongings. Earlier, I shot the dogs that attacked Jacob and forced the demons into the box. Something came over me, and I was speaking in tongues, then before I knew it, I cast the demons into this box Topaz made. We are going to bury it. Lacy is looking everywhere for them, but she can't find them." My mom pushed a big red book over to Charlie. "Topaz's words were coming out of my mouth. I believe she helped me to contain them." My mom was quite proud of herself.

Charlie grinned as big as the Cheshire cat. "Now is the time. We need to cross Lucy over while Lacy is merely a witch and her demons are locked away.

"This is exactly why we are here." My mom was proud, as she had the idea first.

Charlie went into Mia's room, got the doll out, and began calling me. As I surfaced, they both felt my presence and were elated. No, I wouldn't live again, but my mom would be able to rest her head on her pillow at night knowing I was finally safe—finally free of running and hiding in the dark shadows evading capture.

As I entered the house, there was a knock on the door. Charlie and my mother looked at one another, unsure of who it could be. The winds picked up, and the door slammed open as leaves blew into the house. It was as if a tornado blew in as things started falling over. An unsettling feeling came over us as we saw Lacy standing in the doorway.

"There you are, Lucy. I've been looking for you, darling." She cackled like the bitch that she was.

Lacy walked in, and I caught the surprise on her face as Charlie jumped up, tackled her, and began choking her. My mom hit her upside the head, and Lacy lost consciousness. As it turns out, a ghost hunter and a pissed-off mom can take down a witch easily without her hellhounds inhabiting her body, making her nearly impossible to overtake.

As Charlie choked the life from her, something weird happened. I was in my old body again. My soul was naturally drawn, and I couldn't do anything to stop it. I woke up and locked eyes with my mom. She knew in that instant it wasn't Lacy; it was me. I forced Lacy out of my body.

"She's not dead," I explained. "She's just not here anymore." I am unsure if Lacy was pushed out by me reentering my body or if she left purposefully.

Charlie stared at me in amazement. This is not at all what they planned for or expected. My mom was elated beyond words.

"My baby!" Mom hugged me and kissed me. I can't describe in words the sheer joy she felt. I was alive. I was this living dead girl now, no longer lost and no longer slipping away to hide from demons and a witch working her way through the hierarchy of Hell to become the Havacavter.

Then my mom's phone began to ring. It was Mia. Jacob was still in the back with doctors stitching him up, and she was upset and wanted to know where Mom was. Mia was worried about her.

"I'll drive you up there, just don't say anything to Mia yet. We need to get a good grasp on what's going on here. We need to let her focus on Jacob," Charlie explained, and my mom agreed without question.

Mom assured Mia she was safe and on her way with Charlie to the hospital. In addition to the bites, Jacob twisted his ankle from the fall when the devil dogs pounced on him.

I had never felt so sick in my life. I don't know if it was entering the toxins of Lacy's dark life or just a normal feeling of my soul reentering my body, but I wasn't right. I was sick but worried about Jacob, and I couldn't worry about myself. My mom held my hand the whole way in amazement and disbelief that she finally had me back in her life.

The truth is, I was amazed and excited for myself. I was able to begin my life again. I missed out on a big part of my life, but I was so happy to start living again and someday getting a husband, a family of my own, just as Mia had. This was so exciting for me. I always wanted to be a mother and have my own family to love and take care of. Ever since I was a little girl, I knew I wanted those things. Now I would have my chance at life again. A life free of harassment and fear, finally.

As my mom and Charlie drove us to the hospital. We took the dybbuk with us since we weren't sure where Lacy's soul was now. Mom and Charlie explained to me that I had to wait in the car. Everyone still knew me as Lacy, the demon-possessed witch that took my life—the reason Jacob was badly injured and almost killed. Now wasn't the time to explain to everyone. Now was the time to wait until my mom and Charlie were in a position to tell everyone what happened. So that's what I did. I waited. I felt terrible and just wanted to lay down anyway.

Before my mom went in to see Mia and Jacob, I assured her I could see and feel Jacob, and he was OK. I could see his stitches and his swollen ankle. My sister was seething with anger and sadness as she looked over his little bruised body. She felt a sense of rage and hostility. She knew the demons had attacked her son. Tyler did too. They knew Lacy was punishing everyone for wanting to hide me and save me, wanting to cross me over and away from her clutches.

When my mom and Charlie arrived, they got a good report from my sister and Tyler about Jacob, and everyone was relieved and pleased. Charlie and my mom sat in the waiting room. It was quiet; the TV was off and no one spoke. Everyone stayed in their thoughts.

"You have a good group of crows to love and watch over you, Mia." My mom wanted to cheer her up by pointing out all the people who loved her. "Your friend Sophie, who can bewitch any man with her poise and beauty. Lily, who can hypnotize and help you see beyond this world. Dulce, who is so brave and warned you against a witch, even when she was young and scared. The childhood friend, who first warned of the witch. Charlie, who can hunt down ghosts." My mom smiled. "Trina, who protected her grandson from an abuser. Pretty impressive group of women. You, the woman who found your sister—would go to any lengths to help save her. Your wonderful husband, Tyler, who fought off two demon-possessed dogs with his bare hands to save your son."

Charlie smiled and chimed in. "And your mom is the kind of crow that will blow away devil dogs without any fear or hesitation." They smiled, but the feelings were still very somber.

Mia knew my mom and Charlie were only trying to cheer her up, but she felt sad. She would still feel responsible for my passing, to begin with, and she felt responsible for not being able to protect Jacob. Mia was overwhelmed with it all, quite frankly.

Tyler was worried for Mia. "We can't go back in to see Jacob for a while. Sophie is getting some rest. Why don't I take you home so you can relax for a bit? Your mom will be here and call us if she needs us."

Mia was visibly tired and at her wit's end, and knew she needed some time to rest and re-energize, but she had no interest in resting. All she wanted to do was shower, change clothes, and get Jacob's favorite toys to give him when he woke up. My mom and Charlie wanted to tell her about me, but they decided to let her be for now.

As I was sitting in Charlie's truck, I started hearing faint murmurs—something I couldn't understand, but it was strange. I was having a hard time resisting the urge to open the box. I knew I was being lured into opening it by the demons, and it was almost becoming impossible for me to resist the pleadings.

My hands were shaking. I didn't have a way to reach my mom and Charlie. I didn't have a cell phone. So, I scooped the dybbuk box up and headed into the hospital to give the box to Charlie since I was being compelled to open it and release the demons.

I was unfamiliar with the parking garage and wasn't sure which way to head for the hospital elevator. I walked down a flight of stairs. I still wasn't feeling right. My lightheadedness and stomach made me feel wobbly, and my anxiety skyrocketed into a panic attack.

My legs were weak, and I was stumbling around with this heavy-ass box. It felt like it was getting heavier and heavier, almost as if it were pleading for me to put it down and walk away. Fortunately, I knew the game and was too smart and determined to do that. Walking down to the next level, I heard the voices of Mia and Tyler in the parking garage. Their timing was perfect because I needed their help.

Chapter Twenty-One
Unexpected Surprises

I assumed my mom told Mia and Tyler what unsuspecting surprise we had when they choked the life out of Lacy. I was finally me again. I was back in my body. I had to assume, but now she would know. I needed their help, so I had no choice but to hope for the best.

As I approached Mia and Tyler at their SUV for help with the dybbuk box, I could tell from the look on their faces, they were completely unaware of the earlier events that transpired.

I don't blame Mia for anything; she was never responsible for my passing when I was a young girl. She was always an amazing sister to me. Nothing was her fault. She was the best sister I could ask for. All she knew was Lacy and her demons targeted Jacob, he was beaten up and broken, and she was enraged. When I called for her to help me, I admit I was completely shocked when she pulled her gun out of the car and shot me square in the chest. I didn't see it coming. Likely because I wasn't myself, or the demons' whispers and pleadings created so much noise and confusion I couldn't see beyond the moment.

The box fell from my arms as the blood soaked through my shirt, and I dropped down. Tyler called my mom and told her to grab Charlie and then come to the blue level of the garage. My mom worried about Mia because she never heard him cry out like that. He feared now losing his wife to jail for killing a witch. Who would believe something like that, after all?

Mia just stood over me, watching me bleed out. I think the demons in the box affected her and were perhaps telling her to kill me. She was probably so fed up with the Lacy, Ruby, Ramona shit that she reached her breaking point after Jacob's attack.

As she leaned down, she came close to my face and called my name with a good deal of confusion. "Lucy?" she cried out.

I once again felt I was slipping far away and fast. I was not crossing a beautiful ocean; I was at the door of my old childhood home. The sun was beaming through the front door. I was my old self, just a kid, and I felt complete and utter happiness as I began crossing over. There was a lady who was walking up to the porch. I didn't recognize her, but there was no fear or anxiety as she drew near to me.

I didn't think of anyone I was leaving behind. I was focusing on the lady that approached. I knew I was dying. There was no pain or panic this time—not even a little, probably because I have been dead for over half my life already. My crossing over this time felt easy and peaceful.

I don't even remember when my mother and Charlie discovered that Mia had shot me. I do remember hearing my mom shrieking when she picked my head up off the garage floor. "I can't lose my baby again; I can't lose you again, Lucy." She was hysterical!

Charlie screamed to Mia, "We locked away the demons, and Lucy is in her old body. We killed the witch and she left Lucy's body!"

Tyler scooped me up and ran into the hospital to get help as I was dying. I think everyone knew it was a hopeless case after the amount of blood I was losing. I believe everyone was worried about the consequences of Mia shooting me. Could she forgive herself, knowing it was me she shot, and would she be jailed for murder?

Was I really expecting to simply step into a life that Lacy created? She had established a real estate empire; she was wealthy and in control. Sure, it was my body, but it was her life. She created it with her dark magic and sick twisted plans. It wasn't even a life I would know how to live. I was better off being at peace, and I was okay with that. I was at a place of peace.

As I was wheeled back to the room for the doctors to try to resuscitate me. Charlie filled Trina, Dulce and Lily in on the crazy events that just transpired.

Our mom was covered in my blood and crouched down on the floor. Mia was in utter shock. She was trying to make sense of what happened. In a blink of an eye, I was back and then gone again at her very own hands.

Charlie shivered as a chill slid down her spine. "The box!!" she exclaimed to my mother. "You stay here with Mia." Charlie rounded up the other ladies, and they began to hunt for the dybbuk box. To her dismay, it was no longer in the car.

Tyler followed them out to the parking garage. "I think it's still near our car," Tyler called out as he saw them looking for it off in the distance.

Charlie stopped and looked, but the box was not to be found. The ladies walked each floor more than once, but their efforts didn't produce anything.

"Well, let's see if anyone turned it into the hospital," Dulce suggested.

They headed into the hospital, but no one was in the reception area. Lily and Dulce headed up to check on Mia since they were empty-handed, unable to locate the dybbuk box. Our mom sent over a text that Jacob was awake and doing well. Mia and Tyler were with Jacob, but he was still resting. Mia stepped out briefly to check on our mom and to see if there were any updates on me.

The doctors had been working on me and were surprisingly able to stop the bleeding and get me stable again. The doctors gave a positive report and were hopeful I would pull through. It would be a challenge, but they assured everyone I was fighting very hard, which made my mom and Mia ecstatic.

The weird thing is that once the lady in white approached me and sat beside me, I was no longer in my childhood home. I was present at the moment. I was breathing in my body. I knew then that it was a real experience, not my brain dreaming or hallucinating.

Topaz came to me as a vision to heed a warning. "The witch lives," she warned. "She is closer than ever to completing her mission to become a Havacavter." She explained that I had allegiance to my family to save Jacob and rid this planet of the vile filth haunting my family and now I must forever step out of the shadows and face those hunting me.

"You are not the little princess witch your granny taught white magic to in a timid way to not upset your mother. You are an enlightened magical being, and you must sharpen your skills. You must now draw on these gifts. There is no time to lose," she warned me. "It is time for you to prepare for revelations and time for the crows to unite and finish this." Topaz was beginning to fade away. "You must reach in and save yourself. Wake up."

I heard a loud crashing sound that nearly brought me to my feet—so loud that somehow Mia and my mother heard it. The crashing sound was almost as if it wasn't of this earth.

Despite my wounds, it was time for me to get up and get going. Thankfully, my sister missed my artery, and the bleeding ceased after much hard work from the amazing surgeons. The blood transfusions not only saved my life but made me feel better. It gave me the energy I needed to rest and prepare for what the future would hold for me—for us.

Sophie, apparently, had woken up and tried reaching Mia, feeling panicked. The medicine she was taking had given her severe headaches, and she felt uneasy. She was getting especially upset when she called Mia several times and did not hear back. Her gut kept telling her something was off. She would wake up feeling like she was being choked and as if something—or someone—was watching her from the window, but she knew that was not logical since she was on the eighth floor.

Sophie developed tinnitus in her ears, and it was starting to get to her. She couldn't get comfortable and wanted nothing more than to leave the hospital. I think she was also a little frightened by the feeling of being watched. So, she took it upon herself to get dressed then picked up her phone to, once again, try my sister.

In the meantime, Dulce called to check on her, and since she was awake, she headed over to bring her up to speed on the wildness of the day. When Dulce opened the door and walked in, Sophie thought she caught a glimpse of Thomas walking by the door, and her heart almost skipped a beat. The thrill of seeing him was outweighed by the fact that she was upset with him.

She was surprised her frustration with him never reaching out to her started creating a sense of resentment for him. She thought of him every day; she was infatuated with Thomas. Sophie never thought she would be *that* lady that loved someone else's husband. For that reason, she resented herself as well.

Sophie motioned to Dulce, hurrying her in so Thomas wouldn't see her. She assumed Mia told him she was at the hospital, and, truth be told, she felt a little joyous that he made a special trip to check on her. As vain as it was, she didn't want to be seen beaten up and bruised and not herself. Sophie borrowed a brush and started primping in case he came into the room soon.

As Sophie began brushing her tangled, messy hair, she and Dulce continued talking about the crazy events that have been transpiring. Suddenly, Sophie stopped about her appearance. She worried about Jacob, me, and, of course, Mia. Sophie got dressed and urged Dulce to take her to Mia.

They jotted a note for the nurse, saying that Sophie was stepping out with Dulce, and left her number. Essentially, they snuck out so Sophie could be with her friend to help her and to support her.

At the end of the hall, Sophie caught a glimpse of Thomas again. He was sitting in a chair near a bed, and she realized he was visiting someone at the hospital and not there for her at all. She felt relieved before sadness washed over her again. He didn't even know she was there. She then wondered if he even thought of her anymore. Even during a dire time like this, he was at the forefront of Sophie's mind.

As they got into the elevator, Sophie felt weak and had to sit down. Dulce checked her vitals and got her into a wheelchair as soon as they got out of the elevator. They strolled down to Mia and she was greeted with a big hug. "You need to be resting. You have a concussion!" Mia said and then she immediately scolded Dulce. "You know better. She needs to rest!"

Dulce knew better, but Sophie would not sit idly by while Mia needed her. "Sophie is as stubborn and bull-headed as you are!" Dulce said in jest, defending herself for assisting Sophie.

Sophie immediately defended Dulce, letting Mia know she was willing to crawl from room to room and floor to floor if she had to, which brought a small smile to Mia's face.

Some people live their entire life not having a true solid friend.

These girls were blessed beyond measure to have each other. They immediately clicked with one another—no jealousy, no animosity. A murder of crows, standing together just on the edge of the shadows, loving, supporting, and lifting each other up. Facing the unknown for each other. Not many people would do that, even for their own family. I guess blood isn't really what makes people family. Some people you choose as your family.

Charlie and Trina were still on the hunt for the box. They knew this was a matter of life and death. Demons and possession are something you can't and shouldn't take lightly.

Trina said, "You know if there is a human, you can at least fight them or try to. You can see a psychologist for treatment if it's a mental illness." She joked, "But what the hell are you going to do if a demon just gets in there with you and won't get out?"

Charlie needed a good laugh, and Trina was very animated with her explanation. Charlie tried to assure her that she wouldn't let anything inhabit her body. She also said that a priest and a dybbuk box would help if they did.

Charlie and Trina continued to search for the dybbuk. It was very important that the demons stay tucked away until they could be buried. The ladies couldn't take a chance of someone unknowingly opening it and releasing the beasts back into the world—especially where I lay so close between life and death still.

Charlie and Trina didn't have any luck, though, and Charlie was sick about it. As they made their way down the hall, they were greeted by Anthony's ex-girlfriend, Aja. They stood silent, looking at one another in an awkward showdown. Whoever speaks first loses, and Charlie and Trina both knew that.

"Good news, Trina!" Aja said in a sarcastic tone. "My mom is making a recovery! The doctors said she's pulling through. They called it a miracle. Let Anthony know!" She smiled in a bitchy way. "Tell him thank you for checking on me," she smirked at Charlie, trying her best to provoke her.

"I'll just tell him tonight when he comes to see me. I'm sure he will be sad that cunt didn't die, though," Charlie clapped back at her.

Trina ushered Charlie away to check on Mia and get an update on me. "Don't worry about her, just ignore her. She's a shit like her mom."

Trina tried to calm Charlie, hoping she would forget Aja and her drama. After all, there were far more critical things to worry about. Bigger battles to prepare for than a trifling ex-girlfriend.

Aja was still enraged that Anthony quickly found interest in another woman with Charlie. She tried not to think about it and only focused on her mom. Mabel was never cruel to her; that was her flesh and blood. Aja knew Mabel wasn't a fan of Michael, but she didn't know she was abusing him; she just knew she begrudged the little boy and despised Trina and Anthony, so it really complicated the fact Aja was still in love with him.

Surprisingly, Aja was otherwise a decent person. She had many good qualities, aside from making excuses for Mabel. Trina and Anthony didn't bear ill will towards her but simply wanted to close that chapter of their lives for good and move on and write her and her mother out of their lives. Aja wasn't interested in being erased, and she wasn't ready to give up on reconciling with Anthony. She was determined to seduce him back into her life.

Trina was upset that Mabel pulled through. She knew Mabel was a savage and had no reason to hate an innocent child for having a different mother. Michael no longer had a mother and would have welcomed and loved a mother figure in his life. That's how kids are. Innocent and loving by nature.

Charlie and Trina met Mia and were relieved to hear Jacob was fine, and then they were given the additional good news that the doctor was able to stabilize me. I was still in critical care but was alive and hanging on. The doctor warned it would be a tough fight, and the chances of me pulling through for a full recovery were unknown.

"My boss keeps calling me." Mia rolled her eyes and looked at Sophie while shaking her head.

"Oddly enough, I saw him here; he's visiting someone. He didn't see me, thankfully." Sophie shared.

Mia returned his call, and he informed her he wouldn't be in for work and asked if she could lead the conference call the following day. He was unaware that Mia's son had been attacked and in the hospital, too. He explained why he was at the hospital, and she was a little taken aback, curious about why he was at a hospital so far away from home.

When Mia ended the call, she didn't say anything to Sophie, though she could tell Sophie wanted the scoop. Everyone was around, and the timing wasn't right. Mia had way more important things to concern herself with. Sophie knew her bullshit love triangle drama was of little importance in the grand scheme of things.

Lily, who looked exhausted and sad, made her way to Mia and sat with her. She was certain that she was pushing herself too hard. She hadn't told anyone that she had been experiencing morning sickness and was consumed with unhappiness because she just found out she was pregnant. Lily was so early she hadn't told anyone yet, not even her husband. She hadn't even missed her period. The only reason she took a test so early was because of the constant worry about the timing of conception. Worrying herself about the demons that possessed her husband while they were being intimate together.

This time, she was actually hoping she wasn't pregnant, given the messiness of the circumstances. She and her husband had wanted a healthy pregnancy for so long but kept losing the baby when she would get pregnant. She was afraid to allow herself to get excited, and she wasn't ready to share her news.

To add insult to injury, she kept having nightmares about the night her husband made love to her. She knew he was taken over by a demonic entity. She was afraid. What if this was the night she got pregnant?

Lily didn't want the baby to be the result of a night she felt frightened by her husband. She also worried if it would mean anything if the demon were in her husband if the baby was conceived that night. The worry of this would just steal her happiness from the pregnancy away, so the timing wasn't ideal, to say the least.

Dulce's husband called to check on her. Dulce stopped off at the restroom, and to her surprise, Kezziah, our mom, was in the bathroom, sitting on the floor holding her chest. "Oh my goodness, what's wrong, my dear?" Dulce asked as she kneeled to check on her.

Mom was clutching her chest. "My arm and neck are killing me. I'm just trying to give myself a minute before getting up. I'm fine."

Dulce felt she knew better and wanted to get my mom medical

help, but my mom stopped her. She held Dulce's hand and asked her to call in Mia and Charlie. Once everyone got in there, my mom shared something she hadn't shared with anyone before.

"I never knew Ruby was a witch. Unlike my mom, it scared me and made me feel like an outcast, and I had no interest in magic. My own experiences as a child scared me. I didn't want any part of it. I ran from it; I turned a blind eye. I ignored it to the point where I had forgotten about it until Granny came back. She cleansed our home from lingering sadness and darkness."

She went on, explaining to the ladies. "Mom told me after my dealings with my teacher as a child that witches with ill intent are drawn to witches, or people with natural gifts, or a lightness about them that is charismatic and soulful. They covet those gifts. If they win your soul, they consume your essence, your gifts, so that's why they taunt you and eventually take you. They test your abilities, and the more they watch you, the more they want you.

"I'm telling you this so you will understand. If you kill them, well, you get their gifts. It's truly a battle of good and evil. The teacher that haunted me practiced a type of magic and came to people in their dreams. He would be a snake; he could slither around. He would see all. He would hear all.

"Topaz would step into my dreams and watch for him after she did my protection spell. She told me to face him. I did, and I held the python, killing it as she condemned him to Hell, never to rise upon the earth again." My mom was still holding her chest. "I can do it now too. I had this happen to me accidentally when I was a young adult. I realized then what was going on, and your granny, well, she confirmed it. After he died, his ability to morph into a snake was passed to me. I had to train myself not to do it. It was hard not to find myself going into my dream state and changing into a snake. It took a lot of work to dream normally again. It took a lot of work to put that all behind me.

"Truth be told, it was a terrible feeling. I was active in that state, so I would wake up exhausted and with terrible chest pains." My mom shifted herself on the floor, trying to feel more comfortable. "I dozed off, and I guess, by accident, I found myself in Lucy's room watching as she was asleep. It wasn't on purpose; I was in a dream state, and just thinking of her, I guess. Unfortunately, it wasn't just her in the room. The witch was coming towards her. Just her soul, no demons and no body. I think she wanted to get back into Lucy's body but couldn't. The witch is trying her best to hang on. She whispered to someone—or something—that 'she needed a new body because she was forced out and needs a vessel.' She was telling someone this, but I don't know who. I had a weird flash—a vision—something I never had before. There was a man that looking for the dybbuk box for her. She kept urging him to hurry before running out of time. She instructed him to stop and place her soul into the box once he obtained it. She needed him to do the ritual and place her into the new body.

"As I heard the whispers and I saw the vision, I knew she was plotting her next moves. I heard her. As I tried to slither slowly away, she saw something in her peripheral vision and said, 'we're not alone.'" My mom took a moment.

"She's planning. She can't get into Lucy's body because Lucy is too strong, and right now, the witch is very weak. The evil witch plans to inhabit someone else's body that is weak and vulnerable until she rebuilds strength. After that, she will try again to steal Lucy's body and her soul. We must stop her," Mom pleaded. Then she said, "Mia, go to Jacob and guard him with Tyler. Lily, please go with Sophie. I'm worried about your being in the hospital and on medication with a concussion. I think you're vulnerable and you should be resting."

Charlie sat down with my mom. "We are all vulnerable and must stay mindful of her. I will stay with you and Lucy. Dulce will stay with Trina. We need to stick together. Let's make sure it's none of us."

"No matter what, she will be waiting for Lucy," Mia said with a sense of loss in her tone.

Dulce knew what my sister meant, but she also knew there was still hope. "Lucy isn't dying again and she is ready to fight for her life."

No one said anything. It was quiet in the room. Charlie knew there wasn't time to lose. "OK. Let's do this." She said with enthusiasm. "We can't let her win; she will become too strong, and we certainly can't lose Lucy, or anyone else we love for that matter. We need to find that box."

"Mom gained the ability to shapeshift in her dreams into a snake, a python. They could kill her if she gets caught in the dream like her teacher. Lucy has the ability to leave her body and she casts shadows as a way to hide and self-protect. What can the witch, Lacy, do? We must be guarded in both our dream states and our conscious states," Mia urged the ladies before going their separate ways.

"First things first. I'm getting Kezziah checked out by a doctor for her chest pains. The rest of you, be on your toes. Let's get Lacy locked away with her devils for good," Charlie stated.

After my mom received medical attention, Dulce was ready to head out and go home to her husband. Suddenly, the lights began flickering sporadically around the hospital. A storm was sweeping across the area. Leaves were swirling around in front of the exit doors. Dulce stopped short of exiting the hospital, hoping she could reach her car before getting drenched with rain.

An eerie feeling fell across her as she stepped just outside of the hospital doors. As Dulce looked up at the sky, something sinister caught her attention. It appeared that something was watching her, standing in a tree, something unworldly. Dulce slowly broke her stare and stepped back into the hospital, too afraid to make a run for her car. She had difficulty gathering her thoughts.

*****

The ladies spent their nights guarding their loved ones, trying not to dream. Mia took care of Jacob, praying over and loving on him. She confided the wildness of her mother's story to Tyler, who, by now, was a believer.

Sophie kept wondering why Thomas was at the hospital, if not to see her. She wondered why he was so far from home. She kept checking her cell phone without any messages from him.

Thankfully, my mom was feeling better and had a good checkup. My mom knew she was fine; she knew why she felt the way she did and that it would pass. She and Charlie spent the evening sitting with me as I lay in a helpless body, but my soul was strong. Once the witch's evil souls went away from being close to me, I felt so much better. I felt a sense of peace again. I hadn't felt that since I was a child.

I knew the battle wasn't over; it was far from over. Truth be told, the battle was just really beginning. We are always on the brink of revelations, on the brink of doom. Small victories against bad and good provide a small reset until it is time for the ultimate battle. I knew we had to keep Lacy at bay and banish her before she reached the status of Havacavter. I knew I had to sharpen my magic. I had to learn more and prepare. There was a tiny window of time to accomplish this. I knew we were at a big disadvantage, so there was a greater chance of losing the battle before the war.

Across the hospital, Aja was still mulling over the conversation with Trina and Charlie. She kept getting angrier as she rehashed the encounters. Aja tried to put her thoughts of Anthony's new girl out of her mind but struggled with it. She entered the room to see her mom. Mabel looked puny and exhausted.

"Where did you get that beautiful box, Mom?" Aja asked as she gestured to the box on the table next to the bed.

Mabel looked at the box on the small table next to the hospital bed. "My friend Frank came to see me earlier, and he bought it for me as a get-well gift." Mabel smiled. "Frank and I go way, way back."

"Oh, it's beautiful, Mom." Aja went to pick it up. Mabel motioned for her to bring the box to her.

"Bring me my box." She held it in her lap. "I love it. It really speaks to me," Mabel said with a mischievous gleam in her cold and distant eyes.

"You don't seem like yourself, Mama. I'm sure you're tired. Do you want me to get you a cup of coffee or maybe a Monster energy drink? It will give you a pick-me-up," Aja laughed, definitely thinking her mom looked worn out and needed an energy boost.

Mabel's eyes locked with Aja's and chills went through her. She felt sick and freezing cold suddenly. Mabel smiled at her until the smile turned to a cold and crooked grin.

"No, baby. I don't need a Monster," Mabel cackled as the room fell silent. "I *am* the Monster."

* * * * *

I was no longer a little dead girl running in the shadows. I was here; I was alive again. It was time to prepare. It was time to get ready for the battle that was on the horizon. I could see it was going to push me beyond my limits. Something was coming for me and the ladies that saved me. I could feel it watching me; even the shadows have eyes.